She texted "Good morning :)" and I knew it well as I often sent the same; it's a solid text, only my heart didn't jump rope for Michelle. Like a watched pot, the girl (or guy) you achingly want to hear from never texts when you want them to yet the instant you lose hope and look away-Bukka Buuuu! Your heart jumps rope to an incoming text reading: "What's ya doin?" "What's up?" or simply, "Hey..."

After such routine good morning texts, time can eclipse; maybe Michelle and I talked later that day, possibly another or never again. On the contrary, people meet husbands and future ex wife's every day within the slight look between a "passer by" on the street. Accompanied by mirrored hidden smiles, your eyes connect with another to see the first date first kiss first night first kid first wedding and the first night alone.

For tonight IS the first night alone. None of that happen, yet inside that split second your mind lived a lifetime. You saw what could be and built an entire future for the girl (or guy) drifting by you till they exited forever stage "left".

In an attempt to salvage another day alone, I dragged myself to the shower for an idle moment in the eye of the storm where the mind is free to wander amongst the mental playground... Met by a blank lock screen on my phone afterwards, I couldn't force myself to leave the bedroom. One should not allow their moods to be dependent on others but human nature is stubborn to say the least.

...Dreary sets it's sights and I try to keep it in; the heart knows no bounds as the soul continues to sing; I feel tears welling, sun no longer breaking through clouds willing, ready to kill all light and life leaving parallel earth to go it on alone. I try to shift my emotions and passions but cannot find comfort in my own skin's throne; my jaw clenches but one can only bite down sooo hard as thoughts of all I was never given as a child resonate around my brain's room until its too much to take; bag swirling around is too beautiful and I try to hold on but simply must break; my heart beats faster an'transforms to resemble darkened moons while stomachs sink, joining my liver at the bar "pain and suffering" on the backside of my heart and I swoon... I weep for the past and a glimpse of the future. I cannot worry about what I lack, but it's all I can think of sewing up collapsed sutures. I think about those I had wronged at the death of myself and how I'd die so many times over if it led me back to that shelf, with dreams of a passerby laced in such novels and wars that never end leaving Hector to grovel while Achilles lay waiting to play spoiler in climaxes; I'd rather to have found my Helen and fallen victim to hellish romances eventually swallowed by the endless abyss... Embraced by winter's kiss, the pain seeps through my defenseless pores allowing tears t'gracefully stream down in the now frozen sun; having never been love's chosen one, there's painful pleasure living down here with face flushed, eyes run a blood red strained glass window. My veins and arteries remain utterly obstructed by sadness and sorrow's tears; a double bypass couldn't clear out the cobwebs adding to runaway train's fears that spiders have burrowed deep into my emotional immune system and stunted its growth at an early stage in life. I may or may not have burst another blood vessel but neither pain nor blood knows any bounds or strife; the river Hades is full of loss souls and I can prosper down here in hopeless cites; I wish to find my way out but it's ever so easy to bask in one's own self pities. Cry, cry on...

Act 1: Scene 1: "Welcome to the Heights..." (Wednesday: June 18th, 2014)

Q: "This girl on facebook said she was rollin out to a party at the Merlo mansion tonight; sooooo I figured we could-"

Santana: "-I'm out..."

Q: "Big surprise. (turns to Santana pleading) Come on dude; we're gonna 'release Julian back into the wild' and help him get over that one chick. You still out? Why are you such a fuckin drama queen?"

Santana: "Thanks"

Q: (scrunched up face) "Oh come on man, lighten up; that bitch left you years ago and you're still cryin? Get over it already!" (Santana storms out the front door)

Santana Casta danced around graves but never looked the tombstone in the face; never dealt with his head on collision of a relationship with Jasmine Merlo...

Bastion: (picks up bag of chips) “Really dude? That was messed up; we all know how badly she crushed him back in the day”

Q: “Annnnnnd SPEAKing of crushed; (looks at Julian) Arch you still all tripped out over Veronica?” (smiles)

Julian: (pauses video game) “Ha Ha bro; Just cuz you can fuck a girl and never talk to her ever again doesn’t make you a man”

Bastion: (stops chewing chips) “It doesn’t make him a woman…”

Julian: (stands up) “Yeaaaa, but this is 2014 Bass; I mean ever since Sex and the City and Miley Cyrus, woman live like men these days”

Q: “Makes sense both ways; Julian here (slams him on the back) lives like a woman for surrrreee”

Julian: “Fuck you!” (shoves Q)

Q: (shoves back) “Fuck You! Oh, the lover has some fight in him now huh? (looks him up and down) It’s nice t’see some testosterone finally!”

Julian: “Oh unlike you who is a walking-”

Bastion:“-ALRIGHT ENOUGH!!! ALLLL of you are a bunch of fuckin women… Q, what’s up with tonight, you sure about this? Last time we went to a party in the valley we fought some randoms; hashtag wefuckedemup”

Q: “You fuckin know itttt!!! (Hand clasps Bastion) But I wouldn’t worry about it cuz no one ever fights at the Merlo mansion with the police always kickin it in the driveway; besides, Santana isn’t rollin so we’re cool”

Julian: (shaking head) “I don’t know; what if Veronica shows up?”

Q: “Dude, you sound like your brother now”

Julian: “No shit, I AMMMM his brother so of course I’m gonna sound like him”

Bastion: “Score one for the chicks!” (marks imaginary slash in the air)

Julian: “Damn straight! Wait... whatever screw it, who care’s if she’s there or not; let’s roll out. Someone’s gotta grab some alcohol so we’re not drinkin all their shit”

Q: “For sure, Stephan you’re riding with me; Bastion here can take Mopey McMoperson”

Julian: (turns to Q) “...Thanks”

The four walk out to Santana driving away bumping the artist known simply as “Banks”...

Bastion: “Ohhhhh shiiiiitt; he’s playin the sad girly music again; (turns to Q shaking his head) look what youuuuuu did“

Q: "Whatever dude, it doesn't take much to set him off... (starts car) Remember to swoop some alcohol losers!" (drives off)

Julian: (looks at Bastion) "Figures"

Still attempting to talk himself out of heartbreak five years later, Santana continuously debated with his conscious to try and get over her; however, trying to convince yourself of anything is nearly impossible. Try, try on...

("Banks - Bedroom Wall" emits out the car's speakers)

Santana: Ok, She's a bitch. You supported her and threw aside everything and everyone to help her in any way possible yet when she found the confidence and strength to be alone, she left you... And THEN when you're down and out and need her like she needed you, what does she do???.... M-I-fuckin-A; no response, no contact...

Conscious: Why are you such a fuckin drama queen? Its been years and you're still broken up over her??? Suck it up, let it go!!!

Santana: I can't... And every so often the tidal waves shoot down below renewing my hope that-

Conscious: -No you fool, that's just you fabricating shit up in your head again; I should know... If she wanted you she would have come back years ago and not married that one loser. She doesn't want you; get that through your egotistical head!

Santana: I refuse... Yes we fought and have all sorts of issues and obstacles to overcome, but it would be different now; I know it would be... She's who I want and even though its been years I'm still hung up on her... what do I do????

Conscious: I don't know man, I am you.

Santana: Thanks; a lotta help you've been.

Conscious: Hey, I try to help and you don't listen to me at all.

Santana: I triiiiied listenin to you! I stopped hittin her up and look where it got me; she rebounded to that loser. She's such a fuckin bitch!!!

Conscious: ...But you love her...

Santana: ....but I love her......

Act 1: Scene 2:
"What? No applause?"

Anyone can "walk" into a valley party, but most unwanted guests "move along" after seeing the stationed police car at the foot of the driveway, feeling invisible and shunned by the other guests, or enjoying some of the free snickering and whispering insults inside. The latter sends chills of deja vu to the cruel halls of high school where the "cool girls" giggles were always seconds away from slapping the smiles off your face causing your stomach's stomach to churn butter. In turn, your head and confidence fall like the temperature of the dessert from day to night where not even a quick peek to your phone's banner-less "unpopular" locked screen can help shield the blows......... Fuck.

Feeling your eyes tingle and cheeks flush, the next action is impossible to resist; because it's in human nature to embrace extreme emotions on either side of the spectrum, 10 feet past the girls you glance back seeking assurance all your glum is warranted. When you feel incredible and the world's at your finger tips, you'll find ways to take that pleasure and bliss to the greatest heights imaginable. Conversely, while wallowing in the lowlights of your ostracized self esteem, you want nothing more than to cut deeper, bleed harder and dig down as far as possible... And THIS is why you solemnly glance back looking for multiple sets of glaring eyes telling you more than you ever wanted to know: "Frickin loser" "What kinda haircut is that?" "Those clothes don't match at all!" "I can't believe they asked ______ to prom; pshhhh, like they had a fuckin chance". Tell, tell on...

(congregating in the Merlo's "forever an'a day" driveway)

Bastion: "So y'all ready to do this?"

Julian: "Y'all??? Ok Blake Shelton"

Q: "What'd you just say? Blake who?"

Bastion: "Duuuuuudddee... are you talkin bout the voice again?"

Julian: "How would YOU know?"

Bastion: "Because you're always watchin that shit; hello, we live together?"

Julian: "True"

Q: "ANNNYways, (turns to Stephan) You ready to do this? Lover boy here is still stuck on that one chick so I'm gonna need you to step up and tryyyy to wing man tonight"

Stephan: "Ummmmm.... I don't know. (takes a hit of his pipe in the car and turns around to exhale) I'm pretty high bro; I'm like, this high" (puts hand by his forehead)

Q: "Well good thing we brought plenty of alcohol to balance you out cuz you gotta be more drunk than high to hit on the ladies or you won't care enough t'try"

Stephan: "What??? You NEVER try!!!"

Q: "Yea and for Me, and MEEEE only, that ISSS trying"

Stephan: “How does that make any sense?”

Bastion: “Don’t ask Steph, this could take hours”

Stephan: (hands on waist) “What have I told you about calling me Steph?”

Bastion: “Wellllllll Peter Pan, (hand on Steph’s shoulder) when you actually hook up wit a GIRLLLL; I’ll stop callin you one”

(Bastion, Q and Julian erupt into laughter after a second of silence)

Stephan: “Well... I... I-”

Bastion: “-I, I (stutters) ya-ya-you you-”

Stephan: “-Shut up! (socks Bastion on the shoulder) Why Y’all always pickin on me?”

Q: “Good job Bastion, now everyone’s gonna think were some hicks at this party with y’all’s y’all; Fuck dude! Stop sayin that shit...”

Julian: “Damn, don’t have a cow man!”

Q: “That’s better; I can handle Simpsons quotes just no more of this voice shit or your sex and the city sequel garbage”

Julian: “Prequel!!!”

Q: “WHATEVER!!!” (frustratedly shakes head)

Before entering the party, Julian tells Stephan to sag his pants a little bit less because the bunch up on his Creative Rec's "looks retarded" and Stephan advises Bastion to crooked his Pink Dolphin hat a tad more to the side. Bastion "tries" telling Q to lose his unbuttoned LRG striped collared shirt since it looks too preppie with a solid colored polo on underneath but Q laughingly responds: "Fuck NO! One, we're in the valley and two, since when do you know anything about fashion?".

Acting like it's their own mansion, the four walk right in the unlocked door... Severely uninvited, the heights brush off any shots of contempt with a quick dusting of their shoulder and pop of their collar. In public and especially deep in enemy waters, Julian must appear vintage "Casta:" strong, powerful, confident and capable of anything at any time. And to that effect;

Julian: "What? No applause? What the fuck is UP PEOPLE??" (throwing his arms out proudly #crickets)

Bastion: (jets over to the closest group of partiers and turns around excitedly) "Heyyyyy Prince Juliannnn, what uuuppp kiiiiiidddd??? (hand clasp/double back pats Julian) Good to see you man, glad you made it out; (pounds Stephan and Q) make yourselves at home!"

Q: "Thank you thank you... (smiles at a couple ladies he recognizes) We DEFinitely will"

The main room is nearly 8000 sq. feet and split into three levels with two single stairs dividing each area and a yellowish vanilla cake carpet below the white lamps perfectly matching the shades of the white walls. Unloading their non premium alcohol on an unoccupied table in the lower living room, the stark contrast in tastes is evident: from champagne, imported beers, aged wine and high end liquor to the heights two 12's of Pacifico, Sailor Jerry, and Hennessy; no shot glasses necessary. And THAT'S the real difference between the two; the valley show off their "old" money with "la-di-da" clothes, fancy toys, and top shelf liquor all the way down to the "Grey Poupon" like condiments. While opposingly, like many prominent NFL and NBA stars, in many capacities the heights still live like their "pre millions" days; it's what they're a custom to, what's comfortable, and thus what they prefer... Unlike the Merlo family, the Casta's were not always rich, but that's a distant story from a different time; live, live on...

Act 1: Scene 3: "Welcome to the Valley..."

Tyler: (intently staring at the four from a distance) "John. Send one of your boys to keep an eye on our 'guests'. Tonight feels askew; maybe the wine's from an off year or maybe its because Liliana has yet t'say a word to me, but something is a miss"

John: "Miss what"

Tyler: "Something is wrong"

John: "Wrong with what?"

Tyler: (frustratedly looks at John then Nick) "Nick, can you help him out here?"

Nick: "Something IS a miss; I concur"

Tyler: "Thank you Leonardo"

John: "Can't catch me if you can, I'm the muffin man!"

Tyler: "It's GINGERBREAD! Gingerbread man!!! You're like Biff from Back to the Future; always fuckin up your lame ass sayings" (#stillrelevant)

John: "Ha ha-who was I sending t'follow them?"

Tyler: (sigh) "Forget it" (leaves to the dance floor)

Severely jealous of the heights' camaraderie, Tyler hated his daily exchanges with his "friends". Currently in guest room 6 with "random girl 42," Perry (Tyler's bestie) was an emotional vampire who fed off the real emotions of the no esteemed girls he victimized on a nightly basis. Utterly self involved, Perry shut down Tyler's rants about how much he missed his ex girlfriend Liliana Merlo and could care less how maddeningly determined Tyler was to trump the final imprint left on her mind as a broken boy weeping. Pushed around and emotionally abused by those who "loved" him growing up, Tyler became incapable of treating woman or anyone he loved right. Ever fearful of the vulnerability that accompanies attachment, Tyler distanced himself from those he cared for before they could push him away... By subconsciously contorting Liliana's traits into vices and picking petty fights over nothing, Tyler painstakingly convinced himself that he didn't love her.

For Liliana, their relationship was an endless war of attrition: if she curled up to him during movie night or snuck herself into his arms while sleeping he felt smothered; when she gave him space he felt alone and unloved. There was no balance since he favored the moon over the sun, the night over the day and the hurt over the happy. Growing weary of constantly disappointing Tyler and feeling like a failure of a girlfriend, Liliana slowly withdrew... Anyone who feels like they cannot bring happiness to their significant other will eventually shut down; if you can't bring light to your partner's world, the darkness will inevitably sneak into yours and even the brightest of souls will leave those they cannot dance with together in the shine of the sun.

Like a hawk perched above the dance floor, Tyler creepily peers over to his poser bride Liliana and continually scans the room to ensure no one steals her beauty or "passes her by" ;) Once Tyler's surveillance camera lands on his arch nemesis, Q points at a girl dancing in front of him and lips: "Is this your sister?".

Playing to an inside joke that was anything but "funny" to Tyler, none were to stand in his way as he dives towards Q. Yet, like a father sensing someone's adjusted the thermostat, (#familyguy) the queen smoothly sifts through the floor as the randoms almost bow in allowing her to pass by... With her seductive tone and enchanting hypnotic ice eyes, Jasmine needn't ever say much:

Jasmine: (runs outside of her index finger from Tyler's temple t'chin) "You wouldn't wanna ruin your girl's birthday now would ya?" (slightly pushing him on "ya")

With the expansive wing span caged and descent halted, the frightful bird returns to his perch. One talon latches on to the ledge while the second grazes the branch back and forth like a shy school girl. And as if the bubbly soul can feel his gaze, Liliana turns to his defeated eyes, smiles and does an overly excited puppy dog tail waving "HI!!!!" with her left hand. For even after all Tyler's put her through, Liliana still shines down upon him with her glowing warmth as the Merlo's hold the uncanny ability to reign down sun like beams at any moment and brighten up the world with their unparalleled charisma and charm... But as any yang to the yin and any bipolar song to sing, alongside the highest highs comes the lowest lows.

Seeing her kid sister's welcoming wave, Jasmine turns from seductress to devil's caretaker and wickedly drags her ice eyes from her darling sister to throw her disgust towards the tall drink of sour milk at his perch.

Tyler: "Hey! (looks down) I thought you said no drama tonight?"

Jasmine: "Don't you fuckin look at her like that!" (with a wolves like sneer before disappearing into the crowd)

DJ: "Whoa dude... you've been marked"

Tyler: (looks down at his chest and wipes his finger across his Versace laced button down shirt before giving the DJ a "what the fuck is this?" look)

DJ: "Hey hey, (hands up) I don't know man, I just work here"

As if channeling Perry, Tyler's confidence frantically bounces through the crowd looking for a "victim" in which to find solace; finding only an empty chair, Tyler takes a seat and grabs all nearby alcohol. Unable to drown any of his sorrows, Tyler swims in the night's sky pondering how one sister is a sunlit angel while the other tangos under the moonlight leading the devil herself... ponder, ponder on...

Act 1: Scene 4: One

(in the always popular wine cellar)

Dru: "So Tyler walks up to me and is like, who invited you here? And Perry comes in all, 'I DID; what's up?" (arms akimbo)

Bastion: "Siiiiiiiick. (fist pounds Dru) Ya know, don't tell anyone I said this; but that Perry fool is kinda alright..."

Dru: "...I guess"

Tyler relished and even mustarded sitting 3rd on the Valley's depth chart behind Jasmine and his bestie respectively; although he was a year older than Perry, he never exuded his debonair and vampiresque traits. Nevertheless, Tyler's station in life afforded him more than he could handle in the ladies department...

Noel was a pretty young thang who picked Tyler up off waivers and seamlessly entered and departed at his will after placing herself in the channel between the two shores of his heartbreak. And due to her impeccable timing, (and killer ass #letsgetreal) Tyler preferred Noel over the other "lower class" randoms who could only wish to be the queen "stone" on which he stepped. The world is all relative in it's classes, which is relatively classless; step, step on...

Full of liquid courage and weary of the stoner continually excusing himself to the front yard, (#smokebreak) Julian begins the fatal search for his ex Veronica. Wine cellar? No, his friends were drunkenly laughing over something juvenile no doubt. The kitchen in the Viking part of the estate? No, just the "we're old but still cool" ladies scoping some wine; not very cool at all. Out on the balcony of life? No, just the smokers, Julian thought: "Didn't they know that they were killing themselves??? Hmmm, they do look rather cool though". Finally... to the dance floor.

(DJ mixes to "Swedish House Mafia - One (your name) feat. Pharrell")

Sequencing to the beat, the DJ lights flare through the crowd: four white beams flash on and off 7 times in a circular motion to each bass beat before a flood of bright white lights on the 8th beat lead into the 1st again. With no Veronica to be seen (flash) during the first few cycles, (flash) 20 feet forward, (flash flash) mid smile and mid grove, (flash) Julian spots (flash flash) an unknown goddess. (flooooooooooooooood)

His eyes grow wide and the pure bliss of excitement tingles his spinal nerve. Common to a movies romancing, these new ice eyes just so happen t'tip toe in his direction and upon upward looking, Liliana casts a spell or two his way... Levitation is not a magic trick of David Blaine or Chris Angel rising for that night they saw themselves dance on glass ceilings before their eyes reconnect in passing's kiss...

Liliana sees him walk in the door to their egg shell white house with two dogs galloping in their greeting, three kids running from the kitchen gleefully giggling and preparing his favorite meal. As the door's daily gift to them all: the provider, the lover, the father and the order Julian brings is unparalleled in it's windfall; for when the wolves huff and puff at the four, he builds another wall t'block the winds forever roar. Walking towards her, Julian's eyes cannot hide their feelings and collapse with emotions reeling, unable to hold back from the depths of her allure. Intertwined in eye's kiss the moment he enters their safe haven, Liliana sees herself through his mind as he'd dreamt of hours before: staring out at office window panes now healed, Julian envisions a reflective Liliana adoringly gazing back and lips "I love you" into mirrors sprung; evoking Liliana t'smile back down upon with no need to respond any words in return...

Sitting in "bored" meetings, Liliana sees his mind drift off t'last night's reindeer games of waiting for her t'tuck in the kids, so happily ready to dream; for years after meeting, Julian still sits on the bed unsuccessfully attempting to remain tame, unable to contain smiles from leaping off his face knowing her black cocktail dress so elegantly flowing would soon fall to the floor. Involuntarily springing to her side, Julian's left hand moves from thigh to waist while the right pushes Liliana's angelic hair from beside her face exclaiming: "God you're beautiful, have I told you that today?" and regardless she'd always smile, reply and say: "No... but please do tell me at least once more".

From his eyes Liliana sees how touches rile such frenzy from wanting her so crazily as blood boils and scorches Julian's mind with passion normally reserved for novels and movies never read nor seen. And in that moment's dream, the two passerby's saw the future life they'd built; enchanting visions of the pure fantasies of what could be; but nearly ready for time to start on up again, the lights flash on once again in patterns trend...

Trembling to stay strong upon waking in the dark so blind to emotions here, (flash) leaving the worlds of heights and valleys, (flash) Julian jumps to his feet all the while feeling who was near. (flash) And since taste certainly likes to linger, (flash) Liliana wakes to the same flavor (flash) before (flash) reaching out t'grasp (flash) what they'd found on this night of all nights. (flooooooooood) And far beyond dance floors, the two leap up to their royal thrones t'feel the moans of heart's aching breath, soul's yearning lust for each other to possess; and with shallow breathing in duress, both must remind to execute yet the body won't dilute waiting for it's counterpoint to exhale; inhale the pulsing vibes and smiles of all minds on the floor dying to find the breakdown. The DJ knows how to make the orgasm blast, continuously wait and last; the lights pattern faster, so fast; double time, triple time, till the sequence is ridden; adrenaline of random's raving elbows glisten whilst all bodies tense t'listen with open hands beating air drums in anticipation of the orgasmic breakdown. A pleasure drenched instant in silence leaves all breathless until the DJ drops the track unleashing pure ecstasy while white lights flood robustly to the spectacle currently flying off the balcony of life: for standing under the bright white lights lay the prince of hated heights and the princess of valley reich's; lip locked, love tied, sending shockwaves to shatter the moon's deeps and tidal waves to the sun's shores it'll gladly keep. For with all past love's now erased, bore in booming sounds bouncing blissfully they're replaced by a complexity she never could have wished, depths of souls he'd never dreamt to have kissed with neither caution to winds possibly whisked, nor names to have forgotten they'd possibly missed. Flood. Flood. On...

Act 1: Scene 5:
#THEWORLDSNOTREADY

("One" song earlier in the wine cellar)

Stephan: "Hey Bast, you hear what song's playin?"

Bastion: "......Noooooo shit... SHM in this shitty house"

Stephan: (nods his head) "Yup yuuuuuup"

Dru: "...Shall we?"

Bastion: (looks at Stephan then Dru) "You fuckin know it..."

Like moths subconsciously drawn to a cliché'd light, this "one" Swedish House Mafia track draws the masses to the dance floor and even infects a few country oriented wallflowers who refuse t'dance to anything but.

Walking in, Bastion waves his right hand high above his head as if beating a single drum, Dru breaks out his "wanna be raver" dance and Stephan slowly pecks the air left and right like a chicken... Jealousy watching Q singlehandedly entertain a group of girls nearby reminds a few random guys that some men are bestowed "the gift" and involuntarily lure woman in like the song drew the masses to the floor #hesgot99problemsbuta...

Dru: (cupping mouth towards Bastion) "Dude! This is that sick ass remix with Pharrell, let's head down for the break"

Pulses rise and adrenalines skyrocket as the DJ continues to build the track; eyes closed and throwing his own exclusive fiesta in his mind's boardroom, Stephan dances with the other 10 Stephans in his own high world. When the breakdown hits and the final flood of lights reveal the beautiful disaster of a centerpiece, Bastion and Dru's smiles break off their faces like ice shattering their fragile drunken minds in the process: Bastion drops to a crouching position with elbows on his thighs while Dru turns away allowing a slow developing "Faaaaaaaauck" to fall from his mouth... Although the orgasm's complete, the refractory period will last an eternity.

After recomposing himself, Bastion disillusionedly taps Q on the shoulder and waves his index finger in a small circular motion conveying "let's bounce".

Q: "Come on man, I'm just gettin-(turns t'Bastion's "why so serious" stare)-sorry ladies, (shrugs) gotta roll... (walking away Q spins Bastion around) Hey! What the FUCK Bass? This better be some serious shit!"

Bastion: "See for your self" (points towards the centerpiece)

Q: (looks; closes eyes) "Are you kidding me bro? (opens; turns back) You left the prince alone, Drunk and on the REBOUND???"

Bastion: (mumbles incoherent dribble)

Q: "Wha-wha-wha, (slaps Bastion's drink out of his hand; splashing ont'Liliana's toes) I'll do what you losers should have"

Like Leonardo's fall into the bath tub during Inception's first main sequence, the cold liquid wakes Liliana to Q steam rolling towards their embrace;

Liliana: "No time; 408 - 512 - 7XXX"

Julian: "Is that-"

Q: (in Julian's ear) "-We gotta go like NOW!" (puts arm around Julian and escorts'em to the exit)

Julian: (turns back and lips) "I'll text you"

With Julian away at college the last five years, none of Liliana's friends recognize who he is and shoot a million and five questions at her to the tune of: "Who is he? What's his name? Where'd you meet him? Did you know him before tonight? (and) Did you get his number?" ...Yet with the widest "starry eyed surprise" smile, Liliana stares upward picturing her an'Julian dancing on the ceiling moments earlier, catching ceiling Liliana glance down an'excitedly lip: "This is it!" to which grounded Liliana responds;

Liliana: "Yes it isss..."

Random girls: "Yes what is? What are you lookin at? (looks up) You knew him? This is what???"

Luckily, during that "One" song, Perry was off in a guest room 6 with tonight's victim while Nick and John consoled Tyler in the corner. Paramount to how utterly captivated the room was by the DJ's masterful contorting of the track, no one could ID who'd found the sun in the night's sky.

Approaching the door to freedom, Q smoothly flashes a single index finger to Bass, Dru and Steph signaling "give us a minute". In the commotion, Julian stealthily flips out his phone, types in her number and presses send, end call to ensure his phone would not forget.

Q: "Just keep it cool and don't lead on that you just fucked us and yourself in the span of a single track"

Julian: "Wait; Wha-"

Q: (pointing at a random girl) "-Heyyyyyyyy... (blanks on a name) sexy; text me later" (walks out)

Random girl 26: "I will!!! I WILLLLL!!! (turns to random girl 27 and 34 with hands in front of her waist like she's playing an air piano) OH my god! Ohhhh myyyyy GOOOOODDDD!!!!!!" (all three scream)

Julian: (catches up to Q outside) "Whose that?"

Q: "No clue"

Julian: "How'd you know she had your number?"

Q: "Didn't, (smiles) she just looked like a girl I'd hit on"

Julian: "Frickin guy; so what was that shit you said about 'fuckin us?' I didn't do anything, in fact; you'd be proud!"

Q: (looks back ensuring their alone) "Proud of what? Proud that you hooked up with SANTANA'S EX'S LITTLE SISTER??????"

Julian: (stops walking; shaking his head in disbelief) "No... no, she hasn't moved back yet"

Q: "Yes yes; she has..." (walks away taking his phone out)

In pure juxtaposition, Julian's insides explode with competing emotions and feelings; love and lust are quite the strong opponents but betrayal and guilt hold their own with the heart behind the former and mind in support of the latter. There were two opposing trains of thought: Santana and Jasmine's arc ended years before the premiere of his new series yet Julian felt like he betrayed his brother by simply hiring a few of the same writers #funnyjoke

Rotating like the ancient red 3-D picture viewers of the early 90's, (google "retro 3d viewer") the flashing images of his brother aggressive yelling in his mind's eye are eventually trumped by HER loving stare... Smiling without a smile, Liliana seductively looks down and up as the slow blink creasing her perfect skin feeds the sun starved plants of Julian's inner heart with her warming glow; feeling like the world might swallow him up, Julian doesn't know how to imbibe the emotions wrapped in passion and sprinkled with lust such images give him...

Closing his eyes, Julian inhales deeply as if smelling the scent of a goddess who never wore any perfume yet effervesced such sexual beauty... Unable to deny immediate gratification any longer:

SMS: Julian > Liliana
Hey you!!! I couldn't wait any longer! : (

Call: Q > Santana (straight to voicemail)

SMS: Q > Manuel
What up wit the party?

Call: Q > Santana (straight to voicemail)

SMS: Manuel > Q
It's crackin
SMS: Manuel > Q
Come thru

SMS: Q > Manuel
Sick

(back on the valley's floor 3 minutes earlier)

Liliana: "Ok Ok (hands out) ...give me some space, I've danced with a guy before"

Nicole: "Girl, (looks at Jaime and back) you were kissing him like your ship was goin down; wit the violins and everything-"

Jaime: "-Yea yea, you NEVER hook up with random guys; so who was he, who WAS HE!!?? You SURRRRE seemed to know HIM well!!!" (eyebrows raise to ceiling's limits)

Many random girls: "Yea yea, Who was he-Did you know him-Who was he?"

Liliana: "Ok Really. I need a minute; Don't follow me, and that includes you two!" (points at Nicole and Jaime)

Nicole: (despondently looks at Jaime then Liliana as if her dog died) "Us too?"

Slightly tilting her head, Liliana cuts down Nicole and Jaime causing them t'slink away to the living room with the trail of randoms in tow...

Day dreaming of their night's realities, Liliana heads out to the balcony of life for a breather but turns back after being swarmed by drunken jibber jabbering randoms wildly exclaiming: "OH Hi! I love you! Let's be besties! I knew u from blank, helped you with blah and we should yada sometime..." Sifting through the crowd back inside; Bukka Buuuu!

Looking down at her lock screen, Liliana sees a text message from an unknown 650 number and already knows... Looking up to a blurred crowd chattering like the parents of peanuts with their “Wonnn wonnn wahhhh,” Liliana flees through the mansion’s halls determined to ignore any further unwanted advances or comments.

Helplessly awaiting his text, Liliana felt like her life was previously on pause for when you fall this hard, this fuckin fast, the text notification sound/banner on your phone is a breath of relaxation since you become dependent on that feeling and how it floors you, or in this case ceilinged her ;) The anticipation to read any text in the honeymoon stage encompasses all senses and once received allows the mind to freely wander amongst the mental playground with your new love alongside; regardless whether words flowing from phone to eyes ease the mind or ease it into a pool of madness #nothingisworse #thannoresponse

Since the vulnerability accompanying such intensities grows each day, this plague like fear will inevitably chase many off the relationship trail even though butterflies of a “notebook” love hardly fall, rarely fade, and sure as FUCK never wane... Nevertheless, some lose sight of the chemistry endlessly shooting back an’forth between them and bid farewell when the arguments and differences cast shadows over all the good that still resides. Whether parting was the right choice rests in the pocket of time as separation and dating others will tests such notions, albeit it shallow depths or love’s farthest oceans...

Sometimes people can love each other...

TRULY love each other;
but for whatever reason,
it just "Doesn't work".

Period. End of sentence. End of thought.

Whether an unforgivable tragic event remains at the forefront of the mind or unfortunate conditioned patterns of behavior lead to continual irreversible conflicts, such deal breakers may pull the two apart where any remotely similar situation triggers the same horrendous fight/argument... Fight, fight on...

Act 1: Scene 6: The World's Split Personality (Heights Edition)

SMS: Julian > Liliana

Hey you!!! I couldn't wait any longer! : (

SMS: Liliana > Julian

No unhappy face!!! I've been waiting forever to hear from you!!! :)

SMS: Julian > Liliana

I would have text sooner but I got held up ;) Just know that your eyes, your scent, and your warmth have twisted my heart and I fear will never let go...

SMS: Liliana > Julian

Why do you say it like such a travesty? I could only wish to be so lucky to captivate such a deep soul

SMS: Julian > Liliana

Cuz I've never felt so much sooo fast and I feel like I've loss control...

Act 1: Scene 6: The World's Split Personality (Valley Edition)

SMS: Julian > Liliana

Hey you!!! I couldn't wait any longer! : (

SMS: Liliana > Julian

No unhappy face!!! I've been waiting forever to hear from you!!! :)

SMS: Julian > Liliana

I would have text sooner but I got held up ;) Just know that your eyes, your scent, and your warmth have twisted my heart and I fear will never let go...

SMS: Liliana > Julian

Why do you say it like such a travesty? I could only wish to be so lucky to captivate such a deep soul

SMS: Julian > Liliana

Cuz I've never felt so much sooo fast and I feel like I've loss control...

SMS: Julian > Liliana
It's been what... 20 minutes???

SMS: Liliana > Julian
Who knows lol
SMS: Liliana > Julian
But I feel the same way!!! :)

SMS: Liliana > Julian
Don't be afraid!!! You've unearthed unprecedented passions from inside me too!!! #cantexplainit #dontwantto

SMS: Manuel > Q
Yo what up, y'all still coming through?

SMS: Q > Manuel
There in 5

Q: "We got a real party to roll to, lets be out of the lame ass valley"

Julian: "Word, lets DO this!"

SMS: Julian > Liliana
Your words penetrate depths none have traveled and unlock secrets none have unraveled for you're who I've forever chased #amazing

SMS: Liliana > Julian
Awww...

SMS: Julian > Liliana
It's been what... 20 minutes???

SMS: Liliana > Julian
Who knows lol

SMS: Liliana > Julian
But I feel the same way!!! :)

SMS: Liliana > Julian
Don't be afraid!!! You've unearthed unprecedented passions from inside me too!!! #cantexplainit #dontwantto

SMS: Julian > Liliana
Your words penetrate depths none have traveled and unlock secrets none have unraveled for you're who I've forever chased #amazing

SMS: Liliana > Julian
Awww...

SMS: Liliana > Julian
DITTO!!!
SMS: Liliana > Julian
I love your words too!!!
SMS: Liliana > Julian
What's your name???

Q: "Hey J, Roll with me..."

Julian: "Uhhh... alright"

Bastion: "Mannnnn, I don't want him smokin up my car" (pointing t'Stephan)

Stephan: "ShhYea-Yaayyy-Yaaaaa" (nodding and smiling at Bastion)

SMS: Julian > Liliana
Sigh... The name is cursed...

Q: (authoritatively) "He WON'T smoke, (staring at Stephan) WILLLLLL you?"

Stephan: (shakes his head) "Nooooooo"

Q: "Seeee, (hand on Bastions back) we're all good; head to Manuel's, hashtag itscrackin"

Bastion: "Nice"

SMS: Liliana > Julian

DITTO!!!

SMS: Liliana > Julian

I love your words too!!!

SMS: Liliana > Julian

What's your name???

SMS: Julian > Liliana

Sigh... The name is cursed...

SMS: Liliana > Julian
How is it cursed???
SMS: Liliana > Julian
It can't change how I feel!!!

SMS: Julian > Liliana
Julian Casta

(Q and Julian drive away; Bastion and Stephan follow suit)

SMS: Bastion > Julian
Don't let him get on your case about that chick
SMS: Bastion > Julian
If he starts going crazy on you just tell him it's my fault and you didn't know

SMS: Julian > Bastion
Thanks

Q: "Julian Cicero Casta; (slams hand on steering wheel) TELL me you didn't know who she was; I know you're hurtin over that one chick, but yo; (looks over) this shit's fucked up; you KNOW you can't ever see'er again right? I mean (shakes head) You... the heartbreak kid himself; Farrrr more than Derek Zoolander, or; I meannnn; Owen Wilson? No no, ummm..."

SMS: Liliana > Julian
How is it cursed???
SMS: Liliana > Julian
It can't change how I feel!!!

SMS: Julian > Liliana
Julian Casta

A huge net captures all butterflies and replaces them with shrieking bats infiltrating Liliana's internal organs spurring her insides to somersault. Unsure of how to proceed, Liliana reaches out to the only parental like figure in her life besides Jasmine;

SMS: Liliana > Nancy
I need you! Where are you????

SMS: Nancy > Liliana
In the kitchen. What's wrong?

SMS: Liliana > Nancy
Just come to my room

SMS: Nancy > Liliana
I'll be there soon dear

Julian: (chimes in sadly) “Ben Stiller?”

Q: “YESSSSSS!!!!! (startling Julian) But for real, you know what chu gotta do...”

Julian: “I know, I know...” (takes out phone)

SMS: Julian > Liliana
Are you there???

SMS: Julian > Liliana
My body trembles awaiting your reply...

Unequipped to handle new heightened levels of intensity, Julian valiantly tries to keep his composure as anxiety fueled bats soar through caverns inside. Similar to the flashing light beams on the dance floor, Julian’s poses shift from left arm on the center console and right on the door; to left leg straight, right knee up with elbow on thigh; to resting his right foot on the incessantly shaking left knee.

Q: (looks over) “Hey... What’s up with you?”

Julian: (turns to Q) “Huh?..... (high pitch) what?”

Nancy: (opens the door) “Lily, What is it!”

Liliana: “Idontknowwhattodo Nance! I met the man of my dreams tonight and within 5 minutes he touched me in ways no one ever has; But... (looks away and back) I find out he’s the one person, (tilts head) the One person I cannot be with; or well; I should Not be with but is now the one person I cannot live without. I just-(Bukka Buuuu! glances at phone but does not open message)- See! There he is right now! The way he speaks, the way we communicate is on a whole different level... And when our eyes met, That very second I could see our whole future together; I even saw myself from his eyes and I... it’sssss, hard to explain; I just know this is it (Bukka Buuuu! looks at lock screen smiling) That’s all I can say, THIS IS IT!!!!”

Nancy: “Well if that’s the case, who cares what the obstacle is, he sounds incredible!!! Respond child! For if all you say is true, the poor boy is probably freakin out!!!”

SMS: Julian > Liliana
Are you there???
SMS: Julian > Liliana
My body trembles awaiting your reply...

Q: "Fool, you're trippinnn; you need a hit? (offers wax pen) It'll chill you out, I meannnn... I would be pretty tripped out too... (inhales) and t'think, (inhales more) you Finally hooked up with a random chick" (laughingly exhales)

Julian: (sighs) "...yeeeaaaa... (Bukka Buuuu!) Annnnddd, if I see her again?"

Q: (swerves to the side of the road) "IF???" IFFFFF you see her???? (eyes closed squinting) Don't fuck with me right now Jules; (opens) we all know where Santana probably is, (looks over) and you know damn well why...."

Julian: "I Know I Know..." (unlocks phone)

SMS: Liliana > Julian

> I don't know how much you know of our sibling's saga, but I witnessed the beauty and tragedy of their relationship from day one and our meeting will surely send shockwaves... YET I feel like god himself did make us into corresponding shapes like puzzle pieces and this is something from which we can neither run now hide. I feel sooo weird saying such things sooo frickin early, but I can't help what I feel!!! For ever since we danced??? Flood gates........

SMS: Liliana > Julian

> I don't know how much you know of our sibling's saga, but I witnessed the beauty and tragedy of their relationship from day one and our meeting will surely send shockwaves... YET I feel like god himself did make us into corresponding shapes like puzzle pieces and this is something from which we can neither run now hide. I feel so weird saying such things sooo frickin early, but I can't help what I feel!!! For ever since we danced??? Flood gates........

Nancy: "Jesus Liliana, could you type anymore? (smiles) So who is this guy? This all does sound awfully familiar-"

Liliana: "-Wait, (turns to Nancy sharply) who told you, who KNOWS???!!!"

Nancy: "I don't know anything, relax dear; now talk!"

Liliana: "Wellllll.... (glances down at her phone in case a message arrived without an alert) his name is Julian......"

Nancy: (searching her memory banks) "...hmmmm Julian, Julian... I don't know any Julian's, except OH! I do remember Santana had a-(smile hides around the corner)-NOOOOOOOOOOOO!!!!!!!!! (like Monica's high pitch scream #friends) Please, PLEASSSSEEEE Heaven forbid; tell me it's not him...." (Liliana nods in acknowledgment)

Q: "Do you? (sits up tall staring at Julian's phone) Whose that? Is that Bastion? He talkin shit again?" (swipes at Julian's phone unsuccessfully)

Julian: "Chill! It's Dru tellin me how Perry punk'd Tyler"

Q: "Oh alright; ha HAAAAAA" (pulls back onto the road)

Feeling as if he'd just dodged the bullet, Julian jumps back into his delightful phone calling out his name.

SMS: Julian > Liliana

The brother doesn't know yet but please don't allow others to ruin such a night. I once said "Relationships are perfect...... except for other people" meaning two people can be perfectly compatible and set for the happy ending, but it's other people and all they bring that ruins the relationship... And with this in mind, we must cast out such visions of the misery that may befall and the dastardly events that may come before tomorrow's nightfall...

SMS: Julian > Liliana

Tomorrow ain't promised so we should live for the moment!

SMS: Julian > Liliana

And from what I know now, all I want is you...

SMS: Julian > Liliana

Simply :)

Placing hands on her forehead in disillusionment, Nancy envisions Jasmine whispering "You an'I are no more" to Liliana before walking away... In just a few twisted words, Jasmine passively attacks your inner core in ways no physical abuse could ever match.

Realizing the gravity of tonight's events, Liliana silents her phone and buries her head into Nancy's lap as tears begin to surface within her stunning eyes... With depression and guilt swirling around her, similar to Julian the picture show of their passion starts to conquer all and she cannot see anything but him, anything but them; anything but tonight... In her mind, Liliana revisits the scene of love's crime where an orchestral remix of "One" by Swedish House Mafia fills the hall:

Julian stands on one side of the floor in a fitted black Obey graphic-T with light grey "sorta" faded Levi 501 skinny jeans and his infamous black and white Converse all-star high tops he wore at least once a week. His stance doesn't scream "I'm the man," but has a quiet air of confidence with his unique, non "tunnel vision" view of the world; for although most remain stuck on what's directly in front of them at all times, Julian's roving eyes catch the beauty of life few ever see... Deciphering patterns of the flashing lights, Julian holds a cell phone in his right while the left sits in his pocket with only a thumb exposed... alone save for a woman standing across, Julian's eyes eventually fall to her.

Wearing a fitted black mini skirt and a slanted loose red t-shirt, Liliana courtesies; the mini dress rests an inch above her knees while the shirt leaves one shoulder exposed with a smidgen of the mid drift bare. A black heart shaped pendant necklace sophisticates the mini skirt yet accentuates her cleavage... And standing at a mere 5'6 in 2 inch black heels, Liliana shoots a "puppy dog tail waving" HELLO!!!! with her right hand inducing Julian's cool demeanor to hiccup. Feeling the rush of vulnerability whisk by him, Julian looks away as he walks towards her to try an'hide his smile's shame as if it would give away his true self. Realizing she'd eventually have to meet him at the center of the dance floor, Liliana lifts her right foot and takes a step; then the left... then another. Inside, their heart beats power walk; then jog, and with both hearts in full sprint standing 6 feet away from eachother, a total eclipse of the lights halts them in their tracks.

Bowing in total darkness, Julian puts his right hand out awaiting her's in return. Taking two steps forward, Liliana reaches out to graze his fingers an'without hesitation Julian lunges forward as the lights return and gently spins her back to his chest while interlocking their hands. Holding her close, Liliana nuzzles his temple and lets out a feline "mmmmm" exhale allowing her scents and essences to powerfully waft towards him till his insides freeze. After eternity's embrace, Julian's left hand shifts her chin back and kisses her slowly yet deliberate with very little tongue; both bodies writhe in pleasure as evident by the now firm grasp of their interlocked hands below. Gracefully moving her to his left, the two hold eachother side by side like an ice dance couple about to begin their serenade. Turning away to hide her tears of happiness welling up to fall, Julian whispers a soft "no" before swiveling her head t'gaze upon the happiness forming in his own eyes the same allowing smiles to freely blur together as love creeps forth from the shadows... Softly laughing with all reservations now gone, both let happiness glide down passion's slide before the peaceful calm evaporates once tears leave faces up and not down; towards smiles not frowns... Staying true to their name, after exchanging puzzled half smiles enchanted tears fall t'bustling Swedish House Mafia ruled dance floors below... Now contently resting on nooks between his collar bone an'shoulder with eyes closed, a kiss on Liliana's forehead shutters her eyes open to a "starry eyed" Liliana gazing at them from the valley's floor below; and from high on ceilings above to the now shattered grounds below, Liliana wildly exclaims: "This is it!" #sheknows

Act 1: Scene 7: "When will I See you again?" (Heights Edition)

SMS: Q > Bastion
Pick up some beer loser
SMS: Q > Bastion
How's life with the pot head?

SMS: Bastion > Q
Ha
SMS: Bastion > Q
Ha

Stephan: "Should we???"

Bastion: "No..."

Stephan: "I didn't even-"

Bastion: "-NO!"

Stephan: "But how bout just-"

Bastion: "-Read my lips, (looks over) NOOOO!" (#bush)

Act 1: Scene 7: "When will I See you again?" (Valley Edition)

Nancy: "How could you? This is bad... this is really bad..."

Liliana: (sitting up) "...I know, TRUST me, I know... "

Nancy: "Well, how are you going to stay away from him? How will you not fall victim to his spell? (Liliana's eyes fall to the ground) Heavens, you already have! (Liliana flashes an "about to cry" look) Well, we'll figure something out dear"

Liliana: "I'll be right back, gotta fix my make up"

Nancy: "Ok, I'll come"

Liliana: "No no; I got it"

Nancy: (eyebrows suspiciously raised) "...you're gonna text him aren't you (Liliana replies with a "what do you expect" look) Does she know? (Liliana shakes her head) Ok; wellllll tonight is tonight, go child! I'll come back in a little while t'check on you..." (smiles)

Stephan: "Fine... can we stop forrrrrrr......" (stares off blankly)

Bastion: (rolls eyes) "...yessss, we'll stop so you can blaze; we need beer anyways"

Stephan: "Score one for the goood guyyyyysss"

Bastion: (glancing over eyes wide) "You know, every time you take a hit, a fairy dies... "

Stephan: "Well as long as its not Tink from Hook, it's cool... She was hellla sexy"

Bastion: "Uh huh"

Stephan: (eyes closed swinging left fist in the air) "I LOVE YOU JUUULLLIIIIAAAAAAAA!!!"

Bastion: "Yeaaaa you do" (noddingly smiling)

After stopping for beer and a hit or 6, the two embark in Q and Julian's skid marks towards Manuel's party on the east side... far removed from the royal kingdom of the valley.

With her back to the door and knees up in her makeshift sanctuary, Liliana takes out her delightful cell, inhales a deep breath with eyes closed and unlocks her phone to six messages:

SMS: Nicole > Liliana

Girl, where are you? Are you ok? Are you with HIM?????? ;)

SMS: Jaime > Liliana

Lily!! Where are you? I need details!!! Was he a good kisser? You haven't kissed a guy since Ty Ty!

SMS: Tyler > Liliana

Hwey, Whens ourr Dance gonna be? Where yous at?

But only pays attention to:

SMS: Julian > Liliana

The brother doesn't know yet but please don't allow others to ruin such a night. I once said "Relationships are perfect...... except for other people" meaning two people can be perfectly compatible and set for the happy ending, but it's other people and all they bring that ruins the relationship... And with this in mind, we must cast out such visions of the misery that may befall and the dastardly events that may come before tomorrow's nightfall...

Busy tearing apart his calm demeanor t'pieces on the floor of the other car, Julian begins to lose hope; yet the moment he believes she's truly forgotten about him- Bukka Buuuu! Bukka Buuuu!

SMS: Liliana > Julian
Awww... I've only known you for an hour, but I miss you soooooo much!!!

SMS: Liliana > Julian
I just wanna see you! : (

SMS: Julian > Liliana

Tomorrow ain't promised so we should live for the moment!

SMS: Julian > Liliana

And from what I know now, all I want is you...

SMS: Julian > Liliana

Simply :)

After reading his messages twice, Liliana collapses both hands to'er phone, closes her eyes and returns to the ceiling...

Standing alone in his obey shirt and chucks perusing the room with laissez faire grace, Liliana BEGS her mind to fast forward to his eyes meeting hers and magnificently caressing her body to climax... Lighting up her darkened emotional prison, Julian's eyes transpose his blush shortened breath flushed cheeks and trembling heart to her body: now floored ceilinged spun and exhilarated, such adjectives spice up her life in a manner she's never tasted with ingredients she's never heard of in a language unknown to mere mortals. If people can "undress you with their eyes," a Casta can undress your emotional walls and pierce through the strongest doors to enter uncharted waters.

SMS: Liliana > Julian

Awww... I've only known you for an hour, but I miss you soooooo much!!!

SMS: Liliana > Julian

I just wanna see you! : (

SMS: Julian > Liliana

> Such a glorious noise and fantastical feeling to hear your words fall on my vibrantly awaiting ears... I have to, HAVE to see you tonight!!!! But this is not life and death for the breath and beat of my heart now falls in line with yours...

Q: “Hey, McTexty! We’re here...”

Julian: “It’s pronounced, Mc-Lovin; (smiles) and here issssss?” (Bukka Buuuu!)

SMS: Liliana > Julian

> Life hadn’t begun till our eyes met and we’ll surely meet before tomorrow's drama tries to keep us apart :)

Q: “Manuel’s crib in the east hills! You would have known if you weren’t all up in your phone the whole ride up an’ignorin me...”

Julian: “Awwww, I’m sorry girl; didn’t know you were so sensitive. Where’s Bast and Steph?” (turns phone t’silent)

Q: “On their way; they had to stop for beer an’a smoke break”

Julian: “Fuckinnn guuuyyyyy; he needs to smoke less”

Q: “Yea, and YOU need to fall in love less!”

Julian: (glances to his phone an’back at Q smiling) “True”

SMS: Julian > Liliana

Such a glorious noise and fantastical feeling to hear your words fall on my vibrantly awaiting ears... I have to, HAVE to see you tonight!!!! But this is not life and death for the breath and beat of my heart now falls in line with yours...

SMS: Liliana > Julian

Life hadn't begun till our eyes met and we'll surely meet before tomorrow's drama tries to keep us apart :)

SMS: Julian > Liliana

> The words that fall from such succulent lips penetrate my mind's deepest recesses and bring light to previously dormant worlds. I've never met such a beautiful and glorious soul who speaks to me on my own romantically hopeless level... I've walked my whole life with the beat of the bass flowing through my head and only now found it's true treble ;) #imissmytreble

While walking up to the party, a random "acquaintance" of Bastion sees the royal four and moves as fast as possible without running to catch up. Similar to rollin with Vinnie Chase and the entourage, simply arriving with the heights to any party bar or club increases your chances of scoring a random girl.

Random guy 1: "Heyyyy!!!! Sebastionnnnn! What uuuupp! You rollin t'Manuel's?" (puts right hand out)

Bastion: "Oh... hey..." (begrudgingly clasps hands)

Random guy 1: (pulls Bastion in patting his back twice) "Where y'all comin from?"

Bastion: (looks to Q and Julian smirking: did he just say...) "WE ALLLLLLL are comin from the valley-"

Random guy 2: "-Siiiiiiiick, we were gonna head out there but came here instead"

SMS: Julian > Liliana

The words that fall from such succulent lips penetrate my mind's deepest recesses and bring light to previously dormant worlds. I've never met such a beautiful and glorious soul who speaks to me on my own romantically hopeless level... I've walked my whole life with the beat of the bass flowing through my head and only now found it's true treble ;) #imissmytreble

SMS: Liliana > Julian

Your words shoot through my body and continue to break off the doors to my prisons inside...

SMS: Liliana > Julian

Currently free falling, I've jumped off the world and the air of your texts keep me floating, forever to be soaring once we meet in person :) #tompetty

Anxiously awaiting for the bubble with three dots to appear signifying Julian's typing a message, Liliana continues to reread their text stream. Since some phones and social media sites allow you to see whether your message(s) have been "read" and at what time, along with the thrill of seeing them type comes the sadness and anxiety of knowing _______ saw the message but has yet to respond... Maybe _______ Purposely waited because they didn't wanna appear desperate or possibly wanted to start a game of the inevitably dangerous cat and mouse.

Knowing no one would ever invite these randoms to any valley related function, Bastion rolls his eyes and channels his inner Dr. Evil saying: "Riiiiigggggghhhhhtt" #austinpowers ...With Q and Julian continuing on past the random guys to the party; Bastion tries to rid himself of his "friends:"

Bastion: "Well alright alright... I'll see Y'ALLL in there"

Random guy 3: "Wordddd, lets get in that piece" (all leave except for the high space cadet Stephan)

Feeling bad for these random "nobodies," Bastion continues walking towards Manuel's without responding #kingdomhearts ...Always a step behind in life, Stephan constantly assures himself that "Mary Jane" is NOT the culprit and he would function just the same if her were sober; unable to break out of their own smoke filled square, most stoners live their lives in the same denial... Stephan DID however "break free" (#iloveyouariana) of carrying the two 30 rack's of Coors light by handing them off to their new "friends" #wekeepitclassysandiego

SMS: Liliana > Julian

Your words shoot through my body and continue to break off the doors to my prisons inside...

SMS: Liliana > Julian

Currently free falling, I've jumped off the world and the air of your texts keep me floating, forever to be soaring once we meet in person :) #tompetty

With the speed of technology, it takes less and less to justify reaching out to someone else if your "bae" is unresponsive. In the 21st century, people have become so insecure and dependent on other's attention that many will reach out to a new love or lust if their significant other doesn't respond right away. If someone's needs, (not just sexual) are unsatisfied by another, they may find someone else to satisfy that need: if you cannot talk about the meaning of life, what exists in far off galaxies, why the sky is blue, or Any intellectually deep issue, then you may find someone else to converse with in such a manner. Is this considered cheating? Society says no... But cheating is in the eye of the beholder and up to their own interpretation. Cheat, cheat on...

SMS: Julian > Liliana

I wish I was gazing upon your face into stars falling eyes and I promise we'll meet before the day's new sun rise...

Reminiscent of Mike Dexter's entrance to the party in "Can't Hardly Wait," the heights are met by a plethora of guys and girls alike jetting to the door in celebration of their arrival. The complete opposite of their entrance into the valley party which mirrored Amanda Becket's in the same movie with: "I cant believe they're here" and "soft whisperings of the same"... Off in a different realm, Julian auto pilots through the scene...

Q: "What the FUCK is upppp Y'ALLLLL???" (arms open; elbows bent)

Day dreaming of their night's realities and their future meeting, Julian has yet to "announce" himself at the party. After shooting a couple "hey what's up" slight head nods to a few select ladies in the room, Q wakes Julian by slapping his chest with the back of his hand.

Julian: "...We came to CRACK this fuckin lame ass party" (everyone starts wooing, clapping an'nodding their heads)

Stephan: "Anybody order a love burger? Welllll done..." (in his best Breckin Meyer accent #crickets)

Bastion: (looks back at Stephan smiling) "Really?"

SMS: Julian > Liliana

I wish I was gazing upon your face into stars falling eyes and I promise we'll meet before the day's new sun rise...

SMS: Liliana > Julian

When will you leave the world where you stand and return to me waiting on the ceiling with open hand?

Stephan: "Ummmmm...... you fuckinnnnnnn, know it?"

Bastion: "There you go son!" (slams Stephan on the back causing him to stumble forward)

Q: (turns to the random guys) "Bring the beer outside"

Random Nerd 7: (walks up to Stephan) "Dude, love burger? (puts fist out looking for a "I've been accepted by the crew" pound) ...Awesome" (Stephan slowly pounds and highly smiles)

(DJ mixes into "Drake - The Motto feat. Lil Wayne")

Walking up to the lone picnic table in the back yard, Q glares a "Wellllllll?" look prompting the current group to glance at eachother before allowing them t'sit on the table top with their feet resting on the bench's beams. After all, only losers sit on wooden picnic tables normally; "Didn't you get that memo?" #officespace (I'm in the buildin and I'm feelin myself, rest in peace Mac Dre I'mma do it for the Bay, okay)

There's an unused beer pong table in the back, numerous patches of unwatered grass and one large tree providing shade during the day; a various assortment of wooden and metal chain linked fences divide property lines while Mariachi music blasts from neighbors who only drink Bud Light, Budweiser, Bud Light, Tequila and Bud Light con lime. On a couple randomly sized wooden slabs rests a plastic table with two Numark CDJ's and a Non Mac Laptop mixing trendy "top 40" hits which sounds like electro hip hop with voice modulation and "cash money hoes" orientated lyrics.

SMS: Liliana > Julian

Oh no you've disappeared : (

Unlike valley parties, it's always BYOB and BYOD (bring your own drugs) here on the east side. (It's Eastside, we in this bitch) Though talk of the heights arrival currently rain down, standard conversations revolve around: how drunk they or someone else is, who has connects on drugs/more alcohol, options if they leave, how good or bad the music is and stories from the other night(s) of partying. Guys argue over what pack of ladies they should pursue, which exact girls they're "claiming" an'point out "borderline fuckable" girls askin eachother: "Would you?" (with the "fuck them?" implied) ...Conversely, girls debate which groups of guys are attractive and why, what guys they're texting/texting them and whether they should hit up an after party or make it a "girls night". Ironically the "ladies" point out "borderline" girls and judge their hair, make up choices, outfits and boyfriends.

Still carrying the 30 racks of Coors Light and afraid to "fuck up," the random guys await instructions. Without looking towards'em, Q points to the table and puts his hand out expecting 4 beers... After passing them out to the crew;

Q: "Knock yourselves out; have a beer an'go check out the party inside"

Still waiting for a reply, Julian wonders if she's forgotten about him... Sitting on the ledge of his mind with her hands holding onto the edge, Liliana stares forward dangling her legs in silence as she has yet to respond...

Nancy: (gracefully knocks on door) “Lilianazzzzzzyyyyy? Are you in there?”

Liliana: “...uhh, hi Nance... What’s up?”

Nancy: “Are you ok? Did you text him?

Liliana: “OH MY GOD! RELAX! I’m fine, I’ll be out in a minute”

Nancy: “And Julian?”

Liliana: “Well I’m texting him still... or was until he went silent”

Nancy: “Can you open up please?”

Liliana: (neither ready to leave her sanctuary nor face the party and their 8 million questions) “...I just wanna be alone for a little bit longer”

Nancy: “I understand, I’ll be in the kitchen so just text me if you need anything... ok dear? ...Would you like a drink? You know I make the best vodka crans!”

Liliana: (torn between the want for alcohol and the want to be alone) “...Thanks; but, I think I’m good right now. I’ll let you know”

Nancy: “Alright sweetie...”

Somewhat sobered, Julian pictures himself switching his phone to silent earlier and jumps off the bench.

Stephan: “What’s his deal?”

Q: “What the fuck! You sober now? I think that’s the fastest I’ve seen you react in years”

Bastion: (slow claps) “Bravvv-vooo”

Stephan: (bows) “I’ll be here all night people; please remember to tip your bartender”

Bastion: (laughing) “...This guy”

Walking inside, Julian sees four texts from HER on his locked screen:

SMS: Liliana > Julian

When will you leave the world where you stand and return to me waiting on the ceiling with open hand?

SMS: Liliana > Julian

Oh no you’ve disappeared : (

SMS: Liliana > Julian

HELLLLOOOOO!!!!!! ARE YOU THERE?????? ARE YOU OK??????

SMS: Liliana > Julian

The world ceases to spin without hearing from you!!! : (

Fully aware Julian's probably partying with his boys and NOT currently sitting in a darkened bathroom, she didn't wanna continue "blowing him up" yet...

SMS: Liliana > Julian

HELLLLOOOOO!!!!!! ARE YOU THERE??????
ARE YOU OK??????

SMS: Liliana > Julian

The world ceases to spin without hearing from you!!! : (

Jasmine instructed her to use any and all reasons to push significant others away if she ever felt too vulnerable. Taking her advice, Liliana thinks: "How would Jasmine react to the new guy? How would Tyler? How would their relationship affect the whole dynamic of the valley?". Watered by anxiety and given moonlight by lack of control, doubt begins to spring out of her mind's grounds... In an attempt to combat her self defense mechanics, Liliana leaves the bathroom to make herself a drink.

Act 1: Scene 8: "Kodak Moment"

SMS: Julian > Liliana

I'm so sorry my phone was on silent... I thought YOU had forgotten about ME!!!

SMS: Liliana > Julian

LOL never that! I know how y'all party! ;) I was worried Q had started a fight or something...

SMS: Julian > Liliana

Already I can't imagine life without you. I still can't believe I finally found you!

SMS: Julian > Liliana

Haha yea he has been known to get crazy if anyone disrespects us but his reputation doesn't do him justice... Everyone thinks he takes advantage of girls, but they actually take advantage of him! #badreputation #actuallyagoodguy

When the mind frantically shoots out thoughts as quickly as possible because you have sooo much to say, text streams can split into two separate conversations where one responds to the first while the other replies to the second an'vice versa… And since people's tastes refine over time, as you age it becomes harder to find and develop such connections #appreciatethatshit

However, because one cannot convey facial expressions or "tone" via text without attaching an emoticon or "haha/lol," misunderstandings arise when someone takes a comment or joke in a text to heart. Moreover, when you doubt your significant others' affinity for you, hearing the "love" in their voice over the phone reassures you more than any number of texts ever could. Although "lovey dovey" texts normally suffice, days without physical contact creates distance and supplies water to the ever present plants of doubt inside; and since vulnerability increases the deeper you fall in love, the further you travel down the depths the easier it becomes for your plant to grow.

SMS: Liliana > Julian

I know!!!! When will I see you again???

SMS: Liliana > Julian

Wow thats crazy! He gives off this image of being such a bad ass who could care less about his new "girl of the week". It's nice to know that he's nothing like Perry who HAS allowed his inner demons to live up to their own treacherous potential…

Living in his phone, Julian ignores anyone trying to interact with him or throws a half hearted "oh hey what's up" before jumping back into his new obsession... Determined to confront Julian about his incessant texting, Bastion heads inside.

Bastion: "Sooooooo, how is she?"

Julian: "Who the fuc- (looks up) oh, ummmm, she's great... you know me wayyyyy too well"

Bastion: (Julian jumps back into his phone) "...you've been texting her non stop haven't you?"

Julian: (without looking up) "Yup"

Bastion: (leans in) "......annnnnnd, what about your brother asshole?"

Replaced by Santana and his unforgiving stare, the face of Julian's new love fades into the background of his mind... Picturing himself driving up to the over-look t'find a depressively passed out Santana, Julian had grown accustom to saving his brother from his own suffocating heartbreak on a weekly basis... Looking over to his right in disbelief, leafs of doubt brush across Julian's face;

Julian: "...Fuck......"

Santana had never fallen for a love such as her and to prove his devotion he married her quicker than most. Awaking each dawn to the whimsical feeling of a full life, the sweet allure of her scent carried him through the darkest of days; this was a "Matrix" styled resurrection love that could regenerate death into life and breathe beauty into the ugliest of tragedies.

Having never encountered a love like his, it scared her that being apart brought tears to Santana's heart filled eyes due to how much he missed the light she illuminated over his world. Having never known anything but, Jasmine found comfort in her painful life and loathed the lofty throne on which he'd placed her, unable to accept nor conceive that someone could ever see her as HE did... Powerless to change the image she saw in the mirror and utterly incapable of loving herself, Jasmine swam away from such great depths...

Falling in love is waking up in a dark room alone; whether an oasis, mirage or the real thing, the dark is hauntingly heart strickening. But the warmth of your soul's counterpoint waking up the same allows once scared hearts to pump brilliantly without skipping a fatal beat... Wandering the dark alone is the break of the heart; an'although heartbreak stems from true blindness as love knows no eyes, one can only wander without another's warming light for so long until giving in to the hopeless waters below becomes your only option.

In life their are two types of mates: with the same anniversary gleam and sexual routine, the first and most chosen accompanies a love that's never rewritten. This is the safe haven husband or wife; this is the safe havenish sort of life... For with conflict missing in action and smooth open waters to sail, most never chase any other although many will bore of the serene an'resign to live the latter.

The second type can also be the safe haven or forever pin needles away from relationship armageddon. Always sure to spread their voice, this is not the "walk all over" him or her choice; for with accountability each and every date, the'll keep you on course and ensure you'll fly straight. This "notebook" love brings new challenges each day and new place, but together you'll move past various obstacles that you'll both inevitably face. They'll break into boxes on your soul's hallowed grounds, and join the battle against demons we imprison deep down... And contrary to the former, the latter's filled with intense fights; but monumental reconnects will keep your passion in fluorescent lights.

Although stable, reliable, and her best friend, the husband Peter was void of "jump off a cliff" passion; the fights were not as intense, but neither was the inevitable recommence; Peter DID provide much more stability and Jasmine lay content yet occasionally dreaming of the depths she'd glance away and lament. Santana took her to a tea party on the floor of her soul; and by breaking through all barriers and shark filled waters, he'd reached depths she once closed off an'shut down to all others. The lights down here as a guide were no longer alive; but she was. This scared her and she ran; she let go in the dark and swam up to dry land. The vulnerability that he gave her, all too fearful had chased her to the assured warmth of the shallow shores. And while Santana opened another box she'd hid at soul's depths, all lights inside her shut off at his broken heart's expense... That day Jasmine left the tea party down on that shelf; he fell into a hole that now encapsulated himself.

But when currents from the depths wash upon her soul's shores, every moment shared passes an'wisps through her mind with resentment to ashes: she recalls Santana's touches an'his intimate graces, but like a passerby on the street, it quickly erases. Yet these smallest of splashes on the fewest of toes, release earthquake like shockwaves upon Santana's throes, renewing his hope to keep dreaming down below... And reaching out into the dark an'hoping to find her hand, he grasps air instead becoming hard for him to stand; pining for the currents to come shooting through her again, he waits for a life that will never truly begin; but hope... hope can be a dreadfully scary thing...

Bastion: "...I get it, but you gotta talk to him first because it will be THAT much worse if he hears it from someone else. You know where he's at and after you've sobered up you know whats you need to do"

Julian: "Damn... but dude; how can I tell him I've won the heart of the sister he loss???" (Bukka Buuuu!)

Bastion: (shaking head) "...Shit J, I'ave no fuckin clue. Ever since your parents passed, (crosses heart) rest in peace, he's always had your back EXCEPT for when it came to the his ex... Remember when Q and him came to blows over her? After he threw fist to face, Q was ready t'throw down as usual but he took one look at Santana and-"

Julian: "-the one time Q backed down"

Bastion: "Exactly, and he still believes that one day she'll drop that Peter asshole and come back to him... You better be realllll careful how you handle this shit bro"

Julian: (sigh) "I'm utterly loss to the whirlwind of her beauty; the feelings that wrap around me like a tornado carry me off t'distant pleasures and foreign treasures; I can't imagine life without her my dude, I-"

Bastion: "-YOU JUST MET TWO FUCKIN HOURS AGO!"

Julian: "I KNOW!!!! And do you see my entranced nature? My subliminal attraction? She floors me, ceilings me in ways I've never thought possible and I see why he's never let'er sister go...... And now I have to break his heart again? Certain this time it will never mend? I won't divulge lies as to when my time with Liliana is to expire and I'll suffer the consequences of whatever soon transpires"

Bastion: "What... the FUCK... are you TALKIN ABOUT!!! Did you turn into frickin shakespeare in the last 10 minutes???? Who are you??!! (grabs random guy walking by) Hey, have YOU seen Julian?"

Random guy 28: "Heyyyyyyy, what's up Julian, (hand clasps Julian and turns t'Bastion laughing) funny bro..."

Bastion: "You better snap out of this real quick; you're gonna break up the band Yoko!"

Julian: "This love! (points down) Is NOT to trifled, truffled or rifled! No bullets of tongue can deny the war I've won on this night!" (Bukka Buuuu!)

Bastion: (up in Julian's face like a coach arguing with an umpire in baseball) "You've fuckin loss it Jules!!! Did you just talk about truffles and tongue bullets? When did you become a frickin fortune cookie???? What's my lucky numbers this month bitch???" (sarcastically laughing)

Julian: (looks Bastion up and down) "Back up bro. You're over stepping your bounds; for fucked up shit this way comes if you continue these sounds"

(outside)

Stephan: (looking inside) “Hey... (taps Q on the shoulder) ...hey (taps twice) ...hey fool” (taps again)

(inside)

Bastion: “You’ve fuckin lost it! Are you wasted off your ass? You’re about to throw down over some bitch you met 2 hou-”

Julian: (shoves Bastion to the ground)

(outside)

Stephan: “Heyyyy YO! (shakes Q’s shoulder) QUINCY!!!”

Q: “Excuse me girl, (turns to Stephan) WHAT!!!”

Stephan: “Inside!” (pointing to the two)

Q: “Damn Steph, why didn't you tell me sooner? (leaps off the bench and runs inside) What the fuck is this?”

Julian: “He... well, I-”

Bastion: “-IIII insulted his mom”

Q: (turns drunkenly puzzled) “Well frickin A man! You should know better than t’talk about the deceased, (crosses heart and looks up) rest in peace. You’re a fuckin asshole!” (storms out towards the front door)

Stephan: "Yeaaaaaaa..... (looking at Bastion) you; (points at him) fuckinnnnn... ASShole"

Knowing how a drunken Q would have reacted to the real reason of their altercation, Julian understands why Bastion took the blame. Scared of his own actions, Julian realizes just how much he cared for the woman he'd met hours earlier. He should be ecstatic having finally found his Helen but his brothers impending dejection had cracked his core causing new love t'seep out of the newly formed holes... Attempting t'soften the blow, Julian offers to help Bastion up but he passively looks away, stands up under his own power and heads towards the front door shaking his head...

Julian: "Guess he had one too many beers huh? (silence) .....Welllll, (stretching) bout time for me to be hittin the ol'dusty trail..." (with no response Julian leaves #familyguy)

Q: (throws arm around Julian) "Heyyyyy, you cooooool little buddy?"

Julian: "...uhhh shyyeaa" (turns to Bastion)

Glancing at his blown up phone's inbox:

SMS: Great America Girl > Q
You comin back to the valley? :)

SMS: Random # > Q
Heyyyy, still tryin to have you and your boys roll through later???

SMS: Denny's Girl > Q
It's wednesday night baby, you cumin by later? I have your favorite mini skirt on... Mmmmm I want you! :)

SMS: Kristin > Q
Hey

SMS: Random # > Q
You never hit me back last night : (

SMS: Blunt Girl > Q
Q? You there?

SMS: Hand Job Susie > Q
Hey handsome, wyd tonight? :)

Instead of having 3 Michelle's, 6 Jen's and farrr to many Nicole's to count, many ultra pursued guys will enter unique names such as: "Denny's Parking Lot Girl," (met in the parking lot) "Hand Job Susie," (gave a hand job under the table and is NOT named Susie lol) "Great America Girl," (works at...) "Tyler's Sister," (from the valley party earlier) and "Blunt Girl" (always arrives con blunt). On the other side of the sword, an attractive girl uses names such as: "Hot Zack," "Tanned Derek," "Big Dick John," "Drummer guy," "Chemistry James" and "Party Manuel" (host of the party the heights just left). Before using catchy names, people would label duplicate contacts as Nicole 1, 2 or 3 and occasionally mix up whose who. Catch, catch on...

"Kristin" is uncoincidentally the only girl who DOESN'T constantly try to captivate Q's attention by continuously "blowing him up;" and therein lies the secret to texting/messaging in the 21st century: as difficult as it may be, acting as if you have your own life and could care less whether you talk to/interact with any person of the opposite sex increases your attractiveness 8 million fold. Whether Kristin WANTS to see him is irrelevant for the mystery she creates by acting indifferent intrigues Q an'gives him the desire to "know" her and learn what she's all about... Bret Easton Ellis once wrote "No one ever knowwwws anyone... you will never, know me..." #rulesofattraction ...And this is the tragic reality of humanity: you will never truly know who anyone is, what drives their actions and whether your significant other dates you for support money self confidence self worth, or actually loves the fuck out of you.

You can neither step into another's shoes nor send your inner thoughts to anyone as much as you would like. The feelings they give you and the aching pleasures they transpose through their eyes during intimate embraces is the closest you'll ever get to "knowing" another. In such moments, sensations divulge their feelings as their whole essence, body and spirit dance with yours... Yet beyond that "kodak moment" one's never sure what thoughts drip off the leaves of another's mind; for even when you're unsure where you stand in your lover's eyes, you'll remain in troubled relationships due to the inherent need to feel wanted and loved by someone... Anyone...

And to make matters worse, the deeper you fall in love the harder it becomes to read someone since your own feelings eventually transcend your judgement an'overrule common sense; and THIS is the culprit as to why you can analyze everyone else's pitfalls, mistakes, and poor judgement better than your own; for trying to deconstruct your own wants an'actions is nearly impossible... Try, try on...

Act 1: Scene 9:
"I'm in the building and Yes I AM Feelin Myself" #ripmacdre

(Julian throws “The Neighbourhood - 1 of Those Weaks” on Q’s stereo as the three pass around a bottle of Hennessy while waiting for Bastion to grab his car)

Julian: “Fuckkkkk yea!!! NBHDDDD!!!!” (starts C-walkin to the beat)

(Yea I’m stuck in between, if I’m wrong or I’m right)

Q: “Ha-HAAAAAA SONNNN! (swigs Henn and passes it to Stephan) DO it UP!” (hand clasps Julian and starts C-Walkin)

Julian: “OH dayyyymnnnnn fool!!!! (throws arm around Stephan pointing at Q) My boy MUST be twisted, look at him go-give me dat” (steals bottle and swigs)

Stephan: “Hey! I didn’t even hit that yet... Bitccchhh!”

(I’m jus tryin to get by)

Julian: “Quit your cryin” (hands it to Stephan and starts c-walkin again)

Stephan: “Finally!” (raises bottle)

Q: “NOPE!” (grabs bottle and takes a fat ass swig)

Stephan: (high pitched) “Mother FUCKer!!!!”

Julian: (holds a pose) “Come onnn meow” (laughing #supertroopers)

Q: “Alright alright...” (hands it to Stephan)

Stephan: "Finally" (glaring at both while swigging)

Julian: (rappin along) "They call me one take Jake baby... ha ha ha HAAAA" (bouncing left and right)

Q: "I got that big fat snake baby..." (pulls out phone)

SMS: Q > Kristin
Heyyyyy beautiful!
SMS: Q > Kristin
What's you up too?

Knowing how to hold the attention of a "hot guy," Kristin would not immediately reply even though she badly wanted to. Likewise, for "normal" guys to captivate MOST "hot girls," they're to treat them as if their just another chick and even ignore them to a certain extent.

(my daddy is dead, I've got no man to follow)

SMS: Liliana > Julian
Where did you go??? I feel like such a loser texting you 15 minutes later after no response. WHAT HAVE YOU DONE TO ME??? This is just not fair, you're off with your friends and I'm stuck staring at my phone waiting for you to respond : (
SMS: Liliana > Julian
Did you forget about me again? Hellllllooooooo

(It's just 1 of those weaks)

Reassured she's as far off the deep end as he is, Julian drunkenly smiles to himself; nothing like another's frantic texts to boost your confidence in bae's feelings for you ;)

SMS: Julian > Liliana
I couldn't never forget you!!! Pleassssseeee I don't wanna evvvvvver hear such words roll off your tongues again. From here on out.... it's just meeeeeeeee and you. Sooooo if yourrrrrr a loser... than so am I....
SMS: Julian > Liliana
Cuz I feel...
SMS: Julian > Liliana
The exact
SMS: Julian > Liliana
Same
SMS: Julian > Liliana
Way!!!!!!
SMS: Julian > Liliana
:)

Bastion: (walking up) "Hey bitccccheeeeeeees!!! (all three turn back) Whoooooooose drivin??" (jingling keys)

Q: "I'm out... (hiccup) Drunk... I'm... (hiccup) Fuuuuuuuuuuuuuucked-(hiccup)"

Bastion: (waiting a second or two) "Uppppp?"

Q: "...Ahahaha! (hiccup) ...NOPE!!! (swigs Hennessy) I'm jus Fuuuuuuuuuuuuuucked-(hiccup)"

SMS: Liliana > Julian

OMG! I literally jumped out of my skin when my phone went off! Yay!!! You're back!!!! And apparently a little drunk lol...

SMS: Liliana > Julian

When am I gonna see you!!!! I know you're havin "boy time" but still... I miss you loser ;)

Stephan: (shakes head) "Andddddddd THIS guy (points with thumb) is NOT, a drivin... someone get him some weed stat!!!"

Julian: (looks up from phone to Stephan) "Uhhh who you askin? Hook him up moron!"

Stephan: "...Ohhhh, I got you!" (offers electronic pipe)

Q: "Thank you Doctor" (takes it nodding his head)

Stephan: "No problem sir" (both erupt into laughter)

SMS: Julian > Liliana

LOL, wellllll were prob gonna hit the denny's here on the east side by 680...

SMS: Julian > Liliana

If I can loser these guys

SMS: Julian > Liliana

Can yous pick me up? :) dont think I can drive or at least I probbbabbbly should not drive lol I miss you so much : (

Q: "Heyyyy! (inhales) We gonna roll losers?" (exhales)

Bastion: "Well whose drivin? (no response) ...guess I am, (laughs to himself) lets be out!"

SMS: Kristin > Q

I'm over at my girl's house drinking a little wine and catching up on season 6 of Sons... You?

Q drunkenly waves goodbye to his car and all four jump into Bastion's ride. (Q flips to "Bobby Schmurda - Hot Nigga") Driving to the late night eatery or nearest 7-11/Safeway to buy alcohol after a night of drinking is driving with a party in full swing; something about riding around in the car (or cab) drunk off your ass with music blasting causes everyone to act like fools and transforms lame caterpillars into social butterflies partying like its mother fuckin nineteen ninety-nine! #prince ...Busy trying to avoid swerving, speeding and keeping the music under "pull me over" decibels, the driver's job is anything but easy; and along with the peer pressure of the other passengers yelling: "Go fuckin faster!" "Turn that shit up!" and the ever popular "Quit being a bitch!" makes designated driving a fun filled nightmare. Playing the game "how much of my body can I keep outside of the window while yelling at random people," the front seat passenger is a DUI waiting to happen; especially when combined with the two back seat fun bags continuously reaching over the center console to change the music lol... And when they're not fighting over the music the two "DJ's" in the back are stuck on "full blast" arguing over which one of them this "one girl/guy" at the party/bar/club wanted to hook up with. Drive drive on...

SMS: Q > Kristin
I'm drunk

SMS: Liliana > Julian
I can't wait!!! And of course I'll drive cuz I'm NOT drunk lol. Let me know when I can come pick you up!!!! :)

(in the valley)

After confirming their rendezvous, Liliana decides to head back to the currently "host-less" party. (Jasmine passed out during that "one" track ;) Standing up and still sporting a full smile, Liliana adjusts her red slanted t-shirt and pulls down her black fitted mini dress. Finally arisen out of the bubble that was her phone, Liliana hears the faint sound of the DJ blasting a song wit some deeeeeeep ass bass. Although barely able to make it out, Liliana id's it as her favorite Lorde song ("400 Lux") and immediately breaks out into her happy Lorde dance: (similar to Vanilla Ice's go ninja go dance #kraftad)

Placing her right arm straight and pointing diagonally downward towards the floor, her right open palm is about a foot away from her right leg while the left hand rests below her right breast pointing the same direction. For beats 1 and 2 she brings her right hand up to her right breast (still pointing diagonally downward) while simultaneously throwing her left hand down to her waist as if she's covering her _____ #and1and2 ...Then for the second half of the dance she does the complete inverse by placing her right open hand a foot to the left of her face while the left hand almost cups the left breast but not quite. An'for beats 3 and 4 she throws her right hand down t'nearly cup her left breast while the left hand rises up t'land two feet to the left of her face #and3and4 Content with her dance and slowly bobbing her head left and right, Liliana groves out the door an'down the hall singin the repetitive hook: "And I like you".

With the window shattering bass slamming her senses, a floored feeling reverberates in'er mind; having found a love that sends shockwaves down your spine and makes your blood run backwards, Liliana can do nothing but smile while envisioning herself picking up Julian... Eagerly awaiting her phone to vibrate, Liliana glides through the party with a faint hidden smile as if she has a secret no one else knows along with feelings none shall ever experience... Glide glide on...

Act 1: Scene X:
Now THAT'S an Entrance!

Either succumbing to the peer pressure or wanting to join in on his friend's "reindeer games," Bastion flips to "The Chainsmokers - #SELFIE" and turns it up to "pull me over" volume #letmetakeaselfie

Bastion: (turning it down 10 seconds later) "OK!!! Settle down!!! Fuck! I will turn this car around RIGHT now and NO more Denny's!!!" (three look at eachother for a second before breaking out int'laughter)

Q: (slaps Bastion on the back) "Good one fool!!! NOW, Quit being a bitch an'turn that shit up!! But first, (smiles to the back) let me take a selfie" (takes selfie)

(and I don't know if it's a booty call or not)

Stephan: "Are we there yet? I'm not tryin to (inhales) wait t'smoke this" (exhales)

Julian: "Fuck dude, blow it out the window; I don't wanna smell like your smoke!"

(that dress, is so tacky; who wears cheetah?)

Q: (turns around) “Why do YOU care?

Julian: “...well, I may meet up with this one chick later...”

Q: “Shut UP! ...Seriously? Who? ...And don’t you dare say whats her face”

(...but first, let me take a selfie)

Julian: “No no, Sarah...”

Q: “Wait... Who?”

Julian: “Sarah!”

Q: “WHO????”

Julian: “STILL Sarah; FUCK! You don’t even know'er”

Q: “Ohhhhhh Shit! Look at my boy” (slaps Bastion even harder on the back)

Bastion: “I’m tryin t’drive dude! Fuck!”

Stephan: “...yaaayyy (inhales) for Juliaaaannn” (exhales)

(let me take a selfie)

Bastion: (looking at Julian in the rear view) “Good shit I guess...”

Julian: “Thank you, thank you... “ (stares out window)

Q: (switches to “Lil Wayne - Rich as Fuck feat. 2 Chainz” and evilly smiles at Bastion)

Bastion: “No, (frantically shakes head) No dude... not happening”

Q: (looks to the two fools in the back seat nodding crazily) “OH yes... if I play it, we will ride...”

Pulling up to the Denny’s parking lot, smoke rises from cigarettes, pipes, electronic vaporettes, blunts, and even the occasional black and mild. Along with loud yelling and newly bought beers being dranken, all turn to see whose LOUD SLUMPING BASS this way comes.

Q: “Do it”

Bastion: “Q...”

Q: “You better Fuckin do it!”

Stephan and Julian: (chanting) “Doooo it! Doooo it!”

Q: “Come onnnnn man!!! Quit being a bitch and lets DO this Shit!!!!”

Bastion: (sighs, slows car to a crawl an’puts it in neutral)

Q: “You two idiots in the back better be outside the car like five seconds ago”

Opening the door, Q walks/dances next to the car with full swag on display. Begrudgingly opening their doors and stepping out to walk alongside the slow lurching car, Julian and Stephan begin to feel the "ghost ride" infect'em and skip around the car dipping down for an extremely low five like Lebron and Dwayne Wade #RIP ...With sub woofers blowing corporate sized buildings down an'the peanut gallery cheering, all ooze jealousy wishing it was THEIR crew ghost riding around the parking lot, popping collars, high-fiving and giving daps/pounds to all on THEIR "victory lap"... Seeing "Great america girl" who had texted him earlier, Q starts flirting an'completely forgets about the "ghost ride". Realizing the've loss the swag captain, Julian and Stephan head over to Q and the growing crowd...

Great america girl: "Oh my god... Q; that was fuckin dope!!!" (other girls swoon)

Random guy 7: (gives Q daps) "Good shit bro, that Lil Wayne song is a perfect for that shit"

Q: "Pshhhhh, yeaaaa; its alright" (looking for his crew)

Stephan: (yells out towards Q) "Uhhhhh!!! That shit was Siiiiiickk" (points up spurring both to jump and shoulder bump like NFL/NBA players after scoring a TD/killer dunk)

Julian: "ShhYea-Yaayyy-Yaaaaa" (points up to Q with the same result)

Bastion: (parks car, closes doors an'hurries over) "Hellllll yeaaaa!" (points finger up; Q shakes his head)

Bastion: (deflated) "...That shit was sick tho" (hand clasps Q)

Stephan: "I just said that!!!"

Great america girl: (runs over) "Soooo, where we sittin?"

Q: "Wellllll, WEEEE are sitting at OUR table, and you and your girls are sittinnnn... somewhere else... but don't worry, I'll hit you up later, (winks) aight?"

Great america girl: "OK!!!" (still smiling)

Q: "Anyways, (puts arms around Julian and Stephan) shall we gentlemen?"

Celebrating their glorious arrival, Julian looks towards the hills behind them where his brother undoubtedly sits alone yearning for her return...

Act 2: Scene 1: Such Great Depths

After fleeing, Santana ostracized himself and headed into the enclaved mountains; all four knew his final destination atop the overlook along with one woman who tried her best to forget.

Santana: "Hows you doin Jackkkk? (looking at the Jack Daniels bottle) What... nothing to say for yo selfs? Fine fuck you... (throws bottle out the window and stares at the gas pedal) All I have t'do... is turn you on and press down... do ya want me t'floor you?... Damn... no one's answerin me t'night; maybe I should hit up whats her face... but fuck, whats da use..."

(Santana puts one of their old songs on;
"Paramore - All I Wanted")

Admiring his miserable looks and agony induced smiles in the rearview, Santana envisions himself in the same position, same submission, 5 years through... His strength to swim away from the floor was no match for the rip tide of her beauty or the currents of'er eyes; she'd taken the glitz and glamour far up above while he remained at the bar "pain and suffering" in painful waters he'd come to know and love. And as their previous lives sparkle in the moon's view, he sits on his favorite stool having forgotten how t'stop from bleeding thru; with nothing left to adore as he saw all they'd built together fallen t'dust on the floor: the water warped the wood, mind and mirrors of the soul; twisted life's design and cooled the warmth of endless war. The sun dare not rise as Blitzkriegs filled the night's sky... while the moon waltzes by in full roar, reflecting its misery like a basilisk sliding upon the floor...

Awaking alone in darkened rooms all to familiar, Santana savors every inhale as the scent of'er everlasting essence allows pent up bodies to exhale... Heading for the islands of seclusion, his senses travel friendly roads of delusion where sun drenched happiness remains the unreachable illusion; for with no hand to guide the darkened misery, Santana continues in search of the monster he loves so invisibly.

Pining for such a desolate soul, he lay unaware what she'd met crossing tragic seas; an'what she'd left on the floor for none, not all to see. She'd turnt away from love and built barriers to protect against: the large white picket fence, the second story trim; the dream she never dreamt and made sure to keep within. She'd shot the four keys down the four currents of the flow, keeping the hidden boxes surrounding him untouched on the floor below: to the sun's rise in the east and dragon's whelp in the west, to the north's ice barren discs and the south's volcanic mess.

And hoping death wouldn't figure out his true reinvention, Santana travels currents to the final destination; wondering if he'd find his way back as the bar fades from view... Wondering whether she'd return after such time missed; to finally reconnect at such great depths once again in eye's kiss...

Act 2: Scene 2: Quincy Is Human

With all tables taken save for one, the heights walk to their reserved booth to the anger of a few "clueless" patrons waiting...

Random loser 1: "Dude what the fuck is this?"

Random loser 2: "What the fuck is what?" (half asleep)

Random loser 1: (walks up to a waitress) "Why'd they just walk in an'sit down at the ONE empty table?"

Waitress 2: "THAT table was reserved"

Random loser 2: (jumps up from his drunken stupor) "What??? You can't reserve tables at Denny's! This shit's fuckin retarded!"

(Less) random loser 5: "Dude, just drop it; let it go..."

Random loser 1: "No! This shit ain't right! Why do They get special treatment?"

Waitress 2: (flashes universal money sign by rubbing middle finger to thumb)

Random loser 2: "What? How much money do WE need to ALSO 'reserve' a table?"

(Less) random loser 5: (leans towards his friend) "This should be good"

Waitress 2: (glances to the cooks and back) "500 a week"

Random loser 2: "What? Them??? (points towards their table) They don't, (looks closer at their clothes, diamond earrings an'car they arrived in) Welllll; you would charge; hella just to eat at a low class joint; screw this!" (turns to leave)

Random loser 1: (waking up to one of the passed out girls in their group) "Come on, we're going!"

Sleeping loser girl: (eyes open) "Whaaaaa... is our food ready?"

Random loser 2: (helps half carry her out) "Come on we're bouncin..."

Sleeping loser girl: (half asleep) "But I want... pan, cakes..."

After the randoms leave, the heights join the other patrons in sarcastically clapping and waving goodbye. Although typically sympathetic to the lower classes, the heights still occasionally fell into "elitist" stereotypes when drunk... Having done enough damage to their reputation for the night, one random loser's attempts to turn back towards the restaurant were quickly curtailed...

Waitress 1: "Round of drinks?"

Julian: (looks around the table to see if anyone objects) "Thanks Jenn, can you also crack a bottle of Cabernet? (all three look at him confused) ...what?"

Q: “Wine??? I didn't even know we KEPT wine here”

Julian: “I feel like some wine; so shoot me”

Q: “Does it have something to do with your little ‘date’ you have later with... with...”

Julian: “Saaaarah!!!”

Q: “Ok ok... I guessss if its for a bitch then its susceptible to drink wine... (questionably staring at Julian) You meet her at the east side party?”

Julian: “Yup yup, (changing the topic) Niceeee... our drinks”

With three coronas, four shots of Hennessy and a glass of wine from a newly uncorked CAV, (circa 2001) the three still refuse to address the beautiful disaster of a centerpiece they’d seen on the Swedish House dance floor #311 ...The two may or may not believe Julian’s talkin about “Sarah,” but Bastion knows; nevertheless, the three continue with their heads in the sand #ostrich

Stephan: “Cheers to a sick ass night; Q pulled another 20 ladies (clinks Q’s glass) Bastion... Welllll Bastion here learned not to make fun of anyone’s mama (tries to clink Bastion’s glass but he angrily pulls it back glaring at Julian) Ok Ok!... and Julian got over his old flame by hookin up with some random chick (cheers a stunned Julian with an uncomfortable Bastion and Q looking on) Cheers!”

With large amounts of THC running through his veins at any given moment, Stephan could have simply forgotten who Julian kissed or her relation to their fearless MIA leader... Knowing Q would try t'drunkenly snatch his phone to see if he was actually texting "Sarah," Julian leaves to the bathroom.

SMS: Julian > Liliana

I miss youuuu! Whats ya up to darlin??? The funniest shit just happen LOL you woulda have loved it! :) lol Awww... Wish you were here with me... OH BUT youwill be heres soon right! Can you still come pick me up?? Please??? Yes???? Save me a dance ;) #savethelastdance #lovethatmovie

SMS: Julian > Liliana

I can't wait to see you!!!

(valley side)

The magical vibrations from Liliana's phone trigger all the Liliana's in her brain's boardroom to run around screaming "Jump, jump up and get down!!!" #houseofpain #hellaoldschool

Liliana: "I'll be right back ok!?"

Nicole: "Wait, you're leaving again? Where you goin, want us to come?" (Jaime leans in feeling left out)

Liliana: "No no, no need; I'm just gonna get some fresh air on the balcony of life"

Nicole: "K well hurry back!!!" (Liliana forces an "ok I will" smile)

Clueless random guy: "Hey, why's it called the balcony of life?"

Liliana: "Cuz of all the smokers? Get it???? ... AND the 'balcony of death' is soooo not funny" (laughs and smiles)

Anxiously wanting to know what Julian said, Liliana prances off the dance floor only to run into a distraught Tyler around the corner.

Liliana: "Tyler, oh... hey.. (looking left and right for an escape) how are... you?"

Tyler: "You didnttt; save me a dance... where chyu been beautifullll?"

Liliana: "...I wasn't feeling good so I went to lay down" (grazes hand across her forehead)

Tyler: "Welllll how come you are leavin the floor? Canwe catch the end of this song?"

Liliana: "Aww, sorry Ty, I'm heading out to get some fresh air; why don't you go dance with my girls for a little bit and I'll be back soon; you Know they would love it!"

Tyler: (lifting his metaphorical chin and nose in the air) "Ohhhhh I guess I cannnn... Only cuz you asked soooooo nicely" (smiles)

Liliana: "Sweet!" (hurries away)

Tyler: "OH Liliana! (she frustratedly turns around) ...I'll be waiting!" (winks)

Liliana: "Ok!" (turns back with a fake throw up face/ noise)

Moving through the endless crowd of people to the balcony of life, Liliana ignores all attempts to ask questions or hit on her. Picturing Julian impatiently waiting for her response with hands wide open, Liliana scurries to the dark corner of the balcony to read her messages:

SMS: Julian > Liliana

I miss youuuu! Whats ya up to darlin??? The funniest shit just happen LOL you woulda have loved it! :) lol Awww... Wish you were here with me... OH BUT youwill be heres soon right! Can you still come pick me up?? Please??? Yes???? Save me a dance ;) #savethelastdance #lovethatmovie

SMS: Julian > Liliana

I can't wait to see you!!!

(Denny's)

Q: "Soooo... What are we ordering?"

Julian: "I'm good with the uzzzshhhh"

Stephan: "Yea I'm good with that" (nodding)

Q: "Looks like the usual rules the day"

Waitress: "Outstanding!"

Julian: "Sooooooo Q, How's the girlfriend?"

Q: "Hey that reminds me I need to-Ha Ha; Funnnny guy!!! You're a funnnnnny GUY!" (wraps arm around Julian's head #seinfeld)

Julian: "Hey hey!!!! Watch the hair; well she's the only girl you looooveeee right-"

Q: "-Fuck no"

Julian: "Oh, sooo you love many girls and not just one" (loudly smiling)

Q: "Fuck... (drunkenly puzzled) ...Wait, what?... Quit being a bitch, you KNOWWW I don't love'em... Just PARTS of them" (laughs, jabbing Bastion's arm with his elbow)

Bastion: (looks at his arm then towards Q) "Don't touch me; Your elbow DOES NOT speak for me" (Julian and Stephan laugh)

Q: "Y'all some girls..."

Stephan: (pointing at Q incessantly laughing)

Q: "What's so funny y'all?" (all three laugh crazily)

Stephan: (amid laughter) "......Y'ALLL!!!!!..."

Q: "Hilaaaaaaaarious... It's y'all's fault with your frickin voice you Blake Shelton watchin mother fuckers"

(All three continue laughing)

Q: "Whatever, (takes out rarely used phone) I'm gonna hit up my girlfriend-I mean girl-I mean BITCH!!!"

(in full laugh attack: Julian falls on floor, Bastion's forehead hits the table while banging his right fist and Stephan collapses on the booth)

Q: (holds up his lock screen) "LOOK!!! How many of you have over 15 unread messages from at least 7 different bitches at 3 am!!"

Stephan: (places hand on Q's shoulder) "Ooooooooooo, better not tell your girl or she's gonna be heeeeellllla mad!!!" (next booth starts laughing)

Q: (looking at the random's next door) "What the fuck you laughin at?... I gotta make a phone call" (jumps up towards the parking lot)

Julian: (sits up and yells) "Say hi to Kristin for me!!!"

Amazingly enough, Mr. never texts let alone calls was heading outside to CALL Kristin since she hadn't responded to his last "I'm Drunk" text... Never a good idea to leave an "invitation" on the table past 3 AM, Q knows to call instead of text; a call Kristin's been nervously waiting for but would never say or act as such.

CALL: Q > Kristin

K: Well hello there...

Q: Heyyyy you still watchin Son's with your girls?

K: Yeaaaaa, kinda not really; most are passing out and I'm the only one vaguely awake

Q: Word... you sober or nah?

K: Enough. Why?

Q: I was gonna get dropped off atttt, was itttt, Susie's house?

K: Yea. Hey, look at you remembering what I said this afternoon

Q: Hey, I listen to everythings you say..... or text

K: Nice save

Q: Thanks

K: Ill see you in a bit, doors open... you remember how to get here?

Q: Always girl

K: Excuse me?

Q: Uh, of course Kristin

K: See you soon

Q: Peace

Interesting how a true "ladies man" can be reduced to a normal guy by the right girl or in most cases, Woman. Acting as if she was the sought after one, Kristin never asked to see Q and checked him the second he tried to pull the same "smooth moves" that work on lower caliber girls. And this is the case as to how celebrities real (Ben Affleck) and fake (Ari Gold) can be checked by their respective wives #entourage ...Most girl's either try too hard to see such high class men or bitch-like check them farrr too frequently. Yet, normal guys will lose a woman by NEVER checking them when they're out of line; mature woman want to wear the pants in the relationship but desire a guy who WILL check them when they step beyond the realms of sense and reason... Q respects that Kristin won't let him revert to his typical behavior while successfully checking him gives Kristin hope that even the wildcat that is Q can be housebroken; advocating that both Kristin And Q prefer the "notebook" love.

Q: (walking back in) “You ladies done?”

Julian: “Soooooooo... how is Kristin?”

Q: “She’s good, I’m gonna get dropped off at‘er house”

Stephan and Bastion: (drop heads towards each other) “Awwwww-”

Julian: “-how cute”

Q: “Anyways, enough of this madness, lets eat”

Stephan: (mouth full of food) “Wayyyyy ahead of you bro”

Julian: “Cheers” (cheers wing to Stephan’s wing)

Bastion: “No time, (bites into wing) for cheers’ing” (rips off another piece)

SMS: Liliana > Julian

Of course I can come pick you up!!! :) I already stopped drinking a while ago and pretty much danced off all the alcohol anyways

SMS: Liliana > Julian

And you’ll always have a dance waiting for you :) #ilovethatmovietoo

SMS: Liliana > Julian

I feel like I’ve been waiting like a million years to see you!!!!!

Taking a moment from the feast, Julian slides down into the booth, looks to the floor on his right and secretly smiles as he pictures himself jumping into her car...

SMS: Julian > Liliana

Can you leave soonish? Like, 10 15 min? Were finishinnin up then we'll probably just be lounging in the parking lot till you get here lol

SMS: Julian > Liliana

I've waited more than one lifetime for such a soul as yours and I won't mind waiting just a littttttttttttttle bit longer ;)

Act 2: Scene 3: Tyler's Christmas

On the dance floor with her two girls and the entourage in tow, the double (Bzzzzzzz) of Julian's texts awakens Liliana's senses an'enlivens her body; floored by the anticipation that makes life worth living, Liliana steps out of the circle and wakes her phone to the joyous banner of "New Text Message (2)" on her lock screen.

SMS: Julian > Liliana

> Can you leave soonish? Like, 10 15 min? Were finishinnin up then we'll probably just be lounging in the parking lot till you get here lol

SMS: Julian > Liliana

> I've waited more than one lifetime for such a soul as yours and I won't mind waiting just a littttttttttttttle bit longer ;)

When you've jumped head over heels into the abyss and fully embraced the darkness that surrounds you, one continues to ignore the "texting rules" an'reply immediately:

SMS: Liliana > Julian

I will leave from my house soon no longer my home, for my heart lies miles down the road... And as the phone's vibrations rush through my body, my one wish is to gaze upon your face before the sun stretches across tomorrow's forever beautiful sky...

SMS: Liliana > Julian

See you soon!!!

SMS: Liliana > Julian

#cantwait

With the yin to the yang and the ebb to the flow, there's no sunshine without the blizzard like snow: drunkenly waiting for a dance with his "girl," Tyler creepily stares towards the one he could not slay as Nick and John race up:

Nick and John: "Tyler!!!" (Nick an'John look at each other)

Nick: "Ty, I'm sorry to be the one to tell you this but-"

John: "-Liliana was makin out with some guy on the dance floor earlier..."

Tyler: (takes a couple seconds to register) "....wait... (looks at John) WAIT, WHAT??? She made out??? With some asshole???@@@" (angrily stares at Liliana)

John: (looks at Nick then Tyler) "...yes?... That's what we heard..."

Tyler: "From who? No chance, no fuckin way; she hasn't hooked up with anyone since we broke up months ago... No. No way bro. It's not her style, no FUCKin way..."

If you're still in love with your ex after breaking up, you'll hold on to hope that she (or he) will come to their senses and eventually return. However, when they move on and hook up/date again, the sinking realization hits you: "Fuck... it's really over......" Sometimes after a couple months or a year of "seeing what's out there," you'll both conclude that you were "as good as it gets" and return to one another; sometimes only one comes to this dreary conclusion and wakes in a dark room alone... Then sometimes, just sometimes both'll come to the same conclusion yet never reconnect due to the FEAR of possibly waking up alone... C'est la vie #thecrow

Tyler: "Who'd you hear this from?"

John: "Welllll... (looking around) I heard it from random girl 17 and SHE heard it from entourage wanna be # 3"

Tyler: "Take me to her..." (no one moves)

Tyler: "Like, NOW!"

(John guides Tyler to the Liliana-less entourage on the floor and points out wanna be # 3; Tyler taps her shoulder)

Entourage wanna be # 3: "Helllo TY!!%#$@%#!!!!"

Tyler: “Hi d’you see Liliana making out with some guy earlier???”

Entourage wanna be # 3: “Oh my god, you should have seen’em; Swedish House Gangsters featuring Justin Timberlake was playin and they were all up on eachother-(Ty storms off)-and... Ty? Tyyyylllleeeerrrr!!!”

Immediately metabolizing all consumed alcohol, Tyler’s anger overrides his usual calmer than cool demeanor and catalyzes him into an anger ball rolling down black diamond hills on a kamikaze mission after the bastard who stole his girl... In an ideal world, Tyler would direct his hostility away from the unknown knight an’unleash it upon himself since his own issues, lack of attention and maltreatment contributed to the end of their romantic relationship... Failing to notice Tyler’s left, Nick and John remain standing with wanna be # 3;

Nick: (upward head nod) “Hey there” (with a Joey “how you doooooin?” wide smile #friends)

Entourage wanna be # 3: (smiling) “Heyyyyyyyyy Nick (flirtatiously looks away an’back) ...Wanna dance?”

Nick: “Well yes I-(John slaps Nick’s chest pointing his eyes towards Tyler)-save that dance for me ok?” (two walk away)

Entourage wanna be # 3: “.......I will Nikki!!” (Nick turns and smiles before John hits his chest again)

Caught up in the competition to move up the valley's social ladder, Nick brushed aside a girl who not only flirted with him first but even asked HIM to dance. Far too many relationships are put on hold, swept under the carpet or never start due to misplaced priorities... Sweep, sweep on...

With no course of action on his mind's agenda, Tyler will continue his mini rampage through the party until his anger subsides enough to think again. Catching up like two dogs to their master on his second lap around, Nick and John take their rightful place a few steps behind:

Tyler: (grabs random good looking guy's shirt) "Did YOU hook up with my Liliana?"

Random good looking guy: "...uhhhh I wish!" (smiling to his peers)

Tyler: "You what?" (throws fist behind head in pre punch form)

Random good looking guy: (smile hides) "...nothin bro-"

Tyler: "-Fuckin thought so" (releasing a wicked smile an'continuing his rampage)

Nick: "YAAAAA!!!! That's right!!!" (randoms quietly laugh nearby)

Unsure of what would satisfy his thirst for blood or alleviate his newly formed heartache, Tyler asks his good friend "Mr. Alcohol" to heal his pains an'hide his anger as they've done so well throughout his life... Overheating from a couple shots and in need of a breath of fresh air, Tyler heads to the balcony of life...

Elsewhere, a few randoms who witnessed Tyler's "punking" seize the opportunity:

Random girl 56: (running up) "Lily!!!! Tyler just made a total scene! He was asking some hot guy if he hooked up with you and-"

Random girl 57: "-he was helllla angry an'almost punched him!!!"

Random girl 58: (shyly lifts right hand but no words come out)

Liliana: (rereading their text stream) "Uh huh.... wait, he what?... (siggghhhh) where is he now?"

Random girl 58: "He was heading out to the balcony of life last time I saw him" (stoked on herself)

Liliana: "Thanks so much" (places hand on 58's shoulder before power walking towards the balcony)

Random girl 56: (glares at 58) "...Bitch"

With his palms on the balcony's railing and staring at a nearly full moon, Tyler allows his blame to finally fall on the right shoulders. Glancing to the garden below, he envisions the countless days he'd spent bullshitting with Perry and ignoring his former loves request to see the flowers she'd planted... Reminiscent of the "ghosts of christmas" taking scrooge to see his past, Tyler watches as an all too typical scene play out before him...

(standing in the garden a few feet away, Tyler watches himself neglect Liliana to laugh at Perry's sexist jokes until he cannot remain silent any longer)

Tyler: "Look how beautifully majestic she is... Instead of paying attention to your wanna be friend, you could be allowing her aromas to dance on your senses and fill your air with her love for life. (walks up, crouches in front of a digging Liliana and intently stares as if reading her face) What I would give to be in your shoes... able to hold her; feel her skin against mine, kiss her an'look into those adoring sunshine eyes that only see me..... (Liliana longingly gazes towards Tyler's past self) Dude... (stands) Look at her face, (walks towards his ignorant former self) Look how you're killing her spirit! (up in his own face) ...LOOK how she pines for your attention... LOOK!!!!!!!! (points) THIS IS HOW YOU FUCKIN LOST HER YOU FOOL!!!" (tries to push his former self but passes through him on the way to the ground)

Unable to change the past, Liliana is no longer the only one on the verge of tears in this memory... And from such great heights on the balcony of life, Tyler looks down to see himself stand up, brush off some painful dirt and stare up at the banister with a "you fuckin did this" dejected look before stoically shrugging. Soon all disappear into his psyche leaving Tyler gripping the railing harder as he jaw clenchingly breathes in... and out...

Putting the pieces together 6 months too late, Tyler remembered how excited Liliana's mom was when she came home with new exotic foreign plants; how Lilliana regretted never sharing in her mom's vigor for the garden while she was still alive and how she made a point t'find new flowers to continue expanding her mom's garden in honorarium. Tyler's nails dig into the underside of the banister as epiphanies roll off his mind's leaves...

Like most who secretly believe they deserve to be alone and self sabotage their romantic relationships, Tyler holds the horrible gift to be able to hide his true feelings from his own consciousness. Realizing he DID love her far too late, Tyler retraces the breakup and beats himself up over what he did wrong and what he could have done differently; his subconscious finally lets a true feeling float to the surface of his conscious mind: he purposely ignored Liliana AND the garden to push'er away from him...

Since the garden was a sacred and treasured piece of Liliana, Tyler should have shared in her appreciation and made more of an effort to help cultivate it... You may not love what your partner values, but if you don't support and nurture your significant other's passions an'dreams, the simmering resentment will inevitably boil over to burn other aspects of your relationship..... Burn, burn on...

Tyler: (SLAMS hands on banister before furiously turning around) "Did YOU hook up with my Liliana?"

Random Remotely Good Looking Guy (R.R.G.L.G): "No.... No man... Shit no man, I believe you'd get your ass kicked doin something like that man" (#officespace)

Tyler: "Funny Lawrence, crackin jokes at my expenses huh? YOU wanna try this agains?"

R.R.G.L.G: "...it wasn't me"

Tyler: "Ha! Now you makin shaggy references? THAT'ssss it! Let's take this; OUTside!"

R.R.G.LG: "Number one, we ARE outside. And shaggy? I ain't no dog bro and I DIDN'T hook up with your Liliana"

Tyler: "Then WHO stole my cookie from the cookie jar?"

From across the balcony, a random guy whose ex had left him for Tyler back in the day seizes the opportunity:

Tyler hater: (raising hand high) “I ate those cookies brah”

Tyler hater’s friend: (leans in whispering) “Dude, what the fuck are you doing?”

Tyler hater: (tilts his head towards his friend) “I’m tired of this clown... (head returns upright an’tilts again) and I hate this guy... (same action) annnnnnnd the girl I’ve been waiting to hit on once I got drunk already left”

Tyler hater’s friend: (leans back) “Fair enough”

Tyler: (sifting through the crowded balcony of life) “YOU hooked up with her? (points) YOUUUU???? Didn’t I steal your girl like FIFTY FUCKIN years ago?”

Tyler hater: (standing proudly) “Shhhyea... and I just stole yours SON!” (pushes Tyler in the chest causing him to fall backwards)

With Tyler hater’s friend on all fours like a dog behind him, Tyler “fell” for one of the oldest tricks in the book to end up flat on his back... Still bickering with R.R.G.L.G’s crew, the loud crash alerted Nick and John to their fallen leader. As much as Tyler hater and his friend wanted to fight three taller guys ON their home field with Perry and company waiting in the wings, they knew when to dine and dash.

Tyler hater: “HA HA Bitch! I didn't hook up with your girl tonight, but YOU hooked up with the floor!!!” (LOL’s and leaves)

Nick: “Tyler, how d’you end up down there?”

Tyler: (slams right hand on the floor) “Fuckin go after them!!!”

John: “But how d’you-”

Tyler: “-JUST GO!!!!” (gets up, dusts himself off an’walks inside)

Random guy 87: “Looks like YOUUUUU should be hittin the ol’dusty trail”

Tyler: (calmly turns with no expression before shooting a fake smile) “Oh should I? ha ha-” (punches him in the gut causing 87 to arch over grabbing his stomach)

With rage consuming most of his alcohol and the adrenaline sobering him up, “pass out” alarms ring supreme in Tyler’s headache filled head... Sailing an empty vessel named “Numb,” Tyler’s anger diminishes with each step he takes through living room 3 on the way to guest room 6... Bypassing all light switches upon entering the dark room, Tyler walks to the foot of the bed and falls forward... Staring off into the nothingness that was his room an’now heart he closes his eyes...

Before sandman can save him from his own guilty misery, Tyler pictures one of the nights he and Liliana spent in this very room: sitting with his back to the headboard, Tyler sings "shake shake shake du nu na na-na naaaa, shake shake shake daa nu na na-na, shake that bootay... shake that booootay" while Liliana dances around the room flailing her arms crazily, laughing and occasionally trying to remain completely still an'shake just her booty. Never one to conform her actions to the norm or care how anyone perceives her, Liliana excitedly enjoys every minute of his subpar singing and'er weird dancing. Somewhat tipsy, Liliana jumps on the bed gyrating her body left and right before smoothly falling to her knees t'straddle Tyler's feet and smoothly run her hands up his legs to his inner thighs...

On all fours, Liliana walks up his body fully aware that her loose top enticingly reveals everything underneath her shirt save for what lay hidden beneath the black bra; stopping once their waists line up, after trailing her nails down his pecks to his abs, Liliana's eyes quickly smile at Tyler's right before she lunges forward to delicately yet forcefully kiss him...

Far removed from judging eyes, the foreman of the water works starts the wheels an'disallows any anger to survive. Pleading with his mind to stop this mirage of a memento, Tyler forcefully closes his eyes tight in an attempt to stop the now falling tears; drunken as he was and loss as SHE was, there's no fighting the swiftly flowing river... With one reserved table in his heart no one could ever sit, Tyler never allowed himself to fully love another; as a result, although their sex was good, it was never bite their hand lick their sweat nail diggingly fantastical when it could have been had Tyler ever fully let go...

Finally inhaling what he'd never allow himself to breathe, feelings he never felt while thrusting inside her pulsed Tyler's body spurring an eruption of unprecedented emotion to crumple him into a fetal position with knees tucked. Walking by the forever untouched table, the waiter of his heart notices a delightful woman whose eyes break down his core and strip off it's metallic armor'nd all anger all the more; and after glancing away for but a brief second, turning back to an empty table leaves Tyler gasping for air and reaching out into the now darkened room... With no way to escape newly tasted worlds, Tyler pines for her eye's smiles to fall upon him since newly unlocked selfs interject hope that maybe... just maybe he could find her nails softly dragging down chests before leaning in to kiss his still aching lips... maybe she'd find desires could bleed over to a second chance such as this.

Opening eyes to a dark room, Tyler had never awoken alone in such desolation nor seen such stressful cold sweat like perspiration roll down his scrunchfully painful skin. Nervously whispering her name and hoping she'd appear, Tyler sees his words sinisterly returned and burned by rejection on deaf ears; unknown she'd soon awaken in such worlds as these, yet valiantly in search for another's company... Unable to accept that he'd never given her what he could now release, no shadows cast any doubt that had he done so they'd surely laugh at all the time they'd almost missed; and with her no longer continuously pushed aside and dismissed, they'd move forward encased in eternities' delightful an'mighty kiss...

And with faith renewed while flakes of sand quickly fill up his mind's hour glass, Tyler dreams of a day she'd dance and he could once again sing; waiting for a life that will never truly begin, but hope... hope can be a fatefully scary thing...

ACT 2: SCENE 4: SUCH GREAT HEIGHTS

Like Vince Vaughn and the "Swingers" crew, the four walk to their ride in slow motion fame that trails them every step they take but Not every move they make #police ...Congregating outside the car, all four (minus Julian) pass around the peace pipe for Denny's is Still stomach twisting heart burning drunken goodness; like a sit down Jack in the Box.

Standing at love's doorstep an'thankful to leave the rat races behind, Julian waits for what most'll never find in the feelings that rush along side an enchanted embraced divine... An'as if his own shadow he's chasing, his phone's vibrations sends chilling reminders of the sensational mystery that is him loss in her presence: recalling how beautifully they connect, images of the life they could bore eclipse his frazzled an'anxious mind as the Julians inside crash the halls an'shatter walls to uncover hidden rooms she'd opened within...

SMS: Liliana > Julian

I'm two miles from pulling around the corner and I don't know "how it's gonna be" when our eyes meet again... All I know is you floor me, ceiling me in ways I never thought possible! #thirdeyeblind

Q: (leans in towards Julian) "Yooo, tha bitch on her way?"

Julian: (recoils in anger) "Whatthe fuck d'you just say?

Q: "...Whoa whoa, relax bro I'm just say-"

Julian: "-Don't you EVER call'er that again!!!" (walks away smiling victoriously)

Having hit the electronic wax pen 4 or 5 times, Q's too blasted to fight back or even understand what's just occurred. According to the heights, Q had never been in love...... According to Q and ________, he had...

With only a few ratchets and stragglers killing time around their buckets an'scrapers, like a fading camp fire the parking lot is nearly burnt out. Leaning against their year or two old Camaro/Mustangs, a couple "cool guys" wait for the most opportune moment to pull one of the remaining strachets. These are the same "cool guys" who work low paying dead end jobs and live in one bedroom apartments, (with two roommates) yet drive cars, wear clothes and sport accessories as if they live next to the Casta's or Merlo's. Fake it till you make it??? No. Fake it till she spends all your rent money #mybad Fake, fake on...

Taking his phone for a walk down a dead street, Julian notices the disappearance of the shadow he's been chasing; looking left right then up, Julian sees the culprit as a burnt out street light… Lights flash towards him and without knowing, he knew. Closing his eyes an'inhaling a deep breath, Julian opens/exhales to a car stopped in middle of the street; how Liliana knew Julian to be the lone darkened figure is a question not worth asking.

After 5 frozen seconds pass, Julian takes the first step off the curb knowing he'd never look back. Calm as could be on the outside yet trembling and sweating on the inside, Julian flosses his shy card by diving his hands into his pockets as deep as possible… Consciously looking away, he walks up to the car, places his right hand on the roof and dips down;

Julian: "Hey there, (glances to the sidewalk and back) can I get a ride?" (smiling)

Liliana: (flashing a quick smile before getting into character) "But of course sir! Jump in; where ya headed?"

Julian: (gets in) "Why, Neverland of course… second start to the left and straight on till morning"

Liliana: "Awww… (swooning) I just came from there!!! I met the most amazing guy and we danced on ceilings!" (sky high brows on fleek)

Julian: "Shut, Up…" (Liliana drives away turning up the music)

Liliana: “I will not, thank you” (forced teeth-less smile)

Julian: “Dang, (sorrowfully drops head) I wish I could dance on ceilings but I’ve loss my happy thoughts...”

Liliana: “Hey... (Julian looks up) Here” (extends open hand)

Julian: (interlocks hands) “Hey! You found it!”

Liliana: “Ummmm, (rolls eyes) Duhhhh!”

Julian: “What is this fantastical song?”

Liliana: “Saint Raymond, Fall at your Feet”

Julian: “Sweet!!! I love it!”

Liliana: “Of course you do! I mean, (looks over) I DID help write it”

Julian: “Sure you did doll face” (still smiling)

Liliana: “Thank you... I think”

Julian: “No thank you!”

Liliana: “Forrrrrrr???”

Julian: (matter a factly) “Pickin me up”

Liliana: “We’ve been in the car for 5 minutes and you’re just Nowwww thanking me? Pshhhhh... (looks away and back) hellllllla delayed” (still smiling)

Julian: “My mind was tied up for a while and is just now gettin back on track”

Liliana: “Oh yea? Where’s it headed?”

Julian: “Better question, where are WE headed?”

Liliana: “A little place I Like to call; you’ll see” (#kramer)

Julian: “Meannnnniiinnngggg, you have no idea-”

Liliana: (RIGHT AFTER) “-I’ave no idea” (shaking head)

Julian: “I love that place, I was just there yesterday”

Liliana: “Really?” (laughs)

Julian: “Yea, they know me by first name”

Liliana: “Oh yea? Do they know you by last name too?”

Slumping down with his perma smile in hiding, Julian stares out the window to the nearly full moon;

Liliana: (squeezes his hand twice) “Hey...” (lips the word “don’t” before kissing the back of his hand)

Passing by the heart on the way to his mind, this message like kiss evokes images of their meeting on the dance floor hours earlier: loss inside eachother’s world’s, lips intertwined and melded as one with metal no longer the only one.

Julian: (smile finds it's way back home) "Wow... (looks at his hand) I don't think a hand kiss has ever done that much!"

Liliana: (innocent "hehe" giggle) "If that's the case, I can't imagine what more would do!" (throws naughty bedroom smile over t'Julian)

Julian: (feels "something" coming to life) "Oh angelic Liliana, whatever do you mean?" (fondles the middle of her hand with his index finger)

Liliana: (sharply lifts hand) "Stop that!!! (Julian laughs out loud lifting his left knee in full animation) That feels... Just... Weird!!!"

Julian: "Oh come on... It didn't feel Sennsssssssss (runs finger up the outside of her leg) ssssuuuuallllll" (shifts to the inner thigh but far from...)

Liliana: (devilishly pleasured smile forms) "Mmmmmm, (shakes her body back and forth as if there's a bug on it) you're right... that ISSSSS tooo good" (sharply squeezes his leg/thigh)

Julian: "Stop!!! (aggressively flings her hand off; turning her on more) Ok, Ok! Truce!!!" (waves imaginary "white" flag)

Liliana: "No, (looks over) I win!"

Julian: (sigh) "You win... (under his breath) ya, we'll see"

Liliana: "Ahem... what was that Julie?"

Julian: "I didn't say noth-Oh come on... Julie? JUUULie? Really?"

Liliana: "Yes, Julie........ an"

Julian: "I meannnn, my friends call me Juels-" (throws head back closing eyes)

Liliana: (shakes her head) "No no no... your name is Julie, JUUUUUUULIEEE... no E before the L crazy!"

Julian: "Hey baby; whatever you wanna call me; as long as you call me... maybe?"

Liliana: "THIS IS CRAZYYYY!!!!! And THAT is why I called you Julie! What other guy quotes Rae Jepson?"

Julian: "Hey, I just like that Harvard baseball team video" (#shoutouttosleepingguy)

Liliana: "Oh great..... Now We HAVE t'listen to that song; I have to hear it like, RIGHT now!"

Julian: "No no, that song sucks" (Liliana's smile hides)

Always quick to shoot down his significant other's songs an'movies he'd neither heard nor seen, Julian was predisposed to disliking everything his girlfriend (or anyone) suggested by immediately jumping to "I don't like ______" or "_______ sucks"... Those with self worth/ insecurity issues project their own dislike for themselves on anything and everyone.

Liliana: "You know; Just because YOU don't wanna hear it or don't like something, it doesn't mean you should bring someone else down to your level..." (mimicking Jasmine's cold demeanor)

With Liliana's sharp words holding up a mirror he could not break, Julian saw the dejection and saddened faces his negative projections caused on a weekly basis with the last being the death of Liliana's perma smile moments earlier...... In a single powerfully concise statement, Liliana reached into Julian's personality and forced him to address insecure demons he never knew existed; and as a box deep inside him opens, the negative storm clouds revolving around Julian's psyche dissipate into positive air.

Within the first 15 minutes of their first "date," Liliana helped Julian in the battle against himself and he hoped he could do the same for her.

Julian: "You're right..." (kisses the back of of her hand as an apology)

Liliana: (in a demanding tone) "You betta kiss MORE than that..."

Julian: (looks down) "Great... MUST you get him all riled up?"

Liliana: "Get who?" (winks)

Julian: "I dig you Lily; I just dig you... hashtag simply" (kisses her exposed right shoulder)

Liliana: "Lily??? Already tired of saying my whole name huh?" (shakes her head)

Julian: "Oh baby Paaaaleasssseeee! You are farrrr too fine, t'look, soooo sad"

Liliana: "thanksforthekiss; HOW do you come up with all these movie lines so quickly??? (leans in) and I did LOVE love LOOOOOOVE seth green in Can't Hardly Wait... (smiles) fuck, I loved everyone in that movie!"

Julian: "Ummmmmm, cuz I'm an movie genius??? Na, my crew an'I always throw out movie quotes left and right; probbbbbably cuz we all watch the same movies again... an'again... an'again..."

Liliana: "So how many-"

Julian: "-an'again, an-"

Liliana: "-Ok! Stop!"

Julian: (lifts head; mouth open about t'say something)

Liliana: "Don't you dare!"

Julian: (in an asian accent) "Annddd Theeeeeeeeennnn?"

Liliana and Julian: (one second of silence; laughter)

Liliana: (nearly in tears) "Dude!!! That's frickin awesome! That movie's so incredibly retarded the first time you see it but like most beyond stupid comedies, the more you see it the funnier it gets"

Julian: “Dude... did you say Dude on purpose? (laughs) You know what my favorite line of the whole movie is right?”

Liliana: “Dude, where’s my car?”

Julian: “Where’s your car dude?”

Liliana: “Dude, where’s my car?”

Julian: “Where’s your car du-”

Liliana: “-Ok totally killed it”

Julian: “Siggghhhh, I’m sorry...”

Liliana: “It’s ok I still-” (covers her mouth)

Julian: “Whoa, (looks at his watch-less wrist) that has GOT to be a record”

Liliana: (frantically) “No no no no no! (shaking her head) oh my go-no no no no no!”

Julian: “Oh yes, you jus-”

Liliana: “-Shut! Didn’t happen, struck from the record”

Julian: “Well you didn’t actually sa-”

Liliana: “-No! (puts her finger to his mouth) Shhhhhh!”

Julian: “But-”

Liliana: "-I'MMM the girl so you HAVVVE to let me take it back!"

Julian: "Fine... but you can't play the "I'm a girl" card for at least a week"

Liliana: "No dice; 7 days"

Julian: "Deal!"

Liliana: "Sucker!... wait... I'm so flustered on cloud 26 I don't even know what's goin on anymore; what time is it?... and where the HELL are we going?"

Julian: (in a indian accent) "Didn't you get that memo? Hit 17 and we'll head to Le Beach" (#officespace)

Liliana: "OK, enough with the movie lines. You've officially loss movie references for the rest of the day..."

Julian: "Fair enough, the new day starts in (looks at watch-less wrist) bout an hour or two?'

Liliana: "You know what I mean Butthead"

Julian: "Fine Beavis..."

In silence, both go to their phone's GPS! #race

Julian and Liliana: (nearly simultaneous with Julian a Hare quicker than the Tortoise) "DONE!"

Julian: "I soooo said it first"

Liliana: “It was a tie”

Julian: “I can live with that”

Liliana: “Sweet... and thus, (raises chin in the air, eyes closed) I win”

Julian: “This ain’t baseball...”

Liliana: “Damn... you’re kinda smart aren’t you”

Julian: “I’m not ‘kinda’ dumb”

Liliana: “Funny”

Julian: “I try, I try”

Liliana: “Sooooo navigator; are you planning on... uhhh, telling me where to go?”

Julian: “I thought YOU won and had it allllll set up!”

Liliana: “Oh; yea. I do!” (moves phone to driver door slot)

(Julian reaches over to try an’grab her phone; SLAP!)

Julian: “Whoa! what was that for????”

Liliana: “What was THAT!” (mimics failed attempt to grab her phone)

Julian: “You didn’t get directions up... liar”

Liliana: (looks down holding her skirt) “Do these LOOK on fire?”

Julian: “A, those aren’t even pants; and 2, you said no more movie references! You owe me a coke”

Liliana: “What? Hellllll no! You can’t jinx me movie references?”

Julian: “What are we even saying right now? (glances up at the passing sign) Missed the entrance”

Liliana: “DAMMITTT Julie!”

Julian: “Really?”

Liliana: “Yes! You’re giving me directions like a girl”

Julian: “Touche” (types into his phone)

Liliana: “Who are you textin at 4, whatever o’clock it is?”

Julian: “No one... I’m makin sure, ummm; our directions are right”

Liliana: “No you’re hella (BZZZZZZZZZ; looks at her phone) Really? You’re such a loser” (shakes head smiling)

Julian: “Hey, I didn't text you; it must have been your OTHER boyfriend”

Liliana: “Boyfriend? Yea I don't have a boyfriend”

SMS: Julian > Liliana
Your fuckin sexy! Sittin there...... all sexy...

Liliana: "Well thank you, but I'm really not. My make up's half gone from dancing wit the girls all night and-well... (smiles wide) whenever I wasn't texting this new guy I'm talkin to"

Julian: "Oh you're talkin t'someone? ...lucky guy" (typing again)

Liliana: "Yea... he wants to make us exclusive, (sighs) but I just don't know... I kiiiiiinnnnnda wanna keep my options open; (looks over) you know, play the field?"

Julian: (turns away looking out the window) "Ok I don't wanna play this game anymore" (moonlight beams through the clouds)

Liliana: "Chill; relax Julian..." (BZZZZZZZ-BZZZ-BZZZZZZ)

SMS: Julian > Liliana
Yeaaaa
SMS: Julian > Liliana
You kindaaaaa
SMS: Julian > Liliana
Have a bf
SMS: Julian > Liliana
Now ;)

Julian: (brushes off shoulder) "...yea, I'm coo"

Liliana: “No need to get all worked up” (typing)

SMS: Liliana > Julian
Nope!

Julian: “Ok, well you should have taken that last turn an’hit the freeway… I meannnn, you’ve already missed like 8 entrances”

Liliana: (perturbed) “Seriously? Which ones?”

Julian: “Whoa crazy; relax… “

Liliana: “Well?”

Julian: “Oh right, 101 and 87; (staring at phone’s GPS) We pretty much did a loop around San Jose; went down Capitol which turned into Hillsdale...... annnnd will eventually turn into Camden soon… At least we’re gonna hit 17 soon, but who cares as long as I’m with you” (grazes finger from’er ear to chin)

Liliana: “Oh jeezeee; Ok, never do THAT again!”

Julian: “Oh my god it was a joke”

Liliana: “So you DO care!!! I knew it!”

Julian: “Mayyyybeeee… Make a left at the second light right under the freeway”

Liliana: “What’s this (air quotes) freeway you speak of”

Julian: “Really?”

Liliana: “I’m not wired to stay up an’be all delusional; and why oh why am IIIIII still driving?”

Julian: “I thought you’d never ask! Ok, when we pull up” (takes off seatbelt an’puts hand on the door #dontdrinkanddrive)

Liliana: “What!? You’re gonna get us in; oh fuck it, it’s hella late”

Julian: “That’s my girl (looks at her smiling) I know I know... hey put on a Chinese fire drill song, somethin we can dance too”

Liliana: “Done”

Julian: “Annnnnnnnnnnndddd... Go!”

After both jump out of the car, Julian swoops back in t’flip to a track he’d seen earlier on her playlist. (“Connor Maynard - Turn Around feat. Ne-Yo”) Having halted her dancing/skipping directly behind the car, Liliana shoots a “what the fuck” with arms wide open before her body starts quivering to the new infectious beat blasting through her veins... Smoothly exiting the car, Julian glides towards Liliana shaking his shoulders up and down to the beat causing her body to tremble an’ache for him t’move closer, faster...

On cue with the the swooshing flangers at 46 seconds in, Julian grabs her small frame and places her a top the trunk face to face. Following her ribs inward, he tastefully grazes the bottom of her perfectly shaped (thank you Victoria) breasts before continuing down to rest an inch away from her middle, now hot, wet and alive with lust. Sending shockwaves through her body by squeezing her upper inner thighs, Julian arouses her every fiber by moving his lips a heartbeat away from hers. Hovering close enough where either could lick the other's lips, Julian moves her hips towards him an'shifts his fingers down to feel her wet with anticipation causing a moan to jump off'er lips onto his. (floating so high) As the pleasurable pain of his stimulation cast up against the trunk begins t'hit home, Liliana's hands leap off the corner of the car to connect their lips giving her body its breath as if under water gasping for air; and after breathing in his passion an'swallowing his ecstasy, in one swooping motion Julian steps onto the bumper, cradles her head and swings her thighs onto the trunk allowing his knee to pick up where his fingers left off. (I've got you, we won't fall down) Tightly gripping his flexed tricep with Julian's left hand squarely planted on the trunk, feeling his warmth pressed up against her elicits a moaning Liliana to involuntarily slide her left hand down to rest directly on HIM: now swollen, pulsating and dying to be released from the far too tight trendy skinny jeans.

Sliding his hand down'er milky soft skin to her supple not too firm ass triggers Julian's mouth to unlock an'move south resulting in her losing grip of his bulge; yet all is forgiven after ripping down bras lets the cold morning air glide over her sending boundless sensations not normally felt. (we're so high now) Gently biting her left nipple induces Liliana to jump with pleasure an'grunt a shortened high pitched scream like moan; shifting to the now right exposed breast, her hand pushes Julian's shirt up to expose an'wash his cascaded abs. Delicately dragging his nails up and down her left shoulder, Julian forcefully scratches her sending shivers like nails to a chalkboard leaving 4 white marks which scream his want for her with the message well received. (nothing can stop us now) Cupping the left, Julian teasingly swivels his tongue around the right areola leading her hand to aggressively jump from his stomach to his hair an'forcefully push his mouth directly on her nipple; biting down prompts her head to eject up while her body simultaneously sinks down. (no limit to what we've found) With eyes deeply cast into his, Liliana moans a snake like hiss "come here" leaving her mouth slightly ajar; and with her fingers above an'below each ear, Liliana arches her shoulders forward before pressing her passionate lips cries upon him throwing her want, need an'endless desire to have him inside of her. (I wanna feel it all) Needing a moment to catch his breath and a second chance at her soft skin, Julian's lips move down the neck and through Victoria's valley once again...

With eyes closed, the looks Julian shot her in the car an'the images of their night on the dance floor spin like a top in her mind; upon opening, Liliana spots him an'her laying on freeway ceilings above in similar poses yet devoid of clothes as the moment he's to enter her soon approaches. (our home is the sky now) She could only fathom as to how their essences would flow between them like power lines endlessly shooting electricity back and forth; and as if she needed any more teasing, wickedly staring down at her from high above, ceiling Liliana bites Julian's ear before casting his head down the valley's bliss. Mirroring his tongue's slide through her chest moments earlier, skating down her strip on the ceiling lands Julian between'er legs where she assertively pulls his hair and guides him in the pursuit of pleasure... With Julian's hand far beyond mini skirts boundaries on the car, Liliana grimaces in pleasure while biting an'licking Julian's fingers and intently staring into her own eyes above at such great heights... After breaking the spell by glancing to a car rolling up on the ground, ceiling Liliana gazes back to herself below an'lips "never comin down" to which Liliana wickedly smiles before meeting two wide eyed girls jealousy staring on...

Mimicking counter parts above, Liliana bites Julian's ear an'whispers: "baby, (exhale) we have company" prompting Julian to rise from passion induced trances to meet a set of "turned on" headlights... Returning her bra to it's normal upright position, Julian steps down and extends his hand our for HER to join him back on the ground in so many ways more than one.

Julian: "My lady, My queen"

Unable to stop himself after kissing her hand, Julian pulls her in colliding their lips (no tongue) in an attempt to seal their passion; and as he pulls himself away, Julian makes sure to caress his hand down her side an'ass as he glides past...

Needing a moment, Liliana inhales, smiles the world over, exhales and leg shakingly walks to the passenger side.

Both get in;

Gleefully look at eachother;

Flip to song 21,

and jump on the freeway...

Eyes closed, Liliana sits in the passenger seat slightly knocking her head left and right to the beat of "Super Flu & Andhim - Reeves" as the car rolls past 85 and through Los Gatos into the darkness enclaved hills...

Pulsating with desire's kiss, both remain in hearts' passion reverberating on backsides of the car...

(If you're currently listening to this song, quit being a bitch, turn that shit up and knock your head back an'forth with eyes closed picturing yourself driving through the forrest in the middle of the night till the BASS sinks your heart at about 2 1/2 minutes in #trust #youllknowwhen #blastthatshit)

Once the bass drops, Julian caresses his hand upon Liliana's leg while gradually turning his head allowing his lust to follow along. Smiling as if ecstasy driven, Julian's body yearns for it's final permission t'strut down her runway to the Vegas strip... Valiantly wishing to gaze into Julian's love struck mind, Liliana refuses to lean in an'move towards his spirit knowing she'd inevitably jump off the balcony of life an'never live to hear it: Hear the ocean rise while waves crash like the fall; leaving summer's heart at the door while winter laughs at Autumn's uproar...

Julian: "Liana of my Li... I ache for my eyes to kiss your mind's sin for having let go such fire while fantasizing of enchantment's wind; no ashes remain and I cannot allow you to wallow in shadows within. For thanks to your pixie dust ensigning, you send me flying t'stars on high; now can you please turn back t'bask in what we've now found here tonight???"

Beginning to turn t'Julian's facade, Liliana rips back instead to stare out at moon's god; wishing to reach across for the touch she badly craves, Liliana's surrounding engrained misery keeps her blind and stunted; conditioned to push away from such great heights, tragedy stricken lives prefer the pains of faintly low lights... Her heart screams in backlash against all her past dramas yet scars continue to ride deep an'imprison Liliana. And as his confidence grows thin, Julian coincidentally flips to "Bluford Duck - Shoulder To Cry On" which fuels doubts within... Yet accompanying any notebook like rising are such dominos waiting to fall... for regardless, the moon will continue to try an'reign down its beams oh so tall.

Having never faced the altitude of such great heights, similarly to another the thin air instills vulnerability like no other; jumping aboard similar trains, Julian looks for chinks in the newly laden armor as a brother named Santana arises in forefront's mind; becoming harder and harder to sift through the ever growing doubt springing from shadows of the moon on it's treacherously long route.

And with the clouds venturing in t'save the night and soon to be day, Liliana hopefully flips to "Kaskade - 4 AM" and presses play... Praying such a song trumps the melon collie vibes, Liliana places'er hand on his leg to erase all growing doubt; an'sure enough resting his hand on hers allows smiles to return with calm transcendent air they breathe together now in... and now out...

Julian: (laughing to himself) “I can’t believe we did that... ON the car!!!”

Liliana: (turns sharply raising brows) “And-”

Julian: (RIGHT AFTER) “-And it was fuckin amazing! I don’t even know what came over me!”

Liliana: “Um; hello, (turns to him) over US!”

Julian: “Ohhhh, were you there too?”

Liliana: “Ummm Yeaaaa! (laughs out loud) Don’t make me look out the window thinkin again”

Julian: “Ha Ha... hilaaaaaarious”

Liliana: “I try, I try-”

Julian: “-Don’t steal my words”

Liliana: “There’s no stealing, I say that all the time! Besides, I don’t see your name on’em”

Julian: “Look again” (pointing to the air)

Liliana: “Yeaaaaaaaa.... I don’t see it Julie”

Julian: (glaringly pulls hand away)

Liliana: “What?”

Julian: “You know whats you said”

Liliana: "Yeaaaaaaa"

Julian: "Ok then"

Liliana: "Oh come on girl, don't get your panties in a bunch now JUUUUUUlie" (sneakily smiling)

Julian: (snaps glare back on his face)

Liliana: "Finnnnneeeee"

Julian: "Thats what I thought" (interlocks hands again)

With the summit of 17 reached, all was not perfect as harmony was (but for a brief moment) breached; yet all is not rainbows in notebook ties, as sweaters will unravel t'be saved by the soon to be highs.

Julian: "So where are we headed? What's the plan?"

Liliana: "Ummmm... (squint eye "thinking") You're the guy, YOU decide!"

Julian: "Whoa whoa, YOU'RE in the passenger seat (taps her hand on the center console) YOU'RE the navi now..."

Liliana: "Ok Ok... Wellllll we can go to bond-fire beach?"

Julian: "What do YOU know about bond-fire beach?"

Liliana: "Well I know it's down one north and it USED to have a bumpy dirt road that was all crazy before they flattened it out... and of course the infamous white pole"

Julian: “I don't know darling; you’re a little young to know all that... Ok what do you cross over to get there miss I know everything”

Liliana: “Welllll, you cross over the railroad tracks; what do YOU know of it? You describe somethin and quit askin me questions!” (smiles)

Julian: “On the left you can walk under a rock to find a small cove and there’s a tunnel on the right that pirates sail out of at sunrise”

Liliana: “Shut UP! Ya ok weirdo!”

Julian: “No seriously! I’m tellin you; you’ll see a pirate ship sail by the beach stretching... (moves hand from left to right) across... the sky”

Liliana: (briefly believes him) “Noooo, quit being stupid”

Julian: “No you quit”

Liliana: “I don’t ever quit”

Julian: “...You quit being single about 30 minutes ago!”

Liliana: “Ok; now that was smooth...”

Julian: “I try, (looks at’er smiling with his heart) I try....”

With her head now resting on his shoulder and left hand clasped in his, Liliana’s right hand falls to Julian’s still ripped bicep from the workout 30 minutes earlier, 6 feet behind them...

Relationships provide a shower like minute to wander the mental playground and simply swing on the swings or ride the slide; for as adults we strive to recreate those childhood like atmospheres... Yet it's difficult to remain "in the moment" since the new age mind doesn't take breaks and flips channels faster than drugs can be created to slow it down... Yet as she holds her new prince, Liliana's mind does not flip channels and all she sees is their care free spirits dancing in the wavelengths of their new found glory... Though you may encounter turbulent waves with intense fights, never lose sight of such moments or the beauty of those incandescent fluorescent lights...

Checking his emotions on the surface in rare form, Julian's insides cry their eyes out bragging to everyone on the playground that his crush "liked him too!"... Busy playing four square, marbles, kick ball or hide and go seek, the other children couldn't understand his excitement. Most are too busy playing their adult games to ever understand why people do such things in the name of the deceptively hidden abstract notion named love... Some won't let anyone in while others'll never know themselves well enough to recognize what they want; and tragically, some are incapable of love due to inherited biological issues or outside forces having stolen the ability at ages one cannot defend. Yet you must hold faith there is one person who can jump any steeple, any wall an'any trauma to encompass you with that light bulb love: the Ohhhhh That's why nearly all movies, novels, TV shows, fights, disasters, miracles and tragedies continue to encircle around this undefinable feeling/emotion we call Love; yet this stops no one from trying......... I try, I try...

Liliana: (steps out of the car) "Ok, grab the blanket out of the trunk"

Julian: (jumps out) "It's underneath our bed?"

Liliana: "Anddddddddd you killed it"

Julian: "No I didn't!"

Liliana: "Fine, but one more joke and you REALLY will have killed it; just leave it to what it was and it'll remain what it always will be" (walks toward beach trail)

Julian: (lost in what she said till realizing she's left) "Whoa whoa! You're walkin in the dark???? (walks as fast as possible without officially "running") Why'd you just leave by yourself??? There could be, like... (takes 4 steps) stuff out there..."

Diving head first into life, Liliana never looked before hand to see if there was any water in the pool; with the help of her sister, Liliana's as strong as Britney, an independent woman like Beyonce, a fighter like Christina and even lived in her own fantasy like Mariah...

Liliana: "Hurry up! The Sun's not getting any lower!"

Julian: "Thanks for the update big ben!" (#familyguy)

Liliana: (turns back smiling)

Illuminated phone screens help them navigate the rocky terrain down to the desolate beach where shoes are no longer necessary. The dawn counts down while a bluish glow emits from the horizon as if the ocean's lassoed it's dark blue seas into the skies overhead. Stopping at the shore's "field of dreams" like boundary, Liliana looks down at the water as it rushes upon her teased toes, double dog, triple dog daring her t'get in... Turning to Julian with a wicked "I been up all night, high on new love" look, Liliana passes thoughts and emotions without so much of a word: smiling along, Julian knows the conclusion to what she's building to an'beyond; and as if timed or planned, both start disrobing leaving clothes out to roam the sand... And with hands clasped under the new dawn's blue skies, the two run to the ocean with a great and merciless war cry. The ice of polar's cap sends shocking revelations: loss are the lifelong masks as they're cast back on sands with clothes out to past; no longer wishing to'ave restarted life in hopes of finding one who'd bring blissful crying, one whom bereft leaves souls an'hearts dying, eternally screaming at such lungs tops that "I love this person and will not ever stop!".

The rush of the cold is no match for their chemistry; the rush of their love is no match for their destiny as staring across into waves crash, there's no longer a need t'save the last dance. Julian had pined for this feeling, to love and find healing within another's breath; to harness the pain you carry, leaving scars so sorry for ever gracing your body while each passing moment repairs internal scars or burns'em away to forgetful ashes...

And with live's renewed, the two left the ocean that day; yet a small piece remains to wallow in the core of the bay, continuing to frolic and rule the dawn's day. Unable to die, such worlds of passion are truly everlasting; for long after ground's entrusted, breaths continue to swirl beyond caskets dropped an'fallen; long after hearts have stop yet still beat as they'll never cease to pump emotions so warmly nestled an'sound... And like puzzle pieces, the sun's rays of love shatter unbreakable centuries; surfacing countless eternities bleached into passion soaked dreams, allowing their endless infinities to freely dance past moon's countless shooting beams

Act 3: Scene 1: Dressing Room

Santana: “Come out Jazz! Lemme see how fuckin SEXY you look!”

Jasmine: “...Ok! ...One minute... its, a tight fit...”

After pulling up each breast and checking out her flat stomach an’table ass in the fitting room mirror, Jasmine assures herself the black slit dress is not “too hippy”. Having always viewed herself as “cute” but not “god I wanna fuck her” pretty, Jasmine sends a few selfies for Liliana’s approval before stepping outside to face Santana’s judging eyes...

MMS: Jasmine > Liliana

Be honest... Do I look good?

Guys are like cavemen when it comes to girl's trying on clothes or anything that Could show off cleavage, legs, hips, ass or even stomach; ESPECIALLY in public. Even if a girl walked out sporting oversized baggy jeans, an "everything to the imagination" shirt and a dreadful navy sailor cap, the excitement for the next outfit would still power through; whether it's the element of surprise or being a hop jump and a skip away from "role playing," that next outfit may bring the fitting room fantasy to life where the every day jeans and halter top turn into daisy "doesn't cover the lower ass" dukes with a shredded t-shirt and no bra asking "is this too slutty? #nofuckinway

Whatever the case, guys are so effing excited about girls trying on clothes that no woman should EVER feel THAT self conscious since no matter what you come out wearing, they'll still try to picture you with nothing on #winkface ...However, instilling confidence into a woman's self conscious mind is as hard as teaching a monkey OTHER than Koko sign language. Sign, sign on...

SMS: Liliana > Jasmine
You look duckin stunning!
SMSL Liliana > Jasmine
Seriously!

Jasmine: "Ooookkkk... I'm comin out" (peering behind the door)

Santana: "YES YES! Come out you sexy bitch!"

Jasmine: (opens door with hands on hips) "What d'you just call me?"

With an eyes wide drunken smile, Santana moves his head back an'forth tryin t'say somethin... anything...

Jasmine: "What; is it that bad???"

Leave it to a woman t'take a speechless man as something negative; Jasmine knowwwsss she looks good and with any other man (or woman) she would never question nor exude insecurity about her looks. One should never base their own self image on another's view yet the deeper you fall in love, the more dependent you become on their image of you... Base, base on...

("Hannah Georgas - Fantasize"
comes on the fitting room's speakers)

Santana: "Bad?.... BAD??!!" (tilts head; eyebrows raised)

Jasmine: (deflated) "Yes...."

Santana: "You've got to-I mean... I just see you there and I, (steps towards) an'I just, (steps; looks her up and down) I jus-"

Unsure of what he's doing or about to say, Jasmine assumes the worse. Walking straight into her,

Santana's right hand cups the back of her head while the left smoothly closes the door before sliding down the hip to her perfectly bubbled left cheek. With his head slanted to the right and lips pressed against hers on the left, Santana walks/carries her into the wall; surprised and still unsure how she looks in the dress, Jasmine's hands move towards him but do not lock on to any part of his body. If Santana can't keep his hands off her in private, simple math states: public place + black "slit" dress = all restraint out storefront windows... Grabbing her left breast and nearly ripping it off, Santana moves down to try the same with his mouth; playing "hard to get," Jasmine slides to her right but freezes once his left hand walks up'er exposed leg towards the inevitable. Unleashing audacity most women only dream of, Jasmine takes control an'pulls her dress up and to the right while guiding his hand to that which aches for so much more. Inhaling trembling shivers, Jasmine's all natural nails crawl up under his graphic-T an'glide over the V towards his obvious excitement leading her to glance down at "him" and back with a sultry "mmmm, I wanna fuck you" Maxim cover girl look. Her movement into'is waistband prompts Santana's hands to flex inducing Jasmine to jump as the grasp on'er front an'back has revved up both minds for reasons alike. And with the gratuitous dressing room bench screaming her name, Jasmine aggressively guides Santana to stand in front of it before assertively planting her left Chanel heel beside him an'connecting their lips while unbuttoning his pants; after running her left heel down his leg and dipping down to her knees like his very own POV porno, Jasmine enticingly looks at the boxers; naughtily back up at him an'back down at the boxers before sliding-

-Jasmine's eyes open to empty ceilings; laying In her clothes from last night she's cornered by a body mirror on her left and a stranger named Peter on her right. Closing her eyes to try an'fight off the aqueduct's cries for release, Jasmine frightenedly opens to stare up at blank ceilings #iwillnotgivein ...sitting up, Jasmine gazes to unfriendly paintings of disillusion behind her till'er head falls to join her dreams down below... In looking up towards the mirror, Jasmine meets a speechless Santana standing outside the dressing room as the pure lust exuding from his eyes washes upon her feet from currents beneath...

Act 3: Scene 2: "Hard 2 Face Reality"

With prince Julian loss in his brave new world, Bastion had rescued the king from his dreams of old before crashing out in couch heaven: a warehouse sized room where anyone an'everyone freely passed out when parties broke out from inviting a "few" friends over for a "few" drinks. Sitting up with the normal "morning after drinking" traits, (head pounding, hazy and Starving for greasy food) Bastion takes a moment to enjoy the calm before the storm as soon the trojan horse would induce all to proclaim where allegiance's lie when everyone Was on the same side... Although he wanted to find his Helen and start wars that never end, Julian never questioned upon what side his brother would stand.

...Laying asleep, Julian's mind smiles harder than ever before; no need to dream when you're currently living one. (Bukka Buuuu!)

SMS: Bastion > Julian

Dude I know you're probably all wrapped up but you need to talk to your bro. Get over here asap

Expecting to see a love soaked message, Julian's smile falls under siege to the family deviltry on the agenda of the beautiful new day; images of HER peacefully sleeping and happily breathing the same air begin to fade away...

Waking from the dream he breathes every second, Julian walks to the shower head bopping to the new beat she'd shown; standing perfectly in the key of his new love's taste, the water never felt so hot and warm in it's revitalizing embrace as the dance floor they met, the car ride they went, and the beach's waves were all sent trickling down his mind like waterfalls to each level of their pools. Smiling hard at what they'd found, the sounds of her murmurs mid ecstasy chasing and the gazes of her eyes gracefully beat down his mind's pavement. And in turning skyward with eyes closed, Julian's swears never to run from the game he's already won; fuck the world and the acclaim for riches fame an'friends are nothing without someone to share it through... Tears happily cascade torn bodies as he's finally bereft of the misery typically drenching his soul; and although the berlin wall will soon tumble, emotions gleefully clench his jaw as'er feelings scarfully besmirch hearts to shine anew in the eye of life's storm... The whirlwinds could tear down an'surround him as they please for the heart's full whilst the mind basks in waterfall like pools amongst tall trees, embracing magnificent sun's streams that enhance his once thin now thick skin. For only losing her shine within would allow moon's glare to pierce through veils... only losing her touch would collapse beauty into his own treacherous hell...

The cold bathroom air shutters Julian's living day dream for what lay ahead would surely break off Santana's remaining sun beams...

Dragging himself out the front door, Julian prepares himself to push the knife in Santana's back once more as anticipation of events to unfold is far worse than any conversation to behold.

A death march at best, the silent car ride drones on past familiar street signs sneakily laughing at missions in play. The heights had faced two tragedies thru the years: why there's no parents to speak of is one, and two was the Brother of the heartbreak kid stealing his name an'shattering records of HIS heartbreak's fame.

And with each knock Julian shoots on the door, anxiety creeps closer until the fifth leaves him dreadfully sober; sober from the drug he was high on all over; sober from a love he'd wished on four leaf clovers and sober from the world he now must gloss over to the one person who could possibly understand... reduced t'kill the man whom watched his own love swim away from such great depths to dry land...

Bastion: "He's in his room" (Julian lurches by)

Bastion: "Oh hey Jules, (turns around semi-smiling) here, (passes Santana's phone) good luck bro"

Julian: (making first eye contact) "...yea..."

Standing at the mirror structuring his hair for the day, Santana's eyes shift to the left to see Julian in the reflection.

Santana: (raspy hung over voice) "What uuuupp... how was last night?"

Julian: "It was cool; hit up the east side, a little late night ghost riding an'a laugh attack at Q and his 'girlfriend's' expense; it was legit..."

Santana: "Annnnnnnd....."

Julian: "Annnnd what?" (playing dumb)

Santana: (turning around) "Ummm, the valley? Hellloooo, THAT'S why I didn't roll..."

Julian: (scrunched face inhaling air through closed teeth) "Yeaaaaaa... (runs hand through hair) ...about that..."

Santana: "What... did y'all rumble in the bronx??? Without me????" (#jackiechan)

Julian: "Na..."

Santana: "You see Jasmine?"

Julian: "Na"

Santana: "You hook up with Veronica?" (smiles)

Julian: "Na... (scrunched face) but closer"

Santana: (eyes wide, eyebrows raised) "Oh snap! (single clap) You hooked up with someone new!!!! THERE'S my brother; come here, (arms open) lets hug it out bitch"

Julian: "Yeaaaaa... (looking away) I don't think we should beeeee, (looks back) hugginnnngggg...."

Santana: "What? Who could you have hooked up with? (looking down at the bed wandering among the valley playground like a spinning slot machine till landing on-) no... (looks at Julian shaking his head) ...no no... (turns head, eyes closed inhaling) ...Liliana?"

Julian: (nods like a kid admitting to his parents he broke the window playing baseball in the house) "Yeaaa....... I'm in deep"

Santana: "Wait... you hooked up wIth her? With fuckin HERRRR sister????? Of ALLLLLLL the girls in the world you chose the sister of my ex??? THEE EX???!!! Have you forgotten what the fuck happen between her sister an'I? How could I ever be in the same room as her let alone her sister? I have to leave the @standard on the few occasions that fuckin bastard jumps out of his shell an'drags his unworthy ass t'stand next to that goddess... He has NO CLUEEE what dreadful luck he had to grab her on the rebound; just the right bland safe and boring guy to counter my over powering love. (stares at himself in the mirror) ...To see her laugh and them interact, I can't handle myself an'I lose my tact; enraged blood driven anger rips my body apart with only the needle in the haystack able to sew my insides back together. (turns towards Julian) And YOU'VE fallen for her haven't you? (walks closer) HAVEN'T YOU??!! (steps back) Fuck this!

I wont stand by your side and watch you go down the river to meet my own darkened fate; watch her leave you broken down on the side of the road for the fuckin trucker passing by because she quote “needs” a ride. I know she’s a different woman, excuse me, GIRL than her sister whose name I still can’t mention outta fear of being enveloped by’er once again... I can’t bare to think of him touching her with his unworthy hands, (slams mirror) SOOOO unable to satisfy an’leaving her forever in lust.

...I refuse to see you fall down that hole cuz its a purgatory I would not wish upon my greatest enemy. Their floor is NO place for a Casta as we have the means to reach depths others cannot. WE are a dying breed and must remain strong while such adversarial waves crash around us... I don’t know how, but she’ll corrupt your essences within and bring you to your knees asking why your eyes ever graced such a pristine sensual woman as a Merlo; the love that a Casta to a Merlo births is unlike any other with it’s endless attraction and unmatched chemistry; truly unparalleled in its majestic nature... And she will run; just like SHE ran... (runs finger over the newly made cracks) The mirrors that course a Merlo’s veins are jagged born, leaving them crushed before ever gracing this round globe of an earth; their “sunshine” parents saturated their hearts with ill will and sardonic humors in the realm of love causing them to fear the unknown... (faces Julian) And what you see now? What effervesces from her pores? What she says NOWWW??!! You think it won’t change tomorrow or the next DAY???? You believe the words spewed by such a tragic soul???”

Julian: "My dearest brother, my cherished father and my family in all (sits staring off at bedroom walls) ...I was formerly an artist who loss love's definition as the heart of a thousand breaks left me resting at the bottom of waves crashing down upon me. I left Veronica as an Archie not capable of passion and to find feelings that blend the heart an'tend the fire, I cannot help but throw wind to keep its caution; mind to keep its ration for this isn't to be trifled, truffled or rifled... (stands up walking towards Santana) This bares NOT the same world, nor the same plight; this is not your life an'this is NOT your fight!!!!! I feel for you dear brother on whats transpired along, an'I never imagined I'd sing such a conspired swan's song; but sing I do and the will, will be through...

Please help me open such blades of flowers and do not chastise me on such glorious hours for this is my choice an'gift I've found... Now please celebrate my decision of today's declaration for I cannot go on alone without my family's confirmation. (looks to the floor) I now see why you'd have left the heights for her an'why you've been lost in a blur of ecstatic agony as the warmth of such tragedy can soothe or sore; last or fall; beautify or MAUL the lives you built and love you'd spilt on futile grounds below... This is what I now know and fucking truth it be; NOW I demand you join me in my revelry an'taste the snow before sending in the calvary..."

Santana: "You know shit of snow that falls for thou is a mirage of blood against forsaken walls... Do you have any idea the fee demanded from pure white darkness drearily taken and hurled against spry basement floors? To live in the permanent chills of glistening snow having basked in blissful white plains long ago??? (turns to mirror) ...The world never hatches its gleams and like returning to real worlds from Narnia, so dreadful will it ever seem. (turns t'Julian) And t'was better to have loved and sunk? Better to have basked in sunlit floors turned gloom? (looks to bedroom walls) I loss my power to control upon parting and I await for her return; but never... never will she yearn, yet I wait; wait... and wait for my turn" (eyes fall to floors)

Julian: “We are not Thou my dear brother for we are Meant for each other. We’re living life in the bliss of ecstasy and we are NOT your blood soaked aching memory... It is a tragedy all in all, but why desecrate our union for YOUR lonely fall. Selfish it was to claim against new eternal springs, for it’s lit the soul a light, too clean to quickly dirty; tis not your plight, so never you worry... (looks away) This is love of the truest design and it has neither your ghost’s architecture nor bore in your time... (looks into Santana’s eyes) For a merlo and casta CANNNNN coexist in different states of harmony, to thrive together while slaying dragons in a land called Honalee; No smoke is necessary to blind great green dragons for together we slay dreams an’land goals we imagine; lives cannot bleed when hearts aren’t decoys, as this bond’s not for any world’s to taint nor destroy; (in his face) For no NEEEEED to hate or hatch such foul ploys, for cunning as you are and cunning as you be, we shall not! CANNNN Not! Repeat your history...... (shaking head walking away) Love is the most sacred of antiquities, inevitably embedded here in its blind validity. (turns back) So please join our ship as the band’s symphony plays full tempo; know that together we’ve grown wings to touch the skies only mementos; safe from moon’s dark sides an’frolicking with the accompaniment of the sun’s full deride... So pleaaaase, dear brother! For IIII beseech you: heal the frost bite from cold winter’s spells, unlearn the passion driven days of summer and leave autumn’s wretched leafy misery to visualize better days of spring’s new residue”

As his anger appears to lessen, Santana's boil of blood seems to unravel; yet the judge has yet to bang his gavel nor extend its rebuttal... Instead Santana sighs a sigh, worthy of a king; and with eyes down low and head hung, he walks over in the air so fuckin thin... gently grabs his dear brother's head with both hands, face to face from love's eyes to bloodshot's weary cried out eyes:

Santana: "I love you dear brother..." (kisses forehead and walks out)

Thinking he had gotten out with a broken arm and scraped knee, crows peck out Julian's love filled eyes with heartbreaks' treachery; reminding him what the kiss of death entails in a moment all wish to drain from memory...

Sunken to ill fated conclusions, Julian takes out both phones; places one on the nightstand and intently staring at his own (Bukka Buuuu!)

SMS: Liliana > Julian
Good morning Julian!!!
SMS: Liliana > Julian
QOD (Quote of the Day): "When I met you flowers started growing in the darkest parts of my mind and heart"

Smiling somewhere, the body pushes him to respond; yet torn and saddened by the inevitable conclusion, he cannot do so after what's come to fruition... For those very same flowers that grew in Santana had long since withered and past... and he, his own fuckin brother had just forced him to recall how they didn't ever truly last...

And standing for a minute or 5 or 13, he didn't walk away in fear of ending this scene; for to leave would mark the event stamped and done... So he stood there and waited... stood there and waited... stood there and waited..................till the teapot started whistling and his hands did the texting:

SMS: Julian > Liliana

Good morning Liliana...

SMS: Julian > Liliana

When I met you my mind breathed relief as you brought water to dried up wreaths in deep chasms of my heart

SMS: Julian > Liliana

But this is just the beginning...

SMS: Julian > Liliana

...this is only the start!!! ;)

(valley side BZZZZZZZ-BZZZ-BZZZZZZ)

No sooner had a smile waltzed over Liliana's face did "nail scraping chalkboards" lay siege to content ears. An intermittently dual scraping on walls arches closer, tensing and freezing her body, flexing her arms an'twisting the mind until nails scratch her own walls towards the door... Silence...

Turning knobs to Liliana's room, Jasmine swings the door open far too fucking slow for comfort to uncover a face that instills devil like fear into Liliana's fragile shocked body at full alert;

Jasmine: "You fucked him didn't you..."

Liliana: "No... No I; No I didn't Jazz I-"

Jasmine: "-Don't you DARE fuckin Jazz me; I KNOW you fucked him"

Liliana: (in tears) "No, no; we-we didn't do-"

Jasmine: "-Doesn't fuckin matter you backstabbing whore"

Liliana: "Please!!! (head slumped downward, hands on temples) Stop cussing!!! Just; STOP!!!"

Jasmine: (in far too silent of a voice with perfect pronunciation) "I will do no such fuckinggg, thinnggg... You're banished (louder) I don't wanna see you; (louder) I don't wanna hear you... (full yell) I don't wanna ever know you FUCKINGGGGGG EXISTED!!!!!!!"

Liliana: "I... (pleadingly walking closer) You-You know I-I couldn't-help myself! I-I couldn't stop!!! (grabs her hand) Youknow-YouKNOWWW what I'm talkinbout!"

Jasmine: "NO! (flings her hand off hers) I KNOW, that you FUCKed me... (walks away, stops, barely turns her head back an'softer) You fucked the valley (walks an'turns again softer still) ...you fucked us..."

Lunging to the knob, Jasmine violently slams the door. After a second or two of silence a death rattle banshee like scream emanates from the halls frightening Liliana more than lurching nails on walls.

Walking dead faced and emotionless with tears silently streaming, a cold shiver creaks through the recesses of Jasmine's shell like heart; the dreams of him and the mornings of saddened longing gazes to waves crashing upon toes during long winter days had eaten away most of the chains captively imprisoning her inside... and along with blasts of hope from deep down on that shelf had together rejuvenated'er longing for love's everlasting wealth...

So contemptful of Peter's boring and safe manner, no longer did she want to make love to him more than fuck him with a hammer; pulverize his "I love you babe(s)" and "whatever you wanna do is fine" responses, or at least surgically inject some testosterone to give that mother fucker some FUCKin back bone... For with a child like tap Peter would tip over an'lay in his coffin asking "may I have another?" to which she'd frustratedly shriek, "why the Fuck do I even bother..." Oh how she disliked his "you ok?" or "whats wrong babe(s)?" and oh how she HATED such answers bled out like a slave; all leading her to conspire exit strategies or attempts to make light of his ways, and please PLEASE GOD forgive her for what she may do on the next page... For in fighting off disaster with each passing week, she knew he'd slowly kill'er to leave'er woefully sitting in search of currents surging from beneath... In wait for the world to grant'er access back down below, yet sadly she'd hung the guides and killed all light in the after glow; having destroyed the generator an'exhausted all oxygen thinking she'd never dive back down... so utterly convinced she lay in love with the safe an'fuckin sound...

Reduced to a life that was her own dreaded curse, what was she to expect with each day grossly over rehearsed... yet she unknowingly yearns t'dance at such great depths of her soul's weeping sea; while he remains idly waiting by with neither ever truly living, but only her still running away from the why...

Act 3: Scene 3: Brand New

Cold in her once warm bedroom, Liliana breathes a few deep breaths and walks down the halls as the once friendly walls judgingly smile at her... rounding a corner to the three tiered living room;

Tyler: "Hey beautiful! So what was all THAT about? Did you and your sister get into a fight? I'm so sorry..."

With Liliana's emotions crashing into each other like electrons flying through atoms, all systems in'er mind's boardroom shut down;

Liliana: "Oh. Hey... Yeaaaa..." (staring away)

Tyler: "Well, I'm here if you need t'talk, (she looks towards him) I'll always be here..."

Liliana: (puzzled) "O...K, ummm... you feelinnn alright??? You drink too much last night???"

Tyler: (sits back real cool like) "No no; Actually, I've never been better; I feel like I'm seeing clear for the first time... Never been better"

Liliana: "Yea you said that already" (Perry walks in out of sight to Tyler)

Tyler: "Oh, (laughs out loud) fiddle dee meeee"

Liliana: "You meannnn, fiddle dee deeee?"

Tyler: (utterly embarrassed realizing Perry's in the room) "Ummmmm, I guess... I've never said; well, EITHER of those before"

Liliana: "Uh huh... Well I gotta run...."

Tyler: "You're leaving? You can't; hang out for a bit? We never talk anymore..."

Liliana: "Uhhh, yeaaaaaa I do have to... go, soooooo.... I'll see ya later..." (walks out)

Tyler: (much too delayed and awkward in it's timing) "Ok! I hope so!!!! I'll text ya later kiddo! (door closes; murmuring to himself) Kiddo??? What the fuck was that?"

Perry: (sits much too close to Tyler on the couch chewing his gum in silence for 3 seconds till leaning over) "Sooooooo, (chew-chew) what the fucks your deal?"

Tyler: (sits back putting hand on Perry's shoulder) "Pare... I have no frickin clue man; all I remember is feeling really weird last night before I went to sleep an... (squints eyes trying to recall) an'all I can remember is.... (him crying) is I thinnnkkk I just had some funky late night munchies..."

Perry: "Hope so, (chew-chew) I'm havin a couple bitches over tonight, (chew-chew) well actually these are quote 'ladiesssss;' (laughs) high class; (chew) you better bring your A game!"

Tyler: "Yea for sure. (puts arm around perry's neck) I'm about to game YOUUU right now girl! Is it weird that I like you sitting soo close to me? I think I may like it a little toooo much!" (grabs Perry's nipple)

Perry: (jumps up) “Whoa whoa, ok dude; enough. (spits gum in trash) I gotta jump in the coffin an’get some shut eye for tonight. (holds jacket like a cape in front of his mouth) Muaaaahhh haa haa haa haaaaaaaaa” (laughs hysterically)

Tyler: “Ok Bram, let me know what’s up with tonight; I’ll hit up the crew”

Perry: “Alright alright; Dracula Out...”

Oddly enough, some of the biggest “pimps” and “ladykillers” exhibit the same overtly homosexual joking behaviors amongst their friends. Is it comfortability in their own sexual skin that allows men to grab another’s ass twist nipples an’punch genitals without any homophobic reservations? Does the cliché “every girl is a little bi” apply to men as well? Why can girls suggestively hit on/flirt with one another up to the moment of actually HAVING sex yet still be considered 100 percent “straight?” Why are casanova “pimps” welcomed by many while lady “sluts” shunned; why are feminine bi/ lesbian GIRLS loved by many yet bi/gay GUYS shunned... In reality, everyone SHOULD be who they are because that’s the only way you’ll ever find happiness; only after accepting whomever an’whatever sex makes you truly happy will one become fully tolerant of everyone else and THEIR sexual choices; do YOU object to other’s preferences? Maybe YOU should ask why ;) ok; move move on...

Previously incapable of such passions and emotions, Tyler's eyes jump around the room to the surrounding inanimate objects looking for answers... Retracing his steps, Tyler remembers psychotically wandering around the party an'throwing his rage at everyone as if they all found out he had a small ____... In reality he DIDN'T have a small ___, but it really didn't matter since before last night he was just another rich asshole roaming through life treating everyone like garbage save for the vampire and the low smarts duo of Nick an'John... Yet with strange foreign sensations he believes to be "emotions" pulsing his body, Tyler looks at his hands in the metaphorical mirror to see a human being for the first time... and with his estranged heart beating stronger an'louder than ever before, Tyler finally sees Liliana as the forever high on life, care free spontaneous make up all the rules as she goes "GOAL" of a wife; the girl who'd complete a marathon from end to start just to prove she could run against the grain and come out a winner on the other side.

Yet having never awoken in a dark room before last night, Tyler feels hallow inside as if he's missing a part of himself, all too aware of the ever more inviting hopeless rivers surrounding him... In the darkest of times and the hopelessness of love, the heart refuses to give in and carries your body through to the end even when every other fiber of your being has quenched its thirst with the empty waters below...... carry on...

Act 3: Scene 4: JumpingIntoA MomentStuckInTime (#JMST)

With families in (general) disarray, (#butters) each step the younger siblings take away from their former havens is another step towards their union an'ever growing bond. Following such glum, both simultaneously call each other to occupy 4 lines within a single phone call #eventheirphonesbreaktherules

Call: Julian = Liliana

J: Well Hello Darling

L: Sweetums!

J: Awww-

L: -Awww you said Awww; god just hearing your voice has already-

J: -I know it sooo has!

L: You didn't even let me-

J: -Made me feel soo much better an'I needed it sooo badly right now; Muah! (#eatyourheartoutsouljaboy)

L: Ahhhhhhhhh!!!! That's totally everything I was feeling!!! Muah!!! God I

J: Don't you say it-

L: -I didn't say anything, Shuttt up!!! Just for that I'm clicking over an'hanging up on our other conversation

J: NO NO!!! Poor parallel universe us'll be crushed! Since both didn't hang up, one will think the other did an'you will KILLLLL parallel us!!!

L: Ok Ok; somehow that makes sense

J: You bet your sweet I wish I was biting an'grabbing ass it does!

L: Julian-I mean Julie!!! It's barely 2 pm and you're pullin out the big guns! A little teased are we?

J: A little??? You don't know the half of it!!!

L: Do tell!

J: Ok; you got me you called my bluff

L: Yeaaaa... I just get you; come on, you could never lie to me

J: Well, you could; Never... LEAVE Meeeee so we might as well make it official

L: Lets meet up and then we'll "talk" (does air quotes)

J: Hahahaha did you just do air quotes over the phone???

L: How d'you know??? Oh my god that's amazing!

J: You're amazing!

L: WE'RRRE amazing!

J: Ok ok, you win

L: I always do!

J: So where we meetin? I mean; come to my park!

L: Good save; Where? In the heights????

J: Yes!!!

L: Ummm... how bout you come here. After all I'MMMM the lady!

J: After last night? Maybe a lady in the street but a FREAK on the car!

L: HAHAHAHAHA I love that song! Classic!!! Damn can you believe that was like 10 years ago? (#Ludacris)

J: Longer than that

L: Damn! That's fuckin crazy!!! What ever happen to him?

J: I think he got married an'became a priest

L: No that was Ma$e

J: (covers phone "I love this woman") ...that was smooth

L: I try, I try

J: You don't need t'try, cuz everything you say's so effing fly

L: Effing?

J: Yea I try to keep it PG; you know, trick love da kids

L: Trickkkk, Daddy?

J: Ok, can we just drive to vegas like right now?

L: (laughs) But I don't really even like Rap and Hip Hop anymore... a couple top 40's tracks, a little Lil Wayne, Kid Cudi, Chris Brown; OH and Lorde; Lorde's AMAZING!

J: No way! I Just found Lorde the other day! Her songs are incredible and the trendy hits are not even the best tracks!!! I love white teeth teens and bravado...

L: Totally!!!

J: And yea, I'm not into hip hop anymore either. I used to be all about it back in the day when even main stream hip hop was good; but by the early 2000's it just... well, fell off...

L: Yeaaa... Bush was the cause; or not even; just NOT having a Clinton in the Whitehouse

J: What the fuck? How do YOUUUU know about media and music in the 90s?

L: I should have been a teen in the 90s; not the 2000s

J: But yea, I was kidding about vegas. What other genres are you into? What bands do ya like?

L: No you were Hellllllla not jokin dude. If I pushed, you would fly down right now

J: No no; it's drive down in the rental and fly back. That way you have the road trip where you're all stoked and excited for Vegas but when you're hungover slash still drunk, out of money and been up nearly three dayyyys, you can sleep on the quick flight home

L: Anywayyyyssss; I love post-hardcore, alternative and indie; bands like Pierce The Veil, Paramore and The Neighbourhood; well, pretty much anything I can rock out to in the car an'wanna drive like a million more miles

J: Shut the fuck up!!! I love all THREE of those bands!!! You may have just broke the high score for cool points!!! I meannnn; Just last night we were blasting The Neighbourhood's new Mixtape black an'white... Preach, preach on

L: You religious?

J: I meannnn, I have your standard 90's latchkey kid religious views; I went to church cuz I was forced to but I believe in A GOD, or that there is A higher power or spirit, or somethin like that; but I think all this fightin an'killin in the name of quote "religion" is not something ANY god or religious head would ever approve of or support. And THATS's why I don't really identify with a certain religion; let me guess, you're the same too right?

L: Yes and no

J: What's yes and what's no

L; (laughs) Ok. This time you called MYYY bluff. I'm the same and especially don't believe in killing others in the name of an idea or religion

J: Yea I take Kevin Smith's Dogma approach to the world of religion

L: Great fuckin movie btw's

J: Btw's??? Ok, I'll let that slide young'n... at least you can spell via text

L: Wht r u's talkns bout?

J: Nevermind, (laughs) I definitely stole Chris Rock's whole motif in that movie that ideas are better than beliefs and killing people over religions (accent) is bad mmm kayyy

L: (laughs) I love Kevin Smith AND SOUTH PARK!

J: How'd you get that? (covers phone "god she's amazing")

L: Hey. Don't you know who you're talkin to?

J: I do, but I wanna know everything about you!

L: Are you sitting in your car on the phone too?

J: Close, I'm driving around on the way to the valley

L: NO WAY!! I'm driving around on the way to the heights

J: (laughs) Well we should probably meet somewhere in the middle

L: I know this park by my friend's house

J: Wherever you want darling... I just wanna see you hug you hold you kiss you

L: What's that amazin song from that one Batman movie?

J: Which one? The one with two face and Val Kilmer?

L: YES!!! It had that U2 song as the theme?

J: Hold me thrill me kiss me kill me?

L: Ummmm thats close. I'll look it up

J: Awww do you have AT&T?

L: Yea, I can talk on the phone ANNNDDDD use the internet! What's up?

J: Lucky... Well I have, "Can you hear me now?"

L: Yeaaaaa; loss a couple points there, I fuckin hate that guy; never do that again

J: Ok, but Only if you'll be mine forever... OFFICIALLY!!!

L: Whoa quickness, slow down. Like I said, lets TALK first

J: Alright... No air quotes that time-

L: -Ok now THAT'S freaky

J: You ain't seen nothin yet!

L: ......It's on your left

J: What's on your left?

L: The park's on your left

J: How do you know it's me? What color car do I have?

L: Black with blood red trim (smiles)

J: How'd you-

L: -You're sitting at the stop sign not moving on the phone

J: (quietly but forgets t'cover the phone) I love this woman

L: OH MY GOD OH MY GODDDD!!! Whatdidyou JUSSSSTTT SAYYYYY!!!!@@@@

J: Wait; you heard that? How'd you-(realizes he didn't cover the phone)

L: -Nothin. Now we're even

J: I'll even you!

L: Promise?

J: Forever an'always (parks car)

(click) (click) (click) (click)

Stepping out like he owns the fuckin world, Julian slyly looks at her before casually walking around the car with hands in pockets. Confident and calm yet nervously glancing anywhere but her, Julian's heart tries to catch it's breath but cannot inhale enough oxygen from the blood frantically circulating his body... Soon a tingling sensation drains down the back of his neck into his spine t'join in the revelry of his nervousness... Looking to the disguised moon on his left, Julian wonders whether these butterfly like feelings of anticipation would ever wane, triggering a smiling Liliana to appear in the mind's eye to lovingly say "Uhhhh nooo; helloooo, did you not see our future?"

Unable to restrain from her beauty any longer, Julian can't help but glance towards her only to quickly look away as if his smile would give away his true self. Mirroring an elementary school kid skipping out to recess on the friday before spring break, Julian's care free vibes illuminate the cloudy yet sunny three rainbowed sky...

Although Girls of "high class" don't normally lean against cars, Liliana doesn't reside in any class or stereotypical label; and with the guy she'd dreamt about as a kid while running around sporting random pieces of white fabric turned veils currently heading in her direction, the smiles boiling within start to seep out... Like the sun lassoed it's rays upon the beach's horizon, Liliana's skin continually lassoes her heart to try an'keep it from floating over to him; unlike Julian, she would never allow her smile to disappear behind the moon for a woman in love smiles whenever HE is near an'only cries when there's distance While he's near... A TRUE woman whose found the man they wish to marry won't stray and'll be the most caring devoted woman on earth; a woman captured with heart enraptured will be the greatest gift a man could ever have.

As Jasmine's apprentice and a lady of grace, Liliana learned never to strike first an'force men to chase chase chase. Viewing her teachings as merely pirate code like guidelines, after Julian struts past the half way point Liliana politely courtesies before running over without mercy; him being so cool an'calm makes her drool an'spawn to be as close as can possibly be...

Upon colliding they are as two stars falling in the same night sky, and after enveloping eachother all was sooo right felt as if they could die; none wish to leave at the bottom for the top is the way to fly; on and up to skies one limit, with this the place one could always be left to exhibit. The smooth flowing blood gladly jumps from eachother's veins to criss cross as stars no longer fall for they have all but one cost... And with an unbreakable love bore, embracing one another they closely held; this kiss could not be the last for in such great moments spirits will dwell; to remain caught in sun light's shining infamy and dance together on beams of light ad nauseam till' infinity.

...And in a park full of other stories, arm and arm they stood; everyone with somewhere to go and somewhere from whence they came; yet the two standing there did not come and did not even go. As if they ran to a spot where they had been all along; just jumped into the mist for a small epoch of time, and after leaving their embrace would never truly end; to be stuck in that moment again an'again, forever on

Act 3: Scene 5: Out of Love

Shamefully sitting and still staring at mirrors next to his perch, Tyler can only look towards himself, sigh deeply inhale and curse; curse at reflections in foreign gardens with arrogance exuded, all others washed away an'alone as he inevitably concluded.

Having fallen asleep to a shattered mind, Tyler awoke in shadows of his new emotional ways; so unable to release images of his love beyond eye's passing gaze. Wishing to move away from sunken settings of his princess laid beauty no longer, the world continually shakes him without mercy, constantly reminding he's none the worthy to attain the love he pursues... The weights of worrisome thoughts drip off mind's leaves to pool ont'unforgiving rugs an'bleed into floors of his own selfish doing; sinisterly chartering new despicable missions at the behest of his further undoing. For having fucked up so royally Liliana would never see Tyler as anything but the artist formerly known... an'never over run her decision to depart him for the glistening shores of the sun...

Driven by a single lonely fear an'blinded by heartbreak, Tyler turns to the moon and casts farewell to the righteous shine; embracing a wicked touch while inheriting a devil's divine. And in wiping away his shame Tyler brazenly takes up a new cause to his name; for after the next invisible moves, he'd be the last one she'd have a choice to chose in vowing "till death do us part"...

Unable to decipher the next moves nor see the next case, the mind flashes to blank installments; however tragically written, or ironically displaced...

SMS: Tyler > Nick
Yo meet me at my spot

SMS: Nick > Tyler
Which spot?

SMS: Tyler > Nick
My house smart guy
SMS: Tyler > Nick
Hit up your better half

SMS: Nick > Tyler
Oh he's not better
SMS: Nick > Tyler
If anything I'M the better half
SMS: Nick > Tyler
And he's the worse half...

SMS: Tyler > Nick
SHUT UP! Just ducking go!

SMS: Nick > Tyler
No YOU ducking go! Lol

SMS: Tyler > Nick
If you send one more text I swear

SMS: Nick > Tyler
It's not nice to swear ;)

SMS: Tyler > Nick
What are you a woman????? STOP texting STOP flirting and hit up John and roll asshole!

SMS: Nick > Tyler
Word

SMS: Nick > Tyler
Hey lower half… Roll over to Tyler's asap

SMS: Tyler > Nick
You sent that to me dufus!!!

SMS: Nick > Tyler
LOL My bad…
SMS: Nick > Tyler
and no… your the dufus haha

SMS: Tyler > Nick
Clap… Clap… Clap… Now Fuckin Go!!!

SMS: Nick > John
Hey, roll over to Tyler's ASAP

SMS: John > Nick
Why whats up?

SMS: Nick > John
Does it matter? Cuz Tyler said to

SMS: John > Nick
Said to what?

SMS: Nick > John
Dude!!!! Your so annoying!!! Can't you ever just say YES and stop texting hella???

SMS: John > Nick
I could...
SMS: John > Nick
But I won't ;)

SMS: Nick > John
Kasjdfbhksadjhfsiohfsodhfsdhflsakjdhflksdjhfs

SMS: John > Nick
Well that was rude

SMS: Nick > John
FUCKING GO!!!!!

SMS: John > Nick
You fucking go...

SMS: Nick > John
I'm already gone

SMS: John > Nick
Oh yea, well I'm already Gonning

SMS: Nick > John
Clap... Clap... Clap... Good one loser...

SMS: John > Nick
Thanks!
SMS: John > Nick
I try, I try :)

How often does hypocrisy rule the day and teapots call the fuckin kettle black?

Having somewhat regained his prior swag, Tyler drives home casually slow blasting 106.1 KMEL while Nick and John race to their leader's pad. Luckily, the frequent confidence boosts of the "low smarts duo" help Tyler's ever deflating ego act as if it belongs on Perry's unreachably high level; previously a greater caliber being than Bram Stroker himself, Tyler's next moves will throw him off the heaven track an'down to hell to never come back.

Incurable by nothing but time, the disease a desperate heartbroken fool inherits fucks up your sense of reason an'tricks your mind int'giving two huge thumbs up to whatever idiotic plan comes spewed out of lovesick individuals. For even in remission, the smallest of contact or mementos can reopen Pandora's box an'act as a single "hopeful" splash to your toes springing faith that "fuck; maybe one day it'll be 'steady as she goes' and they'll be waiting there at the end of the road"...

Past light seems brighter while living in the dark;
their heart seems bigger when providing a single spark.

Such optimistic thoughts breathe danger an'cast circular traps; for once someone refuses to tread water for their mistakes or consciously chose to leave, it's done; if they let you go once, they may let you go again; and if they didn't fight for you to stay then they didn't value you as much as they should at the end of days; for people DO NOT change until it's too late... Yet even then there's no guarantee they won't revert back to deeply engrained ways an'kill their own joy by casting doubtful shadows over the sun's gleaming shine.

And hardest to keep in the forefront of one's own mind?
Another's poor wiring does not make you any less;

REPEAT: ANOTHER'S BAGGAGE SAVAGELY TEARING YOU APART DOES NOT ACCURATELY REFLECT WHAT RESIDES IN YOUR OWN STILL BEATING HEART.

Sometimes it takes standing on your own two feet to realize such haphazard things; and maybe next time you'll find the one who'll bring you to your knees, together leaving darkness to sway alone in the breeze...

(Tyler pulls up blasting random rap music with Nick an'John sitting on his porch)

John: (yelling like a schoolgirl) "Tyler Tyler! I got here first!" (music drowns his voice)

Nick: (Tyler turns the car off and steps out) "IIIII got here first. (turns to John slamming his head down) IDIOT!!!"

Tyler: (grumbles) "Sigh, what'd I do to deserve these guys?"

John: (jumps up) "So what's up Ty? What's the hullabaloo?"

Tyler: "Uhhhh, John? (rolls eyes) You been watchin The Jungle Book again?"

John: “No no... just A Goofy Movie” (#powerlinerules)

Tyler: (closed eye inhale) “Shut (open exhales) Up dude; no time for jokes”

Nick: (smiles looking at John) “Oh he wasn’t joking haha; (slams head down) IDIOT!!!”

John: “Hey, I was watching it with a chick alright?”

Nick: “Sureeeeee you were; check it... your mom does not count as a ‘chick’ Johnny boy” (laughs; slapping John on the back)

John: “Fuckin funny NicolAAAAASSSSSSS” (slaps Nick even harder on the small of his back causing him thrust his waist forward with a girlish shriek)

Tyler: “HEY PANSY’S!!!! (pushes both in the chest) Got your attention??? Grab your pipes; we got plans t’build bitches”

John: “Allllright, now we’re talkin”

Nick: “Yea yea, I love talkin...”

Tyler: “You’re killin me smalls!”

Nick: “I’m bigger than-”

Tyler: “-SHUTTHEFUCKUP!” (Nick sinks into his shoes an’heads to his car)

Walking into his "yea I gotta a lot of money" house, Tyler grabs a bottle of Jameson, one shot glass an'two beers;

Tyler: "TV ON (TV turns on) ...ESP FUCKIN N (flips to ESPN) ...love frickin technology"

Walking back up the steps side by side, John and Nick hear the racing gun an'sprint inside; shoulder to shoulder at the doorway, both fall to the wooden floor crushing their bags of weed in the process.

Tyler: (shakes his head) "Well it's a good thing you guy's are half brain dead an'did NOT bring your pipes like I asked cuz there would be broken glass allllll over the place"

Nick: "Well maybe his, MINE wouldn't have-"

Tyler: "-That's IT!!!! (slams hand on the table nearly knocking over the Jameson) You're on time out Nick, no talkin for 5 minutes"

Nick: "But I-"

Tyler: "-But NO! That's final!"

John: (snickers but not skittles covering his mouth)

Tyler: "Oh you think it's funny?"

John: "Um, (looks at Nick then Ty) ...yea, it's hilarious!"

Tyler: (straight faced then smiling) "Yeaaaaa it ISSS pretty funny, hahaha... I try, I try............... Now!" (pours himself a shot and cracks open a beer)

John: (Grabs an'cracks 2nd beer)

Tyler: (scrunched face) "Whoa whoa! What are you doin?" (opens hand towards John; slams shot)

John: "Well I thought since you have two you got-"

Tyler: "-Hellllllll no, (snatches 2nd beer and takes a sip) you want a Corona? Go get one! (John heads to the kitchen) ...Oh grab a Stella instead cuz there's only a few Corona's left"

John: (in the kitchen) "DUDE! There's gotta be like 20 Coronas in here"

Tyler: "Fiiiiine, just take one... and grab one for Lil Nikki here too" (smiling at Nick)

John: (proudly sits on the couch)

Tyler: "Ok; Now; I called you guys here t-OH SHIT! Go, GO; GO!!! (stands) RUN!!! TOUCHDOOOWN!!!" (arms up)

John: "You gettin all crazy over college football in June? What the fuck?"

Tyler: "Wolverine's baby!!! Replay of the spring game mother fuckerrrrr!!!" (#goblue)

John: “OHHHH! It’s Michigan Staaaaaaate!!!” (stands up offering high five)

Tyler: (Sitting down glaring at John with no five given) “WHAT? FUCK the Spartans!!!!!! Its UniVERSITY of MICHIGAAAANNNNN!!! ...Come on man”

John: “Yea yea; Thats what I meant-”

Nick: “-IDIOTTT!!!@@@” (Tyler an’Nick erupt in laughter)

John: “Hey, ummm, aren’t you on timeout?” (looks to Tyler for acknowledgment)

Tyler: (still unable to speak from laughter) “No, (laughs) that was awesome; he’s good... (extends hand t’Nick) Welcome back! I always liked you Nikki! (handclasps) ANYWays!!! So I decided this morning, oh hey pack a bowl John; or well, late last night that I NEED to get my ex back” (#packabowljon #insidejokejon)

John: “Ummm boss... I’m pretty sure you’re in the friend zone”

Tyler: “Good point, and what’s another obstacle Nick”

John: (feverishly raises hand)

Tyler: (shakes off John looking at Nick) “No no no; Nick?”

Nick: (looks at John’s floundering hand) “Ummmm, uhhhh, sheeeeeeeee hooked up with that new guy?”

Tyler: “EXACTLY! Wow you guys are so fuckin smart I feel like I’m gonna cry... Now we don’t know what the deal is with this new guy so we gotta act fast cuz she doesn’t just ‘hook up’ with random guys an’there’s always feelings involved”

John: “oooOOOOOooo” (passes packed Greenstar bong to Tyler)

Tyler: “Yes Koko... (takes bong) OOOO is right” (smiles)

Nick: (chuckling) “So what’s you gonna do?”

Tyler: “Well, (hits the bong) I don’t know Nikki (exhales) ...we gotta figure out how into this new guy she is; let me text’er about it...”

SMS: Tyler > Liliana

Hey...

SMS: Tyler > Liliana

Soooooooo I heard you made out with some guy at the party last night...

(minutes earlier at the park where Julian and Liliana sit atop a wooden picnic table #theygotthememo)

Liliana: "No way! If the world was ending and nuclear bombs were all up in the air, we would SOOOO go to my bomb shelter; it's wayyyy better than yours"

Julian: "Well MINE'S up in the hills hella far away from everyone; DEFinitely better to be removed from densely populated areas"

Liliana: "I mean; I guess that makes sense but who cares! If the world ended I'd be happy as long as I was with you when it did!"

Julian: "Welll duhhh, of course we would be! I mean- (Bukka Buuuu! Bukka Buuuu! Julian looks at her purse) Is that your phone?"

Liliana: (rolling eye giggle) "Yea" (takes out phone)

Julian: "Whose it from?" (jealousy ridden)

Liliana: (reading phone) "...no one special"

Julian: "Oh come on; when you say no one it means it's ACTUALLY someone cuz otherwise you would have said who it was darlin"

Liliana: "......it's a friend"

Julian: "Doesss this friend have a name?"

Liliana: "Nope"

Julian: "Come on, lemme see then"

Liliana: "I have nothing to hide, here" (hands phone over)

SMS: Tyler > Liliana
Hey...
SMS: Tyler > Liliana
Soooooooo I heard you made out with some guy at the party last night...

(Julian types a reply)

How much easier were relationships before cell phones, text messaging, social media and the alike joined mainstream culture? No phone hacking, no jealous text messages, no ex's randomly shooting arms back into your significant other's life and NO facebook/instagram stalking just to see how "great" your ex is doing; possibly faking it till they never make it... Since it's human nature to seek out possible tragedy and sabotage your relationships, even the most confident lovers will insist on replying to their significant other's text messages to prove there's "nothing going on;" when in reality you're attempting to prove THERE IS something going on. It's the whole "we pray they don't cheat, But if they DOOOO, we HAVVVVE t'know..." And thus when a person of the opposite sex messages your girl/guy, insecurity/jealousy prompts you to respond yourself to see what, (if anything) is going on between the two; that somehow a simple conversation will divulge whether they "hooked up" or wish t'do so... (No one ever thinks that the most devious and veteran cheaters already have such events well covered : (

And the cliché underlying these insecure actions? "A girl is just a friend you haven't fucked yet..." Such a heinous and sinister catch phrase stating every guy is ONLY friends with a girl for one reason... Sex. (albeit driven by insecurities within yourself/friends, parent issues, abuse neglect or even repressing/running away from inner homosexual tendencies...... or they just wanna fuck the world #thatsnotnice) And although this cliché holds true for many, (Perry and Tyler) it does not hold true for all. (Julian and Santana)

In order to fan their own self validating fire, humans desire as much communication attention an'affection as quickly as possible. Yet ironically the devices an'applications employed to connect one another at light speeds actually tear the true bonds apart farrr too quickly... Yes infidelity did occur before the age of cell phones and even pre PHONES in general; but thanks to 21st century technologies, the endless craving for attention an'communication has grown exponentially and simultaneously made infidelity as easy as: phone 2 3, text 5 6, cheat 8 9, break up 11 12............. followed by phone 2 3... text rebound misery....... cheat text on... cheat message on..........

The best relationships are those with Unlocked phones an'nothing to hide. Period. For when you're happy, treat one another right and in a loving "adult" relationship, there's no need to go through each other's phone because there's neither reason nor need to cheat... yet people still do and that's how fucked up life can sadly be... Unlike most beings on earth, humans have the prime ability of choice making the true question; how strong are YOU at your weakest?

While the significant other wanders amongst the mental playground in the shower and their phone goes off, thoughts of "Hmmm, who messaged MY girl/guy" sound off in your head and therein lies the deeper engrained issue: two people in love can "give" themselves to one another yet paradoxically will not CLAIM to OWN the other; objects are to own while People, (as much as especially guys and girls like to think) are NOT objects... It's these possessive like tendencies that inevitably drive your "bae" away since no independent strong an'capable person wants to be owned; one can give themselves to someone but never wants to be told what t'do, what to wear, and who they can an'cannot talk to/hang out with.

Responding to texts not only possessively stamps "I own you" on your lover's forehead but also portrays the extremely unattractive quality of insecurity. If you're secure with who you are AND your relationship, (in that order) you should never doubt the happiness you bring to your significant other or fret they may venture outside the relationship to satisfy unmet needs... However, if you DO lack qualities your "bae" needs and they DO travel elsewhere instead of communicating those issues, you may not be suited for one another after all... There is not a perfect mate out there for everyone but there IS someone who can BE the perfect person in a relationship WITH you; they may not be the safe haven mate and actually the second; your preference may be the safe haven life but the perfect person for a relationship With you IS the complicated difficult need to work on to persevere "notebook" love... work work... work on... :)

SMS: Liliana > Tyler
Yes I was

Julian: "Why is he texting you?" (hands back phone)

Liliana: "Becausssssee we're friends?" (#hatethatanswer)

Julian: "Why? He's a loser"

Liliana: "No he's not, we go way back..."

Julian: "How far back?"

Liliana: (keepin it "100") "We've known eachother for decades... annndddd dated a couple months back"

Julian: (facial expression turns ugly stammering) "WHAT!? HIMMM??!! An'he's Still textin you?" (Bukka Buuuu!)

SMS: Tyler > Liliana
So are you guys together now?

Liliana: "Yes, we're still friends and he's intertwined in my circle; with my sisterrrr, Perrrry an'everyone... even if I wanted to I couldn't just cut him out; could you cut out, I don't knowwwww, Q?"

Julian: "What'd he say?" (unsuccessfully tries to grab'er phone)

Liliana: "Ewwwww... this is hella unattractive..."

Julian: “Well lemme see then if you guys are ‘just friends”

Liliana: “Ok, I’ll let you see but you need to understand where my heart lies... You must learn to have faith and trust or ALL relationships you have will never work; you can’t go through life sooo insecure that you question another’s devotion to you at the drop of a jealous hat; that’s no way to live...”

Julian heard a variation of this from “Veronica” and a number of other ex’s but never truly understood it or took it to heart. For whatever reason Liliana’s words did not “fall on deaf ears;” an’after opening his stubborn eyes, Julian thought the same thing Santana did about Jasmine years earlier: “Never could someone unlock me the way SHE did. No one could help me open my own tightly clasped doors an’boxes while also supplanting the courage and zeal to deal with that which lay within”

Julian: “Wow... (looks at’er smiling) how do you DO that?”

Liliana: “Do what?” (turns eye to eye an’offers the phone)

Julian: (takes phone still eye to eye) “Break me down an’actually get through to me”

Liliana: “I guess I’m just good like that” (smiles an’shrugs her shoulders in an innocently cute manner)

Julian: “No... You’re fucking great; like amazing!!!!!” (she smiles again)

SMS: Liliana > Tyler
Yes

SMS: Tyler > Liliana
Damn. You serious? Fuck... and I was gonna talk to you about us today before you bounced all fast : (...
SMS: Tyler > Liliana
Who is this lucky bastard?

The stove boiling Julian's blood shoots up t'high causing the pot's top to twerk around #mileycyrus Breathing inward deeply and closing his eyes, Julian tries to keep calm while Tyler's words continually walk across his mind; staring intently at her phone, it's Julian's turn for his emotions to crash into one another like electrons flying through atoms... Refusing to fall where he and so many others typically would;

Julian: (looking away breathing long jealous breaths) "Sooooo... Does he still want you back?"

Liliana: "........yes... (places hand a top his) but it doesn't FUCKinnn matter; you are the ONLY body my eyes see... He could want, hell; EVERYone in the world could want me but it doesn't matter because I, (directs his head towards her) IIIIII only want YOU!!! (clasps hands as Julian looks away again) Look at me... LOOK at me! (solemnly turns towards her) It's you and me; THIS, (holds up interlocked hands) US!!! And that's it; all you need t'know. Who cares about the world him or any of the girls after you..."

Julian: "I love you"

An'with a smile befitting a woman being proposed to by the prince of her dreams, Liliana grabs his face with both hands an'staring deeply into his eyes pictures them dancing on the oceans's sunrise.

Liliana: "I love you Julian"

(kisses him as if the apocalypse floods their world)

Julian: "Miracle number 3"

Liliana: "Awwww, I love The Saint"

Julian: "And I love that you not only love the movie but knew my random quote!!!"

Liliana: "Looks like you have a case of the love you's!" (laughs, adoringly smiling)

Julian: "Love the love you's"

Liliana: "I think you're just in love with love"

Julian: (turns head forward with right hand raised) "Guilty your honor"

While laughing both forget about texting Tyler...

(Back in the house that heartbreak built)

Nick: “Sooo???”

Tyler: “Fuck... “ (gets up)

Nick: (looks at John and shrugs)

John: “Sooo... did sheeee... (cluelessly lookin at Nick) reeeeespond???”

Tyler: (holds up phone towards John) “Did you HEARRR my fuckin phone go off???!!!”

John: (little kid like) “...no...”

Tyler: “We gotta figure something out...”

John: “I conCUR”

Tyler: (laughs) “Thanks dude... (sighs) I needed that, come have a shot”

John: (stands up braggin t’Nick) “Why... don’t Mind if I Do!”

Act 3: Scene 6: Buying Friendships

After storming out in patented fashion earlier, Jasmine text her close "friends" for support; a rare act that plays out only when she's misplaced her confident "I run this bitch" self... Reduced to breathing self denial, most gasps for help stem from burying her past lust and remaining far too proud to admit defeat in swapping fluorescent lights and hollywood fights for shallow depths an'silent deaths. For even with her own hatred an'resentment boiling over to burn'er insides, Jasmine still couldn't break free... Santana's Excalibur like rise out of the waters to offer his mettle could spark Jasmine's heart to unlock itself from tragic prisons, relaxing chains an'unleashing the hidden true self that tearfully hides deep inside the island of her soul; deep in jungle realms she'd barricaded her love due to fears of the moon's eventual full... For if released she'd hover and strike through leafy brush like a bolt, heart turning against her mind to revolt and swim towards open waters so remembered; clinging to hopes that oxygen tanks on buoys survived so she could then dive dive an'descend back to such great depths till darkness encircles... and with faith in love's majesty, her ancient floors electricity would illuminate the dark allowing Jasmine to follow her heart to floors he'd uncovered years before; to approach him pacing or drunk in the bar with pulses racing still staring at the stool as the rush comes through him again, no longer delusional'an havin to pretend she'd return to their throne... And in finally unlocking the last box to'er name, together they'd watch beautiful floodgates crash down chestnut lane with cedars to block out the moon and it's endless reign; for with this, the sun's no longer left to sadly feign; feign that it can shine; feign to be part of love's epic mosaic design...

SMS: Jasmine > Nicole & Jaime
Hey...

The three dots "..." (an ellipsis) has become a silent phenomenon in the world of messaging and ESPECIALLY texting... Although typically symbolizing either an omission of a quotation, a lapse in time or a pause in writing to give the reader a moment to digest the preceding sentence, Jasmine's ellipsis transforms her simple text into a cry for help...... Yet while anxiously awaiting a reply to an unanswered question/text, instead of sending an insecure and desperate sounding: "Hellllloooo???" "Are you there???" or "Where did you go?" Sending "..." can express: "Welllll???? I still haven't heard back from you... just checking in on that, no big deal :)" verbatim...

In emails, messages and texts, some throw an ellipsis' after every other thought... Even in tragic moments of novels one may find a plethora of "..." to help convey the darkened place in which the character's mind currently resides...... truly impacting the reader's emotions in the process an'allowing random thoughts to just... appear...... Why just elongating ellipsis'..............

.....and adding some white space can make............

.....whatever you're saying...........

..............seem like...............

......................like...............

......................the end...............

..........................of the world.........

.........well...

...........................end...

....end..............................

....on.........

*(Group = Jasmine, Nicole & Jaime)

MMS: Nicole > Group
Are you ok? What happen???

MMS: Jaime > Group
What's wrong Jazzy?

MMS: Jasmine > Group
My sister betrayed me... My own fucking sister... Did you guys know about this????

MMS: Jaime > Group
No clue!!! How did she betray you?

MMS: Nicole > Group
What happen???

MMS: Jasmine > Group
My own sister turned her back on the last family she has to join the fuckin family I left!!! Did either of you know who she fucked at the party last night? And she DEF fucked him... I know she did that fuckin slut!!! Will you two help banish her from the valley?

In the gutters of life, one's true colors never gleam for the truth only shines when they're in victory lane... Who do they invite to the afterglow to help celebrate their glory? ...NOT who they commiserate with during tragedies of the worse kind... The lies spewed by a torn soul who continues to run from their own feelings wants an'needs are not as disguised as one would think or hope; karma can see all and eventually so will those you wish didn't #aintthatabitch

MMS: Nicole > Group
Of course!

MMS: Jaime > Group
Always... :)

MMS: Jasmine > Group
Thank you my loves...
MMS: Jasmine > Group
Now... Let us celebrate our new found freedom from that backstabbing bitch with a shopping spree that will make our spring spree look like a quick trip to Marshall's... HAHAHAHA as if we would ever go to Marshall's!!!

MMS: Nicole > Group
LOL... Where to? Great mall or valley fair?

MMS: Jaime > Group
Classic!!! Marshall's... lol

MMS: Jasmine > Group
Lets go slumming... Eastridge...

MMS: Nicole > Group
Are you sureee you're ok? Eastridge is...

MMS: Jaime > Group
...they don't even have juicy or 5th avenue!!!

MMS: Jasmine > Group
Fine, I'll go by myself

MMS: Nicole > Group
No no!!! Please let us come!!!

MMS: Jaime > Group
Or even Nordstrom's...

MMS: Jasmine > Group
Thats my girls!!! Love y'all!!!

SMS: Nicole > Jaime
Can you believe we're going to Eastridge?

SMS: Jaime > Nicole
Who cares!!! The number 2 in command is dead!! That means she needs a replacement... A NEW bestie ;)

SMS: Nicole > Jaime
Aww thanks... Yea, I can't WAIT to take her place!!! ;)
SMS: Nicole > Jaime
Which means ya better be nice to meeeee!!! lol

SMS: Jaime > Nicole
I don't think so bitch! LOL

SMS: Nicole > Jaime
Righhhhttttt... I will console her like its my job Lamey!!!

SMS: Jaime > Nicole
Game on...

SMS: Nicole > Jaime
All is fair in besties and war

SMS: Jaime > Nicole
:)

MMS: Nicole > Group
I'm here for you girl! Don't worry! I cannot believe she hooked up with him!!! I had noooo idea WHO she was hookin up with last night!!! #whatabitch

MMS: Jaime > Group
That is fucking cray cray! How could she do that???? I mean I was like "OMG is this slut seriously making out with another random guy!!! Could she beeeee any loooser?" YAY for shopping!!! #shoppingrules

Girls are cruel to their friends behind their backs;

Guys are just as bad to their fronts...

Act 3: Scene 7: Stephan's Place's Lone's Cameo's

Q: "Bro... Teri hatcher was wayyy fuckin hotter than that Kreuk girl"

Bastion: "Are you kiddin me? (rolls eyes) Dude, Kristin Kreuk's face was fuckin spectacular... Ok; Teri had the boobs on lock, perfect set and a body that just; (drops head) yea... (turns to Q) BUT who would YOU rather wake up to every morning? Teri Hatcher's face or Kristin Kreuk's? Guaranteed without makeup Kristin looks exactly the same; (outlines body with hands) a fuckin flawless beauty"

Q: (stands up) "Hellllllll NO!!!!" I would wake up with a hand resting on Teri Hatcher's glorious breasts!!! I can't even call them boobs they're so nice!"

Stephan: "Wellllll... (intently focused on his joint rolling venture) YOU were never really beyond the physical; I'd rather have Kristin Kreuk" (crouches away from Q bracing for a retaliatory punch)

Q: "Steph... (hand on his back) did you really think I was gonna hit you for having an opinion?"

Stephan: "Huh? (relaxes) You serious?" (turns towards Q smiling)

Q: "It's fuckin Superman!!! They're both hot; I'd take either of them! Any of you would..."

Bastion: "True-"

Stephan: "-Word to your mothhherrrrr" (laughs)

Santana: (laying on the love seat perpendicular with legs overhanging the arm rest an'staring at the ceiling) "...IIII would not take ANY of those fuckin bitches... (sits up swinging feet around to sit hunched over) They're BOTH fuckin ugly; NO one holds a candle to her... (stands up) The days I woke up to HER face angelically sleeping an'mid dreaming were days I woke up to My dream; woke to a life I could never DREAM of... Do you fuckers know anything about that???

Bastion... (starts walking towards) Do you know what it's like to wake up next to someone and be Truly happy? Feel completely at peace and know if the world ended that day that minute that Second you could die having experienced what we were put on earth here t'find? Would you embrace the onslaught of fire enveloping all with eyes closed an'arms wide like an eagle; welcoming the end with a blaring smile having been blessed for every Mother Fuckin Moment you spent with her?

And you... (walks towards Stephan) Have you ever drifted out of your cloud covered life to allow yourself to feel anything? Have you ever fell for someone an'let go of whatever the hell you're escaping from by smoking so much weed? You've been smoking since the day we met... Have you EVER stopped running? Have you ever faced yourself in the mirror or were you too afraid of what you might see? Do you know who you are, what makes you happy and thus what type of girl you seek??? ...or maybe you run and smoke cuz you're afraid you wont ever find it; so you blaze... and blaze... and blaze yourself into oblivion...

And you... (shakes head down at Q) My dearest running mate; (looks up) You finally found someone you actually like; the first girl who brings you a small sliver of the passion that flows on the wavelengths between me an'my ex... The one girl who could Possibly break you of your reckless womanizing ways... (looks away an'back) Did you ever give her chance??? ...Have you even begun to believe she deSERVESSS a chance? Is ANYONE good enough for you!!!??? ...Or do you think so low of yourself that you need an endless supply of adoring woman to try an'fill the enormous void of confidence and self worth that exists inside you-Or should I say, DOESN'T exist inside your core...

(steps backwards; arms wide) You ALLLL judge the fucKKKK outta me; give me shit for being such a pussy an'continually crying over this "wreck" of a human being as you all call'er; you insult her, make jokes and curse'er name yet y'all have never even GRACED such a connection, such a bond, such an earth shattering epiphany love like ours...

My own brother betrayed me last night. Even more so than when SHE left me... Ok, well maybe not more so; but even with his new union, at least he's going after it; at least He's trying! At least HEEE isn't drifting hopelessly through the black darkened space with no trajectory or target in sight.. at least HEEEEEE'S actually living!!!! Which is more than I can say for all YOU losers... (arms drop to his sides) ...I'm over this shit... (stares brokenly at the floor) I have nothing left... (walks towards the door shrugging) ...Nothin left" (steps out into the desolate cruel world)

(all three look at each other in silence)

Stephan: "......Welllll (Q and Bastion look over) ....at least thanks to Mary Jane, (lights and inhales joint) IIIII don't get all emotional like THAT fuckin gu-"

Q: (snaps) "-Shut... the FUCK; UPPPP!!!!"

Bastion: "I don't know if he's right, (Q tilts head down) Ok ok, he's dead on; but he's in bad shape and we gotta bring him outta this... I say we chill at y'all's crib and make it a guy's night, (looks at Q with wide eyes) NO GIRLS!!!! Show him that even with Jules off doin... whatever the fuck he's doin, we're still here for him even WITH his outburst..." (Stephan an'Q nod)

Q: "...How bout IIIIII, invite over some ladies who will surely give it-"

Bastion: "-NOOOO!!! All he needs is some pussy all up on'em to remind him of the one he doesn't have... (Q tilts head) NO BRO!!!! Forget it! Can you put your dick away for one fuckin night? Our boy's on life support; he already loss his girl and now his brother?? Steph... (turns) Roll me up one dude, I need it; this shit's Too stressful"

Stephan: (jumping out of his funk with eyes lit) "Really? Hot DOG!!!! That's the best news I've heard all day!"

Bastion: "Just... do it; this is not a joyous moment to be smokin but I need a break from all this drama. Jesus, ever since last night it's just been drama drama drama... I needa find a girl to take my mind off this shit"

Q: “Well I can get you-”

Bastion: “-NOOO!!!! THAT WAS A TEST Q!!! And you FAILED!!! Complete FAIL!!!@@@”

Q: “You- (pointing at Bastion while glancing at a shrugging Stephan) You-you can’t do that! You’re smokin all of a sudden so I thought maybe you wanted to play wing man since I seem to have loss both of mine... (sighs) Wow, I have no wing man; I’m gonna have t’promote; you? (points to Bastion) ...Or, YOUUU? (points to Stephan) ...Jesus, GOD help me...” (Bukka Buuuu! Bastion’s phone goes off)

Bastion: “Guaranteed; It’s Julian...”

Stephan: (almost done happily rolling up a joint) “How d’you know?”

Bastion: “Trust”

SMS: Julian > Bastion
Hey... you gonna be at the house later?

Q: “What did’e say”

Bastion: “Hold on”

SMS: Bastion > Julian
Why...

Stephan: “Im not givin you this joint till you tell us what he said..... An’what you said”

Bastion: “Fine (typing) ...I wont smoke then” (still typing)

Stephan: (jumps up) “No no; here, I’ll give it to you anyways” (offers Bastion joint)

Bastion: (laughs) “Figured as much, hold on” (still typing)

Q: (swipes joint) “ANNNNY day now bro!” (rolls eyes sparking “Bastion’s” joint)

Bastion: “Ok, I’m done.....“

SMS: Bastion > Julian

> No... I won’t be there, but do you have any idea what your doing to your poor brother? He left lookin like he was about to cry and probably has the sad girly music on again... He’s in bad shape dude... You gotta do somethin...

Q: “Bitch! Don’t make me take your phone like I took your joint” (inhales)

Stephan: “Do it fool! Take that shit!”

Bastion: “Hey! (looks at Steph) YOU’RE supposed to be on my side”

Stephan: “All’s fair in phones and war”

Bastion: (shakes his head) "...That doesn't make a bit of sense"

Stephan: "It does to meee!!!" (said like a little girl whining to her dad; Bukka Buuuu!)

SMS: Julian > Bastion

I will... I'm gonna be at the house tonight after dinner and beyond... Just a heads up... Thanks bro

Bastion: "How much have you smoked today?" (shows text stream to Q an'takes joint)

Stephan: "Just a little bit..."

Bastion: (laughs a loud HA!) "Just like an alcoholic always says 'just a few beers;' How much'ave you had?" (inhales)

Stephan: "Like... a couple bowls..."

Bastion: "And then" (exhales)

Stephan: "...a joint..."

Bastion: "One?"

Stephan: "......well... three?"

Bastion: "Three?"

Stephan: “Well; three...... before the next three”

Q: (scrunched face) “FOOL!!!@@@” (takes joint)

Stephan: “What?”

Q: (sighs; shaking his head) “...we needa find you a girl ASAP!” (inhales)

Bastion: “NO GIRLS!!!!”

Q: “......Bitchessss?” (eyebrows raised exhale)

Bastion: “NO Bitches either!”

Q: “How bout Chic-”

Bastion: “-ENOUGH! No! (Q raises his head) NO! Shush!”

Stephan: “Shush? What are you a woman?” (takes joint)

Q: “NO WOMAN TONIGHT DUDE!!!! (points to Stephan) You gotta bounce Steph... (Steph’s head falls; Q walks over placing his hand on Steph’s shoulder) No woman... No cry...”

Bastion: (laughs and laughs) “Ok that was good...”

Q: “I try, I try” (laughing)

Stephan: “Try what??”

Q: “Smoke more weed turtle... Smoke more weed...”

ACT 3: SCENE 8:
IDK WHT 2 DO WIT MA-SELF

Knowing her sister would not excitedly greet her like a puppy, Jasmine's "high" spirits fall upon reentering the castle doors. Suffering in silence and constantly fighting to keep her emotions hidden from the world, Jasmine couldn't tell her sister how much she envies her ability to quickly jump off the balcony of life without any reservations; even though these same reservations fool Jasmine into believing she's in control of herself...

Yet after their mother an'father exited stage death, by stepping forward to wear the royal gown before the tailor could alter it Jasmine loss herself in'er quest to become Queen Bitch. An'though she now ruled the world, as a slave in her own mind Jasmine never for a moment ruled herself... Once someone broke through her walls an'gave'er the key to such doors; but institutionalized to the core she eventually jetted back to the safety of her own locked prison to remain captive once more; never allowing anyone else to grace'er soul's floor while she's left wallowing in nightmarish purgatories of constantly running from'er own emotional realities......run forrest run...

Jasmine: “Now THAT was some fantastical shopping”

Nicole: “It Totally was”

Jaime: “Oh TOTALLY, you killed that mall” (thinking “did I just say that? God I’m sooo lame”)

Jasmine: (sarcastically like a valley girl) “Oh my god... Like, totally; Totes... Killled, like that mall... Like, TOTALLYYYY!!!!” (glancing over t’Nicole with eyes rolling)

Nicole: (giggles a bit) “Anywayyyysssss, so what’s we gonna do tonight? Bar? Club??”

Jasmine: “Ehhhh... I was thinking we could have a girls night”

Jaime: “Awwwww yeaaaaa!!! That’s what I’m talkin bout!”

Jasmine: (condescending) “Ummmm... I know what I; I meannnn WEEE (points to her an’Nicole) are talkin’bout... but what the fuck are YOU talkin’bout?”

Jaime: (scared) “I’m... talkin bout; the same...”

Jasmine: “You think you know-”

Nicole: “-but you have no idea” (Jasmine and Nicole laugh making Jaime feel 2 feet tall)

Whether a guy or girl, it's your job to insult your close friends by giving them "shit" or a "hard time" 24 ANNNDDDD 7 #suckitbells #politicsmyass ...Yet the stark difference between the sexes lies in their sincerity and whether they're laughing "with you" or "at you:"

Extremely sharp condescending and sincere, girl's truly hurt one another when following the alpha female's insulting leads; an'since many girls neither have the confidence nor the self worth to withstand such onslaughts, simple word play can tear apart one another... In society, close girl friends laugh At you where as close guy friends laugh With you... Although thicker skin helps shield the blows, the general camaraderie between "the boys" keeps insults on a level where they'll hardly cause any long term emotional distress...

While out for blood with fangs unsheathed, Girls attack "friends" to lessen their place in the group while simultaneously raising themselves to a higher level. In true Guy's inner circles, all carry a sense of brotherhood an'abide by the 3 musketeer motto of: "all for one and one for all;" while Girls are more "all for me and me for you as long as it's in MYYY best interest" lol... Being the superior beings in many aspects, there's not much girl's can "learn" from guys; (don't get cray cray) But there is a reason why many girls have "ONLY guy friends" or "don't get along with most woman" #notcuztheirsluts #wellsometimes ...Women could learn alot from guys and their brotherhood mentalities... but since the current status quo allows girls to feel better about themselves as they move up the friendship rankings... Move move on...

(Nicole and Jaime follow Jasmine into the kitchen)

Jasmine: “Hey Nance...”

Nancy: (rushes over to Jasmine with a hug) “My sweet Jazz, I’m sooooo sorry... Are you ok?” (typical mom tone)

Jasmine: “Yea yea, I’m fine... How d’you hear?”

Nancy: “I... (steps back) I talked to Liliana last night”

Jasmine: “And, (steps towards Nancy) Annnndddd (harsher tone) you did NOT tell me?” (Nicole and Jaime look at each other fearing for poor Nancy)

Nancy: (shifting backwards and to the left) “Well... welllllllll, I wanted you to hear it from her; I told her that she needed to tell you ASAP and MUST stop seeing him... I did what was right...” (standing proudly once again)

Jasmine: “Ever since you came in so many years ago we have yet to ever question your allegiance to this house; and though I understand you THOUGHT you were acting in her an’more importantly MYYY best interest; (moves forward) Get this straight... You work for me, You put me first and don’t you ever keep ANYthing from me... If the mailman comes 5 minutes late, you tell me; if you think a mouse has switched living quarters from the living room to the dining room, you alert me; and ESPECIALLY (in her face an’quieter) if you think Gus Gus the mouse has gained 5 pounds; ORR if Gus Gus’ cousin Natalie breaks up with Ray Ray; You best fuckinnn Tell ME!!! ...and MEEEE FIRST!” (#cinderella #iloveyougusgus)

Nancy: “Yes lord. I certainly will... A thousand apologies”

Jasmine: “Make it a thousand an’one... Bitch”

Nancy: “Always”

Jasmine: (turns to Nicole and Jaime’s chagrin) “And that goes for you two as well!!! Don’t let me catch you takin HER fuckin side; and until IIIII say so you are NOT to associate with her unless I’m in your company; Fuck her; Fuck her new guy; and especially, FUCK HIS FUCKIN BROTHER!!!!”

Storming off to resume her hostile an’solitary life, Jasmine thinks: “God I miss him;” swallowing any tears to ensure she remains a royally dry emotional desert.

Act 4: Scene 1: DeSSert

(a nice, but not tooo nice restaurant in Palo Alto)

Julian: "Soooo did you want dessert?"

Liliana: "No... I have mine right in front of me"

Julian: (softer) "Baby, (leans in) there are kids around"

Liliana: (looks to the left an'right like the movies) "No there's not crazy!"

Julian: "Oh; maybe you just make me Feeeeel like a kid again" (cheesy smile)

Liliana: "Awwwww..." (standard head tilt stretching her hands across the white table cloth asking for his)

Julian: "Well... (interlocks hands) what can I say"

Liliana: "Tell me you love me..."

Julian: "I already did like (looks at watch-less wrist) 2 hours an'20 minutes ago"

Liliana: “Not 23 minutes? (looks at her watch-less wrist) By MYYYY watch it says 2 hours an’twentyfourrrrrrr minutes”

Julian: “Ok ok, you win...”

Liliana: “WIN what???!!! A kiss?”

Julian: “Always” (leans in...)

Liliana: “Are people just like absolutely disgusted with us?”

Julian: “I hope so!!!! That means we’re doin somethin right”

Liliana: “How do you always come up with this stuff so fast?”

Julian: (smirks) “It just flows out like water t’wine”

Liliana: “That was deep”

Julian: (snaps his finger) “You ain’t seen nothin yet” (whips his finger around in a circle towards a waitress an’stands up extending his hand to her)

Liliana: “Aren’t you gonna pay?”

Julian: “Just did” (winks)

Liliana (body starts to tingle in places) “Mmmm... Take me away from here” (grabs hand)

Julian: “That was always the plan, but you took me first”

Liliana: “No no, We took eachother”

Julian: (laughs) “Killed it!” (hands Valet ticket)

Liliana: “AHHHH! (high pitch short shriek) I SOOOO did Not! TAKE IT BACK!!!@@@”

Julian: (releases’er hand leaning into another couple walkin by) “She totally killed it didn’t she?”

Random couple guy: “It’s ok, you can’t win em all... But; (checks Liliana out) it looks like YOU’ve won in life!” (pats Julian on the back-

Random couple girl: -Smacks her guy on the head) “Don’t you be checkin her out!”

Random couple guy: “Oh come on, really?” (rubs part she hit)

Liliana: “Serves you right! ...but thank you” (courtesies and smiles)

Random couple guy: (jumps away from his girl) “You’re welcome”

Random couple girl: (open mouth eyebrows down) “Seriously?” (walks off)

Julian: “Uh oh... (points to random girl) you betta go fix that”

Random couple guy: “Two words... makeup sex”

Julian: “Ohhhhh shiiitt... I got chyou I got chyou...”

Random couple guy: “Take some notes kid” (pats Julian hella hard on the back before walkin after his lady)

Julian: “Oh you’re a teacher now?”

Random couple guy: (turns back) “No... but I just taught you! (flashes hand in front of face) SCHOOOLEDDD!!!!”

Julian: “Funny guy...”

Random couple guy: (walks back an’cups hand over his mouth quietly) “...you hear that?”

Julian: “Na I don’t hear shit brah” (growing weary but still smiling)

Random couple guy: “That ringing..... it’s the school bell; class dismissed”

Liliana: (shaking head, clapping an’smiling) “Bravo sir...”

Random couple guy: “Thank you, thank you” (bowing)

Random couple girl: (having returned to the restaurant) “Hey... you gonna cum teach Me a lesson now???”

Random couple guy: “Cumming babe... (turns to Julian) my bad bro, (hand on Julian’s shoulder) but thank you, you just made’er night; thus mine ;)“

Julian: "Yup yup yup" (#landbeforetime)

Liliana: (takes ticket an'turns around to hug Julian)

Kissing Liliana erases any anguish and centers him back into their far off universe to breathe the air of elegance she exudes.

Julian: "Shall we?"

Liliana: "I thought you'd never ask"

Julian: "Blehhhhh!"

Liliana: "HOWW Ruuuuuudeeee"

Julian: "Ok Mary Kate and Ashley Olsen"

Liliana: "Awww, (blinks twice) are you calling me cute?"

Julian: "Ummmmm; no comment"

Liliana: (slaps him on the chest)

Julian: "Fair enough"

Liliana: "Full house my ass!"

Julian: "Soon" (winks an'slaps her ass)

Act 4: Scene 2:
As The Rush Comes

Driving away the two can hardly contain themselves yet couldn't interact and barely even spoke; the air's electrified with intense anxiety as hopeful wishes blend into excitement's possibility of the opportunities that lay awaiting in'is soon to be love packed apartment. The foregone conclusion? Tonight's the night... From underpass glory and the santa cruz beach story, to the moment that was, is, an'forever "stuck in time" exploding with light beams to chase the negativity of moon's gaze away, leaving the righteous sun to freely dance away the day... This was the moment they would now run; no time to deny or leave whispers of wants unspun, undone to inevitably be each other's only one they'd ever moan and thrust with beneath sheets... How could they sit and casually speak knowing they'd soon fulfill their star written destiny; a destiny guided by the sun with shields of love to guard against the moon; for hiding from darkened minds were the tragic binds leading most astray. This was the world they writhed to jump into, awaited to rise and leap thru white cloud's synchronicity wearing the sweat of electricity with all worries and scars dripped off in the process; keeping them in worlds they thrive and live, worlds they'd die to live with the sun god by their side to give his or her's blessing while the poor moon's left distressing over which path to take; which path could erase an'ground them to bask in moon's bliss that's only pretend... giving them fake hope and fake faith that perpetuates, never to end.

(sitting with wine in hands on leather black couches whilst romance rules the land)

Julian: “I sit here with a candle lit heart and wait; my mind’s rolling thunder starts to relax then explodes with what’s to come as now fate; I’ve never seen such beauty staring back at me and there’s no way I could rise to your worth and live at such levels of your warmth”

Liliana: “Never shall you say such blasphemous words; to hear you speak of such drives me up walls; tis a lie and a sin to use such verbs for you live worthy to take our journey as the world has cast us BOTH aside... Yet no worry as love’s gaze stands bewildered; always the fear we’d find eachother to inevitably dance under sun’s protection while the poor moon’s left wounded and suffering”

Julian: “I could only imagine what would happen if I could not see these eyes; (caresses face) could not swallow my pride and have a woman such as you t’grace my side, keeping vices at bay forever caught inside love’s web... I feel tears begin to well, all truly begging to have fell at the thought of such tragic events that could take you an’leave me here to sit and lament; broken down, forever bent on what could drive us apart an’restart the life I now lead... (looks away) Devoid of anyone close to my heart ever again; having also locked out myself to sit alone in dark caverns, refusing to leave such worlds never fathomed... (looks to her) ...a wasteland left where my heart normally sits; with the wind having blown out the last candle ever lit”

Liliana: (painfully closes eyes) "Please do not say such things as my falling tears feel the same, (opens eyes) for I could never leave your side from this moment now on just the same... (grabs his hand) The world's cancers won't seep into our new life and fuck the people who try an'come in between; this is not the real world an'only a dream from which we'll never wake; and if I do it must be to death for only he could take; take me away kicking, screaming, nail torn to shreds against pavements bleeding; for after I leave your presence an'never again recommence? My breath will lose it's oxygen an'my mouth'll forget how to open so severely attached to the moon... So fuck YOU for ever bringing up the remote chance of such earth shattering doom..."

With hands holding her face that ache for so much more, Julian moves towards, closes his eyes and connects lips to hers; no longer fearful, the two soul's blend together an'allow colliding tears t'fall into trailing rivers with such strength an'fervor that the flow drys up having loss it's torrential allure... The lights have blast on; the dark room is now gone; the kiss brings light and any worries of returning t'dark all but disappear; leaving the moon to angrily glisten with the hope they'll soon distance an'fly off sun's beams, or somehow break apart at their now unbreakable dreams... An'though the sun remains strong and a star shines forever long, light years later it may forget the energetic song; might forget how to support their connection's gleam... and maybe, just maybe they'd fall off love's magnetic crystalized beams...

("Motorcycle - As the Rush Comes;
Gabriel and Dresden Chillout Mix" fills the air)

Sitting on either side of the bed, we stare into eachother's love struck eyes. This is not the way life was drawn up t'live nor the love anyone could wish t'give. The eyes can see the moves, the passions possessed; no longer holding onto reality we'll dive into the other's recess. (traveling somewhere) Trembling to speak, words cannot leave mouth's silenced lips; the body will speak for the soul, warrant out for the hips. We cannot begin to understand nor comprehend earth's rotation in such sheets; no longer spinning, moment's can be split and pieced back together through chemistry that floors minds safely; for dancing in their trajectory, stars can only collide and crash so many times over till love's ride down embraced lust leaves reason an'science as but ashes to dust.

Reaching for vibrant colors in the front view, the body starts to collapse as minds lapse with sweeping envy of what's t'come whilst dancing on light beams. (embrace me) The sun casts no shadow yet the moon cannot attempt t'follow, unable to swallow the pleasure that rises nor handle bloods boil of insides to it's highest climaxes... A love spoken none could attempt to inject nor attract is finally left to react and explode in fury laced traction leaving worlds of earth's passion dancing on ceiling tiles. (surround me) With a glide of my hand over the face of'er beauty, she couldn't feel'er heart beat as pure ecstasy awaits to unleash, daring rivers to try an'boldly enter chasms on high from far beneath...

A simple touch triggers worlds no one figured; inside castles the world couldn't have seen, for this was no already chronicled to be epic fuckin dream; he grabs her closer an'pulls her under to feel the pulse of his aching rolling thunder awaken cells unknown to'ave existed until enrapturing spirits from never ending slumbers and casting every fiber into passion's encapsulating fire; raging inferno's light up darkened moonlit paths leaving sun's ever last to wake beasts inching closer towards the inevitable connect. (as the rush comes) With minds a flutter and souls bathed in love's lather, the bodies as water wash out all anger an'barter to transcend normal realms upheld rules, breaking through barriers to rain down euphoria leaving pleasure soaked pools filled with enchanting siren's whispers. (embrace me) An' guiding one another, the lip's trail of lights crashing into eachother sparks glass ceilings underneath'em to shatter

...Arising with hands roving to grace caverns of space's frozen, eachother's heartbeat becomes one an'together enclosen their passions bubble; surely breaking the known order, they'll cast apart mind's synapses to grant access to new enclosures and harness new feelings which allowed them to break through ceilings in rising to such great heights. (we drift deeper) With slow thrusts and heart's trusts pumping succinctly to the sound, the beat engravens a coldness in the air; the rush surrounds them as they drift atop the universe to glow over fields of perpetual bliss; an'as lightning's now forever kiss, they'll soar through galaxy's lovely abyss at heights never seen nor capable in dreams... for even if transfigured to try and clutch passion's throes, the Moon's beams couldn't touch any as their bodies arose to realms outstretched far past infinity... to forever bask in the sunlight's majestic divinity

Act 4: Scene 3:
"I'll Be Thinkin Bout You"

(@thestandard; a club in Mountain View... or Palo Alto; dealer's choice ;)

Anxiously awaiting their return to the dance floor, the two waive goodbye to the Uber and hello to the bouncer before bypassing guest an'VIP lines. Slowly sobering from lack of constant alcohol, jealous impatiently frustrated faces stand in line swearing t'do better yet possessing such weak minds quickly shuts reality's door... Although seen by all an'judged by more, there's not a speck of fret or fear for the two couldn't fall from skies on such fantastical nights...

Julian: (gently pulls her hand) "Hey, I gotta tell you somethin"

Liliana: (whining) "Nooooo Julieee!!! Let's go innnnn, (raspy) we're so closssseee"

Julian: "It'll take two seconds"

Liliana: (rolling eye sigh) "...I love you too"

Julian: "How did you-"

Liliana: "-Come ooonnn! I have no idea what this track is but it sounds Fuckin, EPIC!!@@"

(smiling side by side, "Sun Glitters - Too Much To Lose" floors the senses again; inducing them to dance walk in #dirtyhiddensmiles #jokerlovesharley)

With the bass kicking harder than a mother fucker, strutting down the hallway into the main room of the club for the first time infects the senses and temporarily boosts all egos as if the whole club's been waiting for you an'your crew's "I'm the fuckin shit" arrival... Walking in "slow motion-music video" fame, the build up of getting ready, pre-partying, drunken rides to the club an'the "getting in" rush culminates in the halls of possibility; cuz fuck, maybe YOU could dance on ceilings t'night ;) #itcouldhappen #especiallytothissong

As if forcefield surrounded untouched an'miles above, the two waltz behind red velvet ropes without any reservations ;) ...An'when a new VIP host quickly walks towards the intruders, the owner who'd followed them in shoots a "slow your roll" by shaking his head an'lipping "Their good". (did she really not know who these two were?) Without the gaggle of bottles awaiting, a plethora of diamond rings an'a full entourage in tow they look like two simple kids enjoying a thursday night at the club: "dangerously casual" Julian didn't exude what he's always to portray in carrying a royal essence as a true king of the bay; and following his cue, just call her "Eminem" cuz Liliana didn't "give a fuck" on this night too.

...An'with drinks from "random 23's" bottles a flowing, the booze had no way of knowing they'd already taken shots of eachother with the sun as a chaser;

Julian: "Shall we hit the floor t'dance on ceilings?"

Liliana: "No my love, we shall jump the floor and break THROUGH ceilings as the rush comes through our earlier mementos; they'll carry on so much further than our breaths can last; stuck in moment's that are neither future, present, nor past"

Julian: "How was I so lucky to find such a perfect compliment, a treasured continent that I'll spend a lifetime exploring; an eternity's worth of warring through amazon like jungles discovering every crevice and chasm of the fantastical being that is you... I've only barely step foot into such eyes but will surely never leave" (kisses up on her neck)

With a pleasured smile sealed by shut eyes, Liliana pulls him closer so her lips could grab on an'imbibe what only in eachother could excite; with hands running through hairs to grasp the back of his head, none could hear their soft murmurs of wants an'desires, so dire to return t'space's free galaxies... The two as one could neither see nor feel all stare on to their vigorous public scene, all so fuckin envious to find their own passerby's dream... Jealousy was no longer a feeling but an ongoing reaction to the explosion in the building of an extreme love none could understand except from such great heights, miles an'miles above.

(staring down at the soft core porn from the upstairs VIP)

SMS: Dru > Tyler
What up
SMS: Dru > Tyler
Figured you would wanna know...

SMS: Dru > Tyler
Your girl is here @thestandard
SMS: Dru > Tyler
And she's not alone...

SMS: Tyler > Dru
Thanks for the heads up #onmyway

SMS: Tyler > Perry
Hey get ready, we rollin to @thestandard tonight

SMS: Perry > Tyler
Fuck that I got the ladies comin thru already #betterbringyouragame

SMS: Tyler > Perry
Tell them to hit the club and we can roll back to your crib after #webeclubbin

SMS: Perry > Tyler
Sho #betterstillbringyouragame

SMS: Perry > Assssley
Change of plans
SMS: Perry > Assssley
Meet us @thestandard
SMS: Perry > Assssley
Hit me up when y'all arrive and I'll handle everything
SMS: Perry > Assssley
Then later I'll handle you ;)

SMS: Assssley > <3 PERRY <3
KK!!! Cant wait!!! :)

(house of heartbreak)

Tyler: “Lets roll losers”

Nick: “Hey... Who you callin losers? THIS loser?” (points t’John)

John: “He said loser’sss; plural...”

Nick: “Andddddd you just burned yourself”

John: “No he-you... DAMMMIT!”

Nick: “There it is... IDIOT!!!@@@”

Tyler: “You guys done flirting or should I break out the wrap it up box?”

John: “What the F is the (air quotes) wrap it up box?”

Nick: “What the F? Is this a PG Disney Movie? Are your parents in the other room so you can’t say the word Fuck?”

Tyler: (laughs) “F-in-A, the wrap it up box???? Chapelle show??? Wrap it up B with the mexican guy from half baked???!!!” (#imcubanB! #yes #cubanB)

Nick: “You mean Ezelle?”

John: “That’s friday”

Nick: “WHICH friday loser? The first, next friday or friday after next?”

Tyler: (frustratedly runs hand through hair sighing)

John: “The ONLY Friday, the first one; an’no, YOU’RE a loser!!!!”

Tyler: (leaves out the front door)

Nick: “Me??? A Loser? At least IIIII have hooked up with a girl in the last month. When was the last time You got some?”

John: “Ummmm, the last time I got some waaaassss, theeee... Lasssstt, Tiiiiiime I GOT some!!!”

Nick; “Uhhhh that was clean! (gives eachother daps) Hey Tyler, did you hea-Fuck he bounced already...”

John: “Good job loser“

Nick: (walkin out) “Shotgun! Come on J!”

John: “Don’t tell me what t-fuck it” (power walks out behind Nick)

Pulling up in his far too expensive _______ with “Kid Ink - Show Me, feat. Chris Brown” thumping at “pull me over decibels,” Tyler waives’em over in a single motion without eye contact #realcoollike

Nick: (yelling) “Where we goin???”

John: (yelling) “What??”

Nick: (turns to John) “I’m talkin t’Tyler”

John: “You’re acting like Sylar?” (#heroes)

Nick: “No I’m talkin t’Ty!!”

John: “What’s you tryin t’buy?”

Nick: “Shut up! Just get in the car!”

John: “Fuck you! I’m Comin to the bar”

Nick: (walks up to Tyler) “Hey, where we rollin to?”

Tyler: (points to the front seat)

Nick: (sighs) “Frickin guy...”

After Leaving and turning it down a click or two...

(singin along)

Tyler: “Mami you remind me of somethin, but I don’t know what it issss-”

Nick: “-I don't know”

Tyler: “You remind me of somethin”

John: “-Uh”

Tyler: “Girl you gotta showw meeeee”

Nick and John: “Alright”

Tyler: “You remind me of somethin-”

John: “-Uh”

Tyler: “I don't know what it is right now-”

Nick and John: “-I don’t know”

Tyler: (turns t’Nick with a “that’s fuckin right” look) “Showwww Meeeee”

John: “Uhhh”

Tyler and Nick: “On the real no lie. I don’t know what it is but you just my type”

Tyler: “You can’t sing the verse fool, that’s all me!”

John: “IDIOT!!!!!”

Nick: “Where we rollin to???

Tyler: “...Headin to @thestandard... Dru said SHE’S at the club with the new guy”

Nick: “Ohhhh fuck; Sounds like You need a shot?” (offers bottle)

Tyler: (laughs) “Naaaa... I only drink a drive AFTER the club hahaha” (#dontdrinkanddrive)

Nick: “Well... let me know!” (hands bottle t’John #shots)

(...Improvising the second verse)

Tyler: "Uhhh, so tell me what his name is,
I don't really care who you came wit"

Nick: "Ohhhhh Shiiiiiiiiitt!!"

Tyler: "Her bad if I come try t'fight you"

John: (laughs) "...watch outtttt-"

Tyler: "-Security betta get wit da program"

Nick: "Or you're gonna fuck him up!"

John: "Awwwwww Yeeeeeaaa"

Tyler: (sings last four lines of the second verse lookin around hardcore an'bobbin his head like he IS Kid Ink)

John: "You pickin up Pear?"

Tyler: "You know it!"

Nick: "Hey frickin... put that one Chris Brown song on; the one wit little Weezyyy"

Tyler: "What the fuck? Was tonight sponsored by Chris Brown?"

John: "Hell no! He beat up that one chick"

Tyler: "True... but his songs DOOO crack; gotta give it up... (laughs) and it's only fitting for Pare's arrival"

(flips to "Chris Brown - Look At Me Now
feat. Lil Wayne & Busta Rhymes")

With the track's dirty hydraulics dropping the world to street level, the "gangsta lean" attacks the car infecting everyone... Although this fly ride's whiteness stands at 100 %, this track (and many like it) chew up their "whiteness" and spew it out the exhaust pipe "black"; catalyzed by alcohol and/or drugs, suddenly everyone is a fuckin G on the same level as the rappers beatin out the speakers... A sick ass beat can change the entire vibe of a guy's car and cause everyone to dance an'rap along to the track as if they live "the life"... Funny how a song, adrenaline, testosterone an'a G ride (#optional) affects the confidence an'swag of those inside the car: for even the whitest preppie fraternity "Bro's" who dress in pink polo shirts and near white J Crew shorts'll throw the swag on like they're Lil Wayne or Chris Brown driving down Sunset at 11 pm to some party that's far sicker than yours will ever be #truth

The same type of tracks (and "empowering woman" songs) exacerbate a girl's "I can pull any guy" or "every GUY wants to PULL me-I'm the fuckin shit!" sexitude... Soon the car resembles a strip club where the temporary "strippers" use any and all parts of the interior in their dances #twerk #takeavideo #postittobecool #no Universal in it's effect, it's amazing how something such a music can transform people in the moment... loud, louder on...

With his inhuman senses, Perry's already walking down the corridor to the roundabout driveway as Tyler pulls up; strutting down the final flight of stairs, Perry raps along to Busta Rhymes' acapella intro till

(the beat drops back in #letsgo)

Leaving the bottom step, Perry walks towards the car dipping down every other beat like Katt William's in his "walks int'the club real high" skit where he plays hop scotch and baseball #pimpchronicles ...And when the entire beat drops out mid Busta's verse, Perry acts as if he's running in matrix like slow motion with two fisted hands and eyebrows raised till returning to the Katt Williams strut once the beat kicks back in...

Too cool to react to Perry's antics, Tyler continues staring forward and holding the wheel with a straight flexed left arm while subtlety bobbing his head left and right. After moving his head upward half an inch in his "what upppp" to Tyler, Perry casually walks around the car to silently stand at shotgun... Taking far too long to realize his place in the world, Nick exits an'tries the same charade on John.

John: "No dice"

Nick: (sighs and walks to the driver side back seat)

None should ever approve or condone Mr Brown's actions; (#lovechrisbrown #repteambreezy #eversinceyoandpoppin) but tragedy and drama improves artists musicians actors an'even writers ;)

Look at Chris Brown and Eminem pre an'post issues: Chris used his hatred and new found "bad boy" image stemming from his break up to transform his persona an'style along with a plethora of tattoos #everyonemakesmistakes #howmanyhaveyou #exactly

Even without the drama an'tragic life he lived, Eminem would still be one of the best rappers. (#yeaisaidit) However, over half of his early tracks (when he WAS one of the best of all time ;) revolve around his baby mama drama an'endless growing pains of his upbringing; begging the question: would he be on the same level without it??? ...Exactly... Drama, drama on...

Having almost forgotten why they came to @thestandard in the first place, Tyler steps out, stands tall and straightens his Diesel jacket by abruptly pulling each side downward at the chest. While primping and sporting the no expression dead stare he inherited from the "gangsta" tracks earlier, Tyler glances over to the hottest pack of girls in line and spouts a Busta Rhymes like "let's GOOOO" to the crew... Jumping out third, Nick leaves the onus of parking the car to the last remaining passenger (John) who unhappily pulls away while the other three walk right in like they "motherfuckin own the joint".

And as DJ Kristina Sky mixes into "Calvin Harris - Thinking About You feat. Ayah Marar," Tyler scours the main floor:

While frantically searching, I'm soulfully frightened of what will suspensefully stricken that which my eyes could never prepare for. Upon spotting, I'm bombarded by their insurmountably powerful connection, a deadlocked insurrection against my rule over her. (when I close my eyes you're the one I see) Perched on bar's railings with full view towards my queen, the life breaking theme shatters confidence from alcohol imbibed having never tried in life before moments now arisen. (I'm gonna change my ways) Instilled with a new prism, new view and code of conduct, I see her as gems of the ocean brightly glimmering while ironically my unsightly simmering's loss but a lifetime too late. Closing eyes serves as no defense against the flying daggers of blasphemous scenes ahead since there's no relief having exited scoundrel's cells to lay dying on floors of new found heart's wells instead. (I'll do anything you want me to) Learning to fly and soar across skies are no insurmountable feat; impossible is to be without her innocence engraven, so permanently unable to give in t'leading a life of sin. (no way I could be without you)

Unable to withstand still flying knifes, the beat of my heart falls in line with moon's dark while any attraction to the sun's glow'as fallen out backsides. (I need you every day) What fight could bring us back to pleasure and back to pasts inside shinning suns? What magical potion or spell cast could surpass their love rising high above the night?

...And with unwanted new emotions breaking through walls revived hearts grew, if I only knew how t'stop lusting... dreaming... and thinking about you...

Act 4: Scene 4: What keeps you lying awake at night?

Joining Santana in his queen-less castle, the boys (minus Julian) rescue him from death to barely breathing #duncanshiek ...Feigning happiness and throwing fronts around the room, Santana masks his true emotions by acting as if he's joined in their "reindeer games"...

Soon Bastion takes "too high" Stephan home while Q's low self worth finds him with random girl 41 instead of Kristin since he's scared of following in Santana's wake to continually break his mind while desperately trying to forget'er face... Yet resounding tidal waves surging from above keep Santana hopefully staring up to the sea's emanating blue glow; as crashing shockwaves instill hope she'll one day awaken in search of the depths down below...

How many ex lover's lay awake at night
stuck in mind's past romance?

How many of their loss counterparts ALSO
ponder if there could ever be a chance?

How many lay in bed crying, tearfully fading while the peaceful being next to'em silently sleeps? (too many) How many will reach out next door? (not enough) How many'll wake to continue treading water more? (will you ever stop?)

How many ex lover's lay awake at night
stuck in their mind's past romance?

With Headphones the only connection to a world alone, saddened songs of deja vu magnify falling tears. Sleeplessly laying with one song on repeat, ("Finch - Tarot") Santana cannot erase fears of what nightmares may come...

Why must I remain stuck in your wicked gravity; (I sink tonight) the depravity you've forced upon me leaves me listlessly walking through the days. Please release me of the malaise you've cast down upon and cease nightmares of worlds you brought an'took without just cause, only because you felt too much an'truly loved how my touch shot fibers of life through your body; how ungodly must you be? (it's too late for apologies)

I'll disconnect from hearts taken and the misery you've forsaken forcing a broken me to faking happiness an'smiles throughout the days. (it's all your fault) Your fucked up ways have convinced you to escape vulnerable fears of the treacherous dear in headlights love blinding you with emotions one could neither replicate nor find on earth above; the imperial designs of fate pulse hard in never beating hearts. (is it too late?)

I must stay strong and rid myself of songs (you sing to me) each night and every day full of visions disbursed; you fuckin love to rehearse our shared moments in minds don't you? (It's too late) Please blind me of your memory and bereft me of the gravity trapping me on your soul's darkened floor. The currents hardly fall as often yet I've forgotten how to rise to shores above. (I'll learn to swim someday) The impaling moon's rays overtake any shine from sun's beams an'I am loss in your haunting world below. (shadows dance on the wall)

...I can try as I might an'wish upon falling stars to break curses here tonight, but I'll inevitably remain at such great depths as the mess (you've made) of our lives does not deter; I'm conferred with emotions I can neither run from nor escape; the fuckin sun'll have to wait to shine down as I have faith currents'll shoot through you once again. (is it too late?)

......is it too late?

Act 4: Scene 5: The Moon Shifts the Tide

SMS: Tyler > Nick

Hey yoooo, It's like 3 am or

SMS: Tyler > Nick

I got it

SMS: Tyler > Nick

The plan... get her back

SMS: Tyler > Nick

Hit me tomorrows

Act 5: Scene 1:
Waking to the Sun of the Moon

Waking first, Jasmine reaches out to her "husband" next door but retracts her hand before awaking the thorn... met by soft eyes gazing back on mirrors wall, Jasmine turns away from who she'd become to sit at'er vanity an'stare at the floor. Unable to break out of her own oppression, Jasmine couldn't venture out without the courage to chase HIM in the dark; as fear of vulnerability disallows her to dive in blindly while following the spark...

Waking second to his "way too hot for him" wife, Peter's head sighfully collapses since he couldn't break her out of'er sadness nor was he capable of doing so.

Peter: (sauntering over) "...what makes you wake and always start the day so down?"

Jasmine: (turns away from Peter towards the base of the vanity) "Nothing, I'm fine... just wakin up is all..."

Peter: "Why must I ask every day, and every day you say the same"

Jasmine: "...Nothing, I'm fine"

Peter: "Look at me... (louder) LOOK AT ME!!!"

With Peter standing behind, Jasmine's eyes move up to meet him in vanity's mirror; ironic since he never "stood" tall enough to encapsulate her mind, body and let alone soul. In eyes kiss Peter sees the life he desires: from the kids that never came due to her constant no's and refusal to go off birth control, to her mid smile and laughing having found'er old carefree spirit she'd thrown while coasting down the highway of their "relationship". Recalls how they'd danced for hours at their own private ball, sporting black tie ensembles in the mansion's main hall, breathing the joyous air of a world they once knew.

...Yet now Peter stands alone on dance floors longing for the woman sitting at empty tables; unable to ask his own wife to dance...

Santana could whisk her on to the dance floor, rip out a smile from somewhere within'er an'wake up the sleeping beauty of a person inside; whilst Peter stands begging an'pleading with himself to ask... Yet why should he ask? Having walked down the aisle he should confidently rush over and grab'er as another surely could... Still standing by the all too clichéd punch bowl, Peter looks on to the somber girl sitting alone, legs crossed an'sure to make eye contact with none save for one...

In Jasmine's mind, the moment their eyes kiss did not bring visions of Peter's "anything but" booming life. At first she sees the shell of a skinny man flashing his insecure smile, till showing no disregard, Santana pushes Peter aside to stare deep into'er for a while; an'with elbows bent and hands open, Santana glances down an'back shooting a "yeaaaa, you know you want this" look... Though most would find such overbearing arrogance unattractive, after such a weak mate Santana awakens Jasmine from slumbers on'er once sunny now cloudy shores.

Involuntarily springing to her feet, a "fifth element" like white beam shoots towards the sky from deep down below, uncovering a previously non existent dock encircling the newly formed light show... And upon striking the moon, the beams flood into its hallowed core till it explodes revealing the sun in all it's rejuvenating allure... And by erasing fears of blindly swimming back down in the dark, the illuminated beam could now guide Jasmine back to the spark; yet the lit path's no longer necessary for behind blasts unseen, Santana casually strolls round the dock to place his hand in the beam; an'underneath the reflected light a new dock erupts from out the teal blue, prompting Jasmine t'shoot a "that's fuckin unbelievable" gasp, to which Santana simply shrugs "what do you expect" before removing hands from the blast.

Trying to hide her ecstatic whirlwind of emotions as if they'd give away her true self, Jasmine's eyes dart off to the right before embarking down... Her walk becomes a skip as if heading out to recess at lunch... Her skip becomes a charging warrior like jog; advancing in full sprint with him standing arms wide open at the edge of the dock, Jasmine jumps into his body and upon together colliding fall backwards into oceans inviting; spirits playfully fighting with lips locked an'never to part, whilst hands roam around as if this was only just the start; grasping eachother tightly their bodies writhe while nails tear an'drive down down down towards the floor...

Drifting into the beam the bright white lights eclipse past pains and former dreams, leaving both eyes tearfully closed wishing to remain forever froze in free fall; gleefully carrying them onward to still aching grounds, hearts embrace crashing wall sounds as they break through barriers she had built an'kept; this was no ordinary decent an'knowingly so she wept as they went... The rush he'd held out for shoots straight through him while the spark she came down for lightens up'er soul's skin; she couldn't have dreamt to return so rapidly, enthralled so vampantly till landing on the

chair in her bedroom staring at the mirror with a shell of a man named Peter glancing down upon; shockingly searching round the room an'lost in her bearings, Jasmine frantically leaps up an'runs; alarms blare as locked up tears escape ducts and run... run to getting loss in empty darkened halls, till she fell to meet mansion's floors with a monumental emotional fall; bewildered in disbelief she's not to grace desired souls floor, Jasmine slams down hands in terror as she pictures him standing arms open waiting for what's in store... Yet down the runway she never was to come; an'with legs trembling, spirits broken an'all hope not yet forsaken he dives back down. Lights fly backwards into the ocean and reverse the sun; leaving her on cold shores with the moon back in full tow; eyes screaming, fallen apart an'dying for what she could surely not yet let go

Act 5: Scene 2:
Wheels Set in Motion

SMS: Nick > Tyler
What up, what's the plan!
SMS: Nick > Tyler
Yo
SMS: Nick > Tyler
Fool!

SMS: Tyler > Nick
It's fuckin genius...

SMS: Nick > Tyler
Sickkkkkk
SMS: Nick > Tyler
So what is it???

SMS: Tyler > Nick
Check it out
SMS: Tyler > Nick
So she's all in love with this new guy right?

SMS: Nick > Tyler
How do you know she's in love with him?

SMS: Tyler > Nick

Cuz she doesn't just "date" guys. So I tell her how much I miss her and want her back expecting that she'll turn me down...

SMS: Nick > Tyler

Well why would you do that? That doesn't make any sense

SMS: Tyler > Nick

Shut up! Let me finish

SMS: Nick > Tyler

Ok

SMS: Tyler > Nick

Did you have to say ok?

SMS: Nick > Tyler

Who cares just go!

SMS: Tyler > Nick

So after I tell her I want her back she'll probably say she doesn't want me and is in love with the new guy...

SMS: Nick > Tyler

Why would you try to get her back if she's all about this new guy?

SMS: Tyler > Nick

SHUT THE FUCK UP AND LET ME FINISH!!! Or I'm gonna text John instead

SMS: Nick > Tyler
K I'm done

SMS: Tyler > Nick
So the genius part is I RECORD her saying how she's all into someone else
SMS: Tyler > Nick
Then when we're all partying one night, I'll get her wasted and when she passes out like she always does
SMS: Tyler > Nick
I'll jump into bed with her and get this new asshole to show up... And when he sees me and her in the same bed he'll ask what the fuck is going on and THATS's when I play the recording of her sayin she's in love with someone else...
SMS: Tyler > Nick
So HE will think she's all in love with me and when they break up and she's all depressed, I can pick her up off the rebound and dunk her down into my girl again!!! I'll be the night in shinning armor to save the mother fuckin day! Shhhhyyyyyeaaayyyaaaaaaaa

(time passes)

SMS: Tyler > Nick
Did you get my messages??? It says delivered...
SMS: Tyler > Nick
What's up dude, wheres the hype and excitement???? Isn't this just the sickest plan ever?????

Choices you make (or don't make) define you as a person; although holding extreme reservations to Tyler's plan of "tricking someone" into loving him, Nick believes these types of crazy schemes only work in movies and NEVER in real life. Afraid of losing their positions within the valley's corporate infrastructure, Nick an'John rarely went against "the machine" an'followed Tyler blindly like seeing eye dogs #funnyjoke ...However, this was not a simple "ploy" to out duel another guy by kicking his ass, spreading rumors, talkin shit, or trying to prove how much better he was for her. Taking what didn't belong to him and breaking two people in the process was sabotage of the ugliest variety. At a defining crossroads, Nick chose the path most traveled by... (sigh) Fuckin Frost was right... Wrong, wrong on...

SMS: Nick > Tyler

That IS the sickest plan ever

Loss in his own madness and blinded by heartbreak, Tyler could niether see nor read any sarcasm in such texts #canyoueverseesarcasmintexts

SMS: Tyler > Nick

I know right! It is a little bit shady...

SMS: Tyler > Nick

But fuck dude, all is fair in love and war right? :)

Having lost a good deal of his plan's confidence with Nick's delayed response, Tyler fishes for validation while Nick walks the fence #switzerland

SMS: Nick > Tyler

Yeaaaaa... In principleeeee... All is fair in war and love...

SMS: Tyler > Nick

Why aren't you ultra stoked??? Dude we have to get this plan in motion stat!!! The longer those two are left unchecked the further they'll fall in love!

SMS: Nick > Tyler

Fall in love? Knight in shinning armor? Who the fuck are you bro? Did you turn in your guy card or something? Did I miss the press conference where you announced you have a Va Jay Jay now? lol

Funny how you'll question the words spewed from love sick friends; is it out of jealousy or fear of possibly losing your "friend" to a relationship?

SMS: Tyler > Nick

Ha mother fuckin ha! I've solidified my guy card a million times over! If ANYONE should lose their guy card it's you for being such a pussy about this and not jumping on board full force! #pussyassbitch

SMS: Nick > Tyler

Well, it ISSS a pretty crazy plan… I mean, hoping she says EXACTLY what you want her to and THEN getting her drunk and completely passed out? Last I checked they've been inseparable since wednesday when you flipped out… I mean, were wasted! LOL

SMS: Tyler > Nick

Why are you not on board with this? I'm gonna mark this down on your application for my number two… Maybe Johnny boy will be more in tune with the idea…

SMS: Nick > Tyler

NO NO I am! How you gonna get them apart?

SMS: Tyler > Nick

Leverage

SMS: Tyler > Nick

Jasmine will help me get some time in with her

SMS: Nick > Tyler

Well ok, NOW it's sounding more like a solid plan!

Faking excitement.

SMS: Tyler > Nick

There we go! Roll over to my crib so we can game plan? I'm gonna need all y'alls help on this! Especially Perry #bram

SMS: Nick > Tyler
Why especially Perry?

SMS: Tyler > Nick
Who else would know how to enact such a devilish plan other than the OG vampire himself?

SMS: Nick > Tyler
Yea your right
SMS: Nick > Tyler
It is a devilish plan
SMS: Nick > Tyler
Your dancing with fire here dude

SMS: Tyler > Nick
Dance... Dance on...
SMS: Tyler > Nick
I'll C U when U get here #coolio

SMS: Nick > Tyler
Such a fitting song

SMS: Tyler > Nick
You fuckin know it!!!! Tell John

With a plethora of chances to let his morally designed fibers spread their voice against Tyler's schemes, Nick continuously chose to shoot out vague double entendres and sarcastically dripping texts masking the words: "DONT DO THIS PLAN!!! ITS EVIL!!!" ...He could have steered the sun's tide against the moon, but due his lack of action Nick will never be "the MAN" and just a boy... #tylercanrelate

Act 5: Scene 3: "Come togeeeetherrrrrr, right nowwww... Over me"

Still shaken from her whirlwind waking scene, Jasmine remains emotionally saddened as if woken from a cosmic like dream; determined to revert back to her "I run this bitch" self, Jasmine reinforces her prison doors within...

SMS: Tyler > Jasmine
Hey I'm rollin over... We gotta talk

SMS: Jasmine > Tyler
Whoa, whoa... Are you straight "telling" me what to do? No asking??? Bitch please...

ANNNNNNNND She's back.

SMS: Tyler > Jasmine
No no, never that. I just need your help to gather the valley for a pow wow... Box social status

SMS: Jasmine > Tyler
Box social?
SMS: Jasmine > Tyler
Pow wow?
SMS: Jasmine > Tyler
Who the fuck are you? And what have you done with our Tyler!!!???

SMS: Tyler > Jasmine
Ummm... Yeaaaa, I woke up a little bit different yesterday...

SMS: Jasmine > Tyler
Yea... I woke up a bit "different" today...

SMS: Tyler > Jasmine
Oh really? How's that?

SMS: Jasmine > Tyler
Ummm, na I'm ok

SMS: Tyler > Jasmine
You sure?

SMS: Jasmine > Tyler
Quit digging!
SMS: Jasmine > Tyler
Put...
SMS: Jasmine > Tyler
The shovel...
SMS: Jasmine > Tyler
DOWN!!! lol

SMS: Tyler > Jasmine

Relax! I'm comin over... me and the crew

SMS: Jasmine > Tyler

Are you once again TELLING me what you're doing and not askin ;)

SMS: Tyler > Jasmine

...yes?

SMS: Jasmine > Tyler

Just checking LOL. See you guys soon! XOXO

Although many reply with a "K" or any acknowledgement text, Tyler never responded nor was Jasmine waiting for one. Craving a response to all messages stems from the need for validation, insecurity or not having "much else" going on in your life; if your phone's constantly "blowing up," you wouldn't concern yourself with such small minute details #ihavealifebitch Conversely, those on the other side of the spectrum throw far too much anxiety towards the smallest inconsistencies in life such as non responsive text messages. Yet it's human nature to ask why; why didn't they respond? What's the reason? Is it a conscious decision or are they just busy? Before the advent of modern communication did people allow themselves to become AS consumed by the the answerless self killing questions of why... why? WHY???!!! Were people more confident in their own self worth before the dawn of the digital age? Did we always have such a strong need for constant self validation before social media OR did social media strap you in an'addict you to the "they liked/ commented on my ____! OM effing G!" #IMAWESOME

"It's ironic that the cell phone was created to communicate better, and what has happen is people communicate worse" -Simon Rex aka Dirt Nasty

Since you weren't endlessly supplied with "fake" human interactions on your phone and magnetically drawn to staring at screens 24/7, back in the day people interacted with one another in public. In today's digital age the majority have forgotten how to converse in person and instead prefer to communicate via screens as if face to face is "too intimate" #intamacyisdead #andphoneskilledit ...Just think how intimate YOU and a past love were BEFORE smart phones? #exactly #realsmiles>emoticons

Walking into classrooms teachers WERE once met by talking, jokes about them, laughing, gossiping and WRITING notes to their friends listing who they like and in what order #middleschool #imissit ...And now??? With technology monopolizing the eyes, teachers are met by near silence as if we're machines whose batteries are recharged by staring at screens... Pre "smart/dumb" phones, how often did people make eye contact with a passerby to see "what could be," wonder what they're thinking or try to read their minds while gazing into their soul? How much can you see looking into the pixelated dead eyes of a "snapchat" or a "profile" pic? (#fucksnapchat) ...Can you find "love at first sight?" Can you feel their gaze and heart staring into yours? Can you feel their warmth wash over you and tug at your core? How sad would it be if in the bleak future of our children the norm answer to the question "how did you and daddy meet?" IS online; while in person, through friends, at the bar, and on the street et al. become the rarest of aberrational answers... Please take a moment of silence for the death of humanity... silence silence on....

Since households have always "frowned" on incoming calls past 10 and the reliability of parents or siblings to pass along your message was never guaranteed, unreturned calls were rarely taken to heart as much as today's unresponsive digital communications. It's the unlimited accessibility of modern technology which makes the need for a response to ANY message THAT much greater... And when you don't receive one? Regardless of the circumstance or relationship, many find themselves logging onto social media to try and satisfy their cravings for attention an'validation... Many of these are the same socially inept, low self esteemed no worth masses who beg other's for a "follow" as if having another follower, (especially a celebrity) ignore your posts of what you bought at 7-11 today further validates you as a worthwhile human being. Instilled with a driving need for "likes/comments," the desperate and misguided will actually barter with others to like/ comment their posts if they in turn like/comment theirs; perpetuating both parties struggles to attain "social networking popularity" which save for a very select few means absolutely nothing in "real life"... struggle struggle on...

(> Group = Tyler, Perry, Nick & John)

MMS: Tyler > Group
Roll to Jasmine's

MMS: Nick > Group
Word

MMS: John > Group
Fo sho

MMS: Perry > Group
Why bitch?

MMS: Tyler > Group
Just do it bitch!

MMS: Perry > Group
Fuck you!

MMS: Tyler > Group
Fuck YOU!

MMS: Perry > Group
Lol I'm there

Can someone please invent a group message function with the option for respondents t'ONLY reply to the original sender and NOT everyone? #thatactually #workscrosscarriers ...It's incredibly annoying when there's a large group text, email, social media message and everyone else's endless two word responses blow up your notification banners (Bukka Buuuu!) or flood your inbox (you've got mail) with severely unwanted messages. Although it does lead to hilarious cross friend insults, technology must evolve! #canyouhearmenow

Act 5: Scene 4: "Can't We Just Stay in Bed All Day….."

On the best of days you'll naturally wake with no sadness, no anxiety and no worries falling from cluttered minds causing tension to rise from your pores... Unless your phone's annoyingly yelling at you to wake up where no matter how many times you hit the snooze it will not shut... the fuck... UP!

Next to you is NOT a stranger you met at the bar, nor a woman you eyed from afar; not a guy you called to fill the void nor a random who continues to annoy... Next door rests your counterpoint, fully understanding of how you tick; you'll feel their presence, essence pulsing through the air and in the thick of life they'll calm the senses leaving you breathlessly tied down. You'll look upon them sleeping, dumbfoundedly stare and smile just havin bare your heart whilst surfing on all night talking ventures... an'with all others suspended in their true nature, you'll allow the endless tension to die; finally comfortable with the silence that won't, and can't ever lie...

Awaking such days, Julian saw the girl he had waited, no the woman he was fated to lay next to and hold; fuck the brave, far too bold to run away from such connections an'arrest momentum of love's discretion an'it's wills... Far too difficult not to feel, an'too damn real not t'kill anyone that lay in it's way; constantly attempting to sway the world to stay in it's current state with a love that fucks minds into oblivion having never truly been living till eyes kissed on such darkened days now lit...

Waking in such manners never fades, never delays, and for the briefest of seconds whether you know it or not your smiling somewhere in full...

Yet with such ease you'll forget what kept you together through thick and through thin; feel what you'd forgotten but still lives an'breathes within. Or maybe you wrapped "bored" hands around necks of love as time grew, and what was once never ending could no longer be jumped through; for as the same routine bounced to an'from each day, the soul's depth in essence, slowly died away... And with auto pilot on, zombie like passings led to zombie like passion where sex and kisses flew from eachother because he was hubby an'she was misses _______ with his name. Forgotten were wakings in mornings the same: so excited, insisting an'pleading the other to call in sick t'throw bodies amongst walls; allow love's clouds t'break and fall to rain down moans an'sweat driven actions, so utterly bereft of sensual's love and it's passion; simply takin a walk an'goin to town. Just straight fuckin, ain't no dancin round such words and sex sounds...

Act 5: Scene 5: "Hi. Nice to meet you. My name's awkward"

(Julian walks out to Bastion watching TV on the couch)

Julian: "What uuuupp" (walks by Bastion)

Bastion: "Yoooo... Soooooooo, (Julian turns around) I take it SHE'S here?" (still staring at the TV)

Julian: "Yuuuup!!!! Did you think I'd let her go home?" (shooting a scrunched ESPN "come on man" face; Bukka Buuuu! Bukka Buuuu!)

SMS: Liliana > Julian

QOD: "You give me the kind of feelings people write novels about!"

SMS: Liliana > Julian

So true!!! Morning baby!

Bastion: "Dude (rolling eye sigh) ...don't tell me that's her texting from next door..."

Julian: "I mean... you should know more than anyone that this is not a quote 'Veronica situation' an'is the real fuckin deal; This is it dude!" (smirking like someone who just found a golden ticket to the chocolate factory on the bus)

Bastion: "Blah blah blah. I've heard it before Jules; an'I know, you're sooooooo in love; seen it, lived it..."

Liliana: (walking out of the bedroom) "What!!! (angrily walking towards Bastion) Are you sayin I'm just another Bitch! Another notch on his post???" (standing over Bastion)

Bastion: "I... well NO I, (looking to a smiling Julian for help) I meant"

(Liliana looks at Julian; both erupt in laughter)

Bastion: (realizing she "punk'd" him) "Fuck... youuuuuu bastards!!!" (#ashtonkutcher)

Julian: "She frickin had you Bass!"

Bastion: (standing up with hands in his Jack Daniels pajama pants) "Yeaaaaa yeaaaaaa..."

Liliana: "Sorrrrraayyyyy, what is it... (turns t'Julian and back) Bassss??? or Bastion?"

Bastion: "It's whatever you want it to be bae" (smirking at Julian)

Julian: "Ha. Ha..."

Liliana: (hugs up on Julian an'lookin at Bastion) "IIIIII thought it was funny"

Bastion: (looks t'Julian) "I like her!"

Julian: "Welll, (shrugging) ...what can I say?" (happily staring into new love's eyes)

Act 5: Scene 6: Its Time to Come Home

Fights, arguments, betrayal; no matter the fall out, your shared blood calls you home.

SMS: Jasmine > Liliana
Hey...

SMS: Liliana > Jasmine
Hey

SMS: Jasmine > Liliana
How ya been?

SMS: Liliana > Jasmine
Good...

SMS: Jasmine > Liliana
Where you been staying?

SMS: Liliana > Jasmine
You know where...

SMS: Jasmine > Liliana
Still on cloud 9?

SMS: Liliana > Jasmine
Clouds? ...I've shot 9 million feet above

SMS: Jasmine > Liliana
Oh
SMS: Jasmine > Liliana
No need to rub it in
SMS: Jasmine > Liliana
But yea... I can understand...

SMS: Liliana > Jasmine
Can you?

SMS: Jasmine > Liliana
Yes...

SMS: Liliana > Jasmine
Why did you run away from it then?

(no response)

SMS: Liliana > Jasmine
Why did you run?

(no response)

SMS: Liliana > Jasmine
Why'd you turn you back on something as magical as this?

SMS: Jasmine > Liliana
Please...
SMS: Jasmine > Liliana
Please don't ask me

SMS: Liliana > Jasmine
I miss home

SMS: Jasmine > Liliana
I miss my family, my sister and my life

SMS: Liliana > Jasmine
Well then why did you cast me out with such hatred??? You hella scared me!!! Besides... YOU left him, so why are YOU so resentful
SMS: Liliana > Jasmine
So damn hateful...

(time passes)

SMS: Jasmine > Liliana
You were too young and a teen at home in the throes of young fun to know the realms of horror I lived and what kept me sleepless for countless nights after the siege... When dragons cast spells on the other half of our family I witnessed events you couldn't possibly imagine, leaving scars no flames could burn through an'marks no cries could wish to soothe.... And now?

SMS: Jasmine > Liliana
No period of time can break ice off frozen eyes; blind forever after to love's mosaic design

SMS: Liliana > Jasmine
You STILL'ave never told me
SMS: Liliana > Jasmine
...what the fuck happen

SMS: Jasmine > Liliana
I'm not done...
SMS: Jasmine > Liliana
You think you could ever understand? I've passed along walls I built due to tragedy befallen since no words could replace our parents so solemnly taken from the world we must still walk upon... Please, you'ave no clue what words slivered out of graveyard's mouths to mine ears which fell deaf that day... Nothing can resurrect worlds dead lived, worlds I wished real life could give for I'm trapped apart from a love I'd give ANYthing to return to... But alas HIS waiting's through, and I'll continue t'soothe my heart's scorching burn with the moon's stealth like view.......

SMS: Liliana > Jasmine
HOW CAN I UNDERSTAND IF YOU WON'T TELL ME!!!!
SMS: Liliana > Jasmine
We BOTH loss the only world we ever knew; why won't you let me see it through your broken eyes???

SMS: Jasmine > Liliana
And I won't...

(time passes)

SMS: Liliana > Jasmine

You've fated me t'dark's mercy, barred me to cluelessly sit and plead to parlay the pain you endure daily... Fuck this shit! You've truly forsaken me AND you by unfairly holding events deep below in tightly clasped boxes; divulge what you saw and remains unseen in fires caskets; let me learn an'discern my own conclusions, own endings an'self healings in preparation for the next chapter's NEW new beginnings...

(time passes)

SMS: Liliana > Jasmine

Please!!!

SMS: Jasmine > Liliana

You have matured and grown into a woman far beyond innocent years, yet I'll never take you back to battlegrounds t'hear such treacherous battle sounds... You've brought up pains resembling events you'll forever seek me to send; and fuck YOUUUU for bringing both unspeakable tragedies to the forefront of shattered minds bend...

(no response)

SMS: Jasmine > Liliana

No words of forgiveness will be spilt; for thanks to you blood of past love continues t'gush and feed flowers forever wilt; you've brought pain to numb paralyzed organs now active and revived; cast moons back on windows sills to reflect images I can neither handle nor hide; an'blasted my heart with blood fires I never thought would freely roll down like candle to dripping wax...

SMS: Liliana > Jasmine

Please!!! Just stop!!! Stop how I've hurt you so!!! I cannot gain one love to lose another!!! It leaves me half devoid an'tragically off kilter!!! I am not the earth and cannot relax on such slanted axissees...

SMS: Liliana > Jasmine

I miss the world whence we grew, the world I threw aside by jumping off balconies to a love you once knew and KNOW I could not undo once walked down upon... One you amazingly broke off course since the moon looked brighter than the sun... to unfortunately leap onto paths I cannot relive, retrace, or ever rerun...

SMS: Jasmine > Liliana

Come home...

SMS: Liliana > Jasmine

I want to

SMS: Jasmine > Liliana

Can you?

SMS: Liliana > Jasmine

WIll you forgive for what I could not control?

SMS: Jasmine > Liliana

No promises... Return to your spot by my side and then we'll deal with the great divide

SMS: Liliana > Jasmine

I'm sorry...

SMS: Jasmine > Liliana

Do not cast such lies; even technology cannot hide your words that die before falling on deaf ears...

SMS: Liliana > Jasmine

Then let me prove my worth in person; allow me to come an'give my calling...

SMS: Jasmine > Liliana

Call, call on...

(Liliana walks out to Julian and Bastion bullshitting on the couch)

Bastion: "Nooooo!!! Really????? You started drinking some random chick's bottles? Ahahaha that's fuckin legendary dude!!!"

Julian: (laughing) "I know... We didn't give a fuck about-(see's somber eyes)-what is it darling?"

Liliana: "Soooo.... (sits next t'Julian) I'm gonna go home"

Julian: (sits up) "You're leaving me?"

Liliana: (looks over) "...we have to deal with it sometime Julian"

Julian: "I guess... (stands) well... here goes nothin" (takes phone out, walks to the bedroom, doubles back and kisses Liliana on the forehead before crookedly smiling an'vanishing into the dark room)

SMS: Julian > Santana
What up

SMS: Santana > Julian
Yo yo

SMS: Julian > Santana
Been a minute

(no response)

SMS: Julian > Santana
So you gonna leave the kiss of death on me or we gonna talk this out like men?

SMS: Santana > Julian
Men stab you in the front
SMS: Santana > Julian
Not the back bro

SMS: Julian > Santana
I came to you the next day!

SMS: Santana > Julian

And THAT was the moment you learned who she was?

(no response)

SMS: Santana > Julian

Well???!!!

SMS: Julian > Santana

I knew the night before when Q told me

SMS: Santana > Julian

Loyal Q... You left me out on that cliff an'if not for Bastion I'd still be there...

SMS: Santana > Julian

And you STILL haven't "picked me up"

SMS: Julian > Santana

What's you talkin bout? (#willis)

SMS: Santana > Julian

Don't play dumb bitch, you know what I'm sayin

(no response)

SMS: Santana > Julian

You're loss to her as I was to mine... Each second you live and breathe disgraces my name an'my blood, my heartache an'my love that died a thousand deaths and die again each day... YOU of all people brought such feelings flooding back in full to where I still sit staring at the stool, intently holding on till may

SMS: Santana > Julian

Discharges continually drift by till one day touched'll burst, inevitably sending me to the hearse YOU helped bring forth... Yet still you dance with daggers you've disperse towards my back an'continue to glisten in the glow... Where as I remain moon darkened, melon collie and low... You live in sun ridden world's you took from me; stolen moments, such thievery of the sun's rays that she, SHEEEE!!! ...once gave me...

SMS: Julian > Santana

Your hurt and sorrow shutter insides, but your tragedy's neither today nor 'morow but past; yet your heart CONTINUES to mask what you've seen, never dealt; still swallowing what she no longer felt but you did; what she didn't want, but you lived, so desperately desiring to exhale her scent once more

SMS: Julian > Santana

Live your life my brother; please discern what you couldn't capture for it won't heal burns left in wake of'er rapture... So please! I beseech you to STOP! And cursedly so... My love is here to stay so fuck you AND your living rocky horror show... I will come hither to make peace an'amends for whats been done behind backs whilst you cried; now please let me home an'take thou kiss away from empty seats throne...

SMS: Santana > Julian

You're too young to'ave known her slaying of mine was linked to other's death you DID see but not witness; the moon's light DID cast down, only not to your focus; for sitting in pockets of safety you never saw what endlessly replays through dreams turnt nightmares... You'll never see nor feel, and I'm thankful still for it's where tragedies are bore and souls live to steal. I fear it's what shut'er down t'leave me sitting here in limbo at depths I wish you‘ll never gaze... yet the lingering pain keeps me breathing, so utterly afraid of moving past an'forgetting her love wouldn't last...

SMS: Julian > Santana

I've asked yet you've promised never to tell...
And ALL I know now... is well...

SMS: Julian > Santana

I've finally stopped the bleed an'found a true counter point to balance my sleeve holding life's pestilent emotions... Fuck your blame for not being killed like you in the same since I never shared occurrences your eyes kissed; disallowing me to witness or know what I gladly missed... Allow me to help break your daily cycle and relive massacres you promised never to convey. You must move forth from behind banished love's exhale an'cease to desire the essences you've loss, desist from hangin yourself on your OWN fucking cross!!! ...or you'll forever walk alongside the wicked moon's shadow; for with the sun's rays exorcised? ...Gone is all hope of ending such futile internal battles...

SMS: Santana > Julian
The words sent through technological lines
cannot soothe the pain you've brought

SMS: Julian > Santana
Im comin home...

SMS: Santana > Julian
Leave you may, but in the depths I still sit...

SMS: Julian > Santana
Sit, sit on...

(Bastion takes off with Liliana already gone;
while Julian remains in idle moments as he showers...
and showers on...)

Act 5: Scene 7: Meeting of The Round Tables

Before walking in to what WAS her safe haven, Liliana breathes a couple breaths at the door to what's now quoth the raven; "Nevermore".

(Jasmine stands directly across from the door at bar one, Perry's stage right and comfortably on couch four whilst Tyler sits stage left on the counter of bar three)

Jasmine: "Why hello dearest sister" (smiles)

Liliana: (sigh of relief) "Hey sis..."

Perry: "Well look who came crawllllling back-"

Tyler: "-HA!"

Liliana: (glares at Perry) "Am I on my knees? (Tyler laughs) Oh is something funny asshole?"

Jasmine: "ENOUGH!!! Liliana, my love, my life; whatEVER the case, we simply want you back..."

Perry: "Amen"

Tyler: “Whoa whoa, hold up-(jumps off the bar with a hidden smile)-are you... back?”

Liliana: “I-”

Jasmine: “-No one’s back on nothin-”

Perry: “-That’s what she said”

Jasmine: “LEAVE US! (waves right hand) ...and tell the others to go in the side door; or else”

Perry: (laughs) ”Ohhhhhh Shiiitt, watch out for-(Jasmine glares) Ok Ok! We’re going... Geeeze mom... (hitting Perry in the back as they leave) ...hahaha I called’er mom” (slam)

Jasmine: “Have you forgotten who you are and where you belong???”

Liliana: (scrunched face) “Are you kidding me??? Do you NOT remember how YOU were when you were with-”

Jasmine: “-Don’t you dare!!!”

Liliana: (leans in) “With SANN-TAANN-NAAA” (staring her in the face)

Jasmine: (body deflates; head drops) “Still... strikes me with just a name”

Liliana: “Why don’t you tell him?”

Jasmine: "Never, not after what I did; I can't risk it without knowing he's still there... waiting"

Liliana: "How will you ever know if you don't try!" (steps towards her)

Jasmine: (sharply shakes head) "...ANYways tomorrow, Tyler's, 9 pm... you need to be there and NOT fashionably late... you'll show up with Nicole an'Jaime as if all is right in the valley"

Liliana: "And... this willlll... (steps closer) help bring us back together?" (closer still)

Jasmine: (steps towards an'grabs her hand) "It'll be a start... You still have no clue what you've done in striking up a romance with one of THEM"

Liliana: (flings her hand off an'jumps back) "JAZZZ!!! FUCK!!! Let me live my life!!! No more tryin to protect me from the world!!! If I, (walks to the right) IIIII want to break down my own walls-NOOO!!! (turns t'Jasmine) The walls YOUUUU put up, then so be it..."

Jasmine: "I hear you my love; no more; I'll let you do what you're gonna do"

Liliana: "Thank you"

Jasmine: "Now Tyler wants t'talk to you about tomorrow"

Liliana: "No... no no no, (moves back) he's unstable, didn't you hear what he did at our party??? I refuse"

Jasmine: "You Will talk to him; he's a part of this circle and has always been there for us; you need to accept that he will be around... Regardless"

Liliana: (begrudgingly) "Fineeee... Where is he?"

Jasmine: "No clue, text him"

SMS: Liliana > Tyler
Where are you?

SMS: Tyler > Liliana
No hello, no how have you been?
SMS: Tyler > Liliana
We haven't talked in days...

SMS: Liliana > Tyler
It's been AAAA day lol and we're gonna talk now, where are you?

SMS: Tyler > Liliana
In Perry's room

SMS: Liliana > Tyler
Which one is that?

SMS: Tyler > Liliana
Guest room 6

SMS: Liliana > Tyler
K

(on high)

Rolling up to the Casta mansion, Julian sees all four in the garage: Stephan and Q are on the couch passing a double percolating ROAR Bong, Bastion's fishing in the refrigerator for a couple beers while Santana waxes his 1967 ________.

Bastion: "Julian!!! Welcome brother!" (Santana looks up an'down quickly before shaking his head)

After receiving "good t'see you" hand clasps from the "high kids" an'cheering a newly cracked beer with Bastion, Julian turns to Santana;

Julian: "Hey yo; what... too cool t'say what's up to your baby bro?"

Santana: (glances towards him an'back down) "...Naaaa"

Met by "don't look at me" shrugs and "you're on your own" smirks from the crew, Julian cracks an extra beer an'bravely walks over to Santana:

Julian: "Hey..." (offers beer)

Santana: "I'm good..."

Julian: (sigh) "Come on; enough..." (holds side door open allowing Santana to follow outside)

Julian: "Look... I'm sorry (Santana looks away) ...I should have came to you the second I knew and not left you on high where your mind flew far from body with none to know where you go an'I can hardly guess... Please understand from whence I arrived; from where you yourself still hide having lived and breathed yet remain dying to relive"

Enraged and possessed, Santana turns to Julian's shutter with hand t'throat; an'with firm grasp on his voice's motor, Santana chokes; transposing fears he's lived with since in every moment over... an'as his eyes imbibe an'swallow Santana's hateful sorrow, Julian's uncertain how to proceed as Santana knows neither on any days of future morrows.

Santana: (rest come outside) "How DARE you waltz in so casually to the land IIII FUCKIN CLAIMED!!!! Swiftly walking back in as if NOTHINGS fuckin changed... You are no longer my brother an'the kiss remains pressed and steadfast!!! (shakes head downward) ...and for you to say you understood the backlash??? (eye to eye) Uncompre-fuckinnnn-hendable that you'd think such thoughts an'attack the very blood running through your ungrateful veins; arteries mid laugh, unable to contain having heard such words you've allowed to jump off lips and strike me with no defense; shieldless; yet STILL you fuckin persist..." (releases and turns to walk away)

Julian: "I love her-" (Santana throws fist to Julian's right cheek; shooting daggers upon his body before Q pulls Santana's warring arms back)

Santana: (shrugs off Q with tears forming face flushed) “How DARRREEEE you throw your love in my face an’dance around laughing at me, your own blood brother an’last remaining family... (walks away turns) Don’t come back!! (powerfully rushes towards Julian causing Q to intervene) Imagine if you loss her, If she Crushed you an’she Broke you... (pushes Julian sharply)-SEEEEE IT???-(Julian slams against walls) ...Now; envision what you’d do if I dated her sister YEARS later... See it??? Fuckin DO YOU???? (Julian slumps down an’sits against the wall with knees up dejectedly staring away) SEEEE!!! (voice starts to crack) Do You FEEEEL the RUSSHH OF ANGER AND BETRAYAL??” (storms off to the front of the mansion)

Shortly after Bastion hits Q’s shoulder an’points towards Santana, Q flexes back on Bastion causing him to flinch before heading towards the front... Grabbing a wax pen from his pocket, Stephan feverishly smokes before sheepishly offering the pen t’Julian who remains frozen... Knowing how Julian feels, Bastion neither moves nor tries to console; when one attains an earth shattering love or new heights of success, the rush sends many into easily offendable waters along with obligatory waves of entitlement.

Breathing the air of a world Santana once lived, how could Julian have audaciously reminded his brother how fucking sweet it tastes? How incredible such winds feel against your skin in evoking a refusing t’disappear grin under a refusing to ever set sun? Forgotten was his support throughout Julian’s endless run of revolving door romances, having picked Him up after each an’every recurrence of his perpetual love’s cancer.

...Pondering himself in the day's sky, Julian retraces the crashing and family thrashing due t'new love's shattering of a cold frozen man into two million pieces again... Yet the warmth she brings begins to trump his guilt, unable to disallow smiles from overtaking blank stares of hidden faces in downward tilt... slowly caring less and less about his own blood he'd once again spilt... Bleed, bleed on...

SMS: Santana > Caitlyn

Come see me tonight! Cuz It's friday... You ain't got no boyfriend; you ain't got not plans; and you ain't got shit to do! ;) #friday

Act 5: Scene 8: Confessions of a Devil's Advocate

(the valley; guest room 6; 20 minutes earlier)

Although the ultimate plan relies on her rejecting his declaration of love, Tyler still anxiously debated what his pose should be when Liliana walks in; shifting from sitting laid back on the couch to standing up leaning against the dresser, to laying on the bed acting as if he's on his phone when he's actually just shifting through various apps tryin to "look busy" #obsessmuch

(Liliana enters with Tyler bent over the bed having frustratedly slammed his hand down due to his indecision)

Liliana: "Uhhhhh hello??? Are youuuuuu, (giggles) ok?"

Tyler: (embarrassingly swings up) "I'm amazing, just... playing some bed drums, (shrugs shoulders) ya caught me right in the middle of a breakdown!" (smiles wider #thatlldodonkey #thatlldo)

When your broken heart's desire sets eyes on that which hath broken it, the emotional floodgates can easily crash through any walls you've built up against. Although she rolled out of bed, makeup less and redressed in the clubbing clothes she'd worn last night, Tyler could only see the woman he'd dreamt about as the entire reason of their meeting's pushed aside by the world he loss and the future woman he vows to gain:

In his mind's eye Tyler pictures her shooting an "oh there you are my love" gaze before gliding over to place'er hand on the small of his back with lips awaiting his... after an American or French following, his body sighs a great relief in allowing senses to fall out pores an'pockets, rocketing adrenalines to full bloomed heart realms only love could justly describe... And as these powerful images streamline his body, unknown connections of minds synapses trigger new feelings leaving Tyler wishing to reinhabit his former empty vessel's aimless drifting; wishing for days before altered selfs picked up the novel "Tyler" off that now truly infamous shelf...

Liliana: "Soooo... What did you wanna talk to me about?"

Tyler: "Welll......" (places recording phone on the dresser)

Liliana: "Wellllll, what?"

Tyler: "...I don't really know what's going on; or why I've just now awoken, orrr; felt the need to... t'tell you..."

Liliana: "If this is what I think it is, please stop... (backing away) you must know by now that I'm with-"

Tyler: "-Wait wait, hold on... (looks over at his phone ever so fast) I, I just needa say this... (paces once before facing Liliana) I never knew what I had in you... and I really don't know if I've Ever loved anything or anyone up to this point..."

Liliana: "Tyler I-"

Tyler: "-No! (looks away) I need t'get this off my chest if we're gonna be cool around eachother; (turns to Liliana for acknowledgment to which she begrudgingly nods) ...I never treated you right... I ignored you; neglected you... Fuck, I mean; (shrugs both hands up in the air in disgust) I paid more attention to Perry's jokes than your few needs which I SHOULD'ave put first... I didn't know what I had in you, (looks in'er eyes) an'what wonderful spirit and essence you carry in everything you do... How you have this uncanny ability to arise happiness in all whom you encounter... I never understood what you were but in the wake of us you brought out that which I was never capable of before; that which all men were taught at such a young age to withhold and keep locked up inside due to the fear of "not being a man..." (looks away to the left in shame) I've lived for others and succumbed to social pressures my whole life; an'never allowed my own identity to shine through... (looks at'er) Yet I now see the error of my ways an'how I let you throw your wants and pleas into the winds that carried our relationship away as well... I know I've probably lost my chance but I had to let you know; so maybe you'd see how magnificent we could one day be..." (turns his back to Liliana staring at the wall on the left)

Liliana: "I...... I don't want you. I'm in love with someone else... I'm finally happy. I'm sorry..."

Tyler: (thankfully smirking before shifting back into character) "I, I just.... I don't; (turns to her) know what t'say... Are you seriously in love with him?" (fighting a smile)

Liliana: "Yes, I am... You need t'get over me and move on with your life... find someone new..."

Tyler: (in an "ok whatever" tone) "Well, I guess there's nothing left t'say; (grabs phone, shrugs) it is what it is..." (moves to the door)

Liliana: "Soooooo, you're really ok?" (half smiling #wtf)

Tyler: "Yes... (dreaming of their future together) I said my peace... but if he EVER does ANYthing to hurt you; I will be there for you in anyway you need" (leaves as all the different Tyler's in his mind celebrate, pop champagne and party like its 1999 #game #blouses)

Liliana's confusion ends once HE enters the forefront of her mind to say: "Hello darling! I'm still waiting for your text; for your love; for you... simply..."

SMS: Liliana > Julian

> My love!!! Where are you? How did it go??? Mine was rough but she's being more understanding than I could ever imagine! :) I hope yours went ok too!!! Text me!!! I love you!!!!!!! #missuloser

(> Group = Tyler, Perry, Nick & John)

MMS: Tyler > Group
Done and done y'all! I have more than enough! That fucker is dead in the water and he doesn't even know it!!!

MMS: Perry > Group
Kill, kill on

MMS: Nick > Group
Yea... SOMEONE is done...

MMS: John > Group
#dontknowshit

MMS: Perry: > Group
Hey!!! look at you Johnny boy!!! I didn't even know you KNEW what a hashtag was!!!
#yourallgrownsupandyourallgrownsup

MMS: Tyler > Group
LOL classic #swingersliveson

MMS: John > Group
What's a hashtag?

MMS: Perry > Group
Hahahahahaha.... "You're still the king Kelso!"
#michaelkelsoforthewin

MMS: Nick > Group
I love you John!!! #hashtagcentral

MMS: Tyler > Group
The "king" reigns on

MMS: John > Group
Kelso??? Who the fuck is Kelso???

MMS: Tyler > Group
I love you too John!!! :)

MMS: Perry > Group
Kelso = Ashton Kutcher #that70sshow

MMS: Nick > Group
Bless you group messaging! #weloveyoujohn #whatwouldwedowithoutyou

(Tyler screenshots the group message stream)

SMS: Tyler > Dru
Dude you gotta see these text messages
MMS: Tyler > Dru
(screenshots)

MMS: John > Group
Ohhhhhh OK! Yea I love that 70s show!!!!

MMS: Tyler > Group
"So there's this car man... that runs on water man" (everyone throws stuff at Hyde) "It runs on Water MAN!!!" #bestsceneever

MMS: Perry > Group
I miss that show, you still have all those seasons somewhere?

SMS: Dru > Tyler
HAHAHAHAHAHA thats fuckin awesome!!! #whatamoron

MMS: Tyler > Group
Somewhere lol

MMS: Tyler> Group
We can just Netflix it

MMS: Perry > Group
Yea if they have it... They always have every show I DONT wanna watch and never the shows I WANNA watch

MMS: Tyler > Group
Typical #fuckthatshit

MMS: Nick > Group
What's up with tonight?

MMS: Tyler > Group
I'm gonna meet up with Noel so I'm out

MMS: Tyler > Group
But party at my crib tomorrow! #itsfuckinon #restupkids

MMS: Perry > Group

Yea... I'm out too. Got a couple different ones lined up... you know... no big deal #justanotherfriday

MMS: John > Group

I'm meeting up with this one girl too. So sorry Nick, I cant hang out with you

MMS: Nick > Group

@Tyler good shit @Perry pass one down my way lol @John hahaha your lie was not only hilarious but also rhymed!!!

MMS: Tyler > Group

Alright, alright... Leave poor John alone! I believe you lol! But tomorrow it's on!! Seacrest out!

MMS: Perry > Group

Get'er done!

MMS: John > Group

I'll hit you up about tonight Nick

MMS Nick > Group

Word

SMS: Tyler > Noel

Hey what's up, I'm tryin to bring sexy back... Oh wait, I already have ;) Come over! I want you!

SMS: Tyler > Noel

Yes, drop everything! #jtgotnothingonme #neitherdoeskingkong

Act 5: Scene 9:
"He loves her; he loves her too... he LOVES her; HEEEE loves her TOOOO..."

Dating someone on the rebound is a bad idea... Dating someone on the rebound whose still in love with their ex is even worse since they'll eventually realize you'll never BE their ex an'grow to despise you for giving them false hope #chalkittothegame #happensallthetime

(Noel's apartment; 10 minutes earlier #sisterrivalry)

SMS: Santana > Caitlyn
Come see me tonight!!! Cuz It's friday... You ain't got no boyfriend; you ain't got not plans; and you ain't got shit to do! ;) #friday

Caitlyn: (runs to Noel's room with an "OMG" smile) "Guesssss who just Texted me!!!" (holding up phone)

Noel: (frustratedly sighs an'throws pen at'er journal having written the word Santana) "I know, I know"

Caitlyn: "Ummmm, do you?"

Noel: (sighs again) "Uhhhh Yeaaa! Your Dreamy Mc Dreamy Santana?" (continues writing)

Caitlyn: "Ummm, (scrunched up face) Ewwwww! Number 1, he wasn't even That good looking; and 2, Grey's Anatomy was SO a decade ago" (#whenitwasgood)

Noel: (looks up) "...oh shit, it WAS a fuckin decade ago..."

Caitlyn: “Yeaaaaaa; at least throw out something relevant like a Tatum or Gosling reference; hashtag Seriously!!! How old are you???”

Noel: (head tilt) “You KNOW how old I am”

Caitlyn: “No, I know how DUMB you are; hello, rhetorical question?”

Noel: (gets off the bed) “Hey heyyyyy, (eyes wide sarcastic smile) look at you!!! I didn’t even realize you KNEW what rhetorical meant”

Caitlyn: “Do you?”

Noel: “Of Course I do! And sis??? Tatum? Gosling? If ANYONE looks like either of them, it’s MYYYY Ty Ty!” (blushes and smiles)

Caitlyn: “He’s NOT even with you... why just two nights ago he was tryin t’beat up whoever’s dating-”

Noel: “-Shut!!! Shut up!” (shaking her head)

Caitlyn: “Well I’m just saying; he’s not (air quotes) yours”

Noel: “Whoa whoa, back up missy”

Caitlyn: “Missy? (throws head back) MissssYYYY???!!! Am IIIII overweight, short and black???”

Noel: “No, but she’s rich, can dance, an’has a better chance with Tatum/Gosling than you!!!” (laughs out loud)

Caitlyn: "Ohhhh Helllllll No!!!! ...AnyWAYSSSS, Sanny hit me up an'wants to seeee MEEEEE tonight" (proudly)

Noel: "...yayyyyy" (waves finger in a circle #cliche)

(Bukka Buuuu! Bukka Buuuu!)

SMS: Tyler > Noel

Hey what's up, I'm tryin to bring sexy back... Oh wait, I already have ;) Come over! I want you!

SMS: Tyler > Noel

Yes, drop everything! #jtgotnothingonme #neitherdoeskingkong

Noel: "Well MYYYY guy just texted me too; (holds up phone) annnnnnd What?" (two handed "suck it" motion)

Caitlyn: "And what?"

Noel: (shakes her head like "duhhhh" #hello)

Caitlyn: "Mr Tyler Tatum?"

Noel: (smiles proudly) "Mmmm... myyy Ty Ty..."

Caitlyn: (eyes closed heavy sigh) "Oh My Fucking God!!! HE IS NOT, YOURSSSS!!!"

Noel: (deflated) "Well...... at least Tyler and whats her face Just broke up; Santana's still stuck on that one chick from Hella years ago"

Caitlyn: "...that was low bitch"

Noel: "Whoa; chu tryin to get crazy???"

Caitlyn: "No, no one's gettin cray here cray"

Noel: "Anyways, can we respond to these texts already?"

Caitlyn: "Ummm; I'm not stoppin ya" (takes out phone)

(Caitlyn throws on
"Calvin Harris - I Need Your Love
feat. Ellie Goulding")

SMS: Caitlyn > <3 Sanny <3

Hey love! I have a couple different plans in the air... but maybeeeee I can squeeze some time in to see you tonight ;)

SMS: Noel > Ty Ty #bae

Ty Ty! Mmmmmmmm that sounds amazing!!! I need to get ready and then I'll be over... But ONLY cuz your bringing sexy back! My little JT... #lovemesomejt

SMS: Tyler > Noel

Hey! Who you calling little? lol

SMS: Noel > Ty Ty #bae

Ohhhh Ty Ty... We both KNOW you're not little ;)

SMS: Tyler > Noel

Thats right!!!

SMS: Noel > Ty Ty #bae

So when do you want me to come over baby?

SMS: Tyler > Noel

Cum over now...

(Caitlyn looks at Noel waist deep in'er phone an'back at her quiet banner-less lock screen)

Caitlyn: "...why is he not texting me?"

There's always a million sensible reasons why someone isn't responding to a message: busy, working, dealing with drama, driving, or phones on silent/dead etc... In this case, Santana's phone was loss in translation while he washes his anger in alcohol's depths at the bar "pain and suffering" on.........

SMS: Noel > Ty Ty #bae

Babe!!! I can't right now! I need to shower and get ready! Don't you want me so fresh and so clean ;) #outkast

Noel: "What?" (staring intently at her phone #recharging)

Caitlyn: (whining) "He stillllll hasn't responded..."

SMS: Tyler > Noel

You can take a shower here! Then I'll get to see you undress, dry off and put on your lotion which you'll lose on my sheets soon after anyways ;)

SMS: Noel > Ty Ty #bae

If you're lucky ;)

Noel: "I'm sorry... he'll respond; just don't text him... don't make yourself look desperate"

SMS: Tyler > Noel

LOL see you soon

As her self confidence continues to fall, the stunning Caitlyn sifts through her numerous unread facebook/snapchat/text messages from guys she never responds to and opens her Instagram to see whose commented/direct messaged her in the last two hours; even with all these guys (and girls) hitting'er up, her confidence an'self worth continues chilling at rock bottom since'er heart's desire has yet to respond #cestlavie #humannatureatitsbest

...succumbing to the beast;

SMS: Caitlyn > Random guy 1

Hey... sorry I was busy yesterday

SMS: Caitlyn > Random guy 1

How are you?

SMS: Caitlyn > Random guy 2

Hey, how ya been?

To try and resist texting Santana, (or another random) Caitlyn puts her phone on silent, throws it on the bed next to Noel and promises not to check it for at least 30 minutes... although she'll inevitably check in 10.

......Naturally, less than a minute later;

Noel: "Your phone's going offfff; (sees "<3 Sanny <3 Text Message" banners) it's your LOVVEERRRR!!"

Caitlyn: (Power walks in spilling her Vodka-OJ to have Noel snatch her phone right before she can grab it) "GIVE IT BACK!!!! Oh MY GODDDD!!!"

Noel: "Give what back?"

Caitlyn: (head drop) "...REALLY???@@@"

(Noel's phone vibrates)

Noel: "You're lucky I have a text" (hands phone t'Caitlyn)

SMS: Santana > Caitlyn
Make it happen
SMS: Santana > Caitlyn
10 pm
SMS: Santana > Caitlyn
My house

SMS: Random Guy 1 > Caitlyn (unread)

SMS: Random Guy 2 > Caitlyn (unread)

Considering it took Santana 20 minutes to respond, Caitlyn must wait at least 10 minutes before replying...

Noel: “Soooo???”

Caitlyn: (snootily) “WE’RE gonna meet up later; (rolls eyes) no big deal”

SMS: Random Guy 1 > Caitlyn (unread)

SMS: Random Guy 2 > Caitlyn (unread)

Noel: “Nice! So we BOTH get t’see OUR lovers” (smiling in agreement before turning away smile-less)

In synchronized disillusionment, the sisters believe capturing a “made man” will magically transform themselves from empty anxiety ridden girls into 100 % confident independent an’validated WOMEN... #asif #doesntworklikethat #manysettleforittho #settlesettleon

(exactly 10 minutes later)

SMS: Caitlyn > <3 Sanny <3
I’ll be there Sanny! 10 pm! :)

SMS: Liliana > Julian

Julian... Where are you??? Are you ok??? What happen??? We never go this long without talkin... It's been hours : (

Act 6: Scene 1:
"Love the one your with?"

While perfecting potions awaiting ears of his now greatest enemy, bottled words continuously remind Tyler “she loves me not” #damnpetals ...Having loss command of his empty heart and lacking soul, Tyler can no longer control emotions coursing his stoic veins an’asshole arteries as foreign feelings of sympathy invade his body... Most would be downright “giddy” with such a dime piece/relationship goal of a woman en route; but if it wasn’t HER heartbeat outside chamber doors, then happy an’excited Tyler would be quote the raven, Nevermore...

SMS: Noel > Ty Ty #bae

I’m here!!! Little pig little pig, let me in!!! :)

SMS: Tyler > Noel

Doors open :)

Emotionless emoticons: helping people fake it since 1999.

Noel: (with left hand high on doorway and the right on’er disjointed hip) “Heyyyyyy... (glances down and up) you rang?”

With an “I’m ready to do this” smirk, Noel walks in flaunting a “straight sex” ensemble spurring Tyler’s locked up horn balls to celebrate; wearing a “fuck me” black mini skirt an’a loose grey slanted 80’s t-shirt showing off the “good” shoulder, her “no need for a bra” chest glistens through the fine fabric leaving nothing to the imagination #score

Forcefully trying to feel what he did not, Tyler throws Noel onto his lap and obligatorily grabs her nearly exposed breasts with his left hand while cupping her toned yet full ass with the right kissing her deep… hard… like she IS her; IS whom mind's have erected devious plans designed by companies specializing in tearing down lower income housing t'build strip malls or another parking lot… but fuck; the greatest plans ARE laid with the best of intentions #getit #laid #haha #horrible

Noel: "Well it's good t'feel-I mean (hehe) see you too!!!"

Tyler: "You know it!" (fading smile)

It doesn't take long after opening the eyes to realize who sits on the thighs: NOT the love he yearns nor object of his lust, but just another woman atop the tangled web like mess; why must one weave while stuck on the other? Having called Noel to cushion blows of life's stormy weather, Tyler passes time on this lowly bystander needing to feel loved again; a sin farrrr too many commit throughout all our generations…

Noel: (standing up straightening her shirt) "Sooooo, where are our drinks?"

Tyler: (flustered then cool and composed) "…they're on the counter"

Noel: "I was gonna sayyyy; they're always made upon arrival" (giggles walkin towards the kitchen)

Tyler: (jumps up) “Whoa whoaaaaaa (assertively pulls her waist; turning her on more) what kinda gentleman would I be if I let YOUUU grab our drinks? (swag making a guest appearance) Take a seat missy”

Noel: (did he just say? Nm) “...Hurry back! And bring those lips too!”

Having completely forgotten about their drinks, Tyler throws ice goose an’sprite into two cups on the counter. Sighing a breath of calm before the sexual storm, Tyler glances at the gratuitous four pained window above the sink to see Liliana’s face reflecting back at him with her wondrous smile and “only having eyes for him” stare... Looking down at their drinks with HER name on neither, Tyler sighs an’looks up in hopes of returning to’er gaze he misses more than his former “I could give a fuck about anyone” self... After meeting the reflection of a frightened boy instead, a shiny object in the adjacent window silently yells for his attention; scared like a boy who’d seen a monster, Tyler turns to a nearly full moon staring back as bright as the sun;

Tyler: “What are YOUUUU lookin at???” (#bitch)

Premeditating the future sex, Noel strategically lays on the couch with her back to the arm rest, right leg flat and left knee bent shooting her best "mmmm I wanna fuck you" Maxim cover girl look. Recalling moves of his former self, Tyler interlocks their arms at the elbows an'intimately drinks as if celebrating their 25th wedding anniversary (#classy) with drinks that are strong enough t'drunken but not too strong t'sip #notclassy ...Fantasy's of ripping shirts open to lunge atop in the "easy access" mini skirt flash in one mind while the other's unable to press "Live TV" as earlier DVR'd scenes of his poser bride's rejection play on a continuous loop; most would never wanna know the images that fill your lover's mind mid kiss... Fill, fill on...

The whirlwind of sex can be the beauty and the beast: one couldn't pick their session out of a sex lineup at the police station while the other'll be fantasizing an'masterbating with vibrating objects in future nights ahead... Fantastically moaning, Noel eagerly wishes t'gaze into the closed doorways of the body arising inside her; the body that sent her an'bent her in two t'joyfully writhe in agonies pleasure with no measure of time spent; hopelessly wishing it'll never end, mind repeatedly rewinding again an'again to relive moments with whom she pretends love to be true... The one she weeps for an'boldly allows arms tattoo'd with another to collapse down upon; internally knowing he's actually elsewhere all along...

Laying motionless on her back in bed, Noel savors the dance of what denial's hidden as'er only romance; allowing shaking legs to convulse an'feel no remorse since he loved her as sex SURELY shows; an'though he does not throw any words of "love making" nor thoughts of heart's beating FOR her to feel mid moan, Noel basks in the everlasting sensations shooting through'er as he masters an'breaks her body to puddles of quickly evaporating passion on the ground... An'while HE desires to dive down another, she remains hopefully wishing to rewind time an'never fast forward...

Having dirtied his soul, Tyler must wash away betrayed sweat falsely conveyed in darkened rooms before blindly searching for sparks he never knew he'd left behind... so valiantly trying to wash away his self sins before bottled potions awaken a loss divine...

SMS: Liliana > Julian

Love of my life!!! Where are you!!! Are you ok??? What happen!!! Please answer me!!!!!!!

SMS: Julian > Liliana

I'm here

SMS: Julian > Liliana

Sleeping

SMS: Julian > Liliana

Not ok

SMS: Julian > Liliana

I'll text soon. I love you don't worry...

SMS: Liliana > Julian

Ok baby...

SMS: Liliana > Julian

I'm sorry...

SMS: Liliana > Julian

Text me later!!! I love you too!!

(no response)

Act 6: Scene 2: "Come on now; Don't say you haven't done it before..."

Tyler: (walkin out of the bathroom) “I’m gonna take a shower”

Noel: (on her knees gleefully wearing only an “after sex glow” smile) “Oh nice! WE’RE gonna take a shower?”

Tyler: (grabs a towel from the closet) “I’MMM takin a shower”

Deflated and fallen backwards, Noel’s body and mind frantically search for the “after sex glow” he’d just stolen... From unable to breathe exhilaration to a used tampon, Noel’s tearily clouded eyes haplessly dart around the foolish room she swore to be painted the color love #mindswillrace ...Becoming a robber in the night, Noel creeps to the bathroom to regain the “piece of mind” Caitlyn stole earlier; praying Tyler hadn’t changed the passcode denying access to the holy grail of truth which typically DOES result in death after drinking: the cellphone of the person you just slept with #indianajones #damnyouandyourhat

Though one could easily delete texts and calls knowing YOU were coming over, passcodes give people a false sense of security against attempts of breaking into your life’s bible... And since snooping an’hacking loves company, Noel texts the sister she desperately hopes to prove wrong...

SMS: Noel > Caitlyn

Sigh... Thanks to you and your LIESSSS I’m about to go through his phone! : (

(on high)

Santana: "Soooooooo, was that gunna beeeeeee... one shot or twoooo?" (#drunk)

Caitlyn: (head tilt down) "You already KNOW the answer!"

Santana: (drunkenly stumbles over to her) "I shureee doooo!!! (hugs up on her an'grabs'er ass) Thassss my girl!" (#noshesnot #falseadvertising)

Caitlyn: "You fuckin know it!"

Santana: (pours two double shots) "WellOk Lets doooo these shots then hittt the parrrrrrr-(Ding Dinggg!)-tyyy (points to her purse) Hey heyyyyy, Bitch! Don't you be cuttin MEEEE off wit chur alarms!!! Chu wanna fight???"

Caitlyn: "Relax baby it's just my sister, her text ring is glass"

Santana: (looks at his shot glass quickly an'back at her slowly) "Whyyyyy Yes!!! (takes shot an'holds it up to his eye) It ISSSS glass! Thanks for noticing... hashtaaaag, we keep it classy here mon amie"

Drunkenly staring into her eyes, Santana delicately kisses Caitlyn's hand before flinging'er back towards him an'wrapping his arms around her waist.

SMS: Noel > Caitlyn
Sigh... Thanks to you and your LIESSSS I'm about to go through his phone! : (

Santana: "Liessss? Whose lied? Did YOU lie???" (poking her ab laced stomach twice)

Caitlyn: "No no hold on! Let me see what happen" (slams her shot)

Santana: "Hold ONNN? (stares down at her black yoga pants "table" ass an'firmly grabs it with both hands) Oooooookkkkkk!!! I'm holding onnnn!!!"

Caitlyn: (rolls eyes) "Ohhhh geeezzee" (#thasaboutright)

SMS: Caitlyn > Noel
Wellll???
SMS: Caitlyn > Noel
What did you find out? lol
SMS: Caitlyn > Noel
Me and MYYYY guy wanna know! ;)

Santana: "Wait... (lets go of her) Wait, she wit that asshole Tyler again???"

Caitlyn: (turns around towards him) "Now don't get mad Sanny... but yes, yes she is"

Santana: "Mannnnnnn... Fuckkkkkkkk him; (throwing motion) he straight sucks...."

Caitlyn: "Suck or not, she is-" (Ding Dinggg!)

Santana: "WELL????? Whatdidhesay???"

Caitlyn: (puts open hand on his chest) "Hold on, Let me seeeee" (moves away)

SMS: Noel > Caitlyn

> OMFG!!!!!! He's totally still in love with her!!! OH MY GODDDD!!!

Caitlyn: (eyes grow wide joining Noel in the same OMG expression)

Santana: "What????? What happen?????" (moves to look)

Caitlyn: "Na uhhhh!!!" (brings phone to her chest; Ding Dinggg!)

Santana: "Oh comeeeee onnnnn! (throws hands down) We botttth KNOWWWZZ you're gonna tell meeee, (Ding Dinggg!) once I..." (points towards her ______ an'circles his finger up to her now smiling face)

Caitlyn: "Mmmm... Got me a little wet there..." (moves closer)

Santana: "Come on wit it you sexy bitch!" (smile disappears recalling another he called the same)

Caitlyn: "OK!!! (backs that ass up #juvenile) ummm; put your arms around me, Hellllooo!" (Ding Dinggg!)

SMS: Noel > Caitlyn

HE'S TOTALLY STILL IN LOVE WITH HIS EX AND MADE UP THIS WHOLE FUCKED UP PLAN TO GET BACK WITH HER!!!!!!

SMS: Noel > Caitlyn

THE FUCKIN ASSHOLE DOESN'T GIVE A FUCK ABOUT ME AT ALL IM HAVIN A PANIC ATTACK!!! I CANT BREATHE!!!

SMS: Noel > Caitlyn

EARLIER TODAY HE CONFESSED HIS LOVE TO HER AND TRIED TO WIN HER BACK

SMS: Caitlyn > Noel

Calm down sis!!!

SMS: Noel > Caitlyn

AND HE FUCKIN RECORDED THEIR CONVERSATION????? WHO DOES THAT?????

SMS: Noel > Caitlyn

THEN HES GONNA EDIT THE RECORDING AND PLAY IT FOR THE BOYFRIEND TO BREAK THEM UPPPP!!!! HOW FUCKIN HORRIBLE IS THAT!!!! MY ANXIETY'S OUT OF CONTROL I HAVE TO GET OUT OF HERE I NEED YOU!!! IDK WHAT TO DO!!!!

Like being pulled over by a cop, the stoic Santana stumbles three steps backwards and falls onto his bed as the world spins for more reasons than just alcohol... Unfit to compute lines of texts flashing through drunken minds, Santana's eyes jump around the room trying to erase himself from the world... With the new transfer of power, Santana could reverse what will murder the man he vowed on deathbeds to protect; formidable allies of resentment an'jealousy stand guard against the onslaught of loyalty's prose he bestowed upon caskets to parents gone; promising to block the moons beams from bleeding int'Julian's realms; leaving only himself an'another's hopes t'die before giving dreams a chance to fail...

If Santana doesn't jump into the present discussion, the repercussions'll throw younger brother to despair with no ability to repair what lack of action's caused; no amounts of gauze could cure diseases Julian'll inherit from such gods as none could be forgiven for allowing such truths to remain so hidden... The latter having never knew the former could've prevented the grounding of prince's throne from ironically falling like the king's too.

Act 6: Scene 3:
"This ain't the valley... Bitch."

(heights mansion; 35 min earlier; the main room as "Living Legends - Flawless" plays)

There's no wine yet there's Cristal. There's no Stella Sierra Nevada or Fat Tire, but there ISSSS Modelo Especial an'Mickey's. Grey goose? There's some; but only for the laaaaaaddddiiiies #hollaatme ...And at every bar, table, kitchen, freezer an'night stand there's Hennessy. Sailor Jerrrrrryyyyyyy is floatin round here somewhere; tattoos are a near necessity an'every car that arrives is certainly NOT a LEX BENZ or higher #suckitvalley

Even in the heart of Los Altos, the socioeconomic rules do not apply to the mansion on the hill; built by hustle an'sponsored by "keepin it one hundred..."

Q: "Yezzzirrrr; I mean, we all go wayyy back: we got King Santana, (looks around the main room) my fuckin DAWG is Somewhere in this Bitch! Young prince Julian; (looks around) well shit, (laughing) he's MIA too but my boy Bastion's right there, (raises beer) wit young Stephan next to'em (currently staring at random thick girl 5's massive cleavage on the couch) ...but yea... THAT'S the crew; (leans in) We fuckin own this town; hashtag dontfuckwitus"

Random girl 78: "Oh for real? (starry eyed) Sooooooooo where's this dance floor I heard about?"

Q: "Oh girl! (checks out her thick as fuck legs while throwing his arm around her neck) The floor will get goin-whassup dog (head nod to a random homie)-when it gets goin; THEN we'll have t'see whassup" (flashin the "ohhhh we fuckin t'night" smile)

Planning to "test" him by randomly showing up later in the night, Kristin leads Q to believe she would be a "no show" at the party #notfair #yourenotexclusive

Stemming from insecurities an'lack of confidence in one's ability to fully captivate another, most "testing" revolves around pushing someone away to see if they'll eventually leave #ourgreatestfear ...Clouded by delusions of desiring happiness, many actually WANT to perpetuate their own misery by proving they're not worthy of love nor good enough to be with someone who "has their shit together"... And it's THESE popular self defeating mentalities that catalyze vicious cycles of landing and pushing away the WRONG mate resulting in a more broken you... but isn't that just what you subconsciously wanted in the first place? Break break on...

(Julian's old room)

SMS: Liliana > Julian (unread 40 min earlier)
Well I hope you're feeling better! I miss you!

SMS: Liliana > Julian (unread 15 min earlier)
I'm getting worried!!! Are you ok???

SMS: Liliana > Julian (unread 10 min earlier)
Sigh... I just wanna hear from you!!! Hear your voice... see you smile... taste your lips and feel your hands on me...

SMS: Liliana > Julian (unread 10 min earlier)
Mmmmm... Great, now I'm gettin all revved up!!! Damn you!!! ;)
SMS: Liliana > Julian (unread 1 min earlier)
HELLLOOOOOOO!!!! WHERE ARE YOU????

SMS: Julian > Liliana
I'm broken... My only family's been splintered into pieces and'll never regain its form since the mercury's forgotten how to pool back together... In the midst of wars our love bore I've fallen from clouds to grounds unforgiving... There exists only one desired sight left in the night's young skies resting in two stars within each of your two eyes; my family's left me and I am no longer certain if I shine in the moon or sun's rise

SMS: Liliana > Julian
Please... From time to time even the BLIND will see the light in all it's white splendor yet'll never surrender with no comparison as to what they see... The world WILL turn again so please please wait!!! Your brother will be patient before acting against blood; for although water turns to wine, blood's thicker by design...

SMS: Julian > Liliana
How can you blend true with the dream? The real with what seems and sew it all back together? I cannot imagine a phone without your face flashing an'no good morning text how you romantically fashion

SMS: Liliana > Julian

Julian...

SMS: Liliana > Julian

The kismet of our chemistry travels through wavelengths without need for electricity... For our love's mosaic design stretches far beyond moon's beams in all it's exclusivity...

SMS: Liliana > Julian

Now Please!!! When can I see your smiles glisten? For my eyes'll listen and usurp all your pain!!! #INEEDYOU

Bastion: (slow yell with random girl 8 wrapped around his waist) "JULIAAAANNN!!! GettheFUUUUUCK out here my dude!!! Stop sitting in the dark textin the new girl, your favorite songs about t'come on son... Youngbloooooodzzzzzzzz..."

Julian: "Uhhhhhhh!!! (strolls up to Bastion with right hand out: CLAP!) YESSSSSS! Lets CRACK this Bitch!!!"

SMS: Julian > Liliana

Darlin, you'll be ok... I can only last so long with neither your skin to take in nor your smell to rake in lies I've lived away from your vision

SMS: Julian > Liliana

I have to try and right what I've wronged but you've already made me feel so much better!!! I can't wait to see you!!! Just be patient, cuz I'm comin to you #youngbloodz

("Youngbloodz - 85 feat. Jim Crow & Big Boi" starts)

Julian: (bouncing out into the main room) "I know you're waitin for daddy, it won't be long shawty be patient cuz I'm comin to you... Ridin dirty on 85; slow, takin it easy I don't want nothin to keep me from you... (2x)"

Having just had random girl 78 "take care of him," the chorus triggers Q t'jump up, buckle his pants an'stroll out into the main room rapping the first verse wit 78 in tow;

Quincy: "......Run the game like she ain't ready But still indeeed, she on her knees, keepin thangs steady like Betty Crocker, the face doctor; (looks back) just as she swallows with passion; So now she braggin laggin behind What questions she now be askin... so time is passin (turns to her) Now I'm mashin on, I'm gone, livin in the world of hoes; So I suppose (shrugs an'clasps Julian before turning back t'78) ain't nothin but hard times now shawty pleassee reallaayy..." (Julian takes over the chorus)

Never seeing eye to pimp eye, Julian couldn't comprehend Q's right of "player" passage in using woman an'treatin'em like shit... Was it Q's lack of self worth or past trauma that leads him to try an'fill the void by seeking validation from woman through sex??? ORRRR was Q just another asshole tryin to sleep wit a girl as quickly as possible to blow up his stats and climb the rungs of the MLP (Major League of Players) from single A all the way up into the big leagues???

Whatever the case, thanks to the whole woman's empowerment movement an'new school mentalities; (#iwokeuplikethis) there's been enough sponsors an'interest to form the WMLP allowing WOMAN "players" everywhere to rise up their own ranks #doublestandard #notreally ...In the WMLP, woman prove they TOO can unemotionally "fuck" like men without any attachment or feelings involved; however the "Samantha lifestyle" consisting of endless parades of revolving door men typically cause damage therapy could only Wish t'soothe #orsmithJared #goodluckfindin #thatguy ;)

According to "science" (#whathefuckdotheyknow) normal humans use 10 percent of their brains... Yet men who understand that the most valued and SHOULD be sought after woman on earth ARE the "Sluts" and "Samanthas" of the world use far more than 10 percent; and in doing so they expand their minds beyond the limits of society's norms which lead the masses to forever condemn "sluts" due to their "dick filled" pasts... Though there are ALWAYS exceptions, the sexually freed woman is sexually freed for good reason: being so independent, strong and in touch with themselves allowed these woman to take control of their sexual lives like Amy did in... "Chasing Amy"... During her "crazy days," Amy was NOT "used" and instead USED THE GUYS she interacted with as Silent Bob reiterates: "it was that time and it was that place and she doesn't think she should apologize because she doesn't feel that she's done anything wrong".

Although a majority of guys will only "fuck" girls in this category, MOST of these amazing woman have depths few can deny an'typically carry an undeniable spark that draws men in which allllll woman WISH they had #jealousmuch ...And since women in this label have "tasted the rainbow," there's a much higher probability of these fantastical woman knowing who they are, what they want, an'more importantly WHO they want in life... Besides, who wants a girl that sees the world in black and white anyways? #tastetherainbowbitch #skittles

Similar to women, some men Also sleep around in order to try an'fill their own void of self worth/ confidence with the sexual validation of others #wrongwaytocurebtw ...Yet sometimes the biggest pimps in the world are just intelligent wounded boys who stockpile woman's love as place holders for loving themselves... An'even though there are men with cruel blackened souls who enjoy the chase an'have no disregard for the feelings or emotions crushed in the process, (#perry) many in this category have their own seed like horror stories from turbulent upbringings which root their actions an'behaviors; possibly having also grown up with womanizing role models or a revolving door of woman comin in an'out of their lives leading "junior" to naturally mimic what they see... mimic, mimic on...

(Santana comes in; No, Santana RUNS in Yelling ;)

Santana: "What the FAaaaaCK IS GOIN ON PEOPLES!!!! WHERE THE FUCK'S DAAAA DANCIN ATTTT??? HEY DDD JAYYY (motions all to follow) HIT ME WIT THAT PURSUIT ONEEEEEEE TIMMMMMMMEEEEEEEE!!!"

With the flanger an'echo effect on, The DJ stutter edits the "you" at the end of the Youngbloodz chorus an'spins the CDJ backwards till perfectly scratching and dropping: "Kid Cudi - Pursuit of Happiness (Extended Steve Aoki Remix feat. MGMT & Ratatat)"

Santana: (leading the party to the 2 foot drop off onto the dance floor) "..........I'm a do just what I want, lookin at it no turnin back; People told me to slow my roll, I'm screamin out fuck that; I'm screamin out fuck that; I'm screamin out fuck that, fuck that, fuck that, fuck that (jumps down) fuck that..."

Landing onto the dance floor right on the last "fuck that," Santana starts pop locking until breaking out into his hard core version of the housing two step when the beat kicks in #alljumpdown ...Having read such texts on technology's screens, Santana needs to cut loose and return to some sense of normalcy; running over to the bar at the corner of the dance floor 3 beats before the next verse begins, Santana casually leans against counters as if he didn't just wild'out and leave a bustling dance floor in his wake.

Santana: (calmly rappin along) "Tell me what you know about dreamin' dreamin'. You don't really know about nothin' nothin'. Tell me what you know about them night terrors every night, 5 AM, cold sweats, wakin' up to the sky-"

Act 6: Scene 4: 4 AM

(the heights; Santana's bedroom; headphones;
"Pierce The Veil - Kissing in Cars")

Laying awake at 4 am, the empty vessel next door cedes no fears an'allays no sadness pouring forth. Staring into nothing and darkness my body relates, so unable to shake haunting realities following each second that I wake. (your face is the first thing I see) Asleep, you're consistently out of reach on that beach awaiting in such sand; every time I dream you fall like beads through shakeless hands; I can't let go of what I felt (she was always the one) as minds melt to puddles of sadness roaming open seas, endlessly searching for the restart yet she won't depart world's so closely held... May she feel my love pierce hardened veils when currents wash upon'er again; valiantly attempting to fend off an'pretend she's content with basking in shallow depths she cannot drown, how can she not feel ocean's tides weigh heavy down on love struck minds? Please let love's bounce of my heart guide her to deepened caverns to find me dancing to faithful beats of'er spark's rejuvenated return. (there's faith in love)

Living in hopeless cities I've seen lights flood chasms surrounded; the world's endless prisms of sun's majestic enclouded an'captured by moon's bitter reflection for only so long can she break off my direction till she can no longer run from… I feel her coming closer to ends of floor's wishing to fall in but stands stuck between walls dreaming of what was and could be again. (second chances wont leave you alone) I cannot let water freely run down cheeks as ocean's splashes briefly grace a love I chase since none else could compare… the saddening stare of mirrors gazing back at my self won't cease till she finds our world still waiting on that shelf; please let hope's gravity bring'er back to soul's ground; I'm ready for the rapture of'er eyes to cast me down and save me from myself… (the last I'll ever need)

Act 6: Scene 5: 5 AM

"Tell me what you know about them night terrors every night, 5 AM, cold sweats, wakin' up to the sky-"

(the valley; Jasmine's bedroom; headphones;
"The Neighbourhood - Staying up")

Toss and turn, I've got time to burn before another sad day without any pleasure blended for none compare to what he brought in a single bounce... There are no dreams left to dream and no world's left to lean as there is only black and dark weighing upon eyes collapsed; I wish to depart islands but sadness' sharks roam an'disallows dreams to relay minds a slumber; I await, but sandman won't call my fuckin number. (how can I sleep) I try to jump into a memory but the worse encompasses me an'blasts me to my roots, no longer allowing love t'shoot down aching legs; no warmth to bless once innocent soft skin since the moon's been cast over with all sun's rays swept deep within. (How can it be?) I have no answers to why I cannot dream; to why nightmares pass through psyche's gates unfazed, so very troubled by the malaise of horrors none can romance; none can bring forth deepened sun lit rays as forgotten were ancient spells to break darkened moonlit days (part of me feels a little bit empty) ...I ask the world of gloom to please forgive me for my sins, outlast the moon's winds that drop down from faces so thinned; (how can I sleep) I try to weep but tears cannot fall, (I don't have dreams) I try to close my eyes but (I just have nightmares) ...I see the world's we once lived pass by; no potion will enable me t'sink down to soul's floor, never to return to where I my self should be (I still believe something is out there)

Santana: “Ill be lost until you come and find me here”

Jasmine: “Still there are darkened places deep in my heart”

Santana: “You will find me dancing all alone”

Jasmine: “I am nothing but a shadow in the night”

Santana: “So if you let me I will catch fire”

Jasmine: "Like the moon we borrow our light"

Santana: "I'll be loss until..."

Act 7: Scene 1: "Please keep chasing me......

Sleepless nights replicate since repetitions of misery no longer comfort cold wakes... Nightmares fixate Jasmine's mind in disarray; the path she's chosen'as lead to thy morning, this day. Sitting up and once again unable to stare at mirror's walls, Jasmine wishes to feel his warmth; yet bereft of sun's disintegrated wings to fly back, she's alone on grey barren moon drenched discs. (please keep chasing me) Faithful he still remains down beneath, there's faith his love flounders on shelves of glorious (southern constellation's) reefs... Stepping out of nightmarish beds, (so dizzy) Jasmine falls to floors not dreamt; flaunting wooden slabs laugh and bathe in sorrow's lament worrying Jasmine that he'll grow cold before morrows wash over life's balconies into the deep; for without sleep her mind wanders, jumps off perches and slovenly saunters into waters sealed. (it's cold) Awaking an'rolling over to meet unrelenting ceiling's blank stares, Jasmine begs to have the feelings his touches brought along with the rushes of waters splashed by waves his clutches sent... She mustn't worry her cold winter's kiss has worn down his throes... for please know... (I'll never let you freeze without me)

ACT 7: SCENE 2:
"I LOVE YOU MORE THAN ME..."

Envisioning beauty within sleeping eyes next to him, Julian's floored mind throws an exaggerated smile upon his face... Checking the time;

SMS: Liliana > Julian

QOD: "Falling in love is like jumping off a really tall building: your brain tells you it's not a good idea, but your heart tells you you can fly"

SMS: Liliana > Julian

I love you!!!! You're sleeping right next to me but I had to tell you in dreams ;)

In his mind, Julian pictures himself carefully place phones on nightstands to climb under the comforter and delicately kiss'er uncovered shoulder; she'd open her eyes to happily cast love's dream down passion's slide while dazedly pulling him towards her body now as one. Yet setting aside his own needs, Julian allows'er to peacefully sleep; admiring her angelic hidden beauty after an emotionally draining week... Laying back down, Julian smiles at bliss drenched ceilings to unknowingly enjoy the calm before the storm... For soon he'll be at the behest of current wheels in motion an'loss to deviants stirring moon's facade like potions in cauldrons ticking... ticking... an'sinking closer to testing durability of life's fabric on those with no defense to such onslaughts; so unaware of the emotions stare about t'break worlds thought to be so vastly strong... carrying designs to obliterate the song tattered souls have finally learnt to sing...... and sing on...

Act 7: Scene 3: "You... You read it wrong, that's NOT me"

According to Eddie Murphy's "Raw," a few hours after catching her "man" walking out of another woman's house...

Girl: “What the hell was you doin in that bitches house today?”

Bae: “wasn’t me”

Girl: “I looked right in yo face”

Bae: “...wasn’t me”

Girl: “Well I supposed t’be a fool right-”

Bae: “-Hey......... wasn’t me”

Girl: “........maybe it wasn’t you...”

And how is this possible? According to Murphy, it must be rare for a woman to find a man who can fuck her world up an’leave her laying on the bed with legs involuntarily convulsing an’frozenly shaking, “Cuz when y’all find one, y’all stick through that man through all kinds of bullshit”.

Yet, somehow EVVVVVERY frickin guy claims to be “god’s gift to woman” an’equipped with a porno sized... well yea... Yet if soooo many woman are having issues orgasming an’are unhappy with the size/motion of the ocean, how can every guy on earth please a woman like guys do in the movies??? #quitplayin #quitlyin & #takeadanceclassbrah...

In the big scheme called life, guys DO have it much easier than woman in many aspects... BUT woman get it allllll back in the bedroom as they'll go from 1st gear t'2nd, 3rd, 2nd, 3rd, 4th, 5th, 4th 4.5th, 4th, 3rd, 4th, 5th and eventually climax in 6th; while GUYS quadruple shift from 1st to 4th (#yesonly4th : (and even then there's NO revving down #cliffjump ...An'although there's tantra or other internal mechanisms like orgasming without cumming, (#britishguyfromgo) men's sexual climaxes are generally short lived at best #greatfuckinmoviebtw

Built differently than men, woman rarely base relationships purely on sexual chemistry and may settle for "ehhhh" sex if the new "bae" has other gleaming qualities #andcanbetaught ;) ...Sometimes a woman's been soooo fucked over by guys who WERE "heart pounding body shaking" lovers that they'll gladly embrace a guy who cannot "rock their world" if they'll stay faithful an'treat'em how allllll woman SHOULD be treated #likefuckinqueens #likesantanatohisjasmine

An'all those woman who claim they DON'T need the "I want chu t'fuck me harrrrd" sex an'passion more often than not have simply never been FUCKED right... Or maybe they keep that one table in their heart reserved OR sadly someone stole that ability from them along the way; Yet this explains why woman'll inexplicably sift through the garbage an'boredom of a "6th gear" guy till someone better comes along... Conversely as the hunters and beggars of society, guys are far less complicated an'will typically "chomp" on whatever comes their way: the longer its been, the lower the standards... Lower, lower on...

Having just slept with a man whose head over another, last night Noel told Caitlyn she would leave while Tyler was in the shower...... However woman don't walk this way #aerosmith ...When a woman finds a guy's mistakes sitting on their red hands, they Must; Have to tell'em they fucked up while secretly hoping they'll care to try an'right the ship; for even if she would never reconcile, she still wants to be "wanted"... Cuz after all, no matter the situation or one's future intentions, in the end EVERYONE still WANTS to be wanted... And though people are NOT objects, the supply and demand of a person works in a similar capacity: if you flood the market with "you," your demand will bottom out... yet if you become a rare commodity and put less of yourself out there, your demand may go thru the fuckin roof!!!! #theroof #theroof #theroofisonfire #wedontneedno...

And thus, although her sister demanded she leave, Noel sat on the bed waiting to confront Tyler with the texts she'd found on his phone... Maybe Tyler was the first lover to really "rock her world" or maybe Noel actually "loves the fuck out of him" ;)

(last night; Tyler walks out of the bathroom drying off)

Noel: "Have a good shower Tyler?"

Facing the dresser and pulling out a pair of boxer briefs, Tyler's body freezes; somewhat sobered by guilty showers, he realizes this is the first time she's ever said his full name instead of Ty Ty or Ty...

Tyler: (turns around) “Well Hello Darling!”

Noel: (mind stutters) “...welll... did-you have, a good shower? (hands on hips #dreadfulsign)

Tyler: (walking towards her smiling) “I had a Great fuckin shower; I couldn’t stop thinkin about us the whole time!”

Her emotions evoked by reading such texts mirror his in the shower: Noel felt betrayed by Tyler while Tyler felt betrayed by himself since they’d “made love” when it was anything but... Not understanding Tyler’s heinous head games;

Noel: “I... (beginning to well up) I, can-not...... believe (looks down trembling) You-” (throws unlocked phone on the bed an’runs out)

Standing over his empty room and smiling a full teethed grin, Tyler laughingly congratulates himself for dodging the sobbing lecture of this “random girl” who completely fell off his radar the second he came... Reaching for his phone, Tyler sees a smiling pony tailed Liliana sitting against the headboard in black boy shorts an’a grey skin tight T with no bra STILL looking like a woman any man would gladly wife in a flash... Yet faces soon frown down when laughter dries up to surround him with a desolate wasteland of emotions in it’s place. For like a passerby on the street, the image of Liliana’s quickly erased as Tyler finally understands what a mistake sex can be; left staring at phone’s potions, so lost in hoping the moon’s oceans can bring’er back to thee...

Act 7: Scene 4: Anything Can Happen

Invoked by whispered currents last night, Santana is ready to do the unthinkable today. Lame husbands would no longer keep him from his prize for there's no worse demise than what currently sits in hardened bloodshot eyes; dream whispers gave him what'e needed, leaving ears bleeding from words thrown at high gain volumes in hanging heart colored rugs in the sun's light... And since he'd finally found her peacefully lying amidst last nights stumbling, depression's no longer rumbling as he's ready to state his case in shallow waters unknown; having truly bled for this moment in aching for the queen's return to empty thrones...

Santana: (walking out to Q's wake an'bake) "Yo yooo"

Q: "What uppppp... (smirking) What happen t'YOUUU last night?"

Santana: (stops mid stride an'closes his eyes) "...Fuck... (opens an'turns) Wha'did I do?"

Q: (leaning in all serious for 3 seconds till erupting) "...you were a Fuckin RIOTTTT!!!@@@" (leaning back in his chair puffin on a cone joint)

Santana: (shaking head) "This frickin guy... But check it; TODAY'S THE DAYYYYYY!!!!" (arms out wide)

Q: (sits up) "Whoaaaaaa; Whats with you dude??? It's like... 1:20 or somethin; how are you so hyper this early in the AM"

Santana: (laughs) "You meannnn PM???"

Q: (dismissively sitting back) "Whatever dude" (inhales)

Santana: "Today's the day!!! ...A day; that will live; in infamy"

Q: (rips joint out) "Duuude... Roosevelt??? This early???"

Santana: "The sun's already past it's highest point! It's all down hill from here!"

Q: "Annnnnnddd..."

Santana: "Annnndd I got Just the answer" (runs to the computer, clicks the mouse twice, types a few words an'slams the space bar flooding the room with "Ellie Goulding - Anything Can Happen")

Q: (sits down rolling his eyes) "Not THIS fuckin song" (sigh; puff puff)

Drunkenly swaying his head back and forth, Santana hops around the room singin along to the first verse and occasionally closing his eyes to picture Jasmine walking out of the gym where he used to kiss her goodbye an'hello...

Santana: (pours an'slams a shot of Jasmine's fav alcohol #goose) "Today's the DAAAYYY BIIIIITCHHHH!!! (pours a second) I'mmmm gonna get my girl back..."

Q: (cliché'd coughing voice) "WHAT???... No! (stands up) Noooo San, you can't be-"

Santana: "-I what? What was that?" (pumps up the volume an'slams his second shot before pop locking to the chorus)

Santana: "After the war; we said we'd figgght together"

Q: (turns music down) "SOOOOO after years of not talkin, you're just gonna go up to her and sayyyyyyyyy what exactly????"

Santana: (presses pause) "Whoa whoa whoa whoa whoa! Hold Up-"

(Last night abouttttt 11:31 pm)

SMS: Kristin > Q

Hey have you ever heard of this indie band from the UK called The 1975???? #yestheirnameis #the1975

SMS: Kristin > Q

Well my friend showed me this one song called "She Way Out" and it totally reminds me of you every time I hear it!!! ;) #stuckonrepeat

(12:05 am)

SMS: Q > Kristin
Naaaaaa... But I'll check it outtttttt!!! :)

(Abouttttt 12:47 am; heights mansion)

While drunken idiots and jealous ratchets stare on to the glamorous Kristin fancily whisking by in search of Q, this "goal of a woman" spots Stephan on the couch smoking with some randoms in the main room;

Kristin: "Heyyyy Stephaaann... (he slowly turns back) Where's Q at?" (buzzed smiling)

Stephan: "Heeeeeyyyyyy Kristiiiiiinnnnnn!!!@@@ (stands up completely blasted an'reaching for an awkward hug over the couch) Q will be sooooo happy you made it!!!" (overly smiling)

Kristin: (weirded out) "Cool... soooooooo, where is he?"

Stephan: (blankly stares for 5 seconds) "......Oh HEEEE'S in HIIIIIIISSSSSS room... (turns back to the homies) yea, HEEEE gets a room, (Kristin leaves) but IIIIII have to always sleep in couch heaven or in one of the guest rooms (sighs) ...you would thinnnkkk; THINKKKK I'd get my own room by now, but (turns to Kristin) Nooooooo-"

Random stoner 5: "-Yea, uhhhhh... she left dude..."

Stephan: (sits down) “Damn... she left, heeeeeeeellllllllla fast..... oh shit... I wonder if he’s still with that one chick......” (stunned eyes grow wide; everyone laughs)

Stephan: “Ooppssss, damn... (looks back towards Q’s room) ......maybe I DOOOOOO smoke too much weed” (turns back with head down)

Random stoner 6 on the couch: (pushes Stephan) “NAAAAAAAAA, get the Fuck outta towwwwwwn BITCH!” (laughter rules the scene)

Stephan: “HAHAHAHA!!!! Heyyyyyyy, where’d my joint go??? (spots it in the circle) Pass it back over here dude!!! I barely hit that shit!!!” (#ohhhhstephan)

Heading towards Q’s “room” on the other side of the world, Kristin passes by a 12 pack of pacifico, (Q’s favorite beer) an’grabs two for the road #illtake #13roadbeerstogoplease

With the random dance music fading as she moves into the heart of the mansion, the flowing guitars of “She Way Out” (by) “The 1975” begin rapping on her buzzed ears. Stopping for a second to confirm, Kristin’s floored and beyond excited that not only did Q check out the song but is currently playing it #nofuckinway Knocking her head back an’forth to the infectious beat, for the first time Kristin starts to see a future with Q and not just the gifted present of dating the coolest fuckin guy on the planet...

With guitars painting a pretty picture and soft vocals filling in the color, Kristin sees Q pulling up to'er house t'pick HER up beaming swag you can't buy #twofingers ...Looking away as if smiles would give away his true self, Quincy strolls up the stairs t'swoop his girl down for a "hollywood kiss" from which Kristin would never come back up. She'd finally broken out of her continual loop of lame professional 6 figured demons wishing to hold her at home t'have children an'slowly bleed out from continual boredom... But with Quincy, even menial trips t'gas stations would need a platoon of laughs to accompany for who knows where the fuck they'd go next; maybe Q would whisk her to rest under shady trees in the park, or possibly dance on top of middle school roofs in the dark with only a cell phone's blasting beat t'cut the silence of empty streets... There's no rhyme nor fuckin trail to follow with such a wild card like Quincy to hold each day an'every morrow; living in far off planes at random high altitudes holding unique reigns over worlds most never see... For in sifting through the chaos and bullshit, Q could dive through 3 football fields of shit to stand in the rain embracing any radical change which would normally swerve any joe off course in fully fuckin their poor little brains...

No; He be the prized horse an'celebrity main course to any woman's meal; for only after befriending such a ghetto fabulous high class did he not rise to the tops of caste systems nor use his gifted rhythm an'silver tongue to wrangle the world with each laugh and curl his looks elicit from the hearts of each an'every girl...

Waking up at whatever time they did, Q would certainly reach over or already have a hand a'top HIS beautiful body which she'd given to him, confirming she'd never again feel unloved or beautifully thin... For as a retired all star of the "MLP," a Mrrrrr. Quincy thrived in bedrooms by bringing glory to any somber day; so very capable of wrangling Kristin's inner slut out to play of which she'd always hid so far down an'deep away; always so effing afraid to break out of her own "womanly" type... But with a tyke like Q loving'er after each an'every meal??? Fuck, she could let the ravaging go an'steal any savage moves ever thrown; releasing any an'all moans when his lips rove HIS home with the ability to make her shiver when alone by just THINKING of'is electric touch...

And blissfully she walks until a girlish laugh interrupts the guitars an'covers future stars followed by a voice she knew all too well, but apparently not nearly as well as she thought... Clenching muscles an'stomach aching stares shoot round; with worlds upside down Kristin's caught between walls nearly at doors to bittersweet symphony's rooms... An'for five seconds.... ten..... fifthteen or even a minute long, Kristin stands gazing with'er ears, hearing fears elude an'come true as drunken babbling an'giggling bleeds through walls to ears now stabbed through... The song starts over inviting renewed dread; and though she barely loved the track, hate grows instead as the 1975's can't soothe her cries an'silent tears as stoic gears shift from happy passages to another's betrayed laughing along HER once future route...

Turning to leave, the two beers held against crossed sleeves freeze an'drive her t'knock on doors as she can't leave without guilting HIS sleeves an'truly try t'bring him down to HIS knees for such deceit an'lies she'd swallowed here tonight...

(Knock Knock)

(inside:

Q: "Leave it; who cares"
Random girl 87: "No, I'll get it!"
Q: "Jussss forget it-"
Random girl 87: "-Nope!")

(door opens)

Random girl 87: (topless, wearin a hideous beaming smile an'a thong) "Hello!!!! Welcome to Q's room!!!! How may we help you?"

Kristin: (frozen; doesn't see Q)

Random girl 87: "Ohhhh were you delivering beers to everyone??? Awwww honey! That's TOO sweet (takes beers) ...Hey, (head tilt) have you ever heard of this band called The 1975? I know I know, the name's kindaaaaaaa-whatever, but this song kinda kicks ass; (turning her head) HUH BABE???"

Q: "What? (swings up from laying on the bed) Who the fuc-(spots Kristin)-issss........"

Random girl 87: "Oh I'm SOOOO sorry girl, What's your name? I'm-"

Kristin: “-jus leavin” (jets)

Random girl 87: “Well OOOK! Uh, thanks for the beers!!! (door closes in many ways) ...well she seemed-” (SLAM)

And people HATE putting “labels” on relationships...

Hate, hate on...

Santana (continues): “-Is Mr. ‘I-fucked-up-the-only-relationship-I-cared-about-for-random-girl-87-whose-not-even-a-solid-8’ tryin to give MEEEEEEE relationship advice?” (presses play)

Q: “Fuck... you serious? I KNEW I saw’er last night... (sits down) didn’t know she saw me with randommmm, whatever the fuck her name was...... (grabs end pillow and stares at it in his lap) ...Will YOUUU be my new Kristin?” (starts hysterically laughing towards Santana)

Santana: “Yea yeaaaaa, try an’play it off like it’s no big deal... (walks over) but I gotta say... (sits next to him) you done fucked up kid” (shrugs shoulders up an’down to the Ellie Goulding beat before standing up to continue dancing #iknowitsgonnabe #iknowitsgonnabe ;)

ACT 7: SCENE 5

His brother's ongoing romance keeps Santana's heart swimming as stars twinkle brightly on shattered ceilings in lighting the once darkened floor... Powerfully driven, Santana consents for love to take'im to ill fated desires; the higher the hopes, the lighter he'd pull on said ropes... And from out of fluttering minds falls exacted truths: he couldn't let life survive if he voted himself off his own very tribe; erasing all million dollar winnings an'leaving only darkness to reside... For why let emotions pass slowly by or watch life flash before his own very eyes? No more could Santana stand idly by in allowing brothers' bridal sister to frolic on HER sunny shores, while the face of HIS love quietly bleeds, bleeds... an'bled out on the floor... He MUSTn't be the only one staring at moons from window sills; everlastily yearning for not just one night, an'never just one kiss; Not just one anything for he's ever so selfish.

A tease would hope all dashes in leaving such lustful ashes as this was not a practice to rehearse or a hearse to practice forever in the first... alas, no more withering in winds she'd blown while waiting to reconcile; no more facade like denial nor fake smile to continually mask; ready for the epic conclusion as the series finale's no longer a mirage like illusion... For HE WILL BE reckless, and reckless HE WILL be: swearing t'reach out into thin air for even AIR he'd steal; Steal his radiant bride with hopes no longer dashed, no longer afraid of envelopment within his own waves thrashing crash...

Adjourning to gyms in'er quest to remain thin, Jasmine combats foes named time to ensure her hotness still matches her vivid mind... But the true piece of any Merlo is the enormous heart buried deep below; for with recent night's dreams, Jasmine's toes weren't the only crashed on extremities as'er legs jumped into pleasures of the crash down festivities... And though locks were still hardened and fastened like metals welded shut, eventually the blind wish to see and she'll no longer stand with "eyes (so) wide shut".

Yet no where to be found on these fitness excursions was a stranger named Peter who'd held his aversions... Yet Santana knew what t'do, where to be and how t'shoot arrows to end perpetuated misery; determined to throw love's slingshot round the moon, he hopes not to meet fates of Hanks and Sinise, in casting away all issues and problems to cease; cease from landing on moons and taking one giant step; still possibly losing gravity - "Depravity please enter stage left... And oh wait; insanity HOLD UP! Cuz you're up on deck!"

...Yet he'd gladly take sentences of free falling through space over purgatories now breathed; for if she'd returned he'd divulge fatally hatched schemes an'save his poor brother's back, encasing two families together with impossible missions still intact. And though failure would push for the Witchcraft's return, he'd rather boil in blackened cauldrons than stand forever far from soul's mate... doomed t'living each day conjuring ways to try an'break or free fate...

Jumping into the Rover to range the land ahead; he vows t'bend without breaking, for if broken? Devastation... And if jealousy upends to ride moonsets in for the win, Santana would surely never reveal fatal plans against young Prince Julian.

The tragic conclusion couldn't be worse than intently staring at outlets of his own breathing machines; so very tempted t'pull plugs on his own soul's hopes and crushing dreams... Yet on occasion he'd sit against walls an'bare a faint smile; like a trapped prisoner named Dufrain on roof tops free for a short while. Enjoy hope that came when splashes upon toes reach Santana's love withered frame; so fuckin ready to swim up an'escape savage dragons, for truly madly deeply he can only imagine as life's grown stale from wallowing in twisted chasms.... And while SHE lay basking in sands that kept only one heart warm, the other body swarms with dejection in it's forever sentence of deploying factions of the love he could bore; with waves only crashing in the few and far between..... till his dear brother unknowingly resurrected HIS once pestilent yet now wide awake dream.

Jasmine: (walks out of the gym to stand 3 feet away from Santana with a "why so serious" stare) "...hey..."

With first words spoken towards him in years, autopilot pushes him t'step forward; yet shocked and blindly running, Jasmine retracts;

Jasmine: "No...
(head falls down shaking)
You shouldn't have come"
(looks back up)

Santana: (moves towards) "But I-"

Jasmine: "-You what......" (moves back)

Santana: "I can't live in silence past this minute bore... no more will I live a despondent life at best; no more can I see you with my heart beating straight out of my fuckin chest... I cannot sit idly by an'allow you t'drift through life never alive; for this is NOT to be taken lightly, so please please comprehend: YOU left me for dead, But this is no zombie nightmare and the life I'm force to bred... I showed you love's kiss an'the passionate depths of worlds unbeknownst to mere mortals; but so reluctantly received, each day you grew ever fearful of the bleed; eventually casting you t'weakness and to leave what you thought you'd never need...... I gave you too much causing you to turn your back. The blindness of vulnerability terrified your control; an'once mortality bubbled to the surface, you ran for your sunny, sunny shores... and continue to run, leaving me sinking deeper t'soul's last depths; where I STILL sit alone an'my heart STILL beats out of my fuckin chest.......... Do you know such suffering perched alone in the dark? Staring at empty thrones stoically awaiting for the spark?

You left our wavy black fathoms to surf on designs of your own boards... to bask in the safe waters of your own sunny, fuckin, shores... Never alive, but always the safer as you'd never dive down yet remain perpetually love's chaser; forever secretly pursuing such dreams you'd once lived; and in waiting for you the long? I am no longer love's kid... Aged t'wrinkles casting doubts to my own barely breathing skin; I can no longer live without you an'I beg of you to take my hand an'run away as we should have in the first... I've arosen from the depths for this is NO, Fucking Game..... (looks away an'back) ...You left me years ago yet I still can't bare to say your name"

Jasmine never took criticism well, and truth it still be. For as the rush comes again, crashing waves lead'er heart to run away with the spoon... while her soul reacquaints, with her dearest friend the moon...

Couldn't allow his passion t'come flooding torrentially back in; thus she continues t'live in sin of that which she'd never forgave herself within... Shocked in disbelief, Jasmine truly aches for his touch; yet he an'all who pass knew not any of this, as none shall witness the crash for life continually passes by'em again an'again in a flash... An'to witness such moments would cause any to surely weep: from either having witnessed love an'loss or cry because they'll never meet their soul's cross....

Wanting nothing more than to reawake in the dark and grab ahold of his hand, somewhere inside she knows he's still what she craves; his taste? Still her rave; his arms? Still her cave... Yet only later would she comprehend that this IS the safe haven notebook love and the rarest of such blends; for though she DID want to bend, her own self interjected and stood guard in'er way again... An'as her majestic scent teasingly forsakes him, with the aid of the moon Jasmine lies to herself to awaken on safe shores instead; an'in walking over to her true love, she curses him an'said:

Jasmine: "I don't respond with much as you know I speak with my touch... (takes hand) I cannot be with you... We are not meant to be. Do not remain caught in the lovely floors an'do not second guess for you have NOT died... Yet without question-(pulls hand away)-You couldn't have changed this if you'd tried"

Jasmine walks away. Same conclusion, the same scene. Leaving Santana in tragic grief with not a whimper but silent scream... She cannot've known what she's done as the moon's pull keeps truths hidden from the sun; the common greek tragedy stages are right in effect as all the stage is set for the cathartic to erect... Each person walking out begins t'bump Santana an'eventually knocks him down; rains blow over him, tossing'im onto warm blood's saturated ground; embracing his place on'er floor as he's known for years the long; the river knows he's ripe for the plucking and eagerly awaits with arms wide open......

Yet darkened rooms below are where he wishes to forever stay; t'keep his hope resounding and continually holding on till may... Yet with faith now crashed, waves still fall but only wake at half mast... An'raising arms out to his sides while his eyes fall to close, thoughts of her dance lightly as saddened crooked smiles arose... And in tilting his head down he finally lips Jasmine's name... Yet before falling into roaring rivers an'off the balcony of life, Santana reaches out to grab hold of faint hope's dying light

Act 7: Scene 6: Jealousy Strikes Back

Hours fly; Santana drives... A date with destiny's in the cards but for now driving around aimlessly's the agenda... And with rejections anger dancing on psyches, somewhere the moon lifts its brows as Santana attempts to break "love's cancer" out of remission...

And after hours of silent driving, he puts on one song...

"All Time Low - A Love Like War feat. Vic Fuentes"

Call: Santana > Julian

J: Hello... Is it you?

S: Yes; who else would it fuckin be? (laughingly said)

J: Oh (upbeat) ...And to what do I owe the pleasure?

S: I just heard some news and figured I would pass it on; no big deeze

J: If it has ANYTHINNNGGG to do with the girl, I don't wanna hear it

S: Wellllll... of course it does (laughs)

(I'm Intoxicated by the lie)

J: Then please don't speak... Gwen Stefani said it right... and NO DOUBT, she was right

S: Hahaha... Hilaaaaaarious, but I can't keep this from you my dude...

J: Do you Have to tell me?.....

S: Yes... I do.........

(heart's on fiiiiiiirrre tonight)

J: (sigh) Just say it

(feel my bonnnnessss ignite)

S: Last night Tyler confessed his love to Liliana and tried to win her back... did sheeeeee mention anything?

(feels like waaaarrrr, waaaarrrr)

J: (silence for 8 seconds) ....no...... she didn't...

S: Ooooooo; that's rough son

(we go together or we don't go down at all)

J: I mean----I--’m sure she was... gonna tell me........ you- find out what she said t’him?

(quick sound the alarm)

S: Yeaaaaaaaaa; I couldn’t tell you the answer to that one... you’ll have to ask her yourself

(I am caught in the web of a lie)

J: ......sure...

S: Wellllllll, I gotta run... But be careful my brother (presses mute an’yells “FUCK YOU!!” while flipping off the navigation screen)

J: ....stay up

S: I’ll try....... I’ll try......

(we go together or we don’t go down at all)

SMS: Julian > Liliana
Hey where are you?

SMS: Liliana > Julian
Baby!!!!
SMS: Liliana > Julian
OMG I missed you soooooooo much!!!
SMS: Liliana > Julian
I’m on my way to the house to get ready for tonight. How’s your cheek?

SMS: Julian > Liliana
It's cool... What's tonight?

SMS: Liliana > Julian
lol I have the valley party
SMS: Liliana > Julian
I told you about earlier remember? I was gonna try to get out of it but I couldn't : (

Julian: "FUCK!!!!"

SMS: Julian > Liliana
Anddddd I take it Tyler's gonna be there?

SMS: Liliana > Julian
Well... it's at his house so yea he will

Julian: "Of course it is..." (rolling eyes an'frustratingly shaking his head)

SMS: Julian > Liliana
Def did NOT tell me any of this

SMS: Liliana > Julian
This is not happy to text me, what's wrong?
SMS: Liliana > Julian
Did I miss something??? I thought we were past this Julian...

Julian: "FUCK NO! What the FUCKKK happen last night???"

SMS: Julian > Liliana
We are, I'm just havin a tough day...

SMS: Liliana > Julian
Ohhhh honey, you know I love you the world over

Julian: "I did..."

SMS: Julian > Liliana
I love you too...

SMS: Liliana > Julian
We're still meeting up later right?

SMS: Julian > Liliana
Of course!!! ;)

Julian: "I gotta ask you what the FUCKKK happen last night...!!!"

SMS: Liliana > Julian
You know it's just me and you forever right? And you should never be jealous or down cuz you have the bestest hottest girlfriend in the world!!! :)
SMS: Liliana > Julian
Who loves you to death!!!
SMS: Liliana > Julian
IIIII LLLLLOOOOOOOVVVVVVVVEEEEEEEE YYYYOOOOOOOOUUUUUUUUU!!!!!!!!!!!!!! :)

SMS: Julian > Liliana
love you too

"Old habits die hard" ...The catchphrase SHOULD read "BAD habits die hard" since the worse tendencies are what allows death t'come THAT much faster.

Julian meant to speak up and not let frustrations an'fear linger, but he kept it instead, unable to pull any fuckin triggers... He didn't believe anything was happening but knew better than to fight before sending a loved one into vulnerable waters carrying needs for attention an'affection #trouble ...Independent free and secure in herself, Liliana felt like all was right in the world while HE'd fallen into "old habits" as anger boils an'singes a love that normally instills passion worthy of the gods... Yet having forgotten the like, Julian focuses on negativity's attractive vibes... almost as if he knew "the moon (would soon) divorce the sky".

(30 minutes earlier)

SMS: Jasmine > Liliana
Where are you? You're still comin to Ty's right?

SMS: Liliana > Jasmine
He frickin confessed his love for me last night, I really don't wanna go...

SMS: Jasmine > Liliana
Oooo... rough sledding, but you're still goin sis! :)

SMS: Liliana > Jasmine
Lol it was sooo uncomfortable and awkward... Can't we just make it a girls night? :)

SMS: Jasmine > Liliana
I wish sugar plum, but EVVVVVVERYONE'S gonna be there tonight so we have to go!
SMS: Jasmine > Liliana
Show everyone how the Valley gets down! #getweird

SMS: Liliana > Jasmine
Are you gettin street on me?

SMS: Jasmine > Liliana
Are you not going?

SMS: Liliana > Jasmine
...I'm going

SMS: Jasmine > Liliana
Better be!!! First shot of the night will be us ladies!

SMS: Liliana > Jasmine
I miss ya sis...

SMS: Jasmine > Liliana
I've missed you too! :)

Having dismissed Santana's advances, Jasmine ponders all the mornings she'd awoken an'why she'd never spoken t'Peter while dreaming of past love's kiss; Oh so wondrous as to whether HE was the one she SHOULD have been with...

Sleeping each nightmarish night unless soft dreams of him resonate, she'd heard what she longed to hear in learning he still waits at'er soul's mysterious gate; an'as the perpetual knocking on metal cages reverberates deep inside, she traces it back to where she'd locked herself up with sleeping potions so long ago imbibed...

But if the one who'd fallen to the moon's sight HAD survived, how scary would it be to let'er run off by his side? ...an'let'em start anew in the sun's dawning light.

And so SHE let'er self decide to divulge her majestic mind's rage; she'd close the former book an'together turn the next page... For missions t'find the last key would be one he'd happily recommence; (CRASH) and it all finally clicked together an'made simple "could not hide from anymore" sense...

Act 7: Scene 7: "OMG this ISSSS the Valley Party #perf"

Filled with far too many expensive luxury cars in the driveway, shirts costing more than a bill or two and the average "real" purse's price tag surpassing outsider's pay checks, the "house" was a rockin... Yet most "houses" do not have lakes an'pools, or basketball AND tennis courts to play on an'not use.

Nor do they have gardens with exotic flowers no patrons could ever name; yet the colorful foliage easily answers the question "Does this guy have money?" with "Yes yes and yes" in the same.

This world leaves all but a few wondering how the air feels so high and snootily thin; an'how THEY could arise to such great height yet STILL never be made like Tyler an'Perry in their "troubleless" little lives; on clouds of decked out elegance with an air of arrogance along side...

Glancing at the time on locked screens, Tyler anxiously awaits for his heart to walk in an'join the parties full bloom; ready to throw the first scheming wrench as the full moon rules the night, by further spreading lies t'Tyler's blind insight:

Moon: "This won't hurt anyone! An'she would totally love the you-well, the you she'll finally see tonight... An'who cares how tough this pill will be for loser boyfriend's to fully swallow... Fuck him cuz he'll be nothing come better sunrises of better morrows!"

Entertaining all guests with his former status and #swag on full display, Tyler knows how t'hide his true self while laughing at his own reflection in mirrors break; vigorously attempting t'shake his own head an'ignore exhausts exuding from blackened hearts smoking in the ashes of a person once known as Tyler _____ (who gives a faaaaack)

The recording had been altered set an'timed, now ready to chaos drive; leading to wonton lives an'renewed hopes of recapturing never forgotten wives... For with a soul an'heart to beat as it now fully did? Tyler awakes in darkened rooms awaiting returns to an unencountered bliss; forever reaching out to HER, who knew not any of this...

(Jasmine and Liliana walk into Tyler's mansion as "Tove Lo - Habits (Stay High) Oliver Nelson Remix" flows through the crowd)

Watching all rush up to Jasmine an'Liliana, Tyler throws a single nod to Perry in smirking a devils stare; laughing to one another as they could finally start the war...

Nicole: "Oh My GOD! You guys are back TOGETHER!!!"

Jaime, Nicole an'entourage: (SHRIEKS) "AAAAHHHH!"

Jaime: "I KNOWWW! Shots all around!!!"

Perry: (Looks at Tyler an'lips "I'm on it")

Tyler: (walking up with open arms) "Ladddiiieeessss!!! Welcome!!!"

Liliana: (under breath) "Oh my god-"

Jasmine: "-justsmileandgowithit-TYLER!!! You add in another bar???"

Tyler: (hugs both) "Psssshhhhh, only two; no big deal; but Hey, We got some shots lined up for y'all!"

Liliana: (sarcastically) "Yaaaaayyyyyy"

Jasmine: (slaps Liliana's ass) "Come on sis!! You're goin dowwwwnnn!"

Liliana: "Uhhhh NO! You'll be passed out in like 5 seconds!"

Jasmine: "Whatever you say; shall we?"

Liliana: "You fuckin know it-"

Jasmine: "-What'd you just say?"

Liliana: "...Ummmm, Tyler can you take a picture of us? Here" (hands phone)

Tyler: "Of course of course..." (click)

Perry: (walking up behind an'throwing his arms around the sisters) "Girls, Girls... These shots are a waitin-lets go, lets go" (escorts them to the "fancy room" and looks back at Tyler who pockets Liliana's phone)

Tyler: "...That's my BOY!"

Random guy 37: (passing by) "Aww thanks Ty, I didn't even think we were that clo-"

Tyler: "-Shut the fuck up" (smiles walking out)

(40 minutes later)

With'er sister arm in arm and a few drinks in, all was right in Liliana's stunning eyes... Yet off allowing runaway train's fears to grow, Julian waters warrantless claims a jealous grifter had passed on down; said so perfectly timed that it unknowingly unwound... Holding the world in'er palms Liliana keeps all negativity outside, so very blessed by future moments any an'all would surely enjoy; so very loss in galaxy's forever kiss which she thought none could ever veer off nor destroy...

SMS: Kristin > Jasmine
Hey J
SMS: Kristin > Jasmine
We're heading out to the bars in Palo Alto...
SMS: Kristin > Jasmine
You in? Been too long...

SMS: Jasmine > Kristin
Yea
SMS: Jasmine > Kristin
Pick me up at Ty's in 15
SMS: Jasmine > Kristin
You remember where he lives?

SMS: Kristin > Jasmine
You fuckin know it!

SMS: Jasmine > Kristin
LOL text me when you're outside

Jasmine: "Heyyyyy sister sisterrrr, (walks up to Liliana taking a shot) Whoaaaaaa Lillll!!! Slow down! Jesus what shot is that for you???" (laughs)

Tyler: "Sheeeeeee'sss cooooool; like, three or fourrrr MOOOOOOOMMM... Relax hahahaha"

Liliana: "Yeaaaaa Mooooommm, chilllll out!"

Perry: "Hahaha excellent.... excellent"

Jasmine: (turns to Perry) "Don't you have some random sluts to be attending to???"

Perry: "Heyyyy... You're right! Where RRRRR my manners" (spots two ladies staring at him across the room an'descends)

Tyler: (throws arm around Jasmine) "It is GOOD t'have you back betch!"

Jasmine: "Chyea, I know right... On that note, I'm bouncin in 20..."

Tyler: (spins Jasmine around) "Awwww you're gonna break your poor sister's heart!" (turns Jasmine towards Liliana)

Liliana: "Nicole, NICOLLLLEEEEE!!!! Dudddeee look at this! LOOK AT THISSSSS!!! Is just my ass shakinnn???? Am I doin it???? AM IIII?????" (unsuccessfully trying to twerk)

Jasmine: "I think allllll is back t'normal finally"

Tyler: (loss staring at Liliana's ass) "Uh huh, yea-yea I think this song sucks to-Daaaaaaayyyyyyym, Perrrryyyyy (laughing) Check this shit outtttt!"

(40 minutes later)

Having happily shamed fishes with far too many drinks downed, Liliana's ready to enter dreamland with plans to see the love not around... Having dared'er to take so many shots knowing she'd eventually crash out, Tyler directs Liliana to beds where he'd recently betrayed the girl he now brought... Guiding her up the stairs an'smoothly tucking her in, Tyler's ready to start the misery by sending a single text; his gift to the world aided by skies now fully moon lit...

SMS: Tyler > Perry

Hey yooo... Go talk to your "friend" who I hate...
Throw out whose in bed next to me hahaaaaa!!!!
Lets get this party started #fuckublackeyedpeas

SMS: Julian > Liliana (6th unread text message)

Baby where are you? Are you ok??? Hello!!! Talk to me!!! I'm going crazy over here!!!!

SMS: Julian > Liliana (7th unread text message)

OMG!!! What's going on??? Why are you not responding at all while you are at HISSSSS FUCKIN HOUSE!!!! FUCK THIS!!!!

SMS: Jasmine > Santana

I miss you...

(Perry walks up to Dru with two ladies anyone would "take down" #nogrenadeshere)

Perry: "What's up D?" (hand clasp)

Dru: "You know... just chillaxin, what chyou got here?"

Perry: "Oh.. random girl 89 an'91??? Shiiiiiiittt... Come on D... you know whasssup right?"

Perry and Dru: "Rigggghhhhhttttt" (smiling)

Dru: "What? (confused face) You're not hookin up the permanent wing man no mo? No longer attached at the hip? Whaaaaaa???"

Perry: "Na na na my dude... He's upstairs with Lil... I think they may be (air quotes) done already" (smiling an'laughing)

Dru: (eyes wide) "Wait what? You serious? On boys?"

Perry: (head tilt hands open) "...on boys"

Dru: "Damn... That girl's all OVER the place"

Perry: "Yup yuppppp, you know how girls are my dude, (random girl 89 an'91 fling off Perry's arms in disgust) Oh come onnn now ladies; y'all be cray (laughing) ...and you know thisssss!"

Random 89 an'91 peer past Perry and nod in agreement before returning to Perry's side as his "bitches" for the night #threesomeanyone

SMS: Dru > Julian
Dude... where you at?

SMS: Julian > Dru
Drinkin at the crib

SMS: Perry > Tyler
Hey yo... We're good

SMS: Julian > Dru
You over at Tyler's? You see my girl????

SMS: Tyler > Perry
Thanks bro! One love lol

SMS: Dru > Julian
Yea I'm over at Tyler's...
SMS: Dru > Julian
And your girl disappeared into a bedroom

SMS: Perry > Tyler
She's yours! He'll be here soon! Dru always talks

Dru: (phone blowing up) "Hold up Pear, be right back"

Perry: "No worries son, take your time; I'll try and figure out SOMETHIN to occupy Mine" (looking down at his ladies smiling on cue)

SMS: Tyler > Perry
Thanks lol pick any room you want... Or might I suggest the pool house??? Our old stomping grounds...

Call: Julian > Dru

J: What'syou MEANNNNN Disappeared?

D: Well word is she went into Tyler's room a bit ago-

J: -WHATTHEFUCK!!!@@@ WHAT'SyouMEAN a BITago???!!!

SMS: Perry > Tyler
Damn he works fast... already on the phone with the "dead" ex

D: Well; Fuck dude...... She went into his room like 30 minutes ago or somethin

SMS: Tyler > Perry
Thats so money and everyone knows it...

J: Onmyway (click)

Sometimes when you're so angry hurt an'loss in a twisted "could-kill-someone-break-your-hand-punchin-walls" rage you don't exhibit any anger or emotion at all; simply become red in the face an'clench the jaw... Julian grabs his keys and squeezes, collapsing hands intentionally trying t'draw blood to deflect the pain. Jumping down stairs his hands flash up to faces, pushing skin in all angles before rolling down hairs to contort necks; dragging nails in complete disbelief this is really fucking happening...

The unsightly image of the one you love with another; the sex faces exchanged with YOUR fuckin lips pressed against foreign vessels; the trestles of your bridged connection falling as weight limits begin failing to hold forces laid upon

Starting engines, radios blink on; Live 105 flashes with SubSonic dropping a song you hate to hear but feel it all so passionately an'fuckin clear. ("Fuck Buttons - Sweet Love for Planet Earth; Andrew Weatherall Remix")

All senses an'sounds are heard mid drive: gripping wheels, white knuckles won't ease currents pulsing; with pedals to metal and tires t'dirt; shortcuts're taken, alleyways passing; dodging cars on inverted lanes; swerving through traffic emotions lose grip untamed

Pulling up, tunneled affects remain. People laughing an'leaving said party pass by unnoticed; one mission stands forth; nothing else; the same song blasts from speakers in houses as radio's continue out of cars int'far off enemy territories; the glory's not here and the war's feared to be at an end; last words she sent dance around as texts flash by on grounds of stock ticker tape parades, allowing minds t'run away with train's fears as the ransom; with all checks an'balances already bounced far past pavements of wicked mansions;

Jump in the building, Dru's at the door upward pointing; eyes shifting;

Dru: "Upstairs, second door on the left"

SMS: Perry > Tyler
Knock knock

Door slams open to darkened views, red hues of faces breathless; emotionless; Liliana's under covers with Tyler sitting back to headboards; ironic

Julian: "Liliana!!! Are you-"

Tyler: "-Shhhhhh; keep it down; My girl's sleep-"

Julian: "-She's not your FUCKIN girl!"

Tyler: "...Ask'er bro"

Julian: "Why are you here with him?"

(Tyler plays recording)

Recorded Liliana: "I...... I don't want you. I'm in love with someone else... I'm finally happy... I'm sorry..."

Julian: "What??? Whatttt are youu... (insert fatal adjective) Say-ing? You're really... really in love wit him-with fuckingggg-HIM???"

Recorded Liliana: "Yes, I am... You need t'get over me and move on with your life... find someone new..."

Crash. Walls. Slam. Internal brawls walking lines... I look up, left; momentarily blind; bearings loss, she's... she's supposed t'be... t'be...

Closing doors; standing on alert I look left right up an'(click) sight returns; the soothing burn along with chiseled breaths, that fuckin bitch, fuck this tragic mess... He was right, she was her... fuck this life... it's... blur;

I turn to run the stairs, the first step shakes the wood; cracks erode impaling hearts on crooked slants. Dark earth opens; frazzled nerves sparking, dripping time's barely emitting. I push off my foot as fast as I fuckin can; the blur of the party's not fast but slow motion; what fuckin imbibed cursed potion did she drink? Her name's not Juliet but Liliana, I'm curbing on the brink; the moon steps down halls through gravity infested walls, continuously crashing down on me; repetitively the sun's loss with only jokerish faces beside me; they're outweighing, all linin up t'take turns laughin at me;

All trace round me, slow motion pacers're followin me; I must try to lighting run; no way to retract warring done yet I still stand in depravity back there while she still lays in tragedy I fear whilst all the world's slowed, I must break outta here...

Tumbling forward through chaotic traps of party scenes, I stumble out of our mosaic like dream... weary of the seems she an'he have broken through, please give me wings to fly far... to fly far..........

Act 8: Scene 1

(Ka-Chick, Vrooooooom, NO SOUND;
no sound but an engine;

radio silence till SubSonic
flashes back on with

"Bauer & Lanford - Leave Me Behind

(Daniel Beasley Remix)"

playing as the song)

Backwards stepping, conclusion ending.

Back to the room, darkness in Bloom.

I feel my insides implode, heart now frozen an'blanketed with emotion of lost love's devotion. Alone in the room with no one beside me, I can't rhyme hearts to mend; dejected, I leave the crime and drive...

I drive to nowhere, drive to insanity. Hades rivers flow backwards out of me down clenched blushed cheeks; cluttered dripping eyes cannot cease as fluid oozes from all orifices leaving a warm pool of nothingness to dwell in and play. I feel the horizon ahead but it won't ever rise; the sun has eclipsed, moon sealed all light. With a blurred life to match spinning webs of lies in corrupt minds, I'm delirious with love havin loss the focus I forever wished I didn't find; deceived, for there's no way she'd ever chosen to simply leave.

Shuttered air cries to escape tainted lungs; the screams of blood boil my soul till its cooked to it's ripe an'full gore; the roar of her words and sorrow the've brought cant dispel the suicide simmering adroitly inside. I pull at my hair an'rip nails down necks; I look to my phone for a text that'll never come, but upon lighting I'm struck by her beautiful face, my lips plastered to'er sun shown cheeks while'er eyes dream the world with their wide glee phases; the love from wallpaper's moment jumps out devices and softens blows rained down upon me until reality slaps me with a loud horn ahead; I've swerved out of my lane for the river yearns to be fed. Loss along dotted yellow lines the subconscious alerts me to passing street signs as the moment stuck in time appears in my midst; I fasten the grip as the glowing mist still emits an'I drive off the trail to kneel; elbows bent, a'praying to her will:

"Curse it be that I love her still;

curse my life at thy window sill...

Please let me leave this place

and rid her from basking in tragic mind's embrace"

(promises have turned to lies)

Fog rolling over foothills triggers a blind craze; a rage ensues, woods flipped to shatter on pavements; the wood's design now matches life's beautiful floral arrangement; remnants of broken love break out each bench's side, I sit between them an'place my hands where they lie an'push... I push forcefully as the blood leaves so peacefully; one by one marching down the wooden stair, stoically impressed, I sit back breathe and stare... I feel my essence flow out; ever so slow... the one liquid the river never thought I'd ever give in to let go... I shoot my head skyward, eyes closed to the dark. In tune with the misery, I imagine the spark. The spark of a thousands wars; my Helen of Troy. The spark of my dreams, that I'd loss to a boy.

Monumental words repeated: "I don't want you. I'm in love with someone else... I'm finally happy... I'm sorry"

(so leave me behind; promises have turned to lies)

I play it, hear it, breathe it an'question what I did. With no clue as to where the needle sized hole pierced the bow, I ask how do I right the vast ship? Why now did she trip flip on this night of wasteland's nights? Plight I've been fated, fuck, soooo jaded yet I refuse to live in sin; a sin to kiss another and hold thoughts outside of each other which she broke all 10 times the more… the fuckin bitch left me to ashes as dust on soul's floor… My head aches, pent up heart a flutter an'with only one to unlock me I wait in purgatory like torture; my previous lives cannot compare nor even fathom chased coffins of the grave; her lips were my cave, light Aristotle proclaimed; eyes my safe haven, soothing all sores an'past pains.

I couldn't leave this seat or untangle my amazement, deathly staring onwards towards the breach of life's arraignment: here we once stood, and still glory be; crying out our love in silent glances, endlessly letting out one another's hopeless of romances with mine much experience yet her's never exuded…

I gave'er strength to dance on ceilings without caution as the rush comes over, breaking through glass chasms without fearing in allowing unleashed passions to soar through us… for only we could break skies limits in rising, but now

Pasted together images pan from face to smile t'laugh,

repeating moments with no trace or whisper,

the trees shake off their snow as easy as she simply let

me go...

Shaken breaths out and in, hearts shout to thin

with a knee to bounce eerily along soul's depths within;

no longer amazed,

staring at the glory that was,

glory that is and sad story will be...

Twisting shattering tooth scraping enamel leaves me
heartbreaking,

kill laughing, chopped up and blasting eyes out of my
skull;

my insides dark of the soul,

reaching out an'gasping for the touch I know...

Throat slashes and mad knifes of dashes

keeps me excited t'live if only to end one's demises.

When did life become so technologically driven?

That ending with a dagger was no longer a given.

No more candle left to burn,

the moon stands alone versus the sun.

Fighting the good fight,

until the dark side of moon

reverses its run.

The hallway is quiet. The river has stopped.

The dream is shattered. The glass is so sharp.

The band will keep playing as the ship sinks to the floor,

to join me in forever after as broken dreams wash ashore

(breathe)

(breathe)

Act 8: Scene 2

Walking in Jasmine hears Nancy's lame ringtone sound off;

Nancy: "Hello? ...slow down; what do you mean are you at home? ...It's 1 am of course I'm at home; whats going on?... Yes you can say it; just effing say it! Or should I cuss for the first ti-......wait... wait....... Casta???? ...Is....... gone?????"

Phones involuntarily fall from hands. (Crash) As backs slide down counters to rest against the wood, there is one less life now on earth left to live...

(20 seconds earlier)

"Casta???? ...Is....... gone?????"

Life's new crawl is timeless; as if Jasmine died and HER life flashed before HER very own eyes. Shooting like lightning, visions thunder by the mind's view; with Santana's powerful gaze encapsulating all, through and through; constantly reminding with each passing that till tonight he waited beneath an'still pined; wishing on star covered morrows an'dreaming in mosaic designs. But with no wave left to his name, the soft splish and splash upon Jasmine's feet didn't feel nearly quite the same...

She Imagines returning to depths where silence is accepted and words needn't be spoken for assurance of loves rewoken in every glance touch an'gesture... Bowing as Jasmine gracefully walks in the door, Santana happily fans her atop pedestals an'continues to block the rains pour...

THIS is the love she'd twisted up tossed and rejected by repeatedly walkin away from all attempts at reinfection... And though hours before she'd realized her earlier mistake, only now does she face her self yelling at mirrors break:

"You made the wrong decision... (flushed breaking down) Chose the wroooonnnng one. (crying) And you had a chance!!!! (chest piercing scream) A CHANCE!!! To fuckin right YEARSSSS of torment; but you, YOUUU dealt the final deathly blow!!!" (turns an'runs away sobbing in mirror's distance)

Emanating with his very last breaths, somewhere inside a death rattle calls her name. (Phone hits the floor)

Upon phones crashing, Jasmine opens her mouth to scream but only a whisper of smoke flies forth. Satanically laughing, the little mouse thrashing spins stomachs round as reality sinks in: no longer will warm sensations of love's touch shoot up from her toes; knowing now she'd spurned Peter's poor excuse for advances having never let go of Santana's life struggling romances... And laughing as they twirl, masked contradictions dance in the mind as fate allows inner truths to encircle

Jasmine: "No"

Jetting out the door into dreary's sorrowful black night, Jasmine runs to the street and books right towards the moon; with an eruption of tears she pictures loss embraces knowing HE no longer waits to reconnect, yet soon her mirrored self returns to woefully interject:

"Ran from your love to save future Jasmine that day,
instead you lied and killed your counter point.
Would we allow you to remain in harms way;
and leave you the option for him to appoint?

To ring in your death, for one's blind at such depths,
and the blind can NOT climb back up to secure shores.
Beneath you'd hold him too close to the vest,
and what would you do if he'd found all four?

For if you were with him and left sadly behind,
you could neither drift up nor remember the path;
trapped in depression and lost in the mind;
caught beneath in memories of love's wrath.

We saved your heart from possible breakage;
only now do you see the resulting wreckage"

Stoic and numb, nothing describes what's felt or what's not; neither the catharsis, the epiphany, nor the destructive revelation. Future's bleak; loveless moments commence and all seems dark. With a wide open mouth to catch the sadness of life, Jasmine's heart collapses in on itself and cant run anymore...

(closes eyes kneeling on shallow shores)

"The nights alcohol cannot soften the pain, nor can it numb emotions shooting thru me like a shot gun piercing my soul till I slowly bleed out; I feel life flow out an'dreams evaporate till their loss, loss, loss... Burning eyes an'a burning heart leads to cryless eyes and selfish starts; I'm forced to watch tears run away with my heart to another day and time, a new day and kind of which I can neither find nor join...

And left here is the me I do not know.

The me I cannot let go,

for letting go would cease to breathe

and deceive my own dreams an'crushing hopes......

Please let me leave this place,

for the river Hades steals more than it takes;

and the world of nature gives more than it fates

to those who cannot live beyond their own destiny's true weight.

I wish I could stop the tears I've caused in trusting it was all fake.

Please forever keep me in worlds that I know,

for I cannot leave the depths of the light an'beautiful snow......"

The faintest of glows peaks out from frozen white tides; never to rise and crash on toes for his star's light no longer resides. Yet she'd thrived on his commitment always burning softly in back's burner; for even if she never dove down, the torch he carried always burned so much brighter... And with the forever present flicker always there for the taking, he allowed her to live casually through all darkened times the making...

Yet running through sagas in the mind, maybe the fluorescent lights were worth the price; vulnerability worth the sacrifice... and maybe... just maybe Jasmine wasn't designed to live the safe haven life...

Santana ran to his grave without her return to his side; she'd kept darkness flowing around him by hiding the truth out of love's light; while he passed off cliffs heartbroken an'dying alone in the coldness of love's life...

And with knees underneath her in the middle of the street, all streetlights lay lit save for one overhead. Turning inward an'closing her eyes tight, Jasmine sees no light shinning below... but if she joins him in the afterlife, she may catch the soul's last light show...

No longer basking in the sun's bountiful shine, she cries to darkened skies above having been blinded by moon's cold beams; picks up weights an'oxygen tanks to wade in waters once blocked by fear like gleams: of why she kept all outside an'forever looking in... and why those SHE loved even farther ensuring she'd never self sin...

And finally understanding unlike ever before, Jasmine walks away from the shore to dive back down towards the floor; to wait as he had for countless years the long, a justified sentence having turned away from Swan's song... Dive down to that shelf an'awake in a room; encircled by roaring rivers, darkness still in bloom. Led by the faith that in death HE would at least now know: Jasmine wished never to leave, but t'was her own tilted heart that brought such lies an'such deceit...

She'd never woken the room alone, nor been so cold an'so warm; accepting she too now had the same afflicted open wound of never knowing if she could ever depart from this encapsulated tomb... For after all, it was HER mistakes and self pity that destroyed'er own city by shutting off the lights an'ripping all markers down. Yet descending blindly with no guide, Jasmine finds the floors track to wait for the impossible: a departed love to come rushing back... For this time SHE fell to love and awoke in a dark room alone; freeing her spirit an'taking shackles off'er war like heart's prison of a home...

Now Jasmine sits alone in the dark, so very afraid t'move... pining for the spark to come shooting through HIM again; signifying a return to a life none thought would ever begin; but hope... hope can be a dreadfully scary thing...

And after years in the dark Jasmine feels the essence enter her realm; an'from beyond graves Santana's outstretched hands meet, shooting a blast of light with their body's release. The waters are calm; tidal waves no longer crash. The lost city illuminates; heartbreak heals intact. Encircling mirrors all shatter and collapse together to form a magnificent glass house, an'with new chords of love, sinews are no longer snapped as boxes thought to be loss appear brightly awaiting discovery from the black... And from out of pockets Santana pulls the key she'd hid so mightily; the very key that left him turning back to darkness an'gasping for non existence, hopelessly watching her swim to safer shores...

And with no need to run, both throw shoes into currents flow; ready to pick up where they left off in the sun's ever regenerating glow... To bask in their love and embrace a felicity; enriched by fluorescent lights in all it's enchanted mystery... And in waiting a century for her to return back to him, Santana learned that hope IS a blissfully beautiful thing. For all the torture endured? He'd watch her laugh live an'love another all over to have this moment capitulary ascend; breaking all rules, allowing fate the uncanny ability to bend... He knew she deeply fell, but didn't know if she'd return; and with a few lifetimes spent in proving his devotion, he'd searched through all four oceans an'seven seas in wait for her to break out of self imposed prison's misery...

Yet now they could continue the story as their saga hadn't loss all it's life glistening glory. An'with the end not now to be, they could once again slay dragons in a land called Honalee. For with envisioned images playing out before eachother's very eyes, they needn't live in mementos as the band continues their sweet unfinished symphony full tempo for many chapters here after.

This would not be the easy life by any means; but along with intense fights, monumental reconnects'll keep their passion in those magnificent fluorescent lights: exploring the world in all its grand allure, they'll continue to unlock eachother in their unpredictable human nature... And walking up to the box with her hot on his trail, both laugh as he turns back to glance; confirming that she'd given up imprisoning love's most decadent romance.

Having ruined Julian's fairy tale, Tyler drunkenly drives in excited jubilation; unaware his actions threw not one but four lives off track... And cruising with Liliana knocked out asleep in the back, Tyler unknowingly passes Julian's commiserated earlier scene; passing moments that still stand, still emitting their infinite sun beams... And although Tyler's plans had twisted HER one love's blood out, Liliana unconsciously slept while traveling on this route... Rounding the corner and looking past signs to stop, Tyler murmurs, "Hey Liliana, there's a light out on your block..." Laughing a short laugh, Tyler did think it odd; but continuing to drive without caution an'blind to his own power, the car strikes an object... Disaster.

Turning the key, the box unclicks; but as he opens the lid his sixth sense begins to feel sick; the box vanishes, along with the key; as all lights but one flash off in complete synchronicity. For upon turning to view his lover's adoring stare, Jasmine lay desolate an'fading from breath out stretched on the floor: one hand on his foot, lightly grazing a few toes... just like he'd touched her when hope arose from below... The one faint remaining light lay within Jasmine's two eyes, for having seen the glow he'd brought back it couldn't yet fully die. For finally giving in and returning to his grasp, sadly sometimes the world keeps on it's true mask... She'd thought they'd both passed below shelfs an'off the balcony of life hand in hand; thought they'd reconciled since he waltzed the same design an'taken his own life under the moon's nefarious divine.... but Santana never plummeted past his forever long perch; and up until this now moment both remained alive in full breath...

Earlier she'd sat under one burnt out light... and now her own life, burnt out that very night... And with falling hearts pump beginning to fade, Jasmine realizes Santana had not heartbrokenly fell, but it was his own dear brother who'd passed by in the rearview. Staring deep an'wishing to capture any and all light, Santana bends down to touch her graces before like a passer by on the street it quickly erases... He'd have to carry this moment from here, and here on; remember the light somber gazes she gave; symbolizing her ability to let go of the fear; in falling back to the depths that she'd always revered... To know he'd righteously waited for her here all along, and in holding faith she believed here is where she belonged...

And with'er nearly faded breath, a piece of him would remain at her side for the long; to wallow at such great depths with her here an'the great beyond... For once you've danced and found your life's true love to be, a part of you never leaves like Peter Pan to his Wendy... But this isn't Neverland and growing up fuckin hurts; the thimble like realization that he'll never see her beyond the hearse. He could only imagine truly madly deeply what the fuck had happen back on dry land; how he encountered such miserable luck to lose her once she'd returned to his undying an'shakeless hands...

But miserable it is not, and he wouldn't trade a soul; for to feel such love and beauty he'd gladly take the hurt all too painful; for the pains a reminder of travels to such great depths where both truly fell... where he'd found someone capable of the love he could grow... and that she'd loved him the same over and would forever on after now know

(breathe)

(breathe)

Act 8: Scene 3

(SLAM! Liliana's head hits the back of the front seat and her leg twists under her as she falls to the floor... jostled back to life by a defibrillating blow, Liliana awakes)

With a headache and cramping pain in her leg, she's stuck halfway between drunk and hungover; unaware of her surroundings an'struggling to break out of familiar back seat prisons, Liliana's head flashes upwards to meet a motionless Tyler; white knuckles portray his lock hard grip on the wheel yet the car remains completely standing still. Trying to flee the scene, a trembled breath evades from Tyler's mouth as his shaking legs cannot cease while stoic dead stares drip down stoic dead faces. Pulling herself up, Liliana sees silent tears falling down his abnormally pale cheeks with neither emotion nor facial expression reaching her seat... as if world's flipped and spun in reverse, a painful horror twists Liliana's stomachs inward t'curse'd sirens in far off streets...

Liliana: (softly) "...tyler... (silence) ...tyler... (silence) TYLER!" (reaches out to his shoulder)

Triggering his whole body to exasperatingly inhale, Liliana's touch awakens Tyler from comas to furiously swim up from such great depths an'surface out of deep ends. Ratcheting grips on the wheel, Tyler shrieks out a Banshee like yell as if torn an'dragged piece by piece from the seven layers of hell; subsequently passed out at the bar "pain and suffering" on backsides of treacherous hearts, Tyler cannot face Liliana's wondrous eyes; eyes he'd seen in windows reflection's last night; eyes that gazed while dancin round the bed; tears that flowed in bitter garden scenes for unimaginable were her beams shot by plights resting in tragedy's wake tonight.

Opening doors and placing his left foot down, Tyler's body crumbles, crashing wrists t'pavemented grounds. Through car's warm undersides, Tyler's wide open eyes stare onward to hairs of fate lying amidst guilty pools of blood... Forcefully dragging open hands towards his body ruptures repentant skins, drawing shameful blood to streets that've already taken far too much... Frightened and unsure how to proceed, Liliana tries to hold back the rush of falling from shock's cliff as stomachs confirm the creeping devilish sirens are indeed inching closer... and with computers in frozen minds full of white noised screens, Liliana can't move t'front seats nor eject herself to next scenes... An'after resetting all systems, Liliana pushes front seats forward to face an incoherent Tyler laying amongst the roaring, no longer rushing river; continuing to drag his palms up an'down, the tiny serrations of pavements pull ceremonial bloods from hands that caused such destruction on this night of wasteland's nights #thisisawasteland

Liliana: (achingly whispering) "Tyler... What's go-ing onnnnn??? What; happen?... What's tha-t awful, scraping sound?????"

Tyler: "I... I can't... This is... I-I... (slams hand against car panels wailing) WHYYYY???? (raspily choked) Whhhyyy- (hand out palm open) ..Stayyyy..... (trembling breath out) innn... the car-"

Liliana: (tears falling; shock impaling) "-TYLER!!!!! Your hand!!!! WHERE'S THAT BLOOD FROM????? (softly) what is happening????..... (screams) FUCKINTELLME!!! What HAPPENNNNN???!!!"

Tyler: “Stay; (stuttered breaths) innn.... (flushed face out) the car...”

Liliana: “STOP!!!! (in full yell) TYLER!!!! (whispers) pleeeeaaaase... TELLME!!!!!!” (somber cries emit from Tyler’s lips)

Tyler: “I.... I.. (drags clenched fists emitting familiar scraping noises leaving splotches of blood dispersed throughout the tiny divots of pavement) I... I didn’t....”

Liliana: (entering Tyler’s stoic level) “You what; WHAT??? I’m scared... what d-did...d’you doooo? (peeks head out to Tyler’s flattened body) welllll... (shaking) wha (looks right) did you-(turns left to white and grey speckled shoes-

-Images of Liliana’s sister running through the house in those shoes; the day she tried them on at the mall an’Liliana’s words “they suit you perfectly” met by Jasmine’s goddess smiling face... Walking in to see the line up of kicks always missing only the one-

-Twisting and contorting, Liliana’s body seizures: arms flail, legs kicking anything an’everything nearby; throwing all within reach up in anger’s mercy: empty liquor bottles an’high class dress shoes fall bruising Liliana’s face; commiserating her pain while nails pierce the car’s black leather soul and hers as well...

Mind shuttered an’shattered, frazzled signals fly inside an’she cannot connect the right synapses to will ejection from isolation’s back seat.

Slamming open right hands to center console lids, Liliana pulls herself to knees before breaking it off the hinges sends bolts flying upward into the car's thick air; snakily coiled and tensely broken, upon leaping out Liliana's left foot catches the door's metal lining lip to stumble down on Tyler's back hitting heads against the pavement; (crack) ...Staring at spattered blood on cat like fours, Liliana's tears blend into divots of saddened filled blood. She commands herself, forces herself to look up; face it breathe it, live it see it. The heart beats fast, faster; painfully trying t'send oxygen to short of breath limbs; closing her eyes tighter, tight, the blur thickens; darker, dark; Roaring upwards, rocking heads meet twisted tattered threads of a human being; all happiness tumbles down to floors till knees fall alike; climbing up a steep gravel incline, the four legged beast moves forward... beyond empty vessels an'beyond red trestles cascading past both eyes... Having fallen off shocks cliff and drunkenly unbalanced in'er trip, never fully upright Liliana claws towards faded loves to crash on nearby pavements begging for mercy; her own knees cry blood for Jasmine's beauty while Tyler remains locked in mourning; right face resting an'stuck to the ground; staring at slowly forming rivers of red dancing by unblinked eyes....

Unable to turn away from tragedies befalling:

Tyler: "She'll get up, yes... she will get up; she's fine... just got the wind knocked out of her; she's fine... any minute; any minute she'll wake up; fine; and laughing, we'll all laugh... (trying to inhale forgiveness his lungs cannot find) and we'll laugh! and... and we'll lau-

-Tyler's voice is loss; emotions tossed into wastelands of his own desolate undoing. Replaying dominos so "brilliantly" set up only t'knock down in allowing darkness to erupt; replaying schemes, Tyler sees his own demon standing next to an ignorant mislead soul, recalling moments his world opened up t'love in similar positions as hour glasses filled with sand; wishing t'go back an'reprimand: "Keep THAT table bare, an'never allow emotions to sit for now you lay in street cells, mind a fit an'imprisoned by your own memento's hell in seeing your future star fall and fall, till all dreams of love finally fell... Or continue to fall feet ahead or maybe behind, trickling down rivers in Hades' glorious view; severely fading 30 feet back, off kilter an'askew; sirens capture all light while whispers of your life drift in winds of moon's dreary full night...."

Gazing into her dearest sister's cold motionless cut filled face with the right sides scraped off, pristine soft white skin's replaced by darkened grey an'red undersides of life. Broken bones and disfigured limbs are not easy to ignore, but she cannot look away as most scold lifeless bodies look peaceful in death yet Jasmine appears so lonely... so scared.... Hugging her forever resting body, Liliana lays in the street with her head on Jasmine's chest, softly brushing her hair; whispering:

Liliana: "I love you my dearest sister... you were too beautiful to stay here I guess; but at least you knew love; an'were loved; truly madly deeply... please never leave me; stay with me, stay with me here... I'll see you on the shores; so please wait for me there..." (kisses her forehead)

Laying against heartless hearts and unable to let go, Liliana peers over chins to the sight of'er still wide frightened eyes; closing'em, she hopes to bring some kind of solace inside...

Having loss her parents an'now her last family, the only silver lining is the love she'd found; a binding love that comfortingly surrounds in times where no sounds fly out: when whispers are the shouts for time to turn back, an'for desperate moons to leap off their deadly tracks in falling prey to the sun's majestic beams... Liliana's heart must keep beating for them... beating for the life they'd seen in opposing eyes; beating for the night they'd broken glass revealing worlds beyond unceiling'd skies; forever out past moments never touched in finding such a beautiful fuckin life...

Somewhat healing yet barely breathing, Liliana held it close... warming her heart that Jasmine knew of such love an'such great depths in the same token as her above; and though Jasmine thought she was truly unworthy, she was so undyingly fuckin loved... and as much as her own prisons tried to kept out the truth? She was loved; sought after; desired an'so brave in fighting battles within... And to honor the fallen, Liliana must turn away from moon's glare to bring rays of sun out to play; for the weight of the moon's pull should not trump happiness even on the worse day of all days...

Tears will fall; and they may; but Liliana knew she'd never leave her side and could one day reside on those shores where Jasmine could wait; hoping destiny could commiserate t'give fallen stars breadcrumbs to it's paths so she could leap back to where her sunny shores would still last... to lay in the sand she'd baited with her love and treasured soul she'd hid from all; save for one who danced on'er floor back then that first fall....

Liliana: "Wait for him... wait for him where you basked in his eyes loving gaze; as he will surely go there upon waking... for to live is just to fall asleep; to die is to awake... Maybe we're meant to lose the one's we love, but he fought for you till then..."

Fire trucks sit; outside safe haven houses neighbors stand. Handcuffed Tyler mumbles to himself; destitute salvation gives no last rides before crashing and whispering: "she's ok, she'll wake up... she's ok... she'll wake up......." Escorted to the back seat of his new cell, Tyler remains lying on streets, minds forsaken to remain in such states; stoically brazen an'fucked by his amazing skill to kill the light of his love's last blood out.

Police stand against cars giving her a moment with the star fallen far too young; joining the athlete who died before their time an'shaking heads down with hats off in respect's line; head scratching, mind itching how this could befall a beauty who never lived in full... for wouldn't heaven's gates say heaven can wait? Hardly make her walk past golden rods an'upon seeing such a goddess reject? ...Turn away to breathe new life to splendid bodies? Or a new lease to the misunderstood by all but one?

The life breathed into each soul was never as worthy yet this be the tragedy none could believe nor see. Yet with silence as the ruler, no words drift nor police orders rift the calm as all communication cables are quieted of their roar... And with all sirens finally shut down, all enter idle moments in the eye of the storm; where saddened minds are free to wander amongst mental playgrounds of pouring rains.

And in moments no sounds fly; until Liliana lifts her head, mouth open to let painful screams fly; harshly piercing depths all cringe inviting small slivers of stress fractures to develop in each foundation's spry... And with such cries, all families tug their own heart's chords in realizing how blessed they are regardless of any approaching or oncoming storms... Having witnessed one who'd loss all three that'd awaited'er arrival at birth: the first three fingers ever grabbed, now unclasped an'fallen to haunting rivers below... And in walking utterly alone down sidewalks towards her anything but home sweet home, Liliana's never t'know her dearest sister had run down the same sidewalks in such pain an'misery having lost her true love from tragedy never occurred; leaving life so fucked and blurred; so very rest assured she had no reason to go back... or onward...

Yet the ironic reflections of the moon plays tricks with it's sardonic proclamations of appearing brighter than the sun... For at this point, its near certain the moon's won the war, but final curtains have yet to hit...............

The night's events start to materialize and she realizes she'll never see those shoes by the foray again; never hear patented knocks of sisters tryin to conjure late night reindeer games. Stoic looks and zombie walks shift to uptempo paces; crooked looks as heads collapse to hands; now running an'wiping eyes in trying to steal tears before they fall t'streets that have already taken far too much.... To confirm what occurred, two blocks away Liliana turns back... No sirens, no sounds behind; no lights flash as only darkness surrounds... and with the one street light out above her once delightful sister, Liliana knew she was too... Turning to a full sprint, Liliana fearfully wants only one set or arms; toned arms like towers protecting her, ensuring safety from evils that wish to snatch her beauty, steal her innocence and murder her charm... Yet with cell phones lost in translation, she knew not how to contact the one voice who with a single word could calm an'embalm her sorrow's pain an'desolation, easing consternations of blows repeatedly raining down upon. The voice she'd hear for an eternity far beyond her own lifetime; the eyes to steal her vocal chords like Ursula to Ariel; leaving her speechless, unable to murmur from being so lost to such a spell; So fuckin captivated by his mercurial side, she'll refall once again in each stare cast, remaining at the will of her lover's gaze which forever falls like each one in the last... And for this she yearns, in sacred heart burns to become speechless an'transcend above horror besieged; dance on ceilings they'd broke, eachother's names tattooed on their throats to an exploding love enveloping stars all around; the milky way giving light to where there is no sound... nor is it needed for eyes speak in the loveliest of four nursery like rounds...

The three blocks lay a wasteland of miles far too vast to wait for a single voice; to throw her choice to run far from cursed heights an'valleys; blessed to rehearse vows on the coming day's new light; together to recite true love in century's witness beyond simple life's design; betrothed to one another beyond this or even that life time. Ensuring persevering an'continuing to dance on sunset's bliss; living on rays of sun's first kiss having jettison two stars to the left and straight on till morning... The life they'd seen on those first few glances of love written on shelfs of life's hopeless romances: blossomed on light beams at such great heights, awaiting for the sun to wash away moon's reflections softly laughing on darkened waters..... as if it knew something of future enraptures left to find..

Having entered the code wrong three times before, Liliana climbs over the gate and jumps more determined than an eagle's soar; determined t'reach her house, no longer safe haven as all but one true patron had now moved on before...... Letters whirl in minds but cannot form words; alone till a cell phone found, containing voices to hear, so spellbound... Floating across long driveways, Liliana passes stationed police cars already alerting Nancy of how the moon stole a devilish bounties ransom... Close to her own edge, Liliana leans off the balcony of life: dreaming of arms to catch her safely an'protect from drowning in sorrow's whirlpool of........

Storming into parallel worlds, no longer her home; Liliana's unable to hide such dastardly cries since her sister's name no longer rests along the front route; erased like the sole light pole was so dreadfully blanketed out... How could she lament without her new love's mouth to coax her off the ledge? Losing touch of reality due t'blood spilt on the streets where they'd frolic'ed with family in tow; long before all three fell back into the dark dreary rapids below.... And left with but one voice's salvation to quench her body an'soul's starvation, Liliana dies to hear "hello darling" today an'give her a small sense of normalcy, keeping her sane in realms of sanity an'allowing her to breathe'er first full breath since she stressfully awoke to this calamity in back seats desolation...

The contents inside cannot fathom how to console; the accident just occurred yet Nancy looks to have been crying for hours... Standing commandingly centered, Liliana looks around for any response yet none can look her in the eye an'she loses herself again....

From the door she sees herself's dash forward, bodies tracing as if slow motion captured: slamming fine foreign lamps against innocent walls, uprooting pristine coaster laden coffee tables ont'fabled vanilla yellow cake rugs with color yet to fadden; tearing apart ever so fragile end pillows splashing white feathers throughout the room in stark contrast to the black leather that lay sobbing as their master remains rotting on nearby streets in swoon... End tables fly into chandeliers crystal an'like torpedoing missiles the fixtures shatter, breaking harsh realities of the moon's undoing in vainly murdering lives worth pursuing an'leaving couches to run away with the spoon; leaving this house forever unstable with spiders dancin an'burrowing in emotional psyches of the men who stand in blue... Never ready to depart info resting on heavy minds to a woman hangin by splinters an'ready for the voice on the other end of the call... yet she only knows half of transpired events on such a fucked up nightfall.......

Basking in her devils work reigned down like troubled thunder, the room's now fully fucked raped and plundered. Walking to the upside down love seat, Liliana sits on the floor with her back reclined to undersides of the chair; while usually perpendicular to the floor, its now upside down an'ready for'er full uproar... yet she cannot speak; an'just cries as she sits there...

Running at 10,000 RPM'S and ready to explode, SHE glances over t'Nancy:

Liliana: "Is she gone?"

Looking up at police standing by her side, Nancy cannot instill knowledge to her dear almost daughter, knowing it will inevitably completely shatter any glass that still resides.... After Nancy somberly nods yes with eyes closed, Liliana's returns to staring at the floor between bent knees; tears she'd thought had dried up continue to fall, jumping off foreboding eyes leaving Liliana staring to'er right at open doors: picturing her sister Jasmine tracing through in skipping manners yet the trace of her waltzing in soon fades from view; succumbed by roaring rivers below who've already taken so much more than'er tears knew...

Remembering all is not fools gold and there's sprites of silver to be found in erosion's night, she only needs but a phone to call her love which could save her from jumping off the balcony an'fading from all light; like her sister's tracing did a couple moments past upon bidding farewell an'adieu...

Reaching t'Nancy's knee:

Liliana: "I need, (breathes in) your phone (long sigh out) ...I need t'call him" (Nancy places hand a top Liliana's)

Triggering deja vu to the vision of Tyler's death gripped hands on steering wheels, Liliana latches onto Nancy's hand as her mind rudely awakens the same:

Liliana: "I NEED... (slams other hand on top of theirs) YOUR PHONE!!!!@@@@"

Nancy: “I cant give it to you my dear... please... I... I-Can’t“

Liliana: “GIVE ME YOUR PHONE NOW!!!!!!!” (jumps up unaware that her body has strength an’grabs for Nancy’s phoneless pockets)

Nancy: “Please!!! Calm Yourself!!! I know you’re hurting but I cannot give you a phone right now... I... I don’t know where it is...”

Completely beyond her skin, (flash) Liliana’s own fuse flies to unprecedented ends (flash) shooting multiple versions (flash) of her tracing selfs (flash flash) to their slow motion glory (flash) of unleashing destruction (flash) her identity was never meant to represent (flooooooooood):

Flames unleash sprinklers mists as tables chairs an’stools are broken down t’fan fires dotting ash filled landscapes; romancing them to grow, fiery sparks fly round matching fiery red strained glass window’s eyes of the many doomed selfs encapsulating blame for the world’s blunders on this night... Scanning the room, the woman no longer known as Liliana inhales with closed eyes to envision her tracers in outlined bodies of bright white light surrounded by darkness hurriedly burning the womb... Opening to carpets uprooting in rolling earthquake like waves, white rosed vases flung in molotov cocktail fashion create open chasms of earth exposing the hopeless rivers which thrive in such turbulence... still bereft of a phone, her mind spins off it’s access: Liliana lunges for the gun on blue’s hip, pulls it out from off its lip an’points it towards;

Liliana: (whispers) “I need... A FUCKING PHONE!!!! NOW!!!!” (putting left hand out)

Unleashing his own gun before realizing her fuse is all but burnt, the second man in blue offers cells which she grabs, simultaneously dropping the gun as the war’s now done... After three misdials, Liliana frantically paces through the wreckage now fully a blaze with a plethora of Liliana’s dancin round ceremonial fires; all celebrating the disasterology of wasteland’s night; honoring the world that ceases now to be... bereft of ever returning to a land called honalee...

(Straight to voicemail) Julian: “Hey hey hey, Y’all reached Julian Casta... Well... Ya almost did-” (beeeeeep)

Thinking that he’s on the phone, Liliana calls back (same message) And then calls back again/calls back again/ again calls back; ONE of these times the call will go through; an’though his jubilant voice soothes her soul each call, all versions of’er tracing the room slowly uproar; uprooting from disaster’s possession, eagerly moving towards her...

Realizing she must halt descents into madness or possibly push her off, Nancy’s voice of misery returns...

Nancy: “Liliana... (no response; keeps dialing) Liliana... (stands up from burning couches an’walks over) Liliana-”

Liliana: “-Hold on, he’s gonna pick up”

Nancy: “Liliana...”

Liliana: "...Hold on; HOLD ON!"

Persistently hanging up and redialing, (straight to voicemail) his repetitive words, (hey hey hey) lose all impact leading the devilishly smiling Liliana's to encircle (well) an'descend closer as their thirst (ya) is no longer quenched by the repetitive (almost) voice mail from the beyond. (did-beeeeeep)

Nancy: (glances at a blue then places her hand on Liliana's shoulder) "Liliana... listen...... he's not gonna pick up..."

Liliana: "What???? How the FUCK do you know? FUCK YOU! (flings her hand off an'pushes her to the ground) YOU don't know Fuckin Shit! BITCH! HE WILLLLL pick up eventually... Fuck Off!" (paces to burning wreckage in next tier)

Nancy: (realizing this is the moment to push her off) "...He's gone..."

With all evil laden smiles fallen off her tracer's faces and replaced by cathartic stoicism, the tracers direct their attack towards the messenger while only the true Liliana freezes, lookin away from Nancy towards the door;

Liliana: "Gone?... No, (turns around) He's not gone, He's Just not answering... Probably on the phone with his brother or something........ FUCK YOU!!!! He's not gone!!! How could you say such a thing right now? WHATTHEFUCK!!!@@@"

“Nancy: “The cops found him earlier at _____ park on the benches... He’s gone dear...” (cops nod)

After reading the cops “would not lie” faces, all tracing Liliana's immediately disappear... The fire subsides and all broken chairs, shattered vases, collapsed tables an’disfigured chandeliers revert to pre destruction positions.

Collapsing; Liliana lays silent, motionless on the floor;

The three rush over an’call her name to no avail;

Smiling, Liliana closes her eyes...

Standing in reflections on office windows, she doesn’t see Julian staring back to say “I love you”... Breezing into bedrooms expecting to see Julian eagerly awaiting an’full body thrusting, upon quietly closing the door Liliana turns to empty rooms;

Flowers no longer in bloom...

And with’er three kids beside her in full kitchen glory, the door swings open t’Julian walkin in an’bending down on one knee to catch his two girls an’boy running towards him so happily... But as white walls turn to black, running kids disappear as standing at the door with saddened eye’s kiss between Julian an’her now found, it seems as if he knows the next scenes an’attempts to say “I love you” before fading outside of such dreams.

The house's black and cold walls implode, releasing her to their momentous dance floor three nights before:

Holding no regrets an'standing across floors from his chucks an'obey shirt, Liliana stares on waiting for his eyes to reconnect... but when no eyes descend, she walks over an'begins to call; Yet still frighteningly his eyes do not fall as no eye's kiss warps minds to calm fucked up designs architects satanically erected; infected with depression as eyes she cannot find remain lost in visions unkind... Severely in submission, Liliana waves'er hands in front of his face; an'in desperately screaming out his name she reaches out to shake his core... yet shakeless hands fall through again like once before...

Unable to feel the rush come through his pulse, she throws heads skyward to relentless ceilings yet there's no couple to scream "This is it!" ...an'only sorrow's death rattle whispering "this is it......"

He cannot feel'er around him having loss blood's flow near their moment stuck in time... unable to set eyes forth, Julian shoots down into the floor an'out bottom of worlds below; enveloped by a river that would surely never let such a beautiful soul go...

Alone on the dance floor, Liliana closes her eyes here and is now twice removed; an'in her mind's dreams, arm in arm as ice dancers they stand on ceiling's gleams, with her valiantly wishing to gaze upon his eyes at least once more before................. Julian glances over, eyes meet an'she breathes for the first time since waking in such treacherous car seats.

He transposes his blushing cheeks and trembling heart; his shortened breath an'all he's felt since the start... And with eyes closed his blush washes over, heart bleeds into her pores while shortened breaths whisper quiet nothings to soothe'er lamenting sores, keeping her a glow, for at least a glimmers more... all the while knowing the clock will soon strike midnight t'possibly close'er dreams' doors.......

An'in her dreams of dreams glancing up past shattered ceilings, she gazes remarkably at'em passionately dancing as lightning's forever kiss; still caressing eachother with internal mirrors broken by fields of perpetual bliss... For this was the place they'd so desired an'hopefully waited to find; for like the moment stuck in time, at such great heights they'll continue forever dancing in her own soul's spacious mind... Not ready to let go, Liliana sets'er sights for the beach the night they met as he delicately kisses'er forehead before running off to water's edge as the day's now set... then stops; turns back an'walks back a few steps;

Julian: "I forgot to tell you, my true love's embrace... That if I perish in the sea or any place forever after here we be... that my love'll stretch around you an'keep you eternally warm; for at such great heights you never truly leave, no matter the oncoming storm... That a piece of me'll remain up high as even the beautiful sky could not keep us apart; for not even death could begin to ever divide our now intertwined hearts... So please never fret, if the worse should befall; for we'll still dance like we did on the dawn of night's fall...... but if you ever find yourself, struck with such doubt; simply look out to each horizon t'see how long our love'll rise in the sun's route"

And with that he paced a slow walk out to the ocean through the sand… An'after she calls out "Ditto" he turns back to shoot a smile amongst the land… And once fading from sight to head out an'to the depths; her phone alerts'er to a text, sent from her love that read:

SMS: Julian > Liliana

> Know your eyes, your scent, and your warmth have twisted my heart and I fear will never let go… Your love penetrates depths none have traveled and unlock secrets none have unraveled for you're who I've forever chased…
>
> And all I want is you… simply

(breathe)

(breathe)

Act 8: Scene 4

Upon the overlook in the car HE sits with "Lights - And Counting..." stuck on repeat. Eyes still wide shut, Santana inhales a huge breath of air as if he couldn't breathe at such great depths...

Opening to the valley of lights, he dismisses recent visions whisking through minds as denial's stronger than miles awaiting between truths... After briefly returning, SHE'd quickly flashed back leaving workers shockingly staring towards flashing screens; in wait for moments he'd leap off ledges of denial int'present debacles encircling the only world he'll ever wish to know...

Looking to the forest in his midst, Santana imagines every bottle of Jack Daniels a glow with his tears an'heartache... yet in valleys below, SHE runs freely without pasts weighing'er down; unabashed freedom having thrown off love's chains an'blocking the sun's reigns with her prison like walls... Long forgotten were chasm falls to depths of worlds only heard in rumors an'read with fervor in books crossing locked minds...

Ducking hearts inward she'd cast away such bliss; embracing masked "sun's" kiss in reuniting with her dear friend the moon who aided'er heartless escapes; to leave HIM alone an'staring at doors on backsides of hearts; staring at bar's climatical floor as earlier scenes play out: portraying HER once again walking out having never begun to believe love's truth would ever stand there an'shout:

“Please come back, I know your stare! I know your heart’s locked an’tight behind prison walls; between sheets of ice where our world’s blurry at best; allowing you t’happily rest an’remain in your own safe haven that you’ve built on the run for you’ve never felt the rush come like our connection undone... Yet YOU left blessed waters you wouldn’t dare to dance, having all but banished the chance to thrive by settling uncomfortably in your quaint little silent death of a life....... and though gone are the fights that break your core, you’ll never be reborn nor grabbed so dearly for one must fearfully jump full throttle into worlds knowing intensities can easily breaks hearts... yet losing sight of those fluorescent lights you swam towards moon’s reflection above in the dark; leaving epic mosaic divines to live in sunny facades the moon built in tragic minds; Thinking you’d found love’s designs yet reality’s the prison you still look upon, having scared another victim into regretfully moving on...“

Going no where fast he tries to recompose; the factory inside releases a steady flow of tears out pain an’suffering’s door... leaving him wondering if she still.....................

And after throwing another bottle he’ll soon head down; yet day light’s no where near as fears’ave unwound... (did that happen?) Yet the highway to drive down doesn’t help unwind thoughts or answer guilty pains from which none can run.

With a key's turn an'left pedal to grounds, Santana shifts down highway's nine lives... Furiously confused an'drunkenly loss, Santana swerves round curves an'drifts round bends knowing a single car against the flow brings life to quick ends... Yet continuing much too fast he reaches Saratoga's quaint towns; delayed from future's recourse he jumps forward but fir-

-streets, stop lights read green; green lights read yellow; freeways: 85, 17, 85, 87... 85-85...

"Domino's fell, my mouth didn't open;

I instead yelled muted curse words

an'bless curse'd falls of water from rapids below"

One face appears, please once more over; bewildered by tragedies he unknowingly bestowed an'brought about with jealous silence in dooming allegories he could not rewrite; wonderment in tomorrow's forever morn while scars of scorn trace his barely breathing heart; tracing every walk an'breath of how he didn't reverse his brother's ending to a start... Keeping him blessed with moon's throne to sit and reminisce... sit and reminisce... sit an'remin-

-exits long since been traveled are taken for he'd been banished by the greatest disgrace of no reason; left landing on faces of floors he kept clean while awaiting returns of his once an'only dream. He'd just seen angelic snowflakes fall to rejoin yet truly tumbled down realities stair back to familiar plains; so unable to accept denial reigns on in the now an'beyond, HE awaits to ensure what'e saw had taken place; an'in doing so continues holding on tightly t'dear hope's dying fate;

That soon she'd be standing there...

soon...

Gate's sorely cried for? He simply drove through waking three but not one mid dreaming, sleeping soundly an'living in world's above ceilings...

Smashing into archway steps, all three rush forth knowing something wicked this ways comes; As Lights' stoic vocals fade away, Santana crashes through white doors revealing scenes of Liliana's dystopian destruction.

How could they stand there amidst armageddon scenes? Focus on what you came here t-

Santana: "-Jasmine...... where... is Jasmine...?" ("Incubus - Dig" revs up in his mind as the rush comes on)

All three eyes bloodily dance to one another. Having already announced such horrific tragedies as the devils court recorder, all hearts lay broken an'in no such working order; none able to step forward as the bearer knowing they'd carry flags to it's final resting place; knowing they'd soon sacrifice yet another life #whatafuckinwaste

Stepping up to rebreak his own heart, words he couldn't from conscious shake:

Cop: "She (looking right; down) ... she... sh-."

Santana: "-She what? (nails t'neck) don't you say it... don't you FUCKIN say what I saw!!!! PLEASE!!!!"

Cop: "She... (trembling) ...she passed..."

Santana: (as quiet without whispering) "no... no she didn't... you're wrong..."

In full stride like guns (bang) of 40 meter dashes, Santana glides thru halls; grabbing corners of walls t'fling around darksides of the moon; lookin right an'left havin lost bearings in furious fits, (slamming fisted walls) he lunges left towards rooms of fantasy's dreams; past realities he'd seen an'breathed (breath in eyes closed) t'doors, (open eyes breathe out) THE door...

Somewhere nearby (fuck) a wasted Liliana shutters awake (this is it) and exasperatingly lifts up to open her eyes (fuck) thinking: "Were the tracers at it again?" (just open the door)

Unblinking eyes (As) shivering (The) terrified (Rush) fear (Comes), Santana frozenly stands. Liliana hugs knees int'bodies; full alert; no emotions left as all remains on that beach. He puts hands on doors-(breathes in)-opens t'breach-

-second rate clothes; scattered on beds; suitcases lay nearly filled wit treasured belongings; appearing... as if ready to depart; ready to restart what she'd banished collapses his eyes; releasing 5 years of vanished hope.

No more tea parties to attend,

No more leaves of snow to pretend

that I dont sit alone in the deep end with
only dark chasms to soothe broken spirits,

for the rivers dont care an'no longer want to hear it.

The sorrow that kept him sitting alone at such bars an'kept her apart never spoke for minds continually drifting out to seas; wondering if he was still waiting but could never jump down without knowing'e still resides; convinced of the fake she hid to hide leaving worlds only him an'her could make, so unable to shake'er safe haven life; testing his true mettle as'e wasted away till death does he start; yet sorrowfully repeatedly remarks: "I will wait for you always an'never part".

Striving to beds, minds do not lie as darksides fling int'bed's cruel wombs, burying faces into clothes crying epiphany bled tears; realizing that though she dove back an'met him there, she'd jumped off balconies of life thinking that from death he'd fell... And in turn she'd jumped off the balcony of life to see him if only for just once more before................

But why would she think such things?

Wait. (flash) She thought (flash) I left? (flash) Why (flash) Would she think? (flash) Wait. (flash) What if Tyler's plan-(flash)-turns on phone to a (flooooooooood) of texts;

Unlike himself, Julian couldn't handle being alone... for after finding queens to his throne he would surely die by'er side; an'thus when she "left" him he'd spilled out his own life an'did what Santana contemplated but could never let fly... And now Julian had succeeded in both realms where he could not: he'd captured his true love an'took his life from heart break-Silence was his mista-

-Guilty minds; Phones fly at body mirrors where Jasmine saw him standing but a few nights back; yet before phones break the glass, Santana meets Jasmine's mirrored self with eyes sobbingly wide shut; before opening eye to eye to realize what'as sealed'er now fate.

(crash) (shatter)

"I... I only.......... wanted you back"

Finally broke, the whirlwind of guilt weighs down an'he falls backwards into the ground; falling dreadfully deep till a great an'splashing sound. The river encompasses him. So jealous ridden his eyes remained too hidden; never to have known he'd doomed his world an'queen alike leaving him alone in blackened waters due to resentment's bottomless spite... Valiantly fighting for her till then, her love had kept him above miserable fates yet drove him t'dive off balconies but a moment's too late... And with eyes enveloped by rivers he'd cursed to never cascade, he knew this world was no longer his to live an'he did not onward breathe; unable to face how he'd burned his own sleeve in a single fuckin night; wondering how he loss'em both to the river an'shut out all light.. ("I'm sorry... I love you both") And before last gasps he left his poor ash an'world inflamed; left tragic floors with thrashing waves crash now finally tame... Knowing somewhere in deep chasms his passion an'love'll continue to burn while HE'll never return t'soul's floor to discover the last box ever lasting, unlocking her true spirit, no longer so imprisoned. For she could'ave then given herself to him, leaving rivers saddened as Hades wouldn't have arisen while they thrived in traveling to far off an'distant lands; riding sunsets past once dark lightless rooms now forever far past gone. And as he disappears into river's black, Santana's last conscious thoughts of HER are heard by Jasmine in chasms deep on'er soul's floor; for as she died a piece of her remained there just as he'd waited a million times before... An'though the river swallowed up both, that which could never die reached out to one another t'meet in eyes kiss; sparking a bliss they'd perpetually dance upon from moments they'd met riding tidal waves crash to soul's floor as the rush comes flooding on

---

ACT 8: SCENE 5:

("Super Flu & Andhim - Hasoweh")

(Seamlessly sifting through volcanic materials, all is dark; diving deep into chasms a clearing arises; a gap in space; like Ariel's lair but more like her lounge... moving at a slow submarine pace yet smooth like a beamer you swim towards it:

6...

5...

4...

3...

2................................

1...........

WHITE SPACE ENCAPSULATES YOUR VIEW TILL

You stand on a summer day, 300 greatvine miles away)

(UCLA campus. Westwood. Hollywood. Sunset. Santa Monica. 5th and Wilshire. Sunday stroll day. Sunny sidewalks. Delightening demeanors. The small clearing is now a 4 by 4 block of city streets. You walk up Wilshire on the south side going east. She walks down the north side going west. You both reach the corners directly linking crosswalks. She turns left as you turn left. Your eyes connect with hers. Mirrored hidden smiles. Eyes shatter all previous records. All colors. All past. All thrown out. To the side and about. Transfixed to the entrancement of flashing images)

(You run up the hill and sit alongside her underneath the chestnut tree to relax in sun soaked straw fields. Wine is set and you love to have met beautiful sunsets with no moon in sight; soft music glides down fields holding within it's sight star shot eyes that which none could ever lament. A smile that lasts through the days, fights, phases and love's dialed down gauges. A smile that strips down yours and her's hidden sides, leaving it all out for the sun's cheerful rays to keep dry... with eachother as guides to such great depths deep inside)

(Diving down the deep blue sea you both leave the shores of the calm and safety. Worried but holding on tight to your hand, you and her descend the depths to the lure of her own floor which she'd never dove'n nor left the only worlds she'd ever know'n... and swimming a mile to the floor you meet the lost city she'd closed off from all else who adore; hidden from her own eyes an'her own body the more)

(Driving top down, up from LA t'bay town so convertibly safe in loud thumping bass sounds. Worlds apart from all who'd try to drown what their eyes had seen an'cloak and dagger them away from their majestic new serene... Your hand sits on the thigh of your new bride; her hand rests on top of yours in which to confide her fears an'worry; but your warmth and certainty keep all qualms allayed, allowing her to stay an'play where she could never dare t'rule such vulnerable days... And with random glances over to your new radiant bride, her eyes lovingly gaze at what she never knew she'd find; filling wickedly tragic souls with the divine of wealth that always lives but never breathed in waters so deep of this kind. Left the darkened prison she'd kept locked up so tight and bathed 10 times over in cold dark moonlight... Having left remote controls on the sand, she follows you t'such great depths to unleash what she promised never to give, allowing hearts t'places she'd vowed never to live; yet wars were started upon first encounters on such streets in the LA sunshine... to meet and flash these images throughout far off an'distant minds)

Inside that split second your mind lived a lifetime. You saw what could be and built an entire future for the girl drifting by you till they exxxxittttteeddddddd fffffffffffooooooooooorrrrrrrrrreeeeeeeeeeeevvvvvvvvvvvvveeeeeeeeeerrrrrrrrrrr-

"-No"

Walking to the middle of the street with no words to say an'five feet away, deshielded sunglasses allow eyes to remain transfixed; both smiling softly so excited by worlds that could be, they release quick shortened laughs as if trying to breathe... And with both eyes gleefully chasing eachother on mental playgrounds, an involuntarily outstretched arm extends from him to her: gliding through heavy air, the clasp of their hands sends shockwaves to the floor, shooting adrenaline to bodies unlike anything quite before... An'as if sleeping through life both awaken t'dreams of their meetings; parched are the sun scorched lips forever bleeding; scared of depths few could truly heed, yet having tasted such new worlds both couldn't stop what they so desperately now need...

"I'm"

"Yes?" (leans in more still holding hands)

"I'm..."

"YES????" (smiling harder)

"I'm...... yours"

"Nice to meet you yours, I'm Jasmine"

"...Santana"

Shake, shake on...

Credits
("GeminiClub - BySurprise")

Thank you for taking this journey with me...

I look forward to meeting up with

you again when the saga continues in:

Sometimes the Moon looks Brighter than the Sun (#SMBS)

On the next pages you'll find the FULL soundtrack to:

As The Rush Comes (#ATRC)

Next time you read ATRC, play the designated tracks during each scene the characters's hear'em so you can Truly live the scenes WITH THEM the second time #howitwasmeanttoberead #repeatsongforwholescene #forshortersoundtracksequences #readscenetwice ;)

Or if you just read it WITH all the music playing, read it again without! #totallydifferentexperience

You can start by saving the credits for the SECOND read through OR finish the credits by playing each "credit" song during their respective sections #likerealcredits

The current Gemini Club track ("By Surprise") will also be the first song of the credits in ATRC: The Movie #yestherewillbeamovie #howcouldtherenotbe

Directors I'm open to "talking" with about

As The Rush Comes (#ATRC) are in no particular order:

Christopher Nolan,

David Fincher,

Paul Thomas Anderson,

Darren Aronofsky

&

(the) Coen Brothers

#whowillaskfirst

Oh and Roger Avary and Aaron Sorkin can cowrite the screenplay with one of the directors above ;)

#therealdreamteam

Those who have read the novel with AND without music:

Next time try t'find ALL the references to music,

TV, movies, novels and beyond ;)

Make it a project with your friends

#yup

#ijustgaveyouhomework

#YOBO

And yes...

I purposely left out the Act/Scene of tracks 24 and on of

the soundtrack to NOT give away the last scenes/credits

SO PLEASE don't give it away!

"...And if you don't know,

now ya knowwww, readdeeeeerrrr!!!" #RIP

As The Rush Comes: (#ATRC)

1. Banks - Bedroom Wall 1: 1
2. Swedish House Mafia - One (your name) ft. Pharrell 1: 4
3. Drake - The Motto ft. Lil Wayne 1: 7
4. The Neighbourhood - 1 Of Those Weaks 1: 9
5. Bobby Schmurda - Hot Nigga 1: 9
6. Lorde - 400 Lux 1: 9
7. The Chainsmokers - #SELFIE .... 1: X
8. Lil Wayne - Rich As Fuck ft. 2 Chainz .... 1: X
9. Paramore - All I Wanted 2: 1
10. Saint Raymond - Fall At Your Feet 2: 4
11. Connor Maynard - Turn Around ft. Ne-Yo 2: 4
12. Super Flu & Andhim - Reeves 2: 4
13. Bluford Duck - Shoulder To Cry On 2: 4
14. Kaskade - 4 AM 2: 4
15. Hannah Georgas - Fantasize 3: 1
16. Motorcycle - As The Rush Comes (G & D Chillout Mix) . 4: 2
17. Sun Glitters - Too Much To Lose 4: 3
18. Kid Ink - Show Me ft. Chris Brown 4: 3
19. Chris Brown - Look At Me Now ft Lil Wayne & Busta 4: 3
20. Calvin Harris - Thinking About You ft. Ayah Marar 4: 3
21. Finch - Tarot 4: 4
22. Calvin Harris - I Need Your Love ft. Ellie Goulding 5: 9
23. Living Legends - Flawless 6: 3
24. Youngbloodz - 85 ft. Jim Crow & Big Boi ....
25. Kid Cudi - Pursuit of ... ft. MGMT/Ratatat (Aoki Mix) ....
26. Pierce The Veil - Kissing In Cars ....
27. The Neighbourhood - Staying Up ....
28. Paramore - Part II ....
29. Pierce The Veil - Southern Constellations ....
30. Ellie Goulding - Anything Can Happen ....
31. The 1975 - She Way Out ....
32. All Time Low - A Love Like War ft. Vic Fuentes ....
33. Tove Lo - Habits (Stay High) Oliver Nelson Remix ....

34. Fuck Buttons - Sweet Love ... (Andrew Weatherall Mix) ....
35. Bauer & Lanford - Leave Me Behind (Daniel Beasley Mix) .....
36. Lights - And Counting..
37. Incubus - Dig ....
38. Super Flu & Andhim - Hasoweh ....
39. Gemini Club - By Surprise ....
40. Pierce The Veil - Hold On Till May ft. Lindsey Starney ....
41. The 1975 - Robbers ....
42. A Minor Swoon - Worn ....
43. Courtland Urbano - Red Bull Perspective (Ending Credits) ...
44. The Neighbourhood - Sweater Weather (Little Daylight Mix).

SPECIAL THANKS
("PIERCETHEVEIL - HOLDONTILLMAY FTLINDSEYSTARNEY)

To first and foremost:

PIERCE THE VEIL

To those who DON'T KNOW:

This book wouldn't exist without

PIERCE THE VEIL'S inspiration, songs and themes:

the moon, the sun, the world

......the life.......love.......energy......

This band has saved more lives than anyone'll know...

Go look at any of the band/band
member's posts on ANY social media site
and see the lasting impact of how their music,
mentality an'outlook on the world influence people
on levels most never dare grasp, let alone journey to...

Yet PTV shares the map of how to get there
WITH their vocal chords, guitars, bass an'drums

#thankyou

And to those who KNOW:

You have every breakdown,

every lyric, an'every song memorized...

and you already saw it dritfing across every page,

on the corner of every word,

and behind every action

#isawthemoondivorcethesky

The Bands

(Most Played Songs In Headphones While Writing; "Top 12")

Pierce The Veil (Every Song Ever Made... Ever...
"Kissing in Cars" is # 3)

Paramore (All I Wanted, Part II,
Playing God, Future, Last Hope, My Hero,
I Caught Myself, We Are Broken, Misguided Ghosts)

The Neighbourhood (Warm
Unfair, Staying Up, Honest, $ting,
1 of Those Weaks, Baby Came Home,
Sweater Weather Little Daylight Remix
"Unfair" is # 10)

Lorde (A World Alone, White Teeth Teens, Ribs
"A WORLD ALONE" IS # 4)

A Minor Swoon (I Awoke, Worn,
Silent Heart, Shaken by the Resistance,
Found and Borrowed, Seventeen, I Saw You,
On The Day, The Sacred Songs, Nothing Outside
"FOUND AND BORROWED" IS # 7
"I AWOKE" IS # 1)

Lights (Portal,
February Air, And Counting...
The Listening, Drive My Soul, Cactus in the Valley
"PORTAL" IS # 8)

Finch (New Wave,
Tarot, Inferium, Awake, Ender
"NEW WAVE" IS # 12)

Motorcycle (Gabriel & Dresden and JES) - As, Rush Comes, The, As The Rush, As Comes The Rush, Rush Comes As The, Rush As The Comes, As The Rush Comes)

Banks (Change,
Bedroom Wall, Goddess
"BEDROOM WALL" IS # 6)

The 1975 (She Way Out, Robbers, The City)

Super Flu & Andhim (Hasoweh, Reeves)

Early November (The Rest of My Life, Decoration, This Wasn't In Our Plan, The One That You Hated, Outside, Figure It Out #remindsmeofnermal #sadness)

The Used (On My Own,
Getting Over You, Poetic Tragedy
"GETTING OVER YOU" IS # 9)

Gemini Club (By Surprise, Nothing but History, Candles)

New Found Glory (Dressed to Kill,
The Story So Far, Heartless at Best, This Isn't You,
Tangled Up feat. Hayley Williams #loveyouhayley ;)

Tycho ("MONTANA" IS #2)

Saint Raymond ("FALL AT YOUR FEET" IS # 5)

Usher ("CLIMAX" IS # 11)

Dúné & Alesso (Heiress Of Valentina
Alesso Exclusive Mix #formattingmagic)

Incubus (Dig)

THE "APP" & "THE MOVIE"

SHAZAM

For the gift of music while simply living life.

Over 50 % of the soundtrack was found
by Shazaming anywhere an'everywhere
during the writing months #especiallyshopping

I found Gemini Club by shazamming "Nothing but History" in the "Converse Store" on the promenade in Santa Monica

#truestory

LIMITLESS (THE MOVIE)

For giving me the idea to

"write a novel"

on November 16th, 2013

#thankyou #18monthstotheday :)

The People
("The1975 - Robbers")

My Lost Boy

Kyra - For all your support and help which
lead to the complete reformatting of ATRC!!! like I said
in my first tweet "your query changed my life" #domino

Brentano - For those early morning quotes
at work and all the support during the entire
writing process #alwaysbelievedinme #goodtimes

GIGI - For truly believing in ATRC; you never wavered
and jumped on the revolution the second you learned
about it #couldnthavedonethis #withoutyou #thankyou

Ana - Timing is everything; there are
no words to the inspiration, motivation you
brought and the amazing person that is you...
#thankyou #wedidit

Amanda - You helped me so much
when I needed it most... you were always
there for me... thank you... #yourebeautiful

Lexi - I don't think anyone showed
me more support and inspiration faster
than you did... from the moment we met, you
couldn't have been more helpful and inspirational!
#loveyouroutlookonlife

Rich & Tay - You guys are so fuckin
dope... like for real!!! the chemistry, the
vibes y'all send off an'the supportiveness and ya...
#foreverdownforthecause #thankyou

Shy - You were always there for me
when many were not... couldn't be more
proud to have you in my life... and you give
advice and support from a place others do not!!!
#onelove

Kelly - You're pretty much my idol...
and you're exactly who I WISH I had the
strength and conviction to be at your age...
#neverchange #thanksPTV

Ann Arbor Nick (the professor) - Everyone in
life has that "one teacher" who really connects
with them and changes their trajectory in life forever...
you were mine and took the walls off my writing's room
#iamforeverthankful

Joy - For helping me through the hardest
time of my life in the first half of 2014 #hitmeupdude

Lights - I fell for your music (#februaryair) back
in my touring days during the summer of 2009!
Talkin with you in person (#April2015) about the
book and giving you #ATRC merch was a dream come
true!! Can't wait for you to read it!!! And I would love to
work with you on a track or two for #SMBS !!! #miracle2
#dreamshappen #iknowthisplacelikethebackofmyhand

The Brit - For being so inspirational
in creating "The Credits" and so "bloody"
supportive during the late editing process in 2014
#thankyou #eventhoughyoubouncedonme : (

"Nuf," "Wasted," "Mikey G," "Pass Out P" & "Krazy K" - The Crew #beendecades #andwestillchillin #onecrewftw

Dumbo - No clue where you went #butcomeback #youvealwaysbeenthereforme

Randy - Thank you for taking the time to talk to me about your band's scene and giving me motivation #october2014 #thankyouforyourmusic #iwillneverforget #whatitistoburn #andsoon #allthenewgeneratiosnwill #knowwhatitsliketoburnaswell #finchforever

Too Fly - This would not be possible without all those nights we rode around freestyling and ghostriding in the "freezer" #hyphysummer #thosewerethedays #blazeoneformeyo

Justin Bieber - For your outlook on the world and the inspiration to go after my dreams; the songs "Hard 2 face Reality feat. Pooh Bear" & "Runaway Love;" and for the movie "Never Say Never" #yesijustthankedhim #wannahateonme #feelfree :)

Saara - For being so supportive and strong #courage

Mandy - For actually treating
me like a promising writer and taking
the time to steer me in the right direction
#neverchange #dominotwo

"Query Shark" - Helping me and
so many others find our true "voice"
#dominothree

"Tattoo" Blake - For pushing me
to write however the fuck I want and not be
afraid to do something no one's done before; your
advice helped me break out of myself to write the end
#forreal

Shareen - So supportive and grounding
#lookididit #ididit #thankyou #youhelpedmesomuch

"Natasha Lorde" - Met in a
crazy way but you're still cool as fuck
#hitmeupdude #youreadthesneakpreviewyet #haha

Michaela - For your inspiration and
assistance with the query #youreamazing

"Cassie" - You never responded...
but your outlook on the New Adult
genre and future of literature helped
me understand my own vantage point and
inspired the final query an'blurb for the book
#thankyou #iwonder #ifyouwill #everemailmeback : (

"Sara" - For giving me hope at the most opportune
moment an'being the ONLY one to request a partial
and acknowledge the unique character of my writing
#tillourpathscrossagain ;)

"Moo Moo" - For giving me Tove Lo
and then months later showing me the
Nelson Remix which replaced the Hippie
Sabotage Remix (love all your girly tracks lol!)

and...

Simon "Dirt Nasty" Rex - For your quote
about social media on the Jennifer Tapiero
show #sept26th2014, bringing vine to my life

AND You're the reason why I DVR'd the first episode of
"Happy Land" an'was introduced to the song "Worn" by a
band called...

A Minor Swoon

Your music made this novel possible. I couldn't have done this without you Josh... the emotional vibes your songs exude are unlike anything I've ever encountered...

I would say over 50 % of the poetical parts of the novel were edited with your songs dancing on my ears. (especially "I Awoke")

...If you ever need anything,

please do not hesitate to ask...

Thank you Josh...

From all of me... thank you...

Concerts attended during editing process #motivation #allartists #onthededicationpage #fateistrulyamazing

The Neighbourhood - July 2014/Dec 2014 (Oakland/LA)
Paramore - August 2014 (Concord)
Lorde - October 2014 (Berkeley)
Finch - October 2014/May 2015 (SF/SC)
Pierce The Veil - January 2015 (SF)
Lights - April 2015 (Sacramento)

The ONLY Two TV Shows

FRIENDS

For being there every day
when I took a break from writing or
editing (and all 262 episodes saved on my DVR)

#iprobablywatched #over1000
#episodes #illbethereforrryouuuuuuu

THE VOICE

The only show (besides friends) watched throughout the whole process #season5to8 #bookdebutsweekofS8finale

for your inspiration and bringing so many
great songs to my life AND ATRC's soundtrack

#iloveyouvoice

Blake Shelton - For being you and bringin
"y'all" to the book #keepdrinkin #anddancin

Adam - For being too sexy for your shirts
and being so competitively hilarious! #haha

Adam & Blake - Your guys' interaction and competitive insults make the show #ifoneofyouleft #iwouldnotwatchit

Usher - For your motivation, artistry and your song #climax which was on endless repeat for hours in the headphones during the writing of some of the most epic parts #incredibletrack

Pharrell - For your amazing outlook on life #vibe #andyoursong #one #isinthebook #kickfuckinass

Christina - I don't think I've ever met a woman who was xtremely cute an'fuckin adorable as a teen and then somehow has only gotten more beautiful and goddess caliber pretty as she's aged...

You're fuckin amazing I dont know what else to say... #youarebeautiful #nomatterwhattheysay #uhoh #amigettingacrush ;)

Gwen - Had to put you in here cuz No Doubt is still epic as fuck #new

...and you're kinda sexy lol #sorryguyfrombush

THANKS

("AMinorSwoon - Worn")

The Voice S.7 - After seeing
Ricky do a cover of "Muse - Starlight,"
watching the original version reminded
me of a song from an old James Holden set

James Holden - For your Igloo
set in 2009 which is the only way
"FUCK BUTTONS" becomes a part of ATRC

Mattlemon77 on youtube - For posting the
James Holden Igloo set and the TRACK LISTING!!!!
#score

Lagunitas IPA - Beer of choice
throughout the writing process
#queenbri #whatsyouknowaboutthis ;)

Subway Meatball Sandwhiches -
Food of choice throughout this journey

IMAK - Gloves I used every day from start to finish

Twilight & New Moon (movie) - For your Inspiration
#loveyouboth

The Postal Service - Such Great Heights, Nothing Better,
Brand New Colony & Natural Anthem

All the literary agents who rejected me -
I sent out 14 horrible queries with an awful
sample in July 2014... And 16 GREAT queries
with pretty much the SAME first 10 pages YOU just
read from November 2014 t'February 2015 an'of the
16 queries about 13 NEVER RESPONDED HAHAHAHA
#onlyonepartial #ouch #ohwell #haha #cestlavie #fuckit

Pirates of the Caribbean (Black Pearl) - Amazing flick;
sadly the only good one of the whole series
#thatsnotgoodenough

10 Little Indians and Then There Were None - Reading this book in high school and playing the "311 Transistor" album on repeat forever linked the two. #oneofmyfavbooks

On second thought, this may be the reason why I thought to link music and reading #canthinkofone #withouttheother

Rules of Attraction (book) - Bret Easton Ellis #soinfluential #thankyou

Rules of Attraction (movie) - Roger Avary, your movie and I are forever connected #forbetterorworse

Entourage - #imissyou #iwantahug .... #bitch : (

Good Will Hunting

Eddie Murphy - For Raw #enoughsaid

Shawshank Redemption (movie/book) - Simply amazing

Kevin Smith - For being the only director/writer to actually "speak" to MY generation #sayingwhatweallfelt

Can't Hardly Wait (movie) - Still the best teen movie ever #vivalapoolhouseright #loveburger #likegodssalt #heskindatallandwearstshirtssometimes

The Pursuit of Happiness (movie) - When times were tough and I needed to get inspired... you were always there for me #thankyou

Inception (movie) - One of my top 5 movies of all time; I've seen a total of 3 movies in the theaters since 2010... 2 of them were Inception #nolaniloveyou

Fight Club (movie) - There are no words #iamjacksperception #firstmovietobreakmymind #fincheryoukilledit

There Will Be Blood (movie) - Paul Thomas Anderson revolutionizes the past #wekeepitdark #robberbarons

Black Swan (movie) - Darkingly haunting; simply #epicasfuck

O'Brother Where Art Thou (movie) - Coens you were able to evoke George Clooney's best work besides "Out of Sight"

Tangled #epicasfuck - Can't watch it without tears falling

Beauty and the Beast - #yesthedisneyone Same as tangled ^^^^

Up - Ironic that an animated movie can make you cry within 10 min every time! #amazinggiacchino #absolutelyamazing

(add in other people who helped #placeholder)

Harry Potter (3, 4, and 5) - #Yup

Fed Ex - For flyers/shipping lol

Rock Band 2 and Guitar Hero 3
(on breaks during editing #notwriting)

"give bosh credit???" (found this written
in the novel a month ago and I have no clue what it
means but I told myself to give him credit sooooo...)

Guess (clothing brand) - For shazaming
so many songs in your store an'wearing all your clothes
#noimnotsponsoredbythem #yethaha #butiloveyouguess

SquareSpace

Saltines

Blue Moon, Pacifico & Stella Artois

Oh and I almost forgot...

To the all the girls who left me,
used me and especially those who I bent
over backwards trying to help and STILL
fucked me over - Thanks for the inspiration!!!
#gofuckyourself #smileyface

And...

I am NOT THANKING garbage SNAPCHAT and KIK -

For perpetuating alienation of
people by allowing the exploitation of
others for attention/affection and then
simply "blocking them" whenever they want
#killinghumaninteraction

...And for making cheating and flirting that much more

rampant and easier to do;

FUCK YOU APPS!!!
BESIDES CELEBRITIES, MUSICIANS AND THE
ALIKE, THERE'S NO REASON WHY YOU NEED KIK
OR SNAPCHAT!! FOR CELEBRITIES AND MUSICIANS
IT MAKES SENSE TO CONNECT WITH FANS... BUT
NORMAL PEOPLE #NOFUCKINWAY #FUCKUAPPS
#GIVEYOURPHONENUMBEROUTINSTEAD
#MOREINTIMATE #ANDDOESNTUSEANYDATA

Maybe if the younger generations tried to develop
more PERSONALIZED relationships, actually TALKED
on the phone and IN PERSON/PUBLIC more and
stopped keeping everyone at bay with KIK SC FB and IG
messaging, people wouldn't be so isolated an'alone
#FUCKINNNNN #AAAAAAA

Social Media Section

("CourtlandUrbano - RedBull PerspectiveEndingCreditsBeat" #justputitonrepeat)

I am fully aware of the irony in having a "social media" section within the credits; an'although many believe I am ANTI social media; (isn't that funny Kara?) 1. I am NOT and B. No matter what, social media will be a part of human culture moving forward...

Social media DOES bring alot of good to the world and if we can learn to guard against the self validation aspect of it AND return human interaction to what it was BEFORE social media existed, then we'll be THAT much better off... For without social media, ATRC would not be what it is today:

Banks was a present given to me by an online dating site.. (pause for reader's laughter) LOL, yes during my short lived online dating experience in 2014, (#chillcraycray #nevermetupwithanyone #iwasonforliketwoweekslol) a wonderful woman gave me the gift of Banks (you know who you are... Victoria was it?)

In September of 2014, I was under the impression that Lurk, Unfair and Silver were the only tracks available from the The Neighbourhood's forthcoming Mixtape #000000 & #FFFFFF ...Yet from a conversation spurred by @thenbhd's retweeting of a picture from their concert I attended in August 2014, I learned that Jealou$y, Warm and H8M4CH1N3 were recently released.. Needless to say, having these three songs radically changed my life #yesthenbhdarethatfuckinepic ...Hell the song you're about to hear in the LAST part of the credits is a track I found ON The Neighbourhood's soundcloud; another social media site...

After joining Instagram in November 2014 to a create an account for the novel, I learned that hellllla Neighbourhood fans were all into this band called "The 1975" #whomineverheardof... A couple nights later I started talkin to someone from Europe about'em and a short story shorter; they now have two songs in ATRC and I'm fuckin obsessed with them #iloveyouthe1975

Even "A Love Like War" was found because it appeared as a "suggestion" video on the right side of the screen while watching random PTV music videos on youtube... With a song name of "A Love Like War" featuring my favorite band's lead singer in Vic Fuentes, without even hearing the song I sorta knew it would end up in ATRC... And sure enough the vibe (and especially lyrics) fit perfectly into Santana's scene an'I even ended up downloading 3-4 tracks off ATL's album which I had repetitively listened to while gearing up for the PTV/ ATL/WonderYears tour back in 2013 #ptvislife

Social media COULD be a truly positive part of the new digital world we've created for ourselves... But it's the obsession with amassing a huge audience of "followers," (#fakepopularity) and the bartering for likes, comments, revines, reposts and SHOUTOUTS (aka self advertising) that kills it... On MY social media pages I typically only follow people whose commentary of the world is interesting, inspirational or relatable ensuring my "feed" only contains those whom I respect and wish to interact with (how social media was designed to be)... If you follow hellllla fuckin people, how are you supposed to build a connection with any of them? Imagine if people stopped caring about the # of followers they had an'built smaller social networks where they interacted with a couple hundred people they truly respect ALL the time rather than 1000's of people you don't even LIKE, NONE of the time... Hell would it help if we abolished the "number of followers" box for all under 1000? #interestingconcept #corpswillhate #wonthappen

The reasons for wanting a million followers is obvious but does following 1,000's of random people JUST to get MORE followers actually make you feel "better" about yourself??? I understand that the greater the number of followers you have increases your chances of gaining new followers, but I don't follow for follow/like for like or whatever the fuck because what's the value in a "traded" or "bought" follower/like anyways? Do I feel a sense of accomplishment having 100 likes on a picture if 50 were bought through apps or traded with others? The answer is: Doesn't fuckin matter... I should feel validated because I took a sick ass picture and KNOW it's fuckin dope WITHOUT anyone else's validation; who cares if it has 0 likes or a million #forreal #stopbeggingforlikes

Oh and to all the "Haters" on social media: It IS a free world and everyone's entitled to their own opinion... but just so you know, your jealousy is obvious #burn ...Not to mention in looking over 25 people who hated on one incredible dancer's vine; of the 25 hateful comments, 24 of them were made by people with 60 followers or less #enoughsaid

And to all those who get "HATED" on: just take it as a compliment and know that by hating on you they're saying "I wish I had what you have in _____, and I wanted to let you know that instead of working to better myself or accomplish what YOU have, I've taken time out of my shitty day to displace MY frustration an'anger stemming from MY own shortcomings to hate on you..." Hate, hate on... ;)

I mean, as a true testament to the value of social media, I am writing this whole part of the credits with "Courtland Urbano - Red Bull Perspective End Credits Beat" playing in the headphones which is a song I found from a vine I saw earlier today... And who knows if this whole section would even exist without such a introspective song blasting throughout my skull... Hmmmm... I know! Why don't I just make it so YOUUUU (the reader) are listening to the very same track I'm listening to right now AS I write this... Fuck it, hold on let me go change it... Ok I went and changed it so now YOU TOO will be listening to the same sick ass instrumental track I wrote this too (And yes I do play the same song repeatedly for hours on end while writing/editing ;)

Is it crazy that I'm talking to YOU the reader as I write? ...Kinda weird huh? I mean, granted I did just kinda get to know you or vice versa as you read ATRC... But thats what's so effing cool about the world: when it comes to artistic reality you can break all the rules... Never be afraid t'do something just because "no one else has"... After all, who would have thought to put credits in a novel? Or use hella hashtags and emoticons? Or even bring back Shakespearean prose? #youfuckinknowit For like The Pursuit of Happiness said: "You got a dream. You gotta protect it... People can't do something themselves, they wanna tell you, you can't do it. If you want something, go get it. Period".

And that is something I have learned in my crazy journey to write ATRC: Greatness arises fear and makes people uncomfortable... Maybe that's why so many stopped talking to me when I said "I'm gonna to change the world"... People are comfortable with normal and average while greatness and the pursuit of it scares'em... As I told numerous people in the last year: "If I simply said; 'I wanna be rich as fuck,' people would be all about it... But when I say I wanna change the world and save society from themselves, most scrunch their eyebrows, look at me like I'm crazy and walk the other way..."

To those who kept telling me "one man can't make a difference" or "you can't affect change," fuck off lol; cuz what did I JUST do? And this is me writing before the novel is even fully edited at 7 am on December 22nd, 2014 after writing this whole section between now and 3 am #whenigotup

Greg Evans said he only succeeded because he "was still working after everyone else went to sleep"... I went to sleep at 10 pm as I have for the last week, but every night I just seem to wake up after 5 hours an'get back to work... Why even right now as I sit here on new years eve 2014 making the final edits, I didn't go out... I spent tonight with the family till 11 pm and then edited the novel from 11 pm 2014 till 5 am 2015... While all y'all were partying, getting "wasted" an'raving to everyone else about all the "shit" you're gonna accomplish in 2015, I was at home workin... Call me a loser if ya want... But I WILL continue to... Dream... Dream... On...

Instagram

@ATRCNOVEL

("TheNeighbourhood - Sweater WeatherLittleDayLightRemix")

#ATRCSTREETTEAM

@http.geetheplacenta
(You were the first and one of founders of the street team... it was conversing with you 7 months ago that we came up with the "street team" concept... you're extremely special to me and I'll always be here for you #andyouhavetheukonlock)

@moreanaaa
(So supportive and influential... the chances of us meeting were astronomical... I can't believe I just used that word in a sentence... wow you inspire me still and Kaskade is in the book cuz of your story!!!!! #maizenblueforlife)

@thebignacci
(Hahahaha mustard #enoughsaid... the only guy in
the crew for a FUCKIN reason; you see the world how
I do and wanna fix this shit too #represent #letsdothis)

@jumpingmexicanbean
(I have no words as to how you've
helped me when no one else could or would...
I would thank you but you hate that... so just know
you've always been there for me... #suchabeautifulsoul)

@a.mante
(For your help on the #NBHDMixtapeStreetparty
and that one scene #YOLO #sosupportive #always
#thereforme #youremoneyandihopeyouknowit!
#thebest)

@kellycastro_
(I AM SOOOO jealous of your style and the way
you see the world... you're one of the coolest people
ever and from day one was one of the homies!!! and
I found you through PTV #thatsfuckinsick #soareyou)

@tayyylaaax
(You're such a live wire and
forever stoked on life! Like a bottle rocket of
support and you've always been so stoked an'truly
devoted to the team! Thank you! #seriouslythankyou)

@sweet.disaster
(So close to home yet so far away...
you've always been all about helping me and
wanting to make a difference; know that you have
and I am forever grateful #baylife #letsfixourhomes)

#THEINNERCIRCLE

@me.vs.the.universe
(My first fan!!! #thankyou)

@bae_flexing
(Always there for me in so many ways!)

@ughhxiris
(I love your style and outlook on the world!!!
Let's publish your shit #forreal ;) #writewriteon)

@redneck_babygirl_98
(I'm here for ya always! you kick fuckin ass #inspiration)

@ifuckedyourbitch_98
(You're so strong an'amazing; I can't thank you enough!)

@butterflyfuentes
(Soo supportive and inspiring #youfrickinrule :)

@brianna.the.queen
(Freestyling with you has been one of
the highlights of my social media days!
Don't think I was ever more stoked about someone
following me!!!! #myqueen #iwishlol #ijustadoreyou)

@dashing._.rapscallion
(For being you #simply #hoodlumstatus)

@zzxoxo_1
(Do I have a crush on you? #mayyyyybeeeee ;)

@fucking_hell_jesse
(NBHD NBHD NBDH #NBHD #whatwouldjessedo
#ourpossewilliveon)

@ptvpsycho
(you kick fuckin ass... #simply)

#SUPPORT

@unclecandace
(love your style vibe and how passionate
you are about life! You fuckin rule #simply ;)

@805money
(For being so helpful and inspirational! thank you
for all your advice and support #sostrong #inspiration)

@bright_summer_14
(For liking my pics when no one else did #literallynoone)

@a.sshleyy
(Even though you blocked me for no reason #igotburned)

@mandness
(Finch rules! stay strong!)

@_imnobodyshero_
(You know why #jokerandharley ...still waiting on the
batman pic!!! you have an invitation to the #innercircle
waiting if you ever POST THAT PIC! DAMMIT LADY lol)

@shameless_fangirl
(Your dream will happen #dontworry)

@kitten176 (Thank you!)

@isabelhardesty (You got this)

@alexgilmoreee
(Good timing for this one here... lol you
WERE in the #innercircle but you unfollowed
me lol #noworries #youresweetness #hoodlums)

@3.0am
(So deep and always
inspiring! Aww you left the innercircle
too! #sadness #thankyou #amazingstill
#yourewelcomebackanytime #missyou #comeback)

@christiemckeoghh
(For being a true fuckin Hoodlum
#nbhdislife #000000FFFFFFislife #nbhd4ever)

@justinbieber
(For your many simple inspirational captions
such as: "Don't let your surroundings affect your
beliefs," "Be intentional with EVERYTHING YOU DO"
& "Don't let Instagram define your self worth!" #money)

I will return/post again when ATRC's a NYT Best Seller...
(see second to last post)

Twitter

@MARSTONAJAMES

@lkblackburne
(Keep tweeting those amazing articles #beyondthanks ;)

@dirtnasty
(So many reasons listed above
#ohscarymovie5sonzzzzzzzzzzzz)

@JenniferTapiero
(2015! I told you this was the year!
hit me up yo! been farrrrr too long!)

@orchidstaxx
(Black and white pic +
late night epic tweets = FTW!!!)

@Official_Jes
(What can I say... you gave
me the "RUSH" over a decade ago! ;)

@kristinasky
(You're awesome... simply #wegowayback)

@epeachh
(For being so beautiful #insideandout ...you have a part waiting for you in the movie if you want it :)

@letstrycoke
(Cuz your awesome! don't lose that wonderful spirit #neverchange :)

@woahitsjulie
(You're sweetness... #kit)

@britnigiles_
(For your random tweets #youkickfuckinass)

@askmeifigaf
(Such a sick outlook on the world #shebekillinit)

@cuddlemecarter1
(You're hilaaaaaarious haha #sarcasmcentral)

@marleybookout1d
(You are awesome #simply #losersunite)

@alexis_garcia4
(Love your spirit and positivity #totally)

@KristenStewerrt
(I miss your tweets... where have you gone???)

@ArianaGrande
(My one celebrity crush... I started
crushing on you BEFORE I ever even
knew you were a singer and were just this
funky chick on a disney show... #iloveyouarianalol)

@yelyahwilliams
(I would have a crush on you but outta respect
to the homie (#nfgforlife) I do not... Then again... I
won't go down "without a fight" and would love to be
"tangled" up with you hahahahaha #totallykidding
#ijoke #ijoke #iloveyouhayley #asafriend #imean
#asafellowartist #imean #ok #imgonnaputdown
#theshovel #thisisaconspiracyagainstme
#allweknowisfalling #morelike
#allyouknowisawesome
#heythatrhymed ;)

I will return/tweet again when ATRC's a NYT Best Seller

Vine

VINE.CO/MARSTONAJAMES

@Simon Rex
(For bringing vine to my life an'being fuckin sick and not just "vine famous" but "famous famous" #thanksyo)

@British Girls.
(Support, inspiration, fun and all those hilarious vines!!!)

@Roro and Sophy
(The first viners I really loved... PS Roro I'm gonna hit you up about being the costume designer for the movie & play ;) and I could care less if y'all are together or not... PEOPLE stop askin them!! FUCK!! lol)

@TasiaAlexis
(For not giving no fucks about nothing... wait I just said you give a fuck... you know what I mean #yourule #randominspirationalphrase #keepstaringupatthesunroofbeingweird #iwillcontinuetodothesame ;)

@Alex Ramos
(For your randomness and that one vine
with creed "look at this photograph" #betch)

@Zachary Piona
(Remind me to have you be a
writer for a sitcom I produce later in life
#getalittleloose #wtfwasthat #missedtheexit)

@Cody Ko
(For your idgaf vine and many
others... an'same as directly above ^^^^^)

@A_flexing
(Support and being there for me before all of this)

@Amymarie Gaertner
(For reminding me of great old tracks
such as Baby Bash - Suga Suga and bringing me
Courtland Urbano's music!!! ;) And I'm still gonna
reach out to you for some pop lock help one day!!!)

@Josh Be Like
(Early support, being awesome and real)

@Rudy Mancuso
(Cool tunes dude #yourdope ... #stupad)

@Christian Delgrosso
(You're on this here cuz of your Dora "where's
the bed" vine #fuckinlovethatone #likehella #money)

@Lil Bambi
(You're awesome and seriously dngafbn!
remind me to give you a sick ass job and a
part in the movie #ifyouwantit #nomoresubway ;)

@Ane koval
(For bringing singing back to my life and
reminding me of a better time - 90's R & B #112Cupid)

@//The 1975 Live//
(For that one live vine of 1975
#me which is epic as fuck!!!!!!!!!!!!)

I was on Vine for only 3 weeks... I will
return AND bring back #10badjokesinanhour
when ATRC's on the NYT's........ (see last vine for origin)

I love you all...

And till we meet again...

Never let anyone convince you

that you can't do anything;

"Damn the man"

Marston Out

(End Credits)

Ok...

Absolute last warning

#dontsayididntrytosaveyou

I don’t care if the SOUNDTRACK is in the credits,

read the book WITHOUT the music first

THEN read it again with it!!!

OR just look online if you’re such a rebel!!!

I'm telling you,

you'll spoil it for future you if you keep going!

STOP flipping pages backwards!!!

The credits are coming up

and you need to read the whole book first!!!

No cheating,

Start from the front!

I know the title page is on the back

#imaware

Stop reading,

Close the book,

Open to the FRONT side and start on page 1...

Please?

To my “Lost Boy;” for grounding me when I need to be,

To “Kyra;” for showing me what I couldn’t see,

And

to

“Pierce The Veil”

“Paramore”

“The Neighbourhood”

”Lorde”

“A Minor Swoon”

“Lights”

& “Finch;”

for endless inspiration and support.

AS THE RUSH COMES (#ATRC)

Published in the United States by Skyward Centuries

ISBN: 978-0-692-43411-6

www.skywardcenturies.com

10 9 8 7 6 5 4 3 2 1

PRINTED IN THE UNITED STATES OF AMERICA

AS THE RUSH COMES (#ATRC)

BY

MARSTON JAMES

SKYWARD CENTURIES
San Carlos • Neverland

Made in the USA
San Bernardino, CA
17 May 2015